THE TWO-WAY MIRROR

Five desperate city businessmen asked private investigator Adam Flute for his help. Their managing director, Sir Frank Alva, was missing, perhaps dead or living with a notorious beauty of doubtful reputation. Flute tracked down the girl and met Sir Frank. But, the next day, he discovered his dead body — and someone was prepared to swear that Flute had killed Sir Frank. Deftly keeping one step ahead of Scotland Yard, Flute chases the leader of a vice ring, with international implications.

Books by Drew Launay
in the Linford Mystery Library:

THE NEW SHINING WHITE MURDER
SHE MODELLED HER COFFIN
DEATH AND STILL LIFE
A CORPSE IN CAMERA

DREW LAUNAY

◆

THE
TWO-WAY
MIRROR

Complete and Unabridged

LINFORD
Leicester

First published in Great Britain
under the name of
'Droo Launay'

First Linford Edition
published 2002

British Library CIP Data

Launay, Droo, *1930* –
 The two-way mirror—Large print ed.—
 Linford mystery library
 1. Detective and mystery stories
 2. Large type books
 I. Title
 823.9′14 [F]

 ISBN 0–7089–9763–5

Published by
F. A. Thorpe (Publishing)
Anstey, Leicestershire

Set by Words & Graphics Ltd.
Anstey, Leicestershire
Printed and bound in Great Britain by
T. J. International Ltd., Padstow, Cornwall

This book is printed on acid-free paper

1

I pushed the door wide open, aimed the pistol at the figure behind the transparent plastic curtain and took a couple of steps forward to make sure I wouldn't miss.

'I'm sorry I have to do this,' I said.

Terrified, the girl whipped back the curtain and looked at me in horror. Without hesitating I fired.

The thin, surprisingly powerful jet of water shot across the room and found its mark smack in the middle of her lovely, shining, wet, sun-tanned stomach. She squealed, leapt out of the shower, flung herself at me and tried to wrestle the water pistol out of my hand.

The struggle took us to the four corners of the thickly blue-carpeted bathroom, into the bedroom and onto the custom-built double bed, where I allowed her to empty the magazine at point-blank range all over my face.

I closed my eyes, listened to her gurgles

of pleasure, and wondered, not for the first time, why I had had the luck to land such a pleasant, profitable case.

★　★　★

It had started two days before in the time-honoured manner, me sitting at my desk reading the gossip columns of the daily papers and being interrupted by the telephone.

A man with an educated voice had requested my possible services if I satisfied him that I was the right man to solve a particular problem. He had given me an address where we should meet.

The place was the sixteenth floor of the Alva-Lazell building and the man was the chairman of the company. After a ten-minute wait, in a walnut-furnished, grey-walled reception room with a contemporary desk supporting the silky white elbows of a pert brunette, I had been shown into an oak-panelled boardroom, where five city-suited gentlemen sat round a long oval table waiting to cross-examine me.

Every one of them was desperate, ulcer-ridden, highly strung and unexpectedly put out by the casual way I looked at them and their surroundings.

They were organization men who had little contact with people outside their particular spheres, and, though they could sum up other business men by the way they jockeyed for bargaining positions, private detectives were as unknown a quantity to them as actors or artists or any strange freelance bums who managed to live without going to work regularly from nine till six every day of their lives.

The way I was dressed didn't help them either. Though my clothes fitted perfectly and were obviously expensive, they were not English. I was wearing a dark-blue shirt buttoned at the neck, which I had had made in Switzerland, no tie, well-tailored, Italian-tapered trousers in linen, a good leather belt, moccasins to match and a heavy-knit grey cardigan bought in France. It was a comfortable outfit, ideal for the warm weather but maybe more suitable for rehearsing the Bluebelles through a routine at the

Moulin Rouge than for discussing terms in the Alva-Lazell boardroom.

Their inability to sum me up quickly, however, was to my advantage. They realized that they were incapable of doing what they were going to ask me to do, and I therefore became more important. They were not going to decide whether I was going to be suited to their proposal — *I* was going to decide. I came from the outside world, the world of unpleasantness, uncertainty, insincerity, the world where chairmen and gentlemen directors, shareholders and painstaking accountants were not particularly respected.

The chairman, who sat opposite me at the far end of the table, was sixty maybe, white-haired, public-school-tied and university-blue-complexed. He hated the idea of employing the services of a private investigator, but certain events had placed him and his Board of Directors in a situation that gave him no alternative.

'Mr. Flute, we know very little about private detectives, or how they work, so it is a little difficult to know where we should start.' He had coughed nervously and looked at the gold-plated fountain-pen, which he played with continuously before starting his opening speech. 'I think we should be quite frank with you and tell you that we have already interviewed two gentlemen in your line of business, but that we did not find them suitable for our particular problem. This, unfortunately, has lost us two valuable days. You were recommended to us by someone who knows your work well, but were warned that you used rather unorthodox methods. I hope you will not mind us asking you a few personal questions before engaging you. We feel it absolutely essential to get the right man for this job.'

'Ask me anything you want,' I said genially, which made him feel much better. I was a good deal easier to handle than the others.

'What type of work do you do — I mean, for what sort of people?'

He was dogged by the great English class system, this man. He couldn't come right out with it in case he hurt my feelings, or in case I was left-wing, so I helped him out.

'I usually only accept cases which I feel confident I can solve, involving me with people I can manage and who will not question my expenses. Usually my clients are in the upper-income brackets. You will appreciate that I cannot possibly give you any names, as I do everything in the strictest confidence.'

'Yes, of course.'

I was impressing them, slowly. I was an odd fellow but obviously knew my way around.

'Are you always successful?'

'Most times.'

'You get your man?' one of the young directors suggested with a nervous smile. He watched television every night and was a fan of '87th Precinct'.

'Have you worked on anything really important?' another asked.

'Every case I work on is really important — to my client and me.'

'Are you well known?'

'Not to the general public. The police

know me because I've helped them out once or twice.'

This last remark was a mistake; two of the directors looked at each other and then at their chairman. Maybe they were in trouble with the law.

'I meant important in a famous way — well known to the Press?'

'No,' I said.

'Are you married?'

'No.'

'So you would be free to . . . er . . . free to fraternise with the opposite sex?'

'I can get intimately involved with women when it is necessary to get information, if that's what you mean.'

Three of the directors uncrossed their legs and recrossed them. The youngest one, who watched television, eyed me with envy. He was probably finding it difficult to justify the expenses incurred in taking his secretary out to dinner.

'How do you charge your clients?' This question was from a man who wore steel-rimmed glasses and calculated square roots on his blotting pad while others doodled.

'It all depends on the case, the time allotted, the risks. I like to agree a fee and ask for a 50 per cent advance on that and on the estimated expenses, the remaining 50 per cent on both to be payable on successful completion of the case.'

'Would you be ready to sign a contract binding you to secrecy?'

'Of course, but I usually consider my word is enough.'

'The Government is involved, Mr. Flute; it would be a question of safeguarding ourselves with the Security people.'

I didn't bat an eyelid.

'Do you speak French?' The interview went on.

'Frequently.'

'Are you a member of any clubs?'

'Several.'

'West End clubs?' He was the oldest member on the board and obviously drank port after every meal. The fumes lived in his nose.

'Yes,' I said, 'West End night clubs, strip clubs, gambling clubs, I find them more useful for contacts than the

Athenaeum, Boodles or the Reform. Besides, I could never enjoy the amenities of the latter in case I embarrassed client members.'

There was a pause while everyone thought that one over, then the chairman smiled at his board and at me.

'I must say you seem to be the sort of man we want. Have you any other questions to ask, gentlemen?'

'Just one,' the second on the left said, looking at me. 'You say you've worked with the police. Do they ever check up on what you are doing?'

'Only if my client is involved in a case they are working on.'

'They don't watch your movements, tail you?'

'Not unless I give them cause. The police are very short of men and are glad of help. They usually mind their own business if I mind mine.'

Everyone murmured a bit and turned to the chairman, who took a deep breath before making his closing speech.

'If we are all satisfied, then, and have no more questions, gentlemen, I will ask

Mr. Flute to leave us for a moment while we have a little chat. Perhaps you would show Mr. Flute into my office?'

The younger director, to whom this was addressed, got up and suggested I should follow him.

He showed me into an adjacent room which was typical of any big company-chairman's headquarters. After suggesting that I should help myself to a cigarette, he left me to my own devices.

There was a big desk, three armchairs facing it, a large panoramic window overlooking the East of London. In a corner was the model of a building they were erecting in Puerto Rico, and on the walls various artist's impressions of forthcoming projects. Alva-Lazell's, a little pamphlet told me, was the largest scientific construction company in the United Kingdom, which immediately doubled my price.

I padded around looking at everything there was to see, resisting the temptation of opening the desk drawers. I was curious, of course, to know what they wanted a private eye for and guessed that it would probably be some internal trouble — an accountant embezzling, or the canteen manager selling quarter pounds of tea to members of the staff at half price, though this might be imagining too petty a crime considering government security had been mentioned.

I was back at the window when the young man came in. I followed him into the boardroom and sat down again facing the chairman.

'Mr. Flute, we have all agreed that you are probably the man best suited to help us with our particular trouble, and, as I don't think I can say much more without divulging the problem itself, I suggest we agree now to pay you whatever fee you will think suitable plus your expenses in exchange for your signature on our statement of secrecy.'

Everyone murmured their approval and the chairman then passed a sheet of paper to the young director, who handed it to me. I looked at the solicitor-worded paragraph that swore me to silence on acceptance of an advance of whatever sum I proposed, read in between the lines, saw nothing disagreeable, signed and hoped all the fuss would be worth it.

As the chairman started his second monologue of the day I drew out a small notebook and scribbled down a few incoherent sentences.

'The Alva-Lazell Construction Company, Mr. Flute, is one of the largest companies of its kind in the world. You may have read in the papers recently that we have been approached by the American Government to tender for the contract concerning an underwater atomic reactor station to be built in the Gulf of California. Negotiations are at present in hand and, needless to say, these negotiations are extremely delicate.'

All the directors murmured to themselves rather as though their ulcers were hurting them. I scribbled down a little drawing of an ulcer and frowned.

'We have three rivals, La Compagnie de Travaux Sous Terraine et Sous Marine de France (CTSTSMF), Ferdinand Gratzholpfen of Cologne and another British company, Coven, Gladholland and Butts (C.G.B.).'

I was doing pretty well writing down all

these names which impressed me no end. The young company director alone was probably paid £10,000 a year, which doubled my price again.

'As you will appreciate, the Americans will not necessarily choose the most economical tender, but the one from people they feel they can trust. Already their various bureaux of investigation have been making enquiries about our staff.' He stopped here as though the thought of these enquiries hurt him somewhere.

'George Gladholland, of C.G.B., was onto me this morning,' he continued, 'asking me whether we were allowing them to make such enquiries before contracts were signed. He is not going to make any objections!'

The directors, who had not heard this last bit of news, looked at each other, disconcerted, every one of them. All their hopes seemed to be pinned on me. I waited.

'A week ago, at our last board meeting, the managing director, Sir Frank Alva, put forward the suggestion that we should abandon competing for this project altogether. His reasons were without foundation and hardly made sense. As he failed to get the support of any one of us, his proposition was ignored and, in fact, the whole issue was erased from the minutes book, as we all agreed that Sir Frank was probably unwell, suffering possibly from fatigue caused by the months of negotiations. After the meeting, however, two of us were supposed to dine with him, but he did not turn up, and no one has seen him since.'

I let the significant pause last and looked at each man in turn. All five of them had a lot to gain from the negotiations going through. They were rich men, but, like all rich men, needed double the money they already had.

'I take it that you have called me in to find Sir Frank?' I said, showing a marked degree of intelligence.

'Yes, before the police or the newspapers do.'

'What are you afraid of?'

'How do you mean?'

'You must be afraid of something. He

may simply have been involved in an accident, or have fallen ill.'

The chairman turned to his director on his right, who looked at the doodles on his pad as he put me more in the picture.

'Sir Frank was divorced in 1958, Mr. Flute; you may recall the affair, a not very savoury one. Since parting with his wife he has spent most of his spare time in the company of young women of doubtful reputation.'

'What we're afraid of,' the chairman interrupted, 'is that he may have fallen ill at one of these ladies' homes, and if the police find him first or, worse, the Press, there could be a scandal. Any sort of scandal at this moment would put us right out of the picture. You see, we are not only being examined by the Americans, we must have Government approval — a question of a substantial loan is involved.'

'When did he disappear?' I asked, keeping to the point that interested me.

'The last time we saw him was at the board meeting. He vanished shortly after that. He went to his office and was never seen again.'

'What day was that?'

'Last Thursday.'

'Near enough a week ago. Was he seen leaving the building?'

'Oh yes. The hall porter got him a taxi. There was nothing unusual in the way he left. It's just that since then no one has seen him or been able to contact him.'

'You've tried all the possible places he might be?'

'Yes. Even his doctor. We've drawn a blank. The trouble is that if we go on making enquiries at random, suspicion of his disappearance might be aroused.'

It was a strange set-up. On the face of it there seemed to be no reason for them to be so worried, yet the board of a major British company would hardly waste their time or money hiring me just for the fun of it.

'I'm very sorry,' I said, 'but I haven't enough to go on. You say you are afraid of a scandal, that he may be with some woman. Surely there's more to it than that?'

All of them consulted their pens, writing pads, pieces of blotting paper. Then one by one they turned to their chairman for guidance.

'This is purely supposition, Mr. Flute, but we think he may be living with a woman who was mentioned in his divorce case, a Mademoiselle Babette Boulanger.'

'And?'

'And one of my colleagues has heard some rather disturbing rumours about the young woman.'

The chairman's colleague on his right dug deep into his wallet pocket and brought out a cutting from the Italian magazine *Consuelo*. It was a whole-page article with the translation neatly typed on foolscap pinned to it.

It concerned Babette Boulanger, a well-connected French girl, who had unsuccessfully attempted to imitate a well-known film star compatriot and who, having failed, had made an exhibition of herself at the homes of various famous people in Rome and eventually been deported for obscene behaviour.

There was a photograph of a smiling,

wide-eyed, freckled nymphomaniac of eighteen, and a little paragraph underneath suggesting that she was heading for the high life in London.

Their fears, I now felt, were reasonable, and, after arranging a fee and expenses which I felt could be justified but far in excess of what I normally charged, I promised I would contact them as soon as I had any news. My first step was obviously to find this girl.

* * *

Babette Boulanger very kindly dried my face with a corner of the sheet, lay down beside me and examined the little water pistol which amused her no end.

'Where did you get it?'

'A shop, on the front.'

'I have never seen one before. You could fill it with vitriol and ruin someone's face, couldn't you?'

'You have charming ideas, my lovely. Luckily the vitriol would burn through the plastic and your hand before you had time to use it.'

'Oh,' she said.

Babette had long blonde hair — blonde that particular week, anyway: a very well-proportioned little body about five and a half feet long; dark, penetrating brown eyes and the dirtiest mind I had come across. She was a good-time girl and would stoop to absolutely anything for kicks.

I had traced her address through friends in Fleet Street who were keeping an eye on her since the *Consuelo* story, and I had managed to gain entry into her Brighton flat by pretending I was a millionaire playboy pretending he was a private detective.

Once inside the apartment I had found no signs whatsoever of any man living there, but had decided to take her out to dinner to find out more about her way of life and that of her friends.

I had hired, to impress upon her that I was genuinely from the International Set, an Alfa Romeo 2600, driven her to a London night club at the average speed of 80 m.p.h., returned to Brighton a few hours later, insisted on opening a bottle of Taittinger *Comtes de Champagne blanc de blanc* on the beach in the moonlight, after which she had invited me home. I hadn't left her room since then except to buy more drink, cigarettes and the water pistol. When it came to it I could be as debauched as anyone, or so I thought.

For the first twenty-four hours I had just played the happy-go-lucky lover, then over a picnic of smoked salmon, chicken in aspic and a *Chateau d'Yquem 1959* on the double bed, I had started making tentative enquiries.

She knew many famous people, important people, influential people, but most of them bored her. I felt, however, that if I went carefully she would eventually lead me to Frank Alva. It would take time, but, above all, I did not want to raise her suspicions.

The water-pistol act had not been just fun and games. On the night we had met I had noticed a thin weal on the back of her shoulders and had decided to work along a certain line. With time running short now I got down to work.

'I remember a party once,' I started, gently curling her long gold hair round my fingers, 'when all the male guests were given water pistols each loaded with a different coloured dye. The women were let loose in the garden and the idea was that we should shoot at any of the ones we fancied. After half an hour the women were rounded up and those that were marked had to partner off with the man who had shot them. One girl — Danish I think she was — had eleven dyes on her. She was very tired by the end of the party.'

Babette was sitting up now looking at me with wide-open eyes. She had never heard anything like it even in the company she kept, and wanted to hear more about the rules of this game. She was nearly as fascinated as I was by the possibilities this new pastime presented. So I invented some more.

'Do you often go to parties like that?' she asked when I had finished describing a particularly unpleasant orgy I had never been to.

'No, not often. This one was in Rio.

They don't seem to have them in England — must be the weather.'

'They have them! Mostly indoors, but they have them. Not quite so elaborate of course, but . . . would you like to go to one?'

She was kneeling beside me now, looking at me intensely, her eyes bright with anticipation, her little kick-loving mind working double time.

I hadn't shaved, my eyes were burning with sleeplessness, my features were drawn, my mouth tired, but this was the way she liked her men — dark, sinister, unbearably handsome and dishevelled.

'You know of such a party?' I asked, putting on the enthusiastic act.

'Yes, to-morrow night. I'll arrange to get you in.'

She was off the bed and across the room to the telephone. From where I was I couldn't see the number she was dialling, but it seemed to be local.

'This is Babette. I've just met a fabulous man. He's been to fantastic parties and is full of new ideas. Could I bring him to-morrow night?'

She listened carefully, obviously to a voice of some authority, then turned to me.

'What's your name? Your full name?'

'Adam Fitz-Piper,' I said without hesitating.

She repeated it, listened some more, put down the receiver and turned round to look at me with a great big grin.

'It's all right, you can come. First we meet at a fashionable cocktail party, then get our instructions from there. It should be good — we're to bring whips!

2

We left Brighton the following evening after spending most of the day sun bathing on the balcony of Babette's apartment overlooking the blue sparkling sea.

It was one of those rare hot August spells that made the stay-at-home holiday-makers turn from white to lobster red and the nut-brown foreigners even more unwelcome.

My thoughts, however, were not entirely on blue skies. I was worried. A few years ago, when a carefree young man, I might have looked forward to the prospect of being a guest at an unusual party, but now I was less confident. My physique, for one thing, could be criticised, my stomach muscles had given up the battle against *Tournedos Rossini* at three in the morning and whisky milk shakes for tea. I was still tall, dark, interesting if not handsome and, dressed in elegantly cut clothes, could impress, but in a swimsuit or, worse, without, I wasn't so sure. Maybe everything happened in the dark.

The Alfa Romeo was powerful enough for me to overtake lines of stationary traffic and aggravate the acidity in the stomachs of all the saloon drivers who were sweating their way home after a steaming day in stuffy offices. We reached London in just under an hour, in time to have one drink in a snazzy bar before going on to the cocktail party.

After a couple of brandy sours we drove to Cadogan Square and joined the hundred-odd guests daintily choosing their favourite drink off silver trays passed round by harassed waitresses and their calmer white-jacketed male colleagues.

A quick glance at all the faces assured me that no one knew me and also told me that young Babette Boulanger, despite her reputation, was accepted among the more elegant and important members of London society.

Two people whom I knew by sight were reporters on a fashion magazine and an evening paper. I also recognized three Members of Parliament, two blue, one red, a bearded liberal candidate, a couple of retired but unpublished generals and a handful of better known actors. Apart from these it seemed the greater number of guests were top business executives who had brought their office problems with them.

I followed Babette around as much as I could, but then lost her when the director of a famous wine merchants engaged me in a conversation about the merits of the Amontillado he was drinking. Because he seemed to know everyone personally, and I realized that through him I might get some news about the man I was trying to find, I patiently listened to his lecture.

A large, jovial man with a chubby face and a sense of humour all his own came up behind the wine merchant and slapped him heartily on the back. Six bottles out of the case of twelve Medocs he had been sent were unlabelled and definitely corked and what was he going to do about it?

The big man, dressed in a check suit, white shirt and bow tie, was none other than George Gladholland, the man at the head of C.G.B., Alva-Lazell's rivals. Unlike his competitors Gladholland did not seem very worried about the situation. Life was for living, it seemed — parties, anyway.

While he listened to a description of how bottles of wine were labelled, he glanced at me several times. I made it clear by looking straight back at him that I knew he was trying to place me and this embarrassed him. Covering up, he asked me whether I was a wine connoisseur or thought it all a lot of rubbish. I told him my knowledge on the subject was just enough to know when I was being insulted by my host. He thought this funny and started to roar his head off, but no one turned round. Everyone knew Gladholland was a good audience.

The party was beginning to thin out when a tall, extremely distinguished man appeared in the doorway for a brief moment. There was nothing particularly strange about him except his manner. He had a stoop and seemed extraordinarily tired.

I took a quick summing-up look at him, dark-blue double-breasted suit, white shirt, starched collar, blue-and-red tie, nothing out of the ordinary apart from his socks — red-and-blue horizontal stripes — which struck me as a little eccentric. The photograph I had been given of him by the board of Alva-Lazells was flattering.

Babette joined me for a moment and threaded her arm through mine. When the wine executive had stopped explaining to me how whisky was distilled, she whispered in my ear that it was time we went.

As she edged me towards the door a vivacious six-foot raven-haired brunette, with just about the sexiest figure I had seen in four hours, passed by and smiled at me with her eyes. From a deliberate I-don't-know-you look towards Babette I gathered that maybe we might meet again later.

As I opened the Alfa Romeo door for Babette and got into the cockpit next to her, she lit me a cigarette.

'Where to now then?' I asked.

'Fred Bear's Strip Club,' she replied.

'Is that where the party is?'

'No, we're just going to pick up a girl there for Franky.'

'Franky?' I repeated.

'Yes. He's in one of his moods again. Must have fresh blood.'

I put the car into gear and tried to sound casual and uninterested.

'Franky?' I repeated, as though the name meant something.

'Franky Alva — Sir Frank Alva. You know him, surely?'

'Should I?'

'He was at the party.'

'This last one, the cocktail party?'

'Yes, didn't you see him?'

'No,' I lied.

'But you were standing right next to him.'

'I was?'

'Oh, Adam, the tall man with grey hair — in the dark-blue suit.'

'Oh, him! The one with funny socks.'

'You noticed them?' This was a big giggle. 'They come right up to his knees; terribly sexy when he's not wearing anything else, and so English.'

I drove down Piccadilly, turned up Shaftesbury Avenue, left into Soho and halfway along Wardour Street Babette asked me to stop.

'Fred Bear's is just up here,' she said.

Not wanting to miss anything, I followed my blonde friend into a dustbin-littered, cat-smelling alley to a red-painted door over which hung a sign bearing the legend STRIP CLUB — ALL THAT THERE IS TO BE SEEN CAN BE SEEN HERE.

Pushing the door open, she led the way up some dingy stairs covered with moth-eaten coconut matting, pushed open a badly scarred door at the top and was met by a man who greeted Babette effusively.

'Hazel in?'

'Yes, she's been waiting for you. We'll have to get a replacement for her if you go on taking her away like this. Friend of yours?'

The added phrase was for my benefit to convey that he thought I smelt bad.

'Yes,' Babette said, tweaking his cheek.

He was obviously a very jealous man. 'Shall we wait here or downstairs?'

'I'd go down. Not too much room in here.'

He was joking. We were in a water-closet-sized room that pretended to be an office by having a chair, a telephone and three out-of-date directories.

'How's business?' Babette asked.

'Not bad. The girls are getting bored though. We may have to change the pianist; he doesn't seem to be interested in them.'

The girls, five of them, had their photographs displayed in frames all the way down the stairs. Some had fans discreetly placed so that they modestly showed all that everyone wanted to see, others did the best they could with balloons and silk squares, with the same surprising results.

As I was on the point of dressing a teenage blonde with some imaginary clothes, Babette pulled me by the sleeve and led me out into the street and back to the car.

We got in and waited, with the radio

going full blast to draw the attention of the passers-by who might not have noticed the blonde with dark glasses sitting in an Alfa Romeo. Babette enjoyed being stared at.

Then down the alley minced the Hazel girl looking around as though she didn't quite know what she was doing there. She was the nymphette whose photograph I had attempted to dress.

Babette leaned over me, sounded the horn several times, waved, and took off her dark glasses.

When the Hazel girl saw us she reacted strangely, as though she had hoped it would be someone other than Babette.

Hazel was a blonder blonde; she had nearly white hair piled six inches or so above her head in beehive fashion, a sweet little face under that, with large deep-blue eyes, a well-stencilled mouth, pert nose and figure to match. She wore a neat little outfit of white and green linen, and carried a handbag big enough to hold a G-string.

'Hallo, Hazel,' Babette said, and the way they looked at each other gave me the impression they were sisters, Babette the older by forty years.

'Get in, honey,' she commanded, pointing to the space behind us which was roomy enough for one small stripper.

Like a gentleman I got out and pushed back the seat so that she could slip in. I was wearing dark glasses which maybe made me look sinister enough to warrant the fearful expression she gave me.

She didn't get in immediately, but nervously hesitated on the edge of the pavement.

'Where are we going?'

'A party,' Babette said.

'I don't want to . . . '

'It's worth fifty quid.'

'No . . . really.'

'Don't be silly, honey; fifty quid's fifty quid, and you know what Natalie will do if you don't turn up.'

Hazel didn't hesitate much more. She controlled a shiver, bit her lower lip, and got in.

'What will Natalie do?' I asked, adjusting the driving seat to give her more room.

'You mind your own business.'

Maybe the honeymoon was over, or maybe Babette was like this when organising a party. I switched on the engine and pulled away from the kerb with a roar. The idiots watching from the pavement, who had never driven an Alfa Romeo loaded with two blondes, hated my guts even more.

'It won't be like last time, will it?' Hazel asked, leaning forward and putting her honeycombed head between us.

'What was it like last time?' Babette was a sadist at heart but I hoped the frightened little stripper would answer, all the same.

'Well — you know.'

'Look, sweety, how much are you making now? And who got you the job? Doing this sort of thing once in a blue moon isn't going to ruin you, is it? And it's helping me.'

'It's not natural, that's all.'

I was doing some pretty tricky gear changing down Oxford Street and getting nervous. Any more of this conversation and I would back out of the case.

'You haven't introduced us,' I said, squeezing Babette's twenty-two-year-old knee — she was as jealous as hell of the Hazel girl, all because the stripper was seventeen.

'Hazel, this is Adam Fitz-Piper.'

'Hi,' I said, waving a friendly hand in the air and looking at Hazel in the rear-view mirror. If I accelerated any more her beehive would topple over.

'If you sit right back you'll find it more comfortable,' I said. The younger blonde sat back and for the rest of the journey we didn't hear much from her.

Babette switched the radio programmes, told me to head for Guildford and not to get arrested for speeding. It was a clear starlit night with no moon, warm, even hot, and everything was working out fine.

Along a straight bit of road as we approached Petford she asked me to slow down as we were ahead of schedule. I didn't ask any questions, but did as I was told. Babette was going through a metamorphic change. In the dark, with the green dashboard light shining in her face, she looked positively evil.

'What time does the party start, then?' I asked, stopping the car in a lay-by to put up the hood.

'No, don't stop. Carry on — we don't particularly want to draw attention to ourselves. What we do is drive on for another three miles, then I'll tell you what to do. You've got some money, I hope.'

'A little, why?'

'This isn't for free, you know. Everyone pays a tenner.'

Without batting an eyelid I handed her my wallet, which happened to be stuffed with fivers. She took from it thirty pounds' worth and handed it back to me.

'You can afford to see us all in, darling.'

'Sure,' I said genially. If I couldn't afford it Alva-Lazell's could.

As we reached some crossroads Babette told me to take a road to the right. I did so, and a minute later she asked me to pull up and switch off my headlights.

'What happens now?' I asked, intrigued.

'We wait.'

I offered a cigarette to the silent Hazel, to Babette and myself and lit all three.

Babette then switched off the radio and turned round to look through the rear window.

A large black limousine oozed past unexpectedly with only its sidelights on, and someone shone a torch from the back window. Babette grabbed hold of my wrist, looked at my watch, then exactly a minute after told me to drive on.

Without any lights at all, slowly, I followed the winding bends of the country lane. The three of us were on edge now; the operation was as exciting as a Civil Defence exercise.

After half a mile Babette told me to slow right down, then when a pair of high wrought-iron gates became visible in the darkness she told me to drive through them.

'The drive is straight for about a quarter of a mile, then there's a slight bend to the right.'

I drove, in third, and averaged about twenty along the faintly brighter strip of gravel that unfolded in front of me. At the slight bend I went onto the grass, but navigated off again successfully.

'Now you can turn left anywhere you like and hide the car under the trees,' Babette said.

I swung the car off the road, bumped across some rough ground, felt some branches brush against the roof and stopped.

'This do you, governor?' I asked.

'It'll do.'

Quietly we all got out — Babette independently and very much in charge, Hazel with my help. As I gripped her young arm I could feel her shivering nervously. I squeezed it very gently, reassuringly, but this only made her more tense. I wondered what she thought I had in mind.

Following the all-knowing Babette, we tripped our way further through the trees till we came to a clearing. Looking up against the star-spangled sky I could see the tall sinister turrets of a Victorian atrocity bristling with weather-cocks and television aerials.

As we paused on the edge of the front driveway, Babette handed me a piece of velvet material.

'Put this on, and then leave us. From now we don't know each other. There are two entrances, one straight ahead and one on the left. If you'll take the one on the left, Hazel and I will go in the other way.'

'All right,' I said, trying to control an imminent fit of giggles. The piece of velvet was a Pierrot's mask and I first of all put it on upside-down.

'Excited, Adam?' Babette's voice whispered, unexpectedly close to me.

Then she pulled me toward her and gave me one of those kisses I usually take three hours to work up to.

3

Quite suddenly I was alone. Me, the velvet mask I had been handed and an invitation to an orgy. As I crunched my way across the driveway I looked up at the silhouette of the house hoping that I might recognize it from some book on ancestral homes, but nothing distinguished it from any other edifice of that period. All I knew was that we were on some large estate in Sussex or Hampshire and that the next few hours might prove to be full of entirely new, if not wholly desirable, experiences.

As I turned the corner a tiny spot of light was being waved up and down among some hyacinths. I went towards it with caution. A member of the Klu Klux Klan was waiting for me all dressed in black robes and he asked for ten pounds. I didn't argue, there was no point, but made a mental note to get something in return for my high expenses from Babette.

'Room fifteen, on the left. You'll see the number clearly on the door. Inside you'll find a gown. Wear only that and please yourself when you take it off.'

A black arm then showed me a side entrance and I pushed my way through some curtains to see, ahead of me, two straight lines of phosphorescent numbers on either side of a long dark passage.

The numbers started at forty and went backwards along the corridor. I walked most of the way down before I got to No. 15 and brushed against two people whom I could not see, but by the sound they made I guessed they were robed and bare-footed.

I opened the door of my room and inside found it lit by one electric night light. It didn't take long to see all there was to see, a desk, a chair, a shelf full of school books, two hockey sticks in a corner and a timetable of scientific classes. My whereabouts were explained. I was in a girl's school.

On the back of the chair I found the robe, two pieces of non-transparent green polythene-type material sewn together

41

with holes at the top and sides for neck and arms.

I slipped my jacket off, my shirt and trousers, shoes and socks, but kept on my underwear. Somehow I felt at an advantage cheating like this.

Neatly I bundled the clothes under the desk, picked out a book, read a girl's name and her home address, hoped I would remember it to check up what school I was in, then straightened my polythene sack dress and took a deep breath.

On the back of the door hung a phosphorescent notice. 'Proceed to No. 21,' it read. So I did just that. I traced my way back along the corridor to door 21, opened it and found myself in a comparatively brightly candle-lit stairway.

Here two or three people, masked and clothed in polythene as I was, were making their way down to what I presumed would be a cellar or a torture chamber. The stairs, however, led down to a pair of tall Gothic doors which opened into a panelled dining hall. The house, I realized, had been built on the slope of a hill; this was a lower floor and the promise of dungeons was dashed.

A reception, if it could be so called, was being held in this panelled hall, an elaborate affair with the portraits of ex-headmistresses neatly covered over with sheets of bed linen. The place was lit only by candles and the curtains were carefully drawn. Along one wall was a table laden with a superb buffet; on another table were glasses filled with a dark wine-like liquid — probably high-octane aphrodisiac.

People moved about examining each other in an attempt to identify, though the whole idea of the masks and polythene was to prevent all this.

Despite the disguises, however, much of the person's character was revealed by the lines of the mouth and the voice. Most of the guests were over forty, some men in their sixties even. They were well-built, surprisingly healthy and, apart from a few foreigners, well spoken.

The vanity of some women made them wear their jewellery, bracelets, rings and necklaces — one woman even sported a huge ruby brooch which would enable anyone to recognize her when next she dined out in a fashionable restaurant. Though tempted to make a mental note of these various characteristics, I decided to reserve my sometimes weak Pelmanistic powers to remember anything I could about Alva, if he ever turned up.

I was sipping my second glass of wine cup when the tall girl with raven hair, whom I had seen at the cocktail party, noticed me standing in the corner alone. She crossed the room and unashamedly pressed herself against me Accidentally she jolted my arm, spilling some of the wine on my lovely polythene outfit.

Apologetically she tried to wipe off some of the liquid and suddenly looked up.

'You're not wearing anything under that, I hope!' Her voice was deep and sensuous, but a trifle mocking.

'Only a pair of woollen trunks,' I said. 'I catch cold very easily.'

'But it's against the rules. You must take them off at once or I'll report you.'

She was quite stern, like a sports

mistress reprimanding a junior for not liking cricket. I wondered how I would get out of this one.

'I'll take them off in my own good time, thank you, darling, or maybe you'd like to help me?'

That sounded naughty enough and she raised her eyebrows at the invitation. The great difficulty would be not to get involved in this crazy caper, and not to get too drunk Even after two glasses the wine was beginning to have a stimulating effect.

'You're new here, aren't you?'

'To this house, yes,' I said.

'Were you at our last party in Dorset?'

'Maybe.'

'Did you come alone, or with some-one?'

'That would be telling.'

'I know who you are!' she said, after looking at me more closely. 'You're the water-pistol man. I want to talk to you about that, sometime.'

'There's no time like the present.'

'I intend enjoying myself tonight, sweetie, not talk business!'

'What happens anyway?' I asked, as though bored. 'This is like a cocktail party, very British.'

'Things'll get moving soon. We've got a sacrifice laid on for you later — till then you can do what you like.'

I realized I wouldn't get anywhere unless I did a bit more probing. Taking up another full glass of wine, I moved swiftly in and out of the crowd, looking at everyone, till I came face to face with Babette.

'I hear you're wearing your underwear,' she said reproachfully.

'Well, you must admit it's original.'

'Positively perverted.' Her eyes were wide with excitement, I guessed she might even have taken some pep pills to get through the evening satisfactorily.

I asked her what the sacrifice would consist of, when our brief conversation was interrupted by a loudspeaker announcing by a roll of drums the beginning of the evening's entertainment.

Preceded by some Turkish-type music, a girl came in from what could have been the kitchens, indiscreetly covered by several veils and looking as much like Salome as Hazel.

Presumably to stimulate the company, which the wine had in actual fact dulled, a spotlight was put on the stripper, who started doing a dance. She ran through her routine with unbelievable disinterest, her casualness being the only worthwhile part of the act.

While everyone watched her drop her various nylon kerchiefs one by one, finally ending up wearing only her silver speckled G-string, I noticed a tall grey-haired man edging his way to the front of the circle of onlookers. Though I could not be certain, I guessed that this was Alva.

As Hazel danced on, the black-hooded individual who had guarded the entrance door came in with several of his brothers and started putting out the candles. When Hazel came to the end of her act the spotlight on her was suddenly switched off and curtains, hiding tall french windows, were pulled back. The guests, who now seemed in a high state of frenzy, rushed out into the garden with screams of delight and noises appropriate to Arabs going into battle or Scotsmen about to join an eightsome reel.

Taken aback by this strange barbaric and Anglo-Saxon way of behaviour, I waited a while in the room to see what else might happen. Several people were still moving about in the dark where Hazel had been and I felt that Alva might well be one of them.

Suddenly behind me came a piercing scream. Quickly I moved away from the window where I might be conspicuous and tried to see what was happening in the depths of the hall, but all I could do was hear the heavy gasps of two or three people struggling to keep someone under control.

Somewhere a door opened, and the girl — for it was a girl — started to scream again, but not for long. A gag was placed over her mouth and after a few pathetic mumbles she was successfully silenced.

There was a little more scuffling, a man mentioned the word 'Dormobile', a door closed and then there was silence.

I waited till I was sure I was alone, then

crossed the panelled hall to feel along the walls blindly for a door. Eventually I came to one, opened it and found myself in the hallway stairs face to face with one of the hooded monsters.

'What do you want?' The voice was thick with gin and could have belonged to either sex.

'A cigarette,' I said.

'Haven't they got any in there?'

'I don't know . . . I can't see.'

'Well, they have, on the tables.'

'But I roll my own,' I said.

Not too happy about this, the black hood followed me up the stairs, down the passage to my room.

Once inside I knew I would have to do something desperate, so I turned unexpectedly, hit the robed figure hard and fast in the belly and caught it a well-aimed uppercut under the hood.

As the black shape slumped to the floor with a groan, I wrestled the hood off its face and was temporarily shocked to find myself staring at a fifty-year-old woman. Fat, gross, she might well have been an ex-prison wardress — no chin, no neck, a head covered with a short cut stubble of hair. I wondered what the other hooded creatures looked like.

Quickly taking off my poly-sack, I slipped on my clothes; then, removing the black robe from this monstrous woman, I put that on with the hood.

Pushing my shoes and socks into my pockets, I then left the cubicle bare-foot after gagging the toad with a handkerchief and pushing her heaped body into a corner.

I had no idea who else was keeping watch over the festivities, so I got down to work immediately. Unless people shared the cubicles, it would be a simple matter of visiting some forty of them to find what I was looking for. I started meticulously at one end of the corridor and worked my way down the right, then the left side.

All the rooms were senior girls' studies, similarly furnished, with the added decoration of Mum's picture or boy-friend's photo. Occasionally Elvis Presley smiled at me from a frame, but otherwise it was mainly gym shoes and Swiss calendars.

In room 27 I found what I was looking for: Frank Alva's clothes, socks and all. Quickly I went through his pockets, found nothing whatsoever of interest, so simply swopped his socks for mine and left. At least I knew exactly what I was going to do now, which was a change.

Along the corridor at the entrance I bumped into a naked woman who was sneezing, apologized for treading on her toes and left.

To make sure I wasn't followed, I went straight out into the garden past some tennis courts and got lost in an orchard. A bright moon was now dancing in and out of some puffball clouds and made the going easier but the task in hand more difficult.

I circumnavigated the house, hoping to find something of significance, then heard some music coming from the direction of a gazebo. From various parts of the garden guests, clothed or not, were running towards it. Across the lawn I saw one of my hooded colleagues waving everyone on. Maybe the moonlight was their enemy and from now on all fun and games had to take place indoors, or the famous sacrifice was about to take place.

I waited a while, till the hooded individuals had gone, then crossed the open space to the gazebo. It was a surprisingly large cylindrical-shaped building with shutters at all the windows. These were all firmly closed and not a sound came out, so I started making my way round the building and found that was connected to some outhouses.

Cautiously I started going round these when suddenly a door opened and someone from the darkness shot his hand out and touched my shoulder.

'Locked out?'

'Yes,' I whispered.

A girl's hand came to take mine and like an idiot I let myself be pulled in. The place was dark but the girl's hand was as familiar as her scent.

'Why are you dressed like that?' Babette asked, moving around somewhere behind me.

'I thought the disguise more exciting.'

'But not as exciting as what's going to happen next.'

'No?'

'No! You come with me . . . '

There was no telling whether she had guessed my reasons for being there or whether she still thought me an eccentric out for kicks. I would have to play along till something showed up.

Taking my arm, she started leading me in the darkness across the room. From the smell and the feel of the cement floor I guessed it was used by a gardener for storing apples and potted plants. Suddenly my throat was gripped as in a steel vice and I was pulled down to the floor from behind.

I struggled, but two or three people had got hold of me. With the black robes I found it impossible to move and when I smelt a whiff of chloroform I panicked.

As the pad was brought closer to my nose and mouth I shook my head violently, but someone with huge leather-gloved hands pinned me to the hard gritty floor and forced me to keep still.

The struggle lasted for as long as I could hold my breath, which gave me time to kick out at someone where it hurt and bite whoever was trying to put me to sleep. Then I was released, allowed for a moment to sit up, before I felt a stabbing pain across the side of my face. The room became bright with waves of green and yellow light. My heart thumped once, twice, then I woke up on a stretcher somewhere in broad daylight.

4

Though the ambulance men tried to persuade me not to, I sat up on the thin strip of taut canvas and looked around.

Several people were staring at me and the Alfa Romeo which was being hauled out of a ditch by a motorised crane. From the light I guessed it was early in the morning, and from the people standing around — farm labourers on their way to work — I also guessed that I had probably been found by one of them.

My memory came back very quickly. I remembered vividly the previous night and pieced together what had undoubtedly happened.

I had been slugged, dumped in my car, driven to some distant place and disposed of as though I had had an accident. I put my hand up to feel the bruise and touched dried blood. Maybe they had sapped me rather hard.

'I'd lie back, sir. Now we've come all

this way you may as well make use of our services.'

He was a nice kind man with seven children at home and a wife who made cups of tea for everyone. I didn't want to disappoint him, so lay back and enjoyed the pity that the onlookers were determined to feel for my condition.

'Where am I?' I asked, as they bolted the stretcher into the ambulance.

'Between Yarcombe and Chard, sir.'

'Oh,' I said. 'Where's that?'

'Just inside Devon, sir.'

'Oh,' I said again. They had made a good job of my disposal. 'Anywhere near Exeter?'

' 'Bout thirty mile. Nearer Yeovil. But we're taking you to Honiton.'

I folded my hands on my chest like a dead man and watched the doors close. Babette and company had done the only thing they could; I only hoped they didn't suspect I was after Alva.

I didn't look at my watch till the doors opened because I went to sleep. When they pulled me out of the ambulance and into the cottage hospital's casualty ward, I actually got up and walked around. It was six in the morning and I hoped that I had only been out for a count of four and not twenty-four hours.

A doctor, younger than me, was sympathetic. He understood that I wanted to get away, but, all the same, he examined me for flaws and, finding none, handed me over to a constable who wanted a few details.

I told him I had been driving back from Exeter to London and that I must have fallen asleep at the wheel. He had made up his mind a long time ago that I had had too much to drink; but as it was too late to prove it, all he did was ask me why I hadn't been wearing any shoes or socks.

'I always drive that way. I'm afraid it's a craze on the Continent. These Italian cars are so smooth, it's nice to feel as one with them, you know.'

He didn't, but then he didn't know either what connections I might have. I was a British subject but went abroad a lot, had a foreign car which I had to admit wasn't mine, but all the same cost a lot to hire. He preferred apprehending hikers for littering the countryside.

I asked him how I could get back to London quickly and, after suggesting that I should drive more carefully next time, gave me the 7.24 as a good tip. If I managed to catch that I would be in Waterloo by eleven. Formalities with National Health numbers, doctors' reports and hospital clearance delayed me, however, and I eventually caught the 10.09 after shaking off the local press reporter who had decided I was some sort of film star.

The train had a restaurant car. I had a good meal, hiding my face from a vicar's wife who threatened to have pity on me, and planned my next step in the Find-Alva Campaign. I had plenty to tell my clients already, but first I would call at Franky's address — just in case he went home occasionally.

I took a taxi to 66 Clithfield Terrace, South Kensington, ran up the steps of the neo-Georgian house and rang the bell. It was three in the afternoon — an unlikely time for anyone living in London to be at home, but there was no harm in trying.

As I waited I looked down at my feet. The constable had found my shoes on the floor behind the driving seat and Alva's socks had remained safely in my pockets. Now I wore them and had to admit that they looked splendidly bright in the hot afternoon sun.

They were all I could show as evidence that I had got anywhere near Frank Alva. It would have been nicer to report that I hadn't lost sight of the managing director than to recount what had happened, but I felt sure that the Alva-Lazell board would be grateful, if not very pleased, for the information I had so far on their erring boss.

I was about to turn round and leave when someone pulled back a few bolts and the door opened. To my very great surprise Sir Frank Alva himself was standing there in his dressing gown — a gold dressing gown with a black dragon embroidered in silk all the way down the left side of his chest.

'Good afternoon,' I said cheerfully. I was fingering the blue bruise on the side of my face.

'Good afternoon.'

He was puzzled by my presence, obviously did not recognize me or have any idea who I was.

'I believe you have my socks,' I said with a smile.

'Your socks?' He was astounded.

'Well, I have yours,' I said, and cocked up a leg to display the bright red and blue horizontal stripes.

He glanced at my legs, registered surprise, then opened the door wide for me to come in, suddenly quite concerned.

'How on earth did you get hold of those?'

'Some mix-up last night. Our rooms must have been next to each other, or something.'

'Last night?'

Nervously he bit at a piece of skin on the edge of his thumb.

'You were there then,' he said uncertainly.

'Yes.'

'You're the very first person I've met without a mask. It's strictly against the rules, you know.'

'A lot of things are,' I said.

He showed me into a drawing room which had enough orientana to convince me that he had been to the Far East some time during his life.

'Smoke?'

'Thank you,' I said, accepting a cigarette from a silver box.

'A drink maybe, or don't you in the afternoon?'

'Just a tomato juice, if you have that, with a little Vodka perhaps?'

He left the room and I had a good look round. There was a desk, several glass cabinets, two or three comfortable armchairs, Chinese carpets on the floor and vases everywhere. I couldn't smell opium.

'What happened to the blonde?' I asked when he returned with a tin of juice.

'What blonde?'

'The little one, last night.'

'Didn't you see?'

'No, I had other matters to attend to.'

'Oh, we had quite a struggle. She wouldn't.'

'Wouldn't she?' I said, my imagination boggling.

'There was a slight disturbance which

upset things,' he said.

'Really?'

'An intruder,' he added. Then it dawned on him and he turned abruptly to look at his socks. 'My God! Was it you?'

'Yes, Sir Frank, it was.'

Realizing that there was little he could do about it, he sipped the tomato juice he had poured out for me, making it quite plain that I was no longer his guest.

'What do you want?'

'You,' I said.

'What do you mean, me? Who are you?'

'I'm a private investigator, working for clients who wish to know more about your nocturnal activities. So far, all I can tell them is that you keep strange company and go to debauched parties.'

'Who are these clients?' His manner was scoffing. I could see him now as a managing director.

'I'm afraid I can't reveal that.'

'How much do they want? I presume you are here to blackmail me?'

'No, I'm here to protect you — from yourself.'

'Beautiful words indeed! A private

investigator, eh? Have I sunk this low then?'

For a moment he turned his back on me and started drawing something out of his pocket. I couldn't take any changes so I leapt up, lunged forward and hit out at his arm in case he was holding a weapon.

He swivelled round, momentarily lost his balance and unexpectedly crashed to the floor, hitting his head on the side of a table as he went down.

It had not been my intention to hurt him, or even render him unconscious, but I had succeeded in doing both. A quick examination told me that he was alive but in very bad physical shape, and that he had been about to take a small white pill from a box in his pocket.

Deciding that cold water would probably pull him round as quickly as anything else, I went in search of the kitchen. Sir Frank, I decided, had burnt his candle at both ends for too long and was just about ready for a rest home.

The flat, at first sight, was typical of a

rich bachelor's. The entrance-hall, its walls crammed with sporting prints, led into a square oriental sitting room, while another door led into a kitchen, which in turn led to a bathroom. But here things were different.

It was painted scarlet with a black bath and mirrored ceiling. A long glass shelf extended the whole width of one wall and was packed tight with various toilet preparations, lotions, bath salts, sprays, scents. Under the washbasin a fitted cupboard contained three bottles of champagne and two Venetian cut glasses. It seemed that Sir Frank enjoyed his ablutions.

Apart from the fact that the kitchen led into the bathroom which led nowhere else, I thought it strange that a breakfast tray had been laid for two people.

I retraced my steps through the flat but could see no other door and no sign of any bedrooms, so, ignoring Sir Frank, who seemed quite happy lying spread-eagled on the Chinese carpet, I went back to the scarlet bathroom.

Puzzled, I ran my fingers over the walls

to find possibly a well-concealed entrance to another room. It was logical that the bathroom should be next to a bedroom. Somewhere, I felt sure, there was a way through, but obviously the secret door was mechanically controlled, and without finding the locking device I would have difficulty getting in.

Slowly I started a thorough examination again, pressing here, pulling there till I eventually found the control. Half the wall on the left of the door slid open by putting a little pressure on the towel rail. Beyond the panel was a thick green velvet curtain, and behind that a spacious bedroom which would have done justice to Lucretia Borgia.

The ceiling was a reproduction of Michelangelo's Sistine Chapel — in miniature; the walls were hung with tapestries and the floor covered with a very thick sepia carpet on which lay a number of small Persian rugs and cushions.

In the centre of the room was a huge four-poster bed with all the trimmings in gold, but made up with black sheets.

What I found disturbing were the four elaborate Italian candelabra, burning eight candles each, at the corners of the bed, and the white pall in the middle of it all that covered a body.

5

Around the bed, scattered on the floor, there were a number of diabolical mediæval instruments which were frightening enough for me to hesitate pulling back the white pall and having a look at whatever remains there might be left of Alva's victim.

Slowly I lifted the linen sheet and looked down at the sleeping beauty herself: Hazel, with blonde hair neatly arranged on the pillow around her shoulders, her young white features peacefully smiling, her body clothed in a transparent lace nightdress that might well have belonged to the Infanta.

Gently I took her wrist and tried to find her pulse, but as I did so Alva came into the room behind me.

'She's not dead, she's just asleep. I doped her.'

I turned to look at him. He was dishevelled, his lip was swollen where he had struck the table and his eyes were narrow in the centre of the unhealthy blue circles of loose skin that told the story of too many nights out. I had seen handsomer men.

'Why did you dope her?'

'It was easier that way. She wasn't very obliging.'

'You dressed her up like this, I suppose?'

'Yes.'

'And covered her over as though she were dead?'

'Yes. It's a game I play.'

'A game?' He was beginning to frighten me.

'I'm kinky, you see, I can't help it. I was actually preparing breakfast for her when you rang, but then you wouldn't understand.'

'Understand what?'

'That I really like her, mean her no harm. I'd like her to live here with me.'

'It's a strange way to woo a girl,' I said, more to myself.

He tittered. What I had said was funny. It appealed to him.

'She's coming round, I think.'

Sleeping Beauty stirred, opened her eyes and closed them again, then opened them and looked at her surroundings. As soon as her mind registered where she was she looked frightened, terrified.

She tried to sit up, gasped as though in pain, and fell back on the pillow exhausted by the small effort. Puzzled by this behaviour, I pulled the sheet further back and was appalled to see her waist encircled by a metal contraption which must originally have been designed for pinning down edible Christians in Roman arenas.

'How do you undo this thing?' I asked Alva, who was beginning to smirk at my concern for the girl.

'Why should I tell you?'

I wasn't feeling at all tolerant. I turned round, crossed the room, lashed out with the back of my hand, caught him on the left side of his face and sent him flying sideways against one of his precious tapestries.

In an attempt to stop himself falling he grabbed hold of it, but the great square mass of embroidered material tore from its hooks and came down, enveloping him as he fell.

Like a brave knight in armour rescuing a damsel in distress I went over to Hazel. She looked as frightened of me as of everyone else she had seen in the last twelve hours, till I found out how to release the flexible belt of steel that was holding her to the bed. The two ends of the metal band had been pushed through the thin matress and bolted together under the bed; it was a home-made contraption, but unhealthily effective.

I suggested she should sit up and try to recover. I offered her a cigarette and, after lighting it with one of the innumerable candles, went to the corner where Alva was lying and helped him to his feet.

He was in bad shape, pale, shivering. He tried to say something but was completely incoherent. From his terrified expression I gathered he was begging me not to hit him again.

I led him to the bed and asked Hazel to get off, told him to lie down and once he was settled looked around for an electric light. The whole scene, with only the candles flickering, was macabre. Behind a tapestry I found a switch and a stark clear glass bulb lit up in the high ceiling, making the whole atmosphere even worse.

When I was satisfied that young Hazel could walk steadily, I led her out of the room, through the scarlet bathroom, to the kitchen. There I made her sit down at the table and searched the place for some tea.

'My name is not Adam Fitz-Piper, but Adam Flute,' I said with authority, 'I am a private detective and I am here to help you.'

She did not seem very impressed, but more concerned with her reflection in the glass door of the crockery cabinet. Her honeycombed beehive had come to pieces.

'There's probably some makeup, combs, brushes and scent in the bathroom,' I said. Then, when she didn't move, I went on, 'I can't detain you, nor have I the right to ask you any questions, but, unless you absolutely want to go now, I would like to take you back to my flat and piece together the events since last night.'

Though she was scared of Alva and his particular brand of friends, she wasn't enamoured with detectives, private or public, either.

'If it's all the same to you, I'd like to get dressed and go. Maybe you could give me a ring?'

From the way she got up, strolled back into the bedroom, found her clothes, stripped off her nightdress unashamedly in front of me and dressed, I got the impression that maybe she hadn't put up too much of a struggle against some of Alva's imaginative ideas.

As soon as she could she left the flat without saying another word, but the contemptuous look she gave me as I helped Alva sit up was enough to tell me that she hadn't believed a word I had said.

Hazel, however, was not my concern; she could walk and talk, and that was all that I might have worried about. Alva was my man and I meant to find out for my clients exactly why he had behaved towards them the way he had, though it was clear by now that he could hardly be held responsible for most of his actions any more.

'A private detective, you said,' he muttered as I got him to his feet and led him out of the room.

'Yes.'

'Police?'

'No, this is a private enquiry.'

'Yes, yes. I remember now, you said. American?'

'No.'

All this talk made him grate his teeth and close his eyes. He sat down on the edge of the kitchen table and concentrated for a long time before looking up and accepting the cup of hot tea I had made for him.

'Are you working for C.G.B. — Coven, Gladholland and Butts? That's likely. They'd hire someone like you to find out if I was on the point of cracking up.'

I decided to stop being coy about my clients. 'No, I'm not working for them. I'm working for your own firm, your Board of Directors.'

'What?' He was appalled

'They hired me because they were afraid you might have been involved in an accident, or committed suicide.'

'Ridiculous!'

'Is it? You have been absent from the office some time.'

'I'm having a few days' rest. I've worked hard enough.'

'You didn't tell anyone where you would be.'

'Of course not! I don't want to be pestered all the time. Can't they manage without me then, is that it?' He was fit again, the angry tycoon pacing the floor. But not too convincing. He was putting on the act for my benefit, an act which didn't impress me.

'I think they can manage without you, but there's some question of negotiations between yourselves and an American company being jeopardised by your absence.'

'You don't say! Why do you think I went away at this precise moment? I went away for exactly that reason, so that the negotiations would fall through. The whole project is mad, we won't make a penny out of it.'

I was on the verge of getting involved in business politics which had nothing to do with me, so I decided I would tie up my part of the case and call it a day.

'I'm reporting back to your Board and I would like to know what you'd like me to say.'

'Really? What do you think I'd like you to say? That you found me in a state of acute alcoholism, drugged to the eyebrows, raping a seventeen-year-old virgin I'd tied to a four-poster? I can hardly stop you saying anything, can I?'

'I was hired to find you, Sir Frank. I've found you. I don't have to go into any details.'

He calmed down. He got control of his guilt complex and stopped chewing his knuckles for a moment.

'I've been in the hands of blackmailers, you know that.'

'Who?'

'Who?' He was surprised I should ask. 'The people who got me in this mess. I haven't been decadent all my life. I was tricked into it.'

He said this more to himself than to me, as though wondering whether he was making excuses or whether it was actually true.

'After my divorce I started going out with a strange girl, French she was, mad little thing, quite mad. She took me to a dubious party and, well, when you start that sort of thing it's hard to stop. She was so full of life! So very full of life! She suddenly made things worth while, and I found I had an insatiable appetite for the new. I couldn't resist those invitations to novel forms of sensation, then one day I realized I was in her hands, realized she could blackmail me — and I stopped.'

Unconsciously he had taken my cup and his cup to the sink and had started washing up. Wiping the china now, with long nervous hands, he looked straight ahead, talking in a quiet controlled voice.

'When the negotiations for this Californian project started I met her by accident in the street. I thought at the time it was by accident anyway. Like a fool I went to a party with her and my old thirst for sensations, new experiences came back.

76

They increased with my business activities: the harder I worked the harder I had to play. Maybe a psychiatrist can explain it. Anyway, I allowed myself to be enticed into worse and worse forms of pleasure, and all the time I knew it would end in disaster. She's working for an international vice ring, you see, and they've been blackmailing me.'

'What sort of blackmail?' I asked. Alva was talking to me now as though I were a father confessor; he was unloading all the dirt from his mind and I wasn't going to stop him.

'Straightforward. They want me to stop Alva-Lazell's competing for the American contract so that the foreign companies can have a chance.'

'They're working for the continental firms?'

'It's hardly something the British would stoop to!'

'And what did they threaten to do if you failed them?'

'Expose me to the Press, publish my story. But I'm not going to give them the chance.'

'What are you going to do?'

'I'm going to do the only thing I can do, what I should have done months ago — resign.'

'But then your company will lose the contract. You're the image of the firm the Americans like.'

'They may lose, they may not, but at least they will be able to appoint a new managing director. It will still give the other British company a chance. A scandal now would involve the Government, you see, because of all the people I know. The main thing is to keep the police and the Press out of it.'

'But what is to stop this vice ring exposing you after you've retired?'

'Nothing, but there would be no point. My resignation dissociates me from the company, the negotiations, the Government, everything.'

Alva folded the damp dishcloth neatly, hung it up on the drying rail and asked me to follow him. 'I'm mentally ill, it's the only explanation. I'm a Jekyll and Hyde! Split personality. That girl, she was so young!'

He led the way to the sitting room and, not knowing what he might do next, I watched him carefully as he sat down at his desk, took a piece of paper from a drawer, a pen, then started writing several paragraphs. When he had finished he read what he had written carefully, signed the document, placed it in an envelope and handed it to me. 'This is my resignation. Give it to the chairman when it suits you. I've mentioned your name and asked him to reward you for your troubles. You must have worked, or played, hard to find me.' Then, as an afterthought, he added, 'These parties are fantastically well organized.'

'So I gathered,' I said, slipping the envelope in the fold of my wallet.

'I hope you'll let the matter rest there. I'll probably go abroad. I've stated that I'm retiring through ill-health and, unless word of all this leaks out, a scandal will have been averted. Assure them that I will not take my life — for this is what they fear most. Suicide spells unpleasantness behind the scenes to Americans, and we must avoid that at all cost. It will be a dreadful shock to the shareholders of course, and probably to the Government, but the fact that I've been discovered, that the Board even suspected I was involved in a scandal, forces me to take this line.'

* * *

It was after five when I left Frank Alva in his gold dressing gown sitting in front of the electric fire in his Chinese sitting room. As far as I was concerned my part in the affair was finished. I had been extremely successful in a very short time. More than that, by getting his signed resignation to hand to the chairman I would be responsible for sending every one of the directors into a fit of manic depression.

Apart from the telephonist on the sixteenth floor everyone had gone home. Just in case he was working late I knocked on the chairman's door and a voice asked me to come in.

He was sitting behind his desk with a plate of cakes and a cup of tea at his elbow and a trayful of urgent correspondence which he was trying to check through.

'Hallo, Mr. Flute, I didn't expect to see you so soon. Have you any news?' He seemed relieved to have someone interrupting his work. 'Please sit down.'

'I have news,' I said.

From my voice and expression he realized that I wasn't the bringer of good tidings. 'I spent most of last night with Sir Frank,' I said.

'You did? Where?'

'I don't know that it's necessary for you to know the details. First you'd better read this.' I handed him the envelope and watched him slit it open nervously. He read the letter quickly then folded it neatly before tucking it into one of his pockets. 'I'd like to know a little bit more,' he said calmly. He had been ready for bad news and maybe had expected worse.

I lit the cigarette he offered me and started on the story they had paid me to live through. I began with my routine searches, my stay with Babette in

Brighton; I then led him through the whole sordid episode of the party and gave him every detail. Most of the time he managed to keep a straight face, but when I mentioned parts he could not resist a twisted smile, and once or twice expressed disbelief.

He was my client and I wanted to impress him that I was thorough. The fact that he would probably dine out on the story for the next five years was his luck.

'Do you really believe there's a vice ring behind all this, or is it an excuse he's concocted to save face?'

'Anything seems possible nowadays. Certainly the girl involved was French and could have been employed by an organization, and the girl Hazel was definitely afraid of something. The question is whether you would accept the idea of continental companies using such a ring to work against you?'

'It's rather hard to believe, but when big money like this is concerned one can never tell.'

'It is a bit of a gift,' I said.

'What is?'

'Having the managing director of a rival company behaving like that.'

'Yes.' He didn't want to think about it too much. Reading in the papers that such things happened to other people was fair enough, but to be involved oneself was quite different.

'Who else was at this party?' he asked.

'You're not paying me for that. You hired me to find Sir Frank and I found him.'

The correction jolted the chairman a little and for a moment he didn't like it, then he had to admit he had gone too far and smiled. Promising that the second cheque would be in the post the following morning, he showed me to the door and said goodbye.

In the elevator I started composing the report I had promised to send him on the case, then noticed someone reading the *Financial Times*. I hadn't gambled on the Stock Exchange for a very long time, but it seemed a good idea to invest some of the money I had just made in a few well-chosen shares.

My broker, who hadn't heard from me

for five months, was curious that I should ring him up at all, and when I told him I wanted to buy C.G.B. he strongly advised me against it — then realized I might know more than him. Casually I dropped the hint that I wouldn't be such an idiot as to buy something I didn't think was a dead cert, and he agreed to do his best.

For the rest of the evening I mooched around worrying about my recent experiences. It was unsettling to know that people at the top were behaving like delinquents, that vital Government projects, national and international, were in the hands of unreliable men like Alva and that a crisis could be caused by a scandal motivated by a group of vice organizers.

The idea was worrying enough to make me ring the one contact I had in the Special Branch. He was listening to the last few minutes of a cricket match on a transistor radio at the other end of the line.

'John, I've some information that might be useful to you,' I said.

'Oh yes?' He always managed to damp my enthusiasm.

'Concerns the possibility of a vice ring.'

'Really?'

'Interested?' With difficulty I was controlling a growing aggravation, knowing that I didn't have his full attention.

'If you think it's important.'

'No,' I said, 'I don't think it's important at all, that's why I'm ringing you.'

'We get a lot of calls, Adam, you know. If you think you're onto something drop in; I'll be glad to see you any time.'

'You might just check up on a girls' school,' I said, 'somewhere on the Sussex-Hampshire borders, called The Faustina Private College for Daughters of Gentlefolk, according to my Public School Year Book, 1948.'

'Yes. O.K. Thanks. Drop in any time you're in the district. I've got a new carpet.'

I realized that the acid dancing about in my spleen was due more to mental and physical exhaustion than to John's matter-of-fact attitude, so decided to go to bed with a warm brandy and some soothing music.

By the time I had anointed the blue

85

flesh wound on the side of my face, added lemon juice to the hot toddy, and slipped into my saffron-yellow Cossack style silk pyjamas my eyes were closing.

★ ★ ★

The morning headline on the city page carried the story, and I was surprised just how big an event the affair was to those interested in business.

SIR FRANK ALVA RETIRES
Ill Health after Nervous Breakdown

It was one of those long splashes that would be of little value to the majority of people, but probably spelt ruin to a selected few.

I had hardly got back into bed, after pulling back the curtains, when the telephone rang. It was my broker. He was more intrigued than ever that I should have had a tip-off. C.G.B. shares would be rocketing for the next twenty-four hours, and I was probably going to be one of the few men going around with a smile on my face all day.

I made the kitchen in under ten minutes, goggling at the fantastic affairs of my favourite cartoon strip bird, poured myself a pint-sized cup of coffee and made my way back to the bedroom, where I started getting dressed.

It looked cooler outside so I decided to wear a suit, a lightweight suit, then I changed my mind and put on a pair of trousers, a shirt, a tie and a suede jacket. In the pockets I stuffed a handkerchief, my wallet, my pen-torch, my pen, a small knife, keys, and managed to find my comb under the bed before the telephone rang.

It was Hazel ringing me from an address in West London. Frank Alva had spent the night with her and was now lying on the floor — dead.

6

Hazel's call took me to the Baron's Court area, a quadrangular garden-city block made up of compact maisonettes, painted white on the outside, sporting green-tiled roofs and enclosing pleasant lawns, cherry trees and weeping willows.

Number fifteen had a green door to match the roof, a low rectangular metal casement window to the right and a clarion bell to announce the presence of visitors.

Hazel opened the door. Her hands were shaking; she was cold, sick, very frightened and even her tight-fitting rose bon-bon dress which moulded her neat little figure didn't bring any colour to her pale drawn face.

I stepped inside, closed the door behind me, and she recoiled as though I was going to assault her there and then on the unfriendly yellow-and-white-checked lino floor. I smiled at her with my best doctor's bedside manner and asked where Alva was.

She swallowed the uncomfortable lump in her throat and pointed to the closed door ahead. As though I did this sort of thing every day, I put my hand on the chrome door knob, turned it and went in.

The lino in the kitchen was checked red and green to contrast with the blue plastic curtains above the grey-and-black-patterned formica top of the sink unit. The walls were cream, the fridge old, the gas cooker dirty, and on the floor in front of the broom cupboard, with a broken glass gripped in his stiff marble-white hand, was Frank Alva, looking as though he had successfully taken an overdose of cyanide instead of indigestion tablets.

His tongue was sticking out unpleasantly, which didn't improve his features, and the lids of his eyes were swollen so that he looked like a failed boxer who hadn't done too well as an all-in wrestler either. He was ugly.

The door, on rising hinges, had closed itself, so I wasn't bothered by Hazel looking over my shoulder and threatening to faint. Obviously the poor man had walked into the kitchen to get himself a drink, had never quite made the sink after getting the glass out of the cupboard and had fallen there on the spot and died.

I could not diagnose his death, but since there was no blood, no knife sticking in his back, no bullet holes anywhere, I took it that he had either deliberately taken too many sleeping pills or someone, like Hazel, had slipped him a Mickier Finn than intended. And Alva had told me he wouldn't commit suicide!

The police would have to be informed. They would ask a lot of unpleasant questions because it didn't look like a natural death. For one thing Alva only had on a woman's flowered dressing gown and, for another, he was wearing a pair of green-and-pink-striped socks possibly belonging to some football club.

I opened a window to let in a bit of fresh air, got down on my hands and knees to see whether the people opposite could see in, and, not certain, drew the curtains.

I left the kitchen and found Hazel in

the small living room sitting on the very edge of a hard brown upholstered settee, still shivering.

'Have you had anything to eat or drink?' I asked.

She shook her head. Not a great talker ordinarily, the circumstances had reduced her to a state of temporary dumbness.

'I'll make you a cup of coffee.' Back in the kitchen I managed to get a tin of powdered coffee and two cups from the cupboard, light the gas, boil some milk and add sugar without disturbing the reclining Alva.

In the living room, over the coffee, I tried to find out what had happened. 'Can you tell me a bit about it now?'

She was young — young enough to want her mother's shoulder to cry on, but she knew she couldn't have that. She had left her home in the north to live it up in London, and now what her mother had warned her might happen had happened.

I offered her a cigarette, which did the trick. She had to open her mouth to smoke it and this relaxed her confusion. 'He got up in the middle of the night and went downstairs. I found him this morning . . . ' she said.

'Whose house is this?'

'I don't know.'

'How did you come here?'

'How do you mean?'

'Were you forced?'

'No.'

'You came here of your own free will?'

'I came here.'

'Why?'

She was nervous, rubbing her knees with her young thin fingers, puffing away at the already half-smoked cigarette.

'I think the best thing I can do is take you away from here. But first you must understand that whatever I do is for your own good.'

'I wouldn't have rung you if I didn't trust you, would I?'

It was the strange aggressiveness in her manner that put me off thinking she had some respect for me, though I realized she desperately wanted to be independent and hated being in debt to people.

'Come back to my place, have a rest, and we'll see what we can do.'

'What about the police?'

'Leave all that to me.'

'I don't want to run away. I mean, I didn't do it.'

'Do what?'

'Kill him!'

'You think someone killed him?'

'Yes.'

'What makes you think that?'

'Someone knocked on the door and was let in.'

Maybe it was instinct but I knew that I wouldn't get a clear picture of the events if we stayed in the house any longer. She was the type who might not be able to keep control of herself, and when she cracked she would have hysterics and scream the place down.

'Have you a coat, or a bag, or something?'

'In the bedroom.'

I followed her upstairs and had a quick look round. It was a big place to keep tidy: one bedroom the size of the living room with a double bed, a night table and a pink-shaded lamp; a bathroom the size of the kitchen with all the usual fittings; a

93

large cupboard in which the owner had had the nerve to put another bed. All the curtains were drawn and there was nothing to give away the fact that Hazel had been there.

It was half-past nine when we left; the milkman was just down the street. The semi-detached houses opposite were shaking with the sounds of vacuum cleaners; and unless every housewife was busy listening to their choice and glued to their sinks, there was little hope of not being seen.

I closed the front door, helped Hazel into my car and drove back to my apartment, keeping a lightweight conversation going about this particular vehicle, a secondhand Borgward I had bought cheaply which so far had only had to have its steering renewed, its engine rebored, its lighting circuit rewired and the petrol gauge replaced.

At ten o'clock I rang the police without giving them my name, telling them that I had had a call from a friend who said he was contemplating suicide during the night. I had thought it over and realized that maybe he had meant it, and gave them the Baron's Court address to help them on their way.

In the flat I prepared a delicious breakfast of cornflakes, toast and coffee, gave Hazel a brandy with another cigarette and waited till she smiled at one of my jokes. That took up to an hour to manage, but afterwards the going was easy.

She came from Bolton. Her mother had never had a husband but three children instead, all girls. She was the middle one whom everyone ignored. She had read all about glamorous London in the papers and magazines, and when her boy friend, a man in his forties, had offered to take her there she had readily agreed.

For some reason he had disappeared soon after they had got to Euston, but luckily he had introduced her to a film-producer friend who happened to be in the buffet. Realizing how lonely and helpless she was in the big city, the producer had kindly offered her a room in his Soho flat and then they had become 'friends'.

He had introduced her into show business and she had started her stage career as a strip artist at Fred Bear's Strip Club. She got fifteen pounds a week for that, but the manager kept some of the money to invest on her behalf.

Hazel was beautiful when she didn't speak. Her eyes were perfectly shaped, her face was sweet, her skin unmarked and unpainted. When she was on her guard, or aware that she was being looked at, her movements were abrupt, but when she relaxed she behaved more like a young antelope, at times frisky, at times elegant.

She was not clever, but intelligent enough to know when she was being had. After a while she had suspected the club manager of doing her out of half her salary and had looked around for help. Babette Boulanger had turned up.

First Babette had got her a rise at the club, then found her a flat, which she shared with another stripper, then she had been given free-lance jobs at private parties. It was at one of these parties that she had met Alva, who had paid her fifty pounds to spend the night with him, but as he had rather strange ideas she had tried to refuse when the next occasion arose. That was when she had realized that Babette wasn't such a friend.

If she didn't do what the French girl asked she was threatened with the loss of the flat, money, and it had been hinted that something unpleasant would be done to her.

'Such as?' I asked, intrigued.

'Acid,' she said calmly.

'Yes, that would be unpleasant.' At the thought of Babette and acid I also remembered the water pistol. 'Where do you live now?' I asked.

'The same flat, in Knightsbridge.'

'Big flat?'

'Three bedrooms, one sitting-room. Another girl shares it with us now.'

'Do they have men friends?'

'Yes.'

'And they're on the stage too?'

'One is like me; the other is a fashion model.'

I had met this perplexing type of innocence before. The girls were tarts, but they didn't realize it. They could be kidded into believing that they were doing something else, something respectable. Above all, they wanted to be respectable.

'Now let's get down to business,' I said perfectly innocently, but Hazel had been indoctrinated sufficiently by the company she kept to be suspicious of any such suggestion.

'What do you mean?' Her frown signified that she was frightened I would turn out to be like all the others.

'I mean, let's work out what happened, and what sort of trouble you're likely to be in. Tell me exactly what happened last night.'

'Molly, that's the wardrobe mistress at the club, came to me and asked me if I'd like to make a few extra quid. There was a customer who wanted to ask me out to dinner.'

'Yes,' I said, listening attentively but wondering what a wardrobe mistress would be doing in a strip club.

'Well, I knew what that meant, of course, but I said yes.'

'Why?' I could be dumb sometimes.

'Why not? I send Mum home some money, you know. It doesn't grow on trees!'

'I'm sorry,' I said. 'Carry on.'

'Molly said the customer would like to meet me somewhere private and would I mind going to his flat — I said O.K. She gave me the Baron's Court address plus a fiver for the taxi fare, but when I got there it was Franky. I tried to get away but he threatened me.'

'How?'

'He just said Natalie wouldn't like it.'

'Natalie? Who *is* this Natalie?'

'I've never met her but she runs the business.'

'What business?'

'The club and all the freelance work. She organizes the parties.'

'Natalie,' I said to myself, wondering whether it was one of the black-robed ogres or that raven-haired beauty. Both were potential sadists. 'So you stayed alone with Franky?'

'Yes. He was quite sweet really, didn't try anything funny. I mean, you know, he was normal. Wanted to say how sorry he was that he'd forced me against my will to do things . . . well, you know.'

'Yes,' I said, not knowing, but being brave about it.

'What time did you meet there?'

'About two in the morning, I suppose.'

'Then someone called?'

'Yes, there was a knock at the door. He got up and went downstairs. I heard him talking, then the front door closed, and after that . . . I must have gone to sleep. When I woke up he wasn't in the bed so I thought he'd gone, till I saw his clothes.' I went downstairs and saw him lying in the kitchen.

'And you rang me.'

'Yes.'

'Why didn't you ring Babette, or Molly, or one of your friends at the flat?'

'Why not?' She was astonished at my apparent stupidity.

'They're the ones who are probably going to frame me if things don't work out.'

'Frame you? For what?'

She was standing now, hardly able to bear all my questions; it was like being back home, having to explain everything, having to explain why she went out with boys, or smoked or wore stiletto heels. The reasons were plain enough to her.

After a moment she sat down again, deciding to be patient with me. It was just a pity I was such an idiot.

'It's the papers they're after,' she said at last. 'Babette and the girls were always hoping to get involved in something like this so as to sell their stories to the Press. That's what they used to talk about all the time, selling their stories to the Sundays. There's more money in that than anything else. I mean, it's so easy. You bed down with some famous nob, let the papers know, and they pay you twenty thousand . . . if it's a scandal, that is.'

Hazel was not only ignorant of what was going on but had been tricked by someone into believing she would get into the big money if she behaved as she had done. Life was not going to be easy for her in the future unless I found out more.

'How did he die?' I asked.

'I don't know. I didn't kill him. I mean, the police are hardly likely to accuse me if

I explain what happened, are they?'

The girl trusted me. She hadn't killed Alva so she honestly believed that she would be treated as though she were innocent by everyone. She didn't see that the police would regard her as the prime suspect, because she was a gift as far as suspects were concerned, and that cases like this had to be wrapped up smartly.

I had no proof, of course, that her tale was true, no proof at all. I realized then that unless I acted quickly someone else would make a move which might well seal the girl's fate once and for all.

I went into my study, sat down at the desk and rang up my friend at Special Branch.

'Ah, Flute! Glad you rang, old chap. We made a few enquiries about the matter you mentioned and there seems to be little foundation for worry. We did have a report from a school caretaker, who thought that some cranks celebrated a black mass in the gardens last week-end, but that was all.'

'I see, John,' I said calmly. 'You know,

of course, that Frank Alva was murdered last night.'

There was a long moment's silence at the other end and some rustling of papers. 'Sir Frank Alva, you mean?'

'Yes.'

'Can you tell me more?'

'Why, do you think he's connected with the orgies you've been investigating?' I knew John of old. The fact that he had bothered to check up on my story meant that they were onto this vice ring, maybe had been onto it for some time, that Alva featured strongly in the affair and that my tip had been a good one.

'Perhaps we ought to meet, Adam.'

'Perhaps we ought. How about number fifteen Baron's Court Close? That's where Alva is at the moment, or was.'

'Have the police been called in?'

'Of course.'

'Hell! I'll see you there in ten minutes.'

Satisfied that I had got Whitehall moving, or a little bit of it anyway, I went back to the sitting-room, to find Hazel sitting back on my comfortable chaise-longue nearly asleep.

When I suggested she should settle down in the guest room, she readily agreed. In my apartment, on the sixth floor, overlooking Hyde Park and the Bayswater Road, she felt safe. I told her not to answer the door however long anyone rang, and before leaving I took the telephone receiver off the hook.

There were plenty of people standing around the entrance of Number 15, and even a local Press photographer with his camera was ready to take various shots of whatever the police might bring out of the maisonette.

An ambulance arriving at speed added atmosphere to the scene, and, parking my car immediately behind it, I put on my I-am-here-in-an-official-capacity face.

'I've been asked to meet a certain gentleman from the Yard,' I said to the constable guarding the front door.

'Name, sir?'

'Flute. Commander Flute.'

Just inside the door he gave my name to someone, who mentioned it to someone else, till John opened the door wide and asked me to come in quickly.

John was a tall undergraduate of fifty. He had never left Cambridge and I wondered how he had managed to keep the key post he had, though I was aware that his strange manner probably enabled him to get on with anyone without obliging him to lose his superiority complex.

'The thing is, Adam, you obviously know more about all this than any of us,' he said, waving a hand by way of introducing a detective inspector, whose face I knew but whose name I had forgotten. 'What can you tell us?'

I started my little story from the moment I had been hired by Alva-Lazell's, till I had found Franky on the kitchen floor — omitting, quite by chance, that I was actually hiding the Hazel girl under my roof.

'So you don't think this chap committed suicide?' John asked. He was a little worried by the detective inspector, who stood there silently wearing a black frown, wondering why a private eye like me was telling them what they should already have known.

'I don't think he committed suicide,' I said.

'Well, you're right. We know it was murder.'

'How?'

'The local doctor found signs of needling, if you know what I mean. Friend Alva was given a shot of something at the base of his spine.'

'But what about the witness, sir?' The detective had something to get his own back with.

'Yes, the witness, she's a bit of a problem. There's this woman, lives across the way, says she saw everything happening. Dreadful old bag she is, sort of strong woman one sees in fairs. She watches everything that goes on around here with binoculars and she saw a blonde girl come up behind Alva, while he was having a drink of water, and do something. What, of course, she wasn't sure, but he fell down immediately after.'

'Not only that, sir, but afterwards she saw the girl pour something down the victim's throat, with the aid of a rubber tube.'

'Barbiturates, we think, to make it look

like suicide at the post mortem.'

I said nothing. It was as I expected: Hazel was going to be framed by her pals, and the police would readily believe the story until proved wrong. I thought it highly unlikely that Hazel would ever think of anything so diabolical as thrusting a rubber tube down into someone's stomach to make it look like suicide, let alone shoving a hypodermic needle in someone's back.

'What are you going to tell the Press?' I asked to change the subject.

'Oh, we'll cover everything up. I mean, I think we should, don't you? I'll say that he took his own life, left a note to that effect, then we can work under cover. The main thing is to get the girl. You should never have let her go this morning, you realize that.'

'How could I stop her?'

'She was a suspect.'

'Why, because she was blonde? There are two blondes involved in this set-up,' I pointed out. 'Who's to say that the woman across the way didn't see Babette doing Alva in?'

107

'Yes indeed, I do see what you mean.'

'We have an accurate description of the girl in question, sir,' the Inspector insisted on saying. 'About five feet four inches, wearing a dark-pink dress and with one of those beehive hair styles that's fashionable now.'

'Well, you try and find her, Inspector. I'd best report back to the office.'

I watched John leave the maisonette, talk to the reporter, then get into his Mini parked on the other side of the road. There was nothing for me to do now. The police were not interested in my activities and all the Inspector wanted to do was get the body out of the house.

Though I couldn't trust John not to send one of his men snooping round my flat I felt I should risk that and call on the fat woman across the way.

I drove round the block, knocked on the house I thought it might be, got the wrong person the first time but was re-directed to number thirty-seven, where I found myself facing the very woman I had expected. Either she pretended, or genuinely did not recognize me, I said I was from a press agency and she showed me into her budgerigar-filled room and offered me a gin. Her story, to me, was a little more elaborate than the one she had told John. She took me upstairs to her bathroom, threw open the mottled window and handed me her binoculars. She asked me to look for myself at the kitchen across the way, and in fact she was quite right. If the light had been on and the curtains not drawn, she could have seen Hazel, or anyone else, dealing with Alva quite plainly.

Remembering I was a Press reporter, I started firing a number of questions at her and she replied as though she had learnt the answers off by heart.

'The man you said this blonde killed, did you know him?'

'Nah. Never seen him before in my life.'

'But you knew the girl.'

'No, not her either.'

'Did you see anyone else in the house?' I asked.

'No, not really. Only you this morning, Mr. Flute, not minding your own business — as usual.'

7

She seemed bigger, the fat woman, as she blocked the bathroom door with her repulsive carcass. Her bright-red wig, tightly curled, was badly set on her bald head; and as she looked at me her eyes narrowed and her unkind smile grew unkinder.

'What's your name then?' I asked, moving towards her as though I thought I could leave.

'They call me Molly.'

She was dressed in a green dressing-gown of 1918 vintage, with as many breakfasts as the days it had lived through dribbled down the front. It had the advantage of having a huge collar which made her shoulders look even broader, and large pockets in which she could carry a box of 100 cigarettes, a bottle of gin and maybe a gun.

Her ham-like hand dug deep into one of these and I got ready to get scared.

'I've met some drips in my time, but you just about take the biscuit,' she said. 'Did you think I wouldn't recognize you, or something, coming here like this?'

'Maybe I didn't care? I don't work for the police, you know. I have a client.'

'Yeah? He must be wasting his money, then!'

'What makes you think my client's a man?'

'Don't tell me that Hazel hired you? Poor kid! She doesn't even know what's coming to her. What did you want to take her away like that for this morning? We would have looked after her.'

'We?'

'Oh, mind your own business. Seen these?'

From her pocket she drew out a set of photographs. The moment she handed them to me I knew I didn't want to see them — but I looked, all the same. They were 'artistic' photographs of Babette and Frank Alva; they didn't improve my opinion of either of them, but that didn't worry me as much as the setting they were in. The bed and bedroom were familiar, very familiar. The photos had been taken at Babette's flat in Brighton, where I had spent quite a number of hours.

'Recognize the place, do you, love? Got some of you as well, if you're interested, though they're a bit dull. Not exactly the adventurous type, are you?'

She started down the narrow stairs and for a moment I was tempted to kick her in the back, but just assaulting her wouldn't have helped.

'Had a camera trained on you, you see, that and a tape recorder. We go in for blackmail, very profitable.'

I wasn't sure what all this was leading up to but I certainly sensed an unpleasant feeling down my spine as I thought of the photographs that might have been taken. I tried to remember, too, what had been said. Over twenty-four hours with Babette an awful lot could have been said.

''Course, I don't expect you to pay anything; don't suppose you've got much money anyway. All we want is for you to belt up. Leave us to ourselves and maybe leave the country for a few weeks. Pity if your good clients received one of these through the post, don't you think? Or even that punk you brought in from the secret service? You'd be surprised whom we cater for in that establishment!'

She was helping herself to a pint of gin now in her sitting-room while an old parrot in the corner was running through her obscene vocabulary.

'What did you do with Hazel then? Take her home?'

'No, she went to the Yard,' I said, hoping to worry her.

'That'll be the day! Hazel wouldn't go to the cops. Do you know who her father is?'

'No.'

'Name probably wouldn't mean much to you, but he's in the Scrubs right now. If she went to the cops he'd tan the life out of her. I'm surprised at a bloke like you being taken in by her. Anyway, who do you think rang you up — her? For protection? *I* dialled your number, sonny, and you played right into our hands!'

I tried not to look at her as she sat down, her legs wide open, her elbows resting on her knees, her fat fingers gripping the tankard of gin. She had missed her vocation as a meat porter in Smithfield.

'Of course, when the whole thing blows up in your face through the Press you'll have the pleasure of seeing your ugly mug on the front pages. That'll do your business a lot of good. We're going to frame you proper now, we are. You'll be accused of running a whore house and everyone will believe it. Hazel will say she paid you half of what she earned. So will Babette, and I'll come along and tell them how much you liked being whipped at parties.'

She was the sort that would go on talking for ever if I let her. I felt she was keeping my attention for some reason; maybe someone was coming along to help me on my way somewhere. I decided that, however interesting her conversation might be, I should go. Hazel, for all I knew, might have fled and gone to the papers, and yet I still trusted her.

'You keep on saying 'we' — who are you all?' I asked again. Maybe she was drunk enough now to give something away.

'Keep on trying, ask away.'

'Are you a syndicate or something?'

'We could be, couldn't we? A vice syndicate. Yeah, that sounds fancy enough.'

'Well, I've work to do,' I said. It was as good an exit line as any. 'You'll excuse me.'

'Going, then?'

'I'm afraid so. Duty calls. Besides, if you want me out of the country I'd better make a few plans.'

'I hate your sort,' she said without standing up. 'You're just like that Franky Alva; lecherous, the lot of you, covering up like you were gentlemen. Did you know your flies were undone?'

Naturally I looked. They weren't and she laughed her big ugly head off. It was a big joke, a really big joke, and while she coughed through the gaps between her decayed teeth I walked out of the house.

It was a strange situation, and she knew it. She had said enough and shown me enough for me to realize that I wasn't

115

dealing with one or two people. Molly was working for an outfit like Babette and Hazel. Maybe she was the leader, maybe she was Natalie. Whatever the organization was, they would stop at nothing to achieve whatever they set out to do. Acid, sex photographs, tapes, nothing would stop them, and they had the Press behind them to pay up for their stories. Whether the papers bought their stories or not, the probability was enough for the leaders to entice the young girls with promises of really big money.

I got into my car, half expecting to be shot at from a window, but made the end of the road without incident. The only thing I wanted to do was get back to my flat and see if Hazel was still there. If she had walked out, or even made a telephone call, I would be in trouble. If some of the gang had guessed she was there and called, she would be in trouble. I put my foot hard down on the accelerator.

The door to my apartment was the last one on the right at the end of a long corridor. From the lift gates you could see the whole of the passage and anyone walking down it.

As I reached the top floor and got out of the lift, the silhouette that was leaning against the wall next to my door reminded me of someone I knew. I had held that shape in my arms and been photographed with it. Now, wearing a short-length leather coat over a tight-fitting white dress, she looked too good for me to feel instant regret.

'Hallo, Adam,' she said, purring.

'Hallo, Babette,' I said. 'An unexpected call.'

'I need your professional help. Could we talk together?'

'Certainly,' I said, and took her arm gently to lead her to the lift.

'No!' she protested. 'Can't we talk in your apartment?'

'Babette sweetie, you're out of touch. When did you last talk to Molly?'

She reacted; she tried not to, but she did, then had the intelligence not to try to cover up.

'What's happened then?'

'Is it Hazel you're after?' I asked.

'What's happened?' she asked again.

'The police. You all got me wrong. Whatever it was you thought I was up to. Private investigators deal with all sorts of situations. I was being paid to get a story about Alva by a foreign magazine. We could have worked together.'

She didn't know what to say. She wasn't the boss and she wasn't the one to take decisions, but she tried to find out a little more.

'Can't we still work together?'

'After this?' I said, pointing to my slightly swollen cheek. 'It's too late, the police got onto me. Hazel must have spilled the beans . . . I don't know.'

'But what happened?' She was getting as puzzled about the whole situation as I hoped she would.

'I got a call this morning to go to Hazel's aid, found Alva dead and then got booked by the police.'

'But I thought . . . '

'What did you think?'

She was uncertain, she was puzzled. I squeezed her arm gently and even started leading her back towards the flat as though I had some other idea in mind.

'What did you think?' I asked again.

'Didn't you come back here with Hazel?'

'No. The police thought along those lines as well. They took me to the local station, questioned me and only let me go when I'd given them the keys to the flat. They're probably still in there searching.' I was doing well enough. My inventive powers were improving.

'Don't underestimate the police, honey,' I said, as a bit of worldly advice. 'They use underhand methods as much as we do. I'm a stool pigeon at the moment. All my movements are being watched — timed even.'

That frightened her. She got really scared and drew away from me.

'The best thing you can do is use the stairs and get lost on the first floor for an hour. Whatever you do don't stay here and don't be seen.'

Occasionally I was lucky. This time someone called for the lift and the jerk of the cage as it started its journey down made her jump.

'You'd best go,' I said anxiously. 'All the

119

floors are the same except the first; there's a sort of lounge there — for some reason, nobody ever uses it. You sit tight on one of the uncomfortable chairs. Have a cigarette or two and when it's all clear slip out. O.K?'

The lift was on its way up again and she moved surprisingly quickly in her high-heeled shoes. As soon as she had gone I jammed the key into my apartment door and let myself in. I had worked hard just in case Hazel hadn't double-crossed me; now I was going to find out whether it had been worth it.

I closed the door, double-locked it, chain and bolted it and padded my way across the sitting room to the guest bedroom.

Quietly I opened the door, the curtains were drawn and I peered into the semi-darkness. On the bed was a shape that made sense, but I tiptoed closer to it to see that she was sleeping soundly and still alive. She wasn't. She wasn't even there. Just the bolster and a few blankets covered by a sheet.

It was such an old trick that I didn't

register my surprise when she spoke from somewhere behind me. I turned round slowly, looked at her standing behind the door and smiled.

There was Hazel, looking very attractive, very awake and holding my Colt .25 aimed in my direction.

'I found some bullets in the drawer,' she said sweetly.

8

The way Hazel was holding the pistol gave me the idea that even if she used it she was unlikely to do me much damage. I ignored her therefore, and moved towards the curtains to draw them.

'You didn't go to sleep then?' I said.

'No, I didn't go to sleep.'

The midday sun bathed the room in light and dazzled her a little. I could have rushed her and wrestled the weapon out of her hand but I didn't want to be at all violent.

'Would you like a drink?'

'I'd like you to sit down,' she said, waving the muzzle a bit.

'In here?'

'Yes, on the bed.'

She wasn't too sure what she was doing. She had set out with some idea in mind but was fast losing confidence. I sat down on the edge of the bed and just looked at her. This was unnerving for anybody.

'Well?' I asked after a long minute.

'Where have you been?'

'I went back to the Baron's Court flat and saw a man from Special Branch. I then went to see Molly.'

The name scared her. Her mouth dropped and she looked horrified.

'Molly? Fat Molly?'

'The very one.'

Whatever it was that frightened her about Molly it served me well. Without hurrying I crossed the room and gently took the gun out of her hand. Suddenly, like a little child, she threw her arms round me and started sobbing.

The touching scene lasted for four potent minutes and the feel of her body was remarkably soothing to my shattered nerves. At all costs I knew I would have to save this poor waif from whatever fate she feared.

'What were you going to do with the gun?' I asked. I was being clever behind her back and unloading the pistol. Bullets were dropping all over the place.

'I was supposed to accuse you, tell the police and the papers that you killed Alva.

I was going to double-cross you. Now I've doubled-crossed them!'

'I know,' I said, patting her some more.

'They'll kill me!'

'Not if I can help it.'

Years ago I had thought of becoming a psychiatrist, until a psychiatrist had told me that thinking about becoming one was a sure sign of retarded maturity. All the same I picked Hazel up bodily and carried her to the more cheerful sitting-room, where I laid her down on the chaise-longue.

What I had to do, before anything else, was reassure her that someone, some-where in the world, could be trusted, that not every man was out to rape her immediately and that, of all the people in the world she could have chosen, she had come to the right person.

I gave her a rum and orange with a cherry in it, a cigarette and suggested that music would relax her even more. While she sorted out my L.P.s, and chose one called 'Anthems to Twist To', I careered around the kitchen cooking up a lunch. Because I was a bachelor who always dreamed of having blondes unexpectedly dropping in for a meal, I had a good stock of instant dishes which could be heated up in a few seconds, though in actual fact they took anything up to an hour.

After the first half of the record was over I brought in some steaming Vol au Vents, spinach leaf, cheese butter and a bottle of *Schluck*. I had been given six cases of this petillant Austrian wine by a grateful client for finding his wife after she had apparently lost her memory. The fact that I had found her in the arms of another man was never revealed to him, which guaranteed me a box of cigars for life every Christmas from the even more grateful lover.

Mellowed by the food and the wine, Hazel calmed down and began enjoying my company. In her little mind she began to imagine a more permanent way of life in my comfortable apartment. She moved an ornament, straightened a lampshade, drifted into the kitchen to tidy up the appalling mess, put a bit of order in the bedroom and ended up by washing two of my shirts.

Afraid that she might take my interest in her a little too seriously, I switched on the half-past-two news on the Light and brought her back to her senses.

The bulletin was satisfactory as far as I was concerned. Sir Frank Alva, the reader told us, who had announced his retirement from Alva-Lazell's only yesterday, had committed suicide in a friend's flat by taking an overdose of barbiturates. A note had been found in his pocket.

'Don't they suspect murder then?' Hazel asked, childishly relieved.

'The BBC don't.'

It took a few seconds for the full meaning of my remark to sink in, and when I was about to tell her that I now planned to ring up John and tell him that she was with me, the telephone beat me to it.

I took the call in my study and switched on the automatic tape as I picked up the receiver. I had a small microphone attached to the telephone finding it useful to record unexpected conversations.

'Yes?' I said.

'I would like to speak to Mr. Adam Flute.' The voice was educated, but only recently; it had a slight Midlands accent, maybe Birmingham.

'Adam Flute speaking. Who is that?'

'My name is George Gladholland.'

'Yes, Mr. Gladholland?'

'I don't want to say too much over the telephone, you never know who might be listening, but do you think you could drop in some time and see me, as soon as you can?'

'Yes, what time would you suggest?'

'Could you make it to-day? It's urgent. You can probably guess what it's all about.'

'Any time this afternoon,' I said.

'Four o'clock at my office do you? Thirty-seven Maltravers Street, just off New Oxford Street.'

'I'll be there.'

After a moment's thought I decided I would see Gladholland before doing anything about Hazel. I wasn't sure that Special Branch wouldn't call in the Yard, and the police would have difficulty in keeping a story like this under their helmets. If it was known that Hazel was under arrest, or even being questioned, all that Babette would have to do was ring up the papers and say that she was a friend of both Alva and Hazel and she could tell them a thing or two. Rumours would start and that would be it. While Hazel was safe in my flat, everyone was safe.

After explaining that I was going out to see a client and that it was essential for her not to contemplate double-crossing me, answering the door or making telephone calls, I left Hazel to her own devices with a pile of magazines, tapes, records, photograph albums of my travels and press cuttings and the suggestion that the best place to watch television was from my double bed.

On my way to the C.G.B. offices I bought an evening paper. The retirement and suicide of Sir Frank Alva now put Coven, Gladholland & Butts into first position. Knowing all I knew, it was quite clear that the vice syndicate had completely failed in their Alva-Lazell project and were now moving in on the other

British company. C.G.B. had financial backing from the Government, according to the City page, and no comments had been made on the last few days' events by the Americans. I wondered exactly what sort of trouble George Gladholland was up against.

The headquarters of C.G.B. were not as impressive as Alva Lazell's. It was a terrace house converted into offices. Glass doors replaced wooden ones; the hall and stairs were heavily carpeted; a polished walnut table had all the right magazines displayed, and the atmosphere was small and intimate and not at all one of tycoonery.

The receptionist knew Gladholland was expecting me and took me straight to his office on the first floor.

He was sitting in an armchair with his back to the window reading the evening paper, maybe the article about himself which had told me that George Nathaniel Gladholland had climbed to fortune since the war through sheer perseverance, good sense and business ability, that he loved horse racing, owned a stable, ran a farm in Surrey and had two daughters as well as a wife.

'Hallo, Flute. Glad to meet you. Sit down. What'll it be, gin or scotch?'

I had a scotch with water in a large glass chalice which his thirty-year-old secretary poured for me.

'Wedding present from an aunt, worth about four pounds a piece,' Gladholland said, pointing to the vessel I held in my hand.

The secretary waited to be told she wasn't wanted, smiled at me as though I were her type and left the room. Gladholland was as ebullient as he had been at the cocktail party, full of life, his eyes sparkling with intense enthusiasm about whatever he happened to be doing. He was a likeable man with a sharp sense of humour.

He smoked a cigar, was dressed in a dark well-cut suit, was surrounded by pictures of his family and horses, which gave me the impression that he was perhaps overplaying the part of the typical English gentleman. I sat down opposite him, sipped my whisky and waited for him to make the opening move.

'The chairman of Lazell's put me onto you, Flute; gave me the whole story of Frank's death as you told it to them. I think you might be able to help me.'

'I see,' I said.

'I don't believe in beating about the bush. As you've got a recommendation that satisfies me I take it that all I say to you and show you will be kept between ourselves?'

'Of course.' My expression signified that I was insulted that he thought it could be anything else.

'I got this in the morning post. You'd best read it.'

It was a sheet of quarto paper with a typewritten message printed in the middle.

The enclosed photograph is of Sir Frank Alva. A similar one of yourself with the same girl will be freely distributed to all your business colleagues and contacts in America unless you retire from your present position within a week.

The enclosed photograph was interestingly obscene. It was similar to the one Molly had shown me and had been taken at the same time in the same surroundings.

The head of the bed was familiar; and again, though one could not be sure, I guessed it was Babette who featured, back view.

I handed the letter and the enclosure back to Gladholland, who glanced at the picture again and smiled. 'If I had known that such pictures of Frank were available I would probably have got knighted instead of him.'

It was said as a joke but shook me. It was meant; it gave a great deal away; it made me realize that behind the *bon vivant* façade George Gladholland was a bitter and envious man. He was a social climber; if he had worked hard it had been to boost his ego in the circles he admired. Alva's knighthood obviously hurt him somewhere and this was interesting.

'Have they got such photographs of you?' I asked.

'I doubt it. I think I know who the girl is. My wife knows her. She was at that cocktail party only the other day. I did sleep with her once, but I am sure there was no one else in the room taking pictures.'

'It's not necessary for anyone to be in the room. There are modern devices nowadays such as holes in the walls and ceilings to poke lenses through, you know.'

'Yes, I'm fully aware of that and these people have got to be stopped. The trouble is, I've hit a stumbling-block I didn't expect. That's why I've called you. Whoever is at the head of this organization didn't expect me to call the police, but I did, through a man I know personally at the Yard, but even with his help I've come a cropper.'

Gladholland stood up, turned round and looked out of the window. He was the type who had very little patience with inefficiency and when he got annoyed he became flushed and irritable.

'Calling in the establishment is like trying to wade through a mile of moving sands — red tape, questions, counter questions. By the time they're ready to move these bastards may have sent those photographs all over the country. I'm going to take the law into my own hands and you're going to help me.'

I said nothing. He had gone very red in the face and was promising to have a fit of apoplexy any minute.

'I've just been onto one of the cabinet ministers and, though he suggested I shouldn't be too rash, he didn't try to prevent me from going it alone. As far as I'm concerned that's as good as telling me to ignore the law. What I want to do is find the London headquarters of these people and smash them.'

They were strong words for a man in such a responsible position, but then, top people were beginning to go down in my esteem a little. Perhaps their work affected them mentally.

'What do you propose doing, exactly?' I asked calmly.

'There's a house in Pont Street where this French tart hangs out. I propose going there first and seeing what happens.

They won't expect me to come in person and cause trouble; they'll let me in thinking I've come to settle their demands, or bargain anyway. Once I'm in, you'll follow and we'll get a few questions answered — even if it means using violence!'

I still said nothing, I would follow his plan for as long as it suited me.

'Once they've told us something we can work on, we'll move on from there. I don't believe in long-range planning. I would have been a general in the last war if I'd been old enough. Now what about that stripper girl, where is she?'

'Somewhere safe.'

'You got her? In your flat?'

'Yes,' I said.

'Don't you think the mob might call there? We've got a little time to kill before dark, why don't we take her down to my place? We can have a bite, a bit of a rest, a swim maybe, limber up sort of thing, before the battle. Besides, I'd like to ask her a few questions about these people.'

'All right,' I said.

'What about the money? You'll want to

be paid. A hundred do you?'

'It'll do.' Fifty would have been enough for the part I intended playing in the operation.

Unexpectedly he came round to my side of the desk and, presumably elated by his plans of action, slapped me so heartily on the back that his precious four-guinea vase shot out of my hand and crashed against the desk.

'I am sorry,' he said. 'Have another.'

'No, thank you. I had drunk it all.'

'Don't bother to pick up the pieces, my secretary will do that. That's what she's paid for. Come on.'

His satin-grey Rolls was parked across the street complete with chauffeur examining the spotless tyres for dust. He took the man aside, spoke to him for a few seconds, then got into the driving seat and I got in beside him.

'First evening he's had off for a couple of months. It's been murder recently chasing after this blasted contract.'

We got to my flat in seven minutes, not because he drove fast but because he didn't stop when he was meant to. The car had been designed to impress people that the owner was important enough not to worry whether they crippled themselves against his armour plating or not, and Gladholland wasn't the type of man to worry.

I didn't invite him up but suggested that he should wait right in front of the block of flats so that I could get the girl out of the place without fuss.

Upstairs I let myself into the apartment and found Hazel very composed doing her nails and watching television.

'I'm taking you to the country, a pleasant hideout with a V.I.P. The fact that you're with him will probably help you later when you give yourself up.'

'Give myself up?'

'You trust me?'

'Yes.'

'Then just do as I ask. Next week you can start working for me as a secretary, if you want to.'

She liked that idea. To a stripper the thought of being a secretary was as exciting as the thought of being a stripper was to a secretary.

I pulled a raincoat out of the cupboard and a silk handkerchief from my collection — I bought one every time I went abroad to give girl friends whenever services had been rendered — and told her to tie it round her head.

I didn't give myself too much time to think, but the idea of Gladholland harbouring this girl, who was now death to the reputation of any well-known man seen with her, nagged at me. Maybe I had let myself be influenced too easily by his overpowering personality, yet it couldn't do Hazel any harm, and I was glad to get her off my premises.

When we got down into the street few people looked at us though we climbed into the big Rolls. By sitting in the back Hazel could hardly be seen and the introductions between her and Gladholland were informal enough.

He was behaving like a schoolboy, which was typical of big tycoons. He hadn't had the time to play when he was growing up, being too busy making money. Now any excuse to get involved in an adventure was wonderful. Toy trains, sailing boats, golf, cricket, cops and robbers, it was all good fun and he was going to have himself a grand time.

His country house was bigger than I expected. It was only thirty miles from London, but sat cosily in two hundred acres of land. Probably built towards the end of the 18th century, the house was one of those rambling mock-Gothic places with medieval-styled battlements, Elizabethan chimneys, picturesque gazebos stuck in odd places, all in yellow sandstone and covered with ivy.

Tennis courts, squash courts, a miniature golf course and even cricket nets were all in evidence, and when he stopped the car in front of the palatial steps he pointed to a glass-domed affair one could just see between the trees and proudly stated that it was an Olympic-sized swimming pool. Though his abundance of status symbols irritated me — maybe I was envious — it quite bowled Hazel over. Her eyes were popping out. She had heard stories about such rich men but she had never really believed they existed. As I opened the door for her to get out I reminded her that he was married.

'He can always get a divorce,' was her quick reply, which rather floored me. It was just as well that I hadn't seriously thought of her as a life's companion, though it would have been very pleasant to have her waltzing around the flat doing all the chores for a month or two.

A housekeeper opened the door and Gladholland led the way into a sumptuous drawing room. I realized why he was jealous of Alva's knighthood: he had a better setting in which to live with such a distinction.

'Wife and kids are on holiday, so make yourself at home,' he said, and to Hazel, 'I suggest you settle down in my elder daughter's flat. She has a sort of penthouse on the third floor. The housekeeper will show you up.'

With a good-humoured grin he pinched her bottom, and she squealed, as he hoped she would. I could see that I might soon be engaged by Mrs. Gladholland to follow them both to some shady hotel on the south coast.

'You'll say what you like, Flute, but

these girls are getting prettier every day. Just as well I'm not young, I'd never do any work. Do you?'

'What?'

'Do any work?'

He was looking for more four-guinea glasses in a cupboard somewhere after opening a bottle of scotch.

'I'm kept fairly busy,' I said. I was examining his bookshelves, leather-bound sets of Dickens and Jane Austen.

'Read much?' he asked.

'Papers mainly. Haven't the time for anything else.'

'Time! Time's the enemy, boy. Make a lot of money, it's the only way to combat it.'

'Meanwhile you're not free. Freedom's more important than money.'

'But you're free when you've got money. Really free!'

'What about your wife then?' I asked as a joke.

'She won't be any trouble when the time comes.'

While the housekeeper was keeping Hazel busy I was taken for a tour of the place. The study, the dining room, the kitchens, the cellar, the greenhouses, the indoor swimming pool pink and orange-tiled which made an unwelcome change from the usual green or blue. It was all as impressive as it was meant to be.

Hazel had slipped into one of Gladholland's daughter's cocktail pieces, which the housekeeper had suggested, and looked even more edible. It gave Gladholland the opportunity to say he was displeased because he could not make a pass at her without being reminded he was a father — then suggested she should call him George.

Hazel was sufficiently impressed by the setting to ignore his rather unattractive features and portly figure. When she sat down next to him and allowed him to put his great big hand on her leg I decided that if the vice ring got hold of this story I would also be framed for procuring.

After the meal, about nine o'clock, when it was getting dark and we had had two brandies to Hazel's three creme de menthes, Gladholland went upstairs to change.

He came down a few minutes later in a tweed suit, looking for all the world as though he was ready for an afternoon's sport.

Hazel saw us to the door, as though she owned the place, and we got into the satin-grey Rolls.

He took a road which went round the inner wall of the estate, and as we reached a tall pair of closed gates with a small fort tower on either side he stopped the car and got out, suggesting I should follow him.

I watched him unlock the door of one of the towers and stepped into the damp, cement-smelling gloom behind him. Somewhere he found a switch which lit up a single bulb hanging from the high woodworm-eaten rafters. Opposite the door was a cupboard and he unlocked this, took something from it and turned to face me.

His expression had changed. The humour had gone out of his features; his eyes stared at me intensely and his mouth was now cruelly thin.

'Did it ever occur to you, Flute, that I

might not be George Gladholland, but a member of the vice ring?' His right hand was gripping a narrow black cylinder some eight inches long.

'No,' I said, backing away only to realize that the door had closed behind me.

'Do you think it possible?'

I didn't answer. I didn't know. Now was not the time to worry about possible mistakes but to make sure about not making any more.

'Do you know what this is?' he went on menacingly.

'No,' I said.

'It's a knife, Flute, an old German flick knife.'

So saying he pressed a little button, which released a hideously long blade of cold steel from the black handle, and came towards me.

9

I waited for Gladholland to make the first attacking move. He was grinning now and enjoying my surprise, standing there a few feet from me, holding the knife at hip level, hoping I would rush forward and impale myself on it.

'Ever used one of these?' he asked, quite unexpectedly clicking the blade back into the safety of the cylinder.

'No,' I said faintly, relieved that the ordeal was over.

'Didn't think you had. Better have a Smith & Wesson. I take it you know how to handle one of these revolvers?'

'Yes,' I said, recovering.

Gladholland had a great sense of humour, the sort I laughed at when someone else was the victim. He had guessed I was uncertain about him, without cause, and had tested my reaction to the type of situation he thought private detectives should always be ready for. I could hardly blame him if he was unimpressed. Loading the magazine he handed me the Smith & Wesson and I had a good look at it, judging its weight, tossing it from one hand to the other as all successful cowboys did when handling a new gun. I thought my act was good but he still didn't seem to admire me too much.

'Let's hope you won't have to use it to-night,' he said casually, implying that it was more than likely.

'I have no licence to kill like some I could mention,' I said. I had no intention of carrying a firearm on this particular mission and I tried to hand it back to him.

'I wouldn't have thought that worried you boys,' he said, locking up the armoury cupboard.

'If I was found carrying one of these I'd have my licence taken away.'

'Well, don't get caught carrying it!'

By the way he showed me another Smith & Wesson of identical calibre, I gathered that I would have no option. He was also going to go into battle armed to the teeth. I followed him out of the small tower back to the car, struggling to get the heavy gun into my jacket pocket. As he got into the car I deliberately closed his door for him and leaned on it, poking my head through the window so that I could speak to him really close-to without him hitting out at me, getting up, or overpowering me. Men in cars behind wheels felt strong because of the brake, accelerator and clutch pedals, because of the power they had at their finger tips, but they were more vulnerable there than anywhere else. They could not move, nor get out without losing a certain amount of confidence.

'I don't intend carrying this gun,' I said, extracting with difficulty the revolver I had just put in my pocket.

'No? Why not?'

'Because it's dangerous.'

'Our mission is dangerous, Flute. You don't know how dangerous.'

'Then you should leave it to the police.'

'Pah! I thought I'd explained all that.'

'You're risking an awful lot.'

'Do you think I don't know? I'm not

fighting for myself, Flute, it's the honour of the country that's at stake. If the Americans give France or Germany this job what sort of prestige do you think that will leave us with as far as the world markets are concerned. I haven't asked you to do this for nothing. I guessed that something sinister lay behind Alva's suicide and I also guessed, from what Lazell's chairman said, that you had succeeded in protecting his name and averting a scandal. You're going to finish the job you started — and you're going to protect my name too. I'll pay you plenty once we're through with this whole affair. Now get in and don't act the silly ass.'

I didn't move, but struggled, once more, to put the Smith & Wesson into my pocket. I had to hand it to Gladholland, he was convincing.

'I don't see why we have to meet these people armed.'

'You don't? Well, I'll tell you. This woman Natalie needs to be scared. She's as hard as nails but still attractive enough not to want to be crippled for life. The threat of a couple of bullets smashing her kneecaps should calm her down a bit, and that's the plan I'm working on.'

'Natalie?' I asked. 'Who's she?' It was the first time he had mentioned the woman's name, and I was surprised that he should know of her existence.

'The ring-leader. I thought I'd mentioned it.'

'No,' I said quietly, then decided that maybe I should go along with Gladholland. He obviously knew a lot more about the ring than I did.

I closed my door and sat back to enjoy the ride, the gay happy-go-lucky drive to London that might well end in a blood bath. I was working back in my mind how I had become involved with this particular lunatic and realized that it had all been to save Hazel. Breaking a woman's legs with bullets was hardly likely to help her or me, but I had my pride and now was not the time to try to back out — besides, we were on the open road and the Rolls was doing all of 85 miles an hour.

It was just on midnight when we got to Hammersmith. He got onto the Brompton Road extension and shot straight down there into the heart of Knightsbridge, turned right and slowed down as we got near Pont Street.

'I'm going to park outside this woman Natalie's brothel, leave you in the car and go up and see her. If I'm not down after ten minutes you come up and see what's happening.'

'Yes,' I said. If I heard a shot, or anything like that, I might go up with the gun, otherwise I would just leave it behind. 'Where's the house?'

'Just here. That's the hovel, the one with the black-and-white-panelled door.'

The house was one of those unfortunate tall and narrow Queen Anne creations in red brick, four storeys high.

'Her flat is number 3 on the second floor; it has a blue door with chrome fittings. I'll leave it open if I possibly can; if not, ring the bell, and, if that doesn't do any good, shoot your way in.'

From the way he was talking about the layout it was obvious that Gladholland knew the set-up a lot better than he had let on so far. It was more than likely that at one time he had got as involved with the vice ring as Alva had.

'What do you intend doing when you're up there?' I asked, though he had told me already.

'I'm going to try and talk sense into that woman and ask to see those pictures. If they really exist, which I doubt, I'll get them from her. That's all I want — to show them to the police!'

We synchronized our watches, looked up and down the street to see if anyone was around, and when he thought the moment had come he heaved himself out of the car, closed the door quietly behind him and strode across the street.

I watched him go up the entrance steps, push the main door open and start walking up the black and white tiled stairs, then the front door closed behind him.

I checked my watch with the dashboard clock, moved into the driver's seat to have a better look at the house and wondered some more about carrying the Smith & Wesson in with me.

Gladholland had his own revolver. If in his enthusiasm he shot someone, I would have time to get rid of my lethal weapon before the police arrived. If, however, he was really up against an Amazon who might use violence herself, I would be pretty silly going up to help him with nothing but my doubtful knowledge of judo.

Memories of Fat Molly came back to me and that decided me on taking the risk. I could imagine her carving someone up with a scimitar and keeping her favourite appendages as mementos if given half the chance. I hoped she wasn't up there, for Gladholland's sake.

I glanced up at the window on the second floor and tried to make out whether it was someone standing very still between the curtains and the glass or an effect of shadows. It was not improbable that somebody was keeping an eye on the car and me.

Patiently I watched the hands of the clock ticking by and I watched the shadow at the window. When Gladholland had been in the house nine minutes and fifty seconds I got ready to go.

Quietly I opened the door, stepped out

into the cool street, closed the door and crossed the road. I looked up at the second-floor window, but the shape I had imagined to be a figure was gone. I couldn't be sure, however, that it hadn't been a trick of light.

Swiftly I climbed the stairs to the second-floor landing and paused in front of the blue-painted chrome-fitted door. I pushed it and stepped into a lobby big enough to contain a baby grand piano, a sofa, a card table with artificial flowers in a plastic bowl and two doors: one on the right, one on the left.

No sound came from either of them, so I tried the one on the right first. It opened into a bedroom and this gave me an unpleasant surprise. It was uncanny yet made a lot of sense.

The room was a complete replica of the one Babette had in Brighton — the pink lights, pink carpet and curtains, the wallpaper and the large treble bed with the heavy gilt mirror on the opposite wall.

There was no one in the room, so I crossed over to the window and pulled back the curtain a little. There was no one hiding there, but on the surface of the glass there was a round patch of moisture where someone had been breathing steadily for ten minutes. Hearing a noise behind me, I turned and looked at the door.

She looked disarmingly attractive again, wearing baby-doll pyjamas under a transparent pink nylon gown chosen to match the room.

Slowly she closed the door behind her, locked it and without looking slid open a small hidden panel let into the wall where the light switches normally would be.

'You don't seem very surprised to see me,' Babette said.

'Should I be?'

From where I stood I could see a row of buttons in the middle of the recess, and with one of her long well-manicured fingers she pressed one of these and something metallic purred behind me.

Not altogether happy, I turned to see an automatic blind coming slowly down over the window. Pressing another button, Babette changed the mood of the bedroom. The lights dimmed to a deep pink and orange; the ceiling lit up in blue. I smiled, amused by the effect, then heard soft music coming from hidden loud-speakers. Though it was presumably supposed to make me feel romantic, it only reminded me that Babette was working for a very successful organization, and that Gladholland had probably been right to arm me with his gun.

'More elaborate than your Brighton apartment,' I said, managing a smile.

'You like it?'

She moved away from the locked door, opened up a hidden cocktail cabinet near the bed and looked at the brightly lit selection of booze displayed on the glass shelves. 'What will you have?'

'Nothing for the moment, thank you. I'm not really here on a social call.'

'You came to find Mr. Gladholland?'

'Yes.'

'He's with Mary Ellen, next door.'

'Is he?' I didn't know Mary Ellen and didn't much care.

'You don't believe me?'

'Not particularly,' I said.

As though I were a child and she a

kindergarten mistress, she smiled to humour me, moved barefooted back to the button panel and pressed a selection.

The lights dimmed — the pink and orange ones first, then the blue ceiling till it gave a dark-blue night-like glow. Then, slowly, a strip of light appeared below the heavy gilt mirror.

I didn't at first understand what it was, then I realized that the mirror itself was moving upwards into the wall though the frame was stationary, and that behind it there was a window of dark-green tinted glass. We were now looking straight into the next room.

'They can't see us,' Babette explained, putting both her arms round my neck and pressing her warm body against mine. 'But we can see them. On their side it's a mirror.'

'I see,' I said, seeing.

The room we were looking into was exactly the same as the one we were in, the furniture and fittings were the same, and for a moment I got the impression that I was still looking at our own reflection; but Babette was not there, nor me, only Gladholland wrapping himself round the tall, dark, elegant, raven-haired girl I had seen at the cocktail party and at the orgy. Both were fully dressed and both were drinking champagne.

'That's Mary Ellen?' I asked.

'Yes, that's Mary Ellen and her friend George.'

'We can see you now,' Babette said to the green-tinted window in front of us.

Gladholland and Mary Ellen looked towards us but their eyes focused on their own reflection some three feet in front of them — a strange effect.

Gladholland disengaged himself from the raven-haired girl and lifted his glass with one hand and did the 'thumbs up' sign with the other. Then, to make sure that I had got the message, he turned to Mary Ellen, enveloped her once more in his huge arms and buried his head in the nape of her neck.

Discreetly, Babette left my side, went to the button panel, turned up the lights and let the mirror slide down over the window. I wasn't sure what I was meant to do now, though I presumed that Gladholland was behaving the way he was of his own free will. There was the possibility that someone was aiming a gun at him from a hidden corner and telling him to perform, but he hadn't seemed to be nervous in any way.

Babette came towards me with a laugh and put her arms round my neck again. Her lips were warm and soft, her mouth tasted sweet, her tongue as nervous and excited as her hands, which were now busy undoing my belt. Forgetting, for a moment, where I was and why, I gently tugged at the one knotted ribbon that held the top of her baby-doll pyjamas together, then, looking up, realized that somehow she had managed to manoeuvre me round so that she was between me and the mirror with her back to it. I was facing our reflection.

There was something strange about the whole setup and the sequence of events: the locked door, Gladholland and Mary Ellen posing for my benefit, the mirror. It didn't make sense, any of it.

'Where is Natalie?' I asked, trying

to disengage myself from the heated Babette.

'Would you prefer her to me?'

'I'd like to meet her.'

'Can't it wait? I'm just in the mood now.'

She was pulling my tie away from my collar and undoing my shirt but I was hardly aware of this. I was trying to work out why my eyes felt funny, why the room seemed brighter, and found the solution by watching the shadows the edges of the curtains were throwing onto the wall. The shadows were fading and the room was very gradually getting brighter. I now knew exactly what was going on and had the choice of either playing the game or attempting to get out of the place without losing face.

'Do the lights have to be this bright?' I asked. 'I'd prefer just the blue ceiling.'

'But I want to see you, darling, you know.'

From experience and instinct I knew that the moment hadn't yet come to make a decisive move, so I started slipping her gown and pyjama top off her shoulders as

159

she nestled even closer to me. Then, quite firmly, she stopped me from undressing her any further. 'No, darling,' she whispered, 'there's no point. And please believe me when I say that I really hate doing this to you . . .'

I didn't give myself time to think that one out, but the moment she threw herself to the floor I did the same, hurling myself on top of her as the air was split by a deafening report and the gilt mirror exploded into a thousand pieces.

I rolled over Babette and pulled her on top of me as another shot came zipping through the jagged black hole in the shattered glass. It missed us both by a fraction but the third shot didn't; it hit her and she squirmed on the floor like a severed worm.

Kicking against the bed, I thrust myself towards the door as another shot blazed through the gilt mirror, hitting the very spot where I had been.

Panic-stricken, I got to my feet, reached out for the button panel, slammed my hand flat down hard on all the switches and in the sudden darkness threw myself to the floor and crawled to a corner as another bullet shot out of the merciless gun and this time hit me somewhere in the hip. It stung, but it didn't kill me, and I wrestled the Smith and Wesson from my pocket. If I killed anyone in the next few seconds it would be in self-defence.

I fired two quick shots in the general direction of the other room.

Then I waited, holding my breath, for my opponents to make the next move. I had four bullets left, a burning hip and every reason to be worried.

An eerie silence followed the fearful noise that had filled the two rooms. Then someone stumbled, groaned and gasped for air.

'Mr. Flute?' a voice said. 'Don't shoot, I beg you, don't shoot. He's gone, and he was the only one with a gun, I promise.'

I was getting used to the semi-darkness and felt safe in my corner. I said nothing, but kept quite still. Maybe Gladholland had been shot dead before my assailant had taken a pot at me. Maybe he wasn't dead and just pretending, which meant that two guns were still going to come in handy, his and mine.

Suddenly a bright light was switched on in the next room and lit up the slaughter-house that had once been a pink bedroom. A few feet from me, twisted like a discarded bloodstained bolster, was Babette, looking pretty dead.

The light coming through the jagged remains of the two-way mirror was then partially blocked by the silhouette of the elegant Mary Ellen. She held no weapons but just stood there looking aghast at her colleague.

'Babette?' she stammered, horrified. Then stepped quickly through the gaping hole and crouched down to examine the girl.

Nursing my bruised hip, I just looked at her, pointing the Smith & Wesson in her direction, but not seriously thinking of pulling the trigger.

'Who tried to kill me?' I asked, hardly interested right then whether Babette was dead or not.

'She's badly hurt!'

'So will you be if you don't answer. Who tried to kill me?'

Mary Ellen saw the gun and opened her mouth to speak but couldn't. She knew now what guns could do to people and didn't like it.

'Who?' I asked once more, then added, 'What about George Gladholland, what's happened to him?'

She looked puzzled, frowned, stepped a little closer to me to see if I was all right, then got down on her knees to have an even closer look.

'You were taken in?'

'What do you mean?'

'By George,' she said. '*He* shot you.'

I pushed myself against the angle of the two walls and found I could stand up without any trouble. The bullet that had hit me had only ripped a bit of my trousers away and grazed my pelvis. It was as painful as a half-hearted bee sting, but would make an interesting enough scar to show a few girl friends.

'George Gladholland?' I said. 'He shot at me? That's an interesting idea. How's Babette?'

'I don't know . . . '

I couldn't be sure that all this wasn't a

163

trick, so I moved cautiously to the edge of the broken mirror and peeped round the corner into Mary Ellen's room.

A bright 100-watt clear-glass bulb was casting ugly shadows from its broken chandelier in the ceiling. Fat Molly, clutching the leg of a bedside table, lay in a crumpled heap by the window, a trickle of blood coursing its way down from the corner of her clenched mouth along the gross ridges of her thick neck to her now red-spattered white shirt.

On the bed, unstained, unused, was Gladholland's knife and beyond the bed the open door through which someone had got away with murder.

I turned round after that and looked at Mary Ellen, who was moving the blonde so that she could lie on her back. Her eyes were firmly closed, her mouth open as though she needed more air. From where I stood I guessed she needed a lot more — a lot more air and breathing power and pumping action in her heart.

Mary Ellen looked up and I shrugged my shoulders. They had all been playing with fire too long and someone had had to get burned badly.

As I was about to walk over to have a closer look at Babette, Molly groaned behind me and Mary Ellen looked up in despair at the sight of the crippled woman.

'Molly, are you all right?'

'You'd best get after him, lovey,' Molly whispered through a mouthful of blood. She reminded me of a sick fish.

'George?' Mary Ellen queried.

'There's Hazel, I can't have her on my conscience as well. How's Babs?'

'Hurt!' Mary Ellen said.

'Badly?'

'She's dead,' I said.

Molly opened her eyes a bit more to look at me. She had as much love and admiration for me as she had for a woodlouse.

'I killed her,' she gurgled, 'trying to shoot that lunatic!'

'Who's behind all this, Molly?' I asked.

'Behind all what, lovey?'

'All this — the set-up, the two-way mirrors, the ring?'

'Me, sweetie, I was behind it. But I

won't be for much longer. Is there any brandy?' She was wheezing like a fat toad and bleeding like a pig. I didn't like looking at her.

Mary Ellen left Babette's tomb and came through the jagged mirror with a bottle of brandy from the cocktail cabinet.

'I ran this set-up, lovey,' Molly said, managing to sit up a little to drink some of the brandy. It hurt her as she drank, the alcohol stinging her internal wounds. 'I ran this set-up with Georgie boy's help and he ran it for some tart named Natalie. He's your man. He was behind Franky Alva's death. I did Alva in, but Georgie boy asked me to. Their man in London he is, old Georgie, but he was too ambitious, wanted too much blood . . . so he took some of mine, the bastard.'

She was still strong enough to reach out for the bottle and wrestle it out of Mary Ellen's hand. She stuffed the neck of it into the gash that was her mouth, took one long draught, then fell backwards.

'I'm dying,' she said after a few painful seconds of heaving and groaning. 'I'm dying because of you, you punk.' Her eyelids were heavy now and she couldn't move them; she was going white and shaking in odd traumatic spasms. 'I'm dying because you got under Georgie boy's skin and scared him. He put the bullet in my back, Mary Ellen. Your boy friend, your lover boy, he killed me because I overplayed my hand . . . '

'Overplayed your hand . . . how do you mean?' I asked.

'You're a nut, you really are. You, walking right into every bloody trap that's set. I don't know how you get away with it. You're such an idiot, people don't expect you to be such a bloody fool. I was supposed to rub you out. I was supposed to shoot you through the mirror — but I realized that this was madness, that you had a gun too, and saw the red light in time. If I missed you, you'd probably hit me . . . You didn't shoot me though, you ran and hid, so he had to do the job. He had to do the deed himself.'

'But why, Molly? Why should Gladholland . . . ?'

'Because I double-crossed him. I realized some time ago that I'd be in his way the moment he got on in the straight world. He was a part-time crook, and they're dangerous. When he got what he wanted out of us, his precious contract and no doubt a knighthood, he was going to forget our existence. But he thinks he is a clever man. He's not. He slipped up getting mixed up with you. Wanted to prove his intelligence, wanted to show off his set-up. It cost enough, those all-electric two-way mirrors; he never got much pleasure out of them. Now he'll skip the country and ruin little Hazel. You could try to save her. But fancy him coming a cropper because of a punk like you . . . '

Molly took a deep breath and started laughing. She laughed till the end of her life; she laughed for three seconds and then it was over.

'She died laughing,' I said to myself, then saw Mary Ellen looking at me. She had no idea what sort of person I really was and she was badly shaken by all that had happened. Apart from her and me there were only two dead women in the two rooms. Then I noticed she had picked up Gladholland's flick knife.

10

A screech of tyres in the road outside brought us to our senses. She had released the steel blade from the flick knife and was holding the weapon in a trembling hand. I had gently turned the Smith & Wesson in her direction. It was a stalemate, and the outside noise made us realize we had been acting in self-defence.

I moved over to the window, pulled back the curtain, and watched a police car having difficulty parking between a vintage Packard and a Mini Minor.

'The police,' I said calmly. 'We'd better clear out.'

Without wasting another second I took the knife out of her hand, flung it and the revolver on the bed, grabbed hold of her arm and led her out of the flat. We were down the two flights of stairs and in the hallway by the time the front door burst open and the two constables from the car rushed in.

'They're on the third floor,' Mary Ellen said, button-holing the first officer, 'killing each other! One's drunk and the other's mad,' she went on in an artificially high-pitched hysterical voice. 'I was telling my brother only the other day about them. 'It's bound to end up badly,' I said, 'because of the tea.''

'The tea?'

'Yes, one likes China and the other Indian,' she went on, staring at the officer intensely.

'Well, we'll take any statements later,' the young officer said. He had decided Mary Ellen was a nut.

His colleague pulled him away and then started up the stairs. We rushed out into the street.

We ran down Pont Street, right into Beauchamp Place and there saw a car drawing up. It was a large new Rover with a respectable couple in evening dress about to get out after a good evening. 'I'm terribly sorry,' I said, opening the woman's door, 'but my wife has just swallowed a chicken bone — stuck in her throat — can't get a taxi — St. George's

Hospital . . . could you?'

They were delighted. For one thing the woman had served in the Ambulance Corps in the 1914–18 war and so understood emergencies, while her husband had some pretty good memories of the Blitz. He drove at the frightening speed of ten miles an hour — in case Mary Ellen dislodged her chicken bone — and by the time we got to the hospital at Hyde Park Corner we knew all about them but they knew nothing of us.

I thanked the Rover man profusely, helped Mary Ellen up the steps of the emergency edifice, through the main doors where we waited till the sedate car had driven off some safe distance.

Within four seconds we were out of the hospital and in a taxi heading straight for my flat.

My own car was in the garage below ground and, without stopping to check whether we had been followed or not, we got in and drove out. The fact that lovely Mary Ellen's raven hair was falling down over her eyes and that I had a patch of blood the size of a meat dish down the side of my pants didn't matter. We had to get to Gladholland's place and Hazel before he committed another crime.

I crashed the gears in my anxiety to get away, woke up the whole neighbourhood revving out into Bayswater Road and shot off at a speed which should have brought out all the Metropolitan Police speed boys.

If Mary Ellen was frightened by the way I drove, she didn't show it. There was no reason why she shouldn't be able to cope with such an insignificant type of thrill considering what she'd been up to in the last few months.

'How about a few words on all this?' I said as we got up speed on the dual carriageway.

'What will happen to them?' she asked.

'Who, Babette and Molly?'

'Yes.'

'They'll be taken to a morgue after the detectives have looked the place over.'

'You don't care, do you?'

'I care very much, especially as I should have been in their place.'

'Perhaps Babette wasn't really dead.'

'She was dead all right. She's probably walking the streets of heaven right now — though she didn't do that sort of work really. Did you?'

It was a crazy insult to hurl out at that moment and she only just stopped herself hitting me. Instead she shut up for about twenty minutes and stared ahead in a cold, hating silence.

'How did Gladholland get mixed up in all this?' I asked eventually. To make it clear that her answer would be appreciated I shot though some traffic lights, nearly sending a bubble car skittling up the highway like a ten-pin ball.

'I'm a respectable woman, Mr. Flute,' she started, then burst out into hysterical laughter.

I didn't slow down, or try to control her. I had a fair amount of experience as far as hysterics were concerned and I found that the victim got exhausted soon enough if ignored.

She calmed down quickly. After lighting herself a cigarette from the packet I offered her she apologized for her behaviour. It was the first time she had ever seen anyone shot, she explained.

'It doesn't exactly happen to me every day either,' I said, sympathising. 'Are you part of a vice ring?' I asked, hoping to get an answer this time.

'My mother used to run a drinking club in Mayfair; it was closed by the police and we needed money badly, so I worked for her.'

'Doing what?'

'I'm a prostitute. A respectable one, but in the eyes of the law that's what I am.' She had probably never openly admitted this to anyone and somehow I felt it was a relief for her to talk about it.

'I found that hundreds of perfectly normal men needed something extra, something forbidden, and so I provided it. I also provided them with other talent.'

'Babette?'

'Among others. Babette didn't do it for money, she was a nymph. She was the one who started encouraging clients to want more. As it was against the law, she had to have help to cover up. That's where Molly came in.'

We were in the Surrey countryside

now, not too far from our destination.

'Where did Molly come from?' I asked, fanning the flames.

'She used to run a brothel in Hamburg, came back because she missed London. I brought the big clients with Babette and she provided the kicks.'

I didn't ask for any details. I had seen and heard enough to make up my own. 'How did Alva get involved?'

'Babette brought him in. He liked that sort of thing more than most.'

'And Gladholland?' I asked for the third time.

'He financed us.'

'How?'

'He was a private client of mine, one of the old-time regulars, once a week, Thursday afternoons. I was indiscreet enough one day to tell him that Frank Alva was also one of my clients, and that's how the trouble started.'

'He wanted to ruin Alva-Lazell's?' I said, jumping to conclusions.

'He wanted to ruin Franky. It's the one and only time I have ever given a client away to another client. He had just got his title and I was joking about it, it seemed so extraordinary that a man like that should get honoured.'

'And you talked about it to Gladholland?'

'Yes.'

'How old are you?' I asked suddenly.

'Thirty-nine.'

I glanced at her — it could only be a glance because I was doing ninety and the road wasn't wide enough for that sort of caper — but she didn't look any older than thirty.

'It's a wig and I use American make-up,' she said. 'I also spend a lot of time at beauty parlours.'

'Your figure is still in good condition,' I said by way of a compliment.

'You haven't seen it — yet.'

It could have been an invitation, costing fifty guineas, but I didn't commit myself.

'How come big men like this play with fire?'

'Big men? Don't make me laugh. They're worms, every one of them. Frightened little worms who have the luck occasionally to bark up the right tree at the right time, after which they act their way through life as though they had big characters. In bed they are immature schoolboys still crying for Mummy's apple pie.'

'And you give it to them?'

She said nothing, but from then on I was conscious of her critical gaze. She was older than I was and knew more about life. If I had been in a few scrapes it was more than likely that she had been in many more. Her line of duty was not without risk.

'Why did you try to kill me?' I asked. It was a fairly important question.

'I didn't. I had nothing to do with it. I had nothing to do with Alva's death either — that was all arranged between George, Molly and Babette. Babette and Molly didn't care what they did providing they were paid enough.'

'They were paid enough all right,' I said, taking a corner remarkably casually on what seemed like two wheels. 'Why did Molly double-cross Gladholland then?'

'I'm not sure that she did; she said that because she intended to, but she never got the time.'

'When did Gladholland decide I'd be better dead?'

'When he realized that you weren't as stupid as you pretended.'

'And Molly volunteered?'

'Molly could be bought for a case of brandy. I didn't know what they were up to when they asked me to be friendly with him in front of the mirror. It's the sort of routine I've been through before for clients in the next room. I didn't even know it was you with Babette!'

I was beginning to have my doubts about Mary Ellen. She was managing to clear herself of every possible charge. She was beginning to be the most innocent person I knew.

'Molly shot at you. When she realized she'd hit Babette she threw the gun down and rushed towards the door to go and help her. Gladholland then picked up the gun, shot at you and then at her.'

'But was the whole thing planned? Babette and me in one room, Molly in

179

the other ready with Gladholland's gun?'

'It must have been.'

'But it was senseless. Supposing I had been killed, the two-way mirror shattered like that, they'd never have got away with it.'

'Who would never have got away with it? Molly wouldn't, but George would — with honours. He planned this thing so that you'd be dead, shot by Molly who would go to prison — if not hang — Babette and me involved, and himself as the hero who exposed the vice ring. People in top places knew he was after something, they even knew he was going to take the law in his own hands.'

It made sense, it was a way of ridding himself of the set-up, but an eccentric exhibitionist's way. Maybe that's why it hadn't worked. If it had, the case might have been heard *in camera*, treated by John and his mob as a secret.

'I wonder what he's planning next, then?' I said.

'I wouldn't like to guess, but we'll never catch up with him. He has a helicopter on his estate.'

Instinctively I looked up at the sky but there were no helicopters around just then. As I was about to turn off the main road I glanced in my rear-view mirror, and saw the blazing headlights of a large car behind us. It was the fourth or fifth time I had noticed them but till then had not thought about who it might be.

Immediately after a dip and a bend, when we were out of sight, I turned into a small driveway, switched off all my lights and got out, telling Mary Ellen to get down in her seat.

As the purr of the big car approached I hid behind a tree. The headlights lit up the whole of the countryside, and I saw a satin-grey Rolls shoot past us.

'It's him,' I said to the brunette, getting back into the car. 'We'll have to be quick, but careful.'

I backed the car onto the road and, using my fog lamp, cruised along quietly till we reached the Gladholland estate gates.

'You're very trusting,' Mary Ellen said, out of the blue.

'What do you mean?'

'How do you know I won't help Gladholland?'

'He killed Babette,' I said. 'She was a friend of yours and, anyway, this is your one hope of clearing your name with the police.'

Once more I switched off my lights. The drive, like the one at the girls' school, was gravel, and showed up white against the dark grass on either side. I accelerated, took the only bend easily and then heard the shot.

I jammed on my brakes, but it was useless. The steering wheel spun round uncontrollably in my hands, the punctured tyre jerked the car right round. It hit a boulder, and as I felt it keeling over I pulled back the door handle in case we got trapped.

At forty miles an hour we smacked against a tree. Mary Ellen screamed, and I flung myself sideways to avoid the impact of the snapped steering wheel against my chest. Stunned, I realized the door had been ripped off its hinges. I leaned forward and fell out of the car into some hawthorn bushes, where I stayed immobile till the stars had stopped dancing about inside my eye-balls.

If my hip hurt it was nothing compared to my arm, but I suffered in silence. I had to. Somewhere out there in the black night a man with a Smith & Wesson was waiting to kill me.

11

I didn't move. My right ankle was being treated for rheumatism by an unpleasant crowd of stinging nettles, but I didn't move. I was getting used to the dark, and could make out the shape of my car, its tail sticking up at an angle, the radiator and front wheels nuzzling comfortably in the branches of a purging buckthorn.

The large searchlight headlamps of Gladholland's Rolls were suddenly switched on, and the tall, velvet-blue shadows all around changed to a ghostly negative landscape. The trees and bushes and flowers and grass shone white, a bright white, against the impenetrable blackness of the sky, and the polished satin-grey panelling of the luxury limousine sparkled like Cinderella's coach.

Slowly the Rolls turned so that it faced my car, and moved forward. Taking advantage of the noise the engine made, I pulled my leg out of the nettles, rolled

184

over a couple of feet into some brambles and pulled the heavy revolver out of my pocket.

The large car stopped some ten feet from me, and Gladholland's voice rang out in the still, silent night.

'Mary Ellen! Get out and come here. I can see you and I have a gun.'

Mary Ellen, still apparently in the cockpit of the car, moved. The metal groaned as she struggled to open the jammed door, and I saw her legs dangle down from the wreck before she jumped.

She fell on her knees, picked herself up, straightened her skirt and walked towards the Rolls, more concerned about her appearance in the dazzling light than the circumstances she was in.

'Where's that idiot Flute?'

I didn't hear what she answered, but she got into the capitalist's saloon as though the whole sequence of events had been a rather boring game.

Gladholland didn't get out to hunt me, but drove his car closer to mine. After giving himself plenty of time to examine the surroundings from the comfort and safety of his driving seat, he decided that time wasn't on his side, and backed the heavy vehicle out of the scene. A few seconds later he was accelerating up the drive out of my reach, maybe for ever.

Left to myself in the dark, safe for the first time in four hours, I got up, straightened my clothes, and was reminded of my superficial wound by a jarring pain in my hip.

I took my jacket off, undid my belt, pulled out my shirt and felt around to find out what damage had been done. My hip felt sore, sticky, and was probably unpleasant to look at, but I knew I would live. So, after placing my folded handkerchief on the wound, I redressed and started off towards the house.

Some four or five hundred yards in the distance, the Rolls drew up in front of the main entrance. When the headlamps were switched off and I could no longer see exactly where I was going, I walked off the drive and made my way along the white-painted iron fencing that enclosed the paddock in front of the house. When I was near enough to see the silhouette of the house, I dropped down on my haunches and surveyed the scene.

Gladholland had parked the Rolls very near to the front steps and had gone in with Mary Ellen. There were no lights on anywhere and I figured that he had probably gone in to collect a few things, maybe do something drastic to the poor, unsuspecting Hazel, then make a dash for it.

Cautiously I got up and crossed the wide expanse of the front drive and crept up to the big car. The window was open, and I reached across the steering wheel to run my fingers over the dashboard. Unbelievably, he had not removed the ignition keys and I quickly pocketed these.

Flower beds and a thin strip of lawn surrounded the house, and I tiptoed onto the grass and made my way silently round to the side. All was dark and there was no sign of life, but at the back lights came from several windows on the first floor.

Realizing that someone might be looking out for me from the ground floor, I kept as close to the wall as possible, ducking below the window-sills as I went. Then a window opened above me and I froze, dropping to a crouching position and remaining quite still. If I had been spotted I wouldn't stand a chance. In a cold sweat that started very gradually then made me shake all over, I waited for a shot to ring out and for a bullet to zip straight down into the back of my spine, but the window closed again and all was quiet. As I stood up, breathing deeply to regain some self-control, I noticed a piece of cotton wool caught in the thorns of some climbing roses. It could have been there before, but its whiteness was very noticeable in the night, and I felt I would have seen it. A slight breeze made the wool flap a little, then it detached itself from the thorns and came floating down to the lawn. Carefully I picked it up and shook it. I had the habit, at the flat, of using cotton wool to dispose of large spiders, trapping them in a large wad and throwing the whole lot from my sixth-floor balcony.

There was no spider in this wad, but it was cold with ether. Something remarkably unpleasant was going on upstairs.

Avoiding the open spaces, I kept to the wall, following the T-shape plan of the house till I came to a kitchen door. Without weighing up the pros and cons of my proposed action, I smashed the butt of the Smith & Wesson against the square pane of glass nearest the lock, thrust my hand through the resulting hole and turned the key.

I got in quickly, crossed the scullery into a large kitchen, walked through the dining-room and was on home ground — Gladholland's home ground admittedly, but at least I had been there before and could move in the dark without colliding with too many pieces of furniture.

I opened the door and stood just outside in the hall, the steep oak staircase rising immediately to my right. Boards creaked above and there was a fair amount of movement, then a light was switched on in the corridor and two people started coming down the stairs. I hid in the shadows of a doorway and waited.

The two people didn't talk and the one glance I gave them told me that they were carrying suitcases and that they were not using the front door but some other exit.

I could have stopped them then, but I was more concerned with the ether and Hazel's possible fate. Then I heard them coming back. They went into the drawing-room, not more than three yards from me, opened the french windows and went out into the night, Gladholland wearing a hat and a coat, Mary Ellen with a mack thrown casually over her shoulders.

Safe once more, I raced up the stairs and rushed down the main corridor, flinging open every door to the left and right till I got to the room I thought I was looking for.

On the bed, quite unconscious in a deep ether-sleep, was a female, fifty years old maybe and looking more like Gladholland's housekeeper than Hazel. I didn't bother about her but rushed on up the next flight of stairs to the second and third floors.

The door to the penthouse was locked and I started getting in a panic. I hurled myself against the heavy oak, which had as much effect as hitting a toy plastic hammer against the hull of the *Queen Mary*, apart from changing the shape of my shoulder for life.

'Hazel!' I shouted. 'Hazel, are you there?'

The dead silence that followed made me more anxious than ever to get in. Holding the gun with both hands, I aimed it at the lock and fired at point-blank range.

When the dust and the smoke had cleared and my shattered nerves had stopped shaking, I kicked at the door and at the fifth attempt the splintered wood gave way. I switched the light on and looked across the neatly-furnished room. Hazel was lying on a cosy inglenook bed, asleep but holding an empty bottle of barbiturates in one hand and a note, ready for the police, in the other. All it admitted was that she had taken her life deliberately because she couldn't live with Sir Frank Alva's ghost who had haunted her day and night since she had murdered him. I had no idea how long ago she had been given the drugs, or how they had been administered, but decided that there was little I could do single-handed.

I switched off the light, pulled back the curtains to see what direction the window was facing and found myself looking down at the estate's pleasure gardens, the acre of undulating lawn that Gladholland called his golf course.

In the centre of it two pin-points of light were dancing around and, when I became accustomed to the darkness again, I could make out quite clearly what was happening.

Mary Ellen and Gladholland, with the help of torches were very busy pulling back a tarpaulin which covered an Alouette helicopter.

Forgetting Hazel and her possibly dangerous condition, I ran down the two flights of stairs to the hall, unlocked the front door, ran out into the drive and got into the Rolls. Ramming the keys in the ignition I started the engine and put the large limousine into gear.

I had sufficient knowledge of the property's layout to remember that there was space enough between the house and adjoining buildings to drive the car through to the back gardens. Switching on the headlights, I drove onto the soft, beautifully-laid-out lawn.

In front of me, down a slight slope, Gladholland was climbing into his machine. As I got nearer, the helicopter's blades started spinning. I slammed my foot flat down on the accelerator and the Rolls purred as it gathered speed, its rear wheels spinning and leaving an ugly trail of torn turf.

Mary Ellen, who was standing back from the flaying blades, turned in astonishment as the headlights caught her. Terrified, she leapt out of the way as the helicopter pulled itself off the ground, swinging in the air like a badly-balanced yo-yo.

Ducking behind the steering wheel, I closed my eyes and let the Rolls ram the two hovering skids. The speed and impact of the car brought the helicopter down, its radiator smacking it like a metal fly swat trapping a dragon-fly. Its undercarriage snapped, it struggled a second in the air, then plummeted to the ground, the Perspex cockpit bursting like a bubble, the blades carving up the soft green grass before splintering into a thousand pieces.

The Rolls was scarred, its windscreen white with a network of shattered safety glass, but little else. I got out and looked back at the strewn wreckage; everywhere there were pieces of metal and glass and aluminium. There was a smell of petrol and the danger of an explosion, but I moved closer to see what had happened to the pilot who had tried to escape me.

No one cried out in pain, no one shouted for help but the sound of squeaking metal and heavy breathing told me that Gladholland was still alive, if not all in one piece.

Stepping over part of the instrument panel that had buried itself deep in the ground, I peered into the tangled mess and saw a hand come out to grab me.

I took it and held it as Gladholland

shook himself free of the wires and straps that had held him to his seat and maybe saved him. I pulled, he pushed and after a moment he was out, staggering, breathing heavily, hanging onto me for support.

'My legs!' he cried out, in a strange strangled voice. 'Oh, my legs!'

He was lighter than I expected and I managed to bear his weight long enough to carry him to a space on the grass where there was no wreckage. I laid him down, straightened him out and then realized I had made a big mistake.

The man who was groaning at my feet, clutching at my trouser leg in agony, was not Gladholland at all; it was his chauffeur.

12

Mary Ellen was nowhere to be seen. In the confusion that had followed the crash she had disappeared, leaving me alone with a crippled chauffeur, an ethered housekeeper, a drugged Hazel, and a knowledge that I would have been better off minding my own business.

Leaving the chauffeur to chew on a leather strap I found lying among the wreckage, I made my way back across the lawn to the house, walked in through the open french windows, found a telephone in a corner and dialled 999.

By the time I had called the police, the ambulance service and the fire brigade, and gone upstairs to look at the housekeeper, she was coming round but feeling very ill. I tried to explain to her who I was, why I was there and what had happened but gave up after two attempts; it didn't seem to make much sense to her.

On the third floor Hazel was still

breathing and her pulse was regular, so I stopped worrying. From her breath I could tell that she had also been given a whiff of the old ether, a trick this particular bunch of criminals seemed to use frequently. I covered her over and let her sleep peacefully.

A search around the room revealed that they had used another of their favourite methods for disposing of people. In a drawer of a chest of drawers a damp length of rubber tube indicated that they had poured dissolved barbiturates into the girl's stomach, as they had for Frank Alva. I now hoped the ambulance people wouldn't be too long.

As I turned to go downstairs the housekeeper appeared in the doorway. She was holding a handkerchief to her mouth and trying hard not to be sick. She was Scottish, she was tough and, now that she was obviously needed, she wanted to be available and upstanding.

'You were attacked?' I asked, pretending I hadn't noticed her slightly torn nightdress.

'Ay, in my bed.' This reminded her that

she was not dressed and caused her to run away down the corridor quickly.

After a minute or so she returned wearing a dressing gown, a respectable affair in dark brown with tartan lapels.

'Who attacked you?' I asked.

'I don't know, it was in the dark.'

I felt that even if she suspected Gladholland she wouldn't give him away. He was her master and until it was proved conclusively to her that he was a nasty crook she'd stick by him. Besides, perhaps the chauffeur had done the deed.

Somewhere deep in the house a bell rang and the housekeeper looked up at me surprised.

'It's probably the police,' I said.

'I'll fetch them up,' she said, then added, 'I've got a dreadful headache.'

I was holding Hazel's hand when she came back showing a young doctor into the room. He was fair-haired, in his late twenties, a locum to the district's practice and not over-confident about his bedside manner.

He was nervous because Gladholland was the big fish in the district and this was the big house.

'Now, what can I do for this young lady?' he asked, opening up his medical gladstone and bringing out a stethoscope. 'I understand from the police that she overdid the sleeping tablets.'

'Yes,' I said, 'twenty-five little tablets, if she took the whole bottle.'

He looked concerned, did not of course want to listen to what I thought her trouble was, but in this case had to. As he leaned over her, maybe to look under her closed eyelids, I pulled back the sheet that covered her and watched him step back as though he had never seen an attractive blonde teenager stark naked before.

'It's all right,' I said before he could protest on grounds of decency, 'she's used to it — works afternoons at Fred Bear's Strip Club.'

He wasn't too sure what to do with his stethoscope or his hands, and when he realized that the housekeeper was looking on aghast, he blushed to the roots of his hair.

'Stomach pump,' I suggested, then added, 'It's a lovely stomach.' When it came to embarrassing young doctors I was a genius.

'Yes,' he said, 'you . . . know . . . the patient? I mean . . . you're a relation?'

'You could call me that. I'm sort of her manager.' I was leering. 'I brought her for Mr. Gladholland to have a look at. White slave traffic, you know.'

He didn't, he was confused. Even Emergency Ward 10 doctors had never been made to face this sort of situation.

More bells rang down in the house and the housekeeper left the room quickly. Just as quickly she returned with a police inspector. Like the doctor he had never seen a teenage strip artiste lying asleep under the effect of drugs on one of Gladholland's beds either and reacted as badly as the doctor.

Without saying a word, but telling me with shocked eyes borrowed from his early Salvation Army days that I had absolutely no sense of decency, he covered up the girl before turning to ask a few questions. Behind him, a constable tried to hide his disappointment.

The production of my card didn't give

the inspector a better opinion of me, and when I had given him a number of irrelevant details about how I had come to find her he started on the counter-questions.

'You say you broke into this room?'

'Yes, officer. I knew the girl would be in trouble.'

'You say you shot the lock?'

'Yes, I had to; there was no other way.'

'With a gun?'

'A Smith and Wesson,' I said, producing it from my pocket.

He took it, surprised, as though he had never seen a gun before.

'Have you a licence for this?'

'No.'

'You realize . . . '

'Yes,' I said, interrupting him.

He flipped open the button of his jacket pocket and pulled out a little pad. His constable was watching him very carefully; here a lesson was to be learned.

Before asking me any further questions he ran right through the story again: how I had broken into Gladholland's house; gone upstairs and shot the lock off the door; how I had first seen the house-keeper; how I had discovered the length of rubber tube; how I had dialled 999. After writing all this down he suggested to the constable that he should check up on whether the ambulance was on its way.

'You know Mr. Gladholland?' he asked, expecting a negative answer.

'Yes,' I said, 'I was working for him.'

'So you had permission to be in here?'

'Not really.'

'Do you know where Mr. Gladholland is now?'

'No, I only wish I did. His chauffeur might, he's in the garden.'

'In the garden? His chauffeur?'

'Yes,' I said. 'He's not really very well.'

The inspector walked to the window, pulled back the curtains and looked out into the black night. He couldn't see a thing.

'Constable,' he said as the constable, rather short of breath, came running up the stairs with the news that the ambulance was at the gates, 'will you go down in the garden and find Mr. Gladholland's chauffeur. Ask him if he'd mind stepping up here. I have a few questions to ask.'

'He might not be able to come up,' I said.

'Why not?'

'Well, he's in bad shape, had an accident. You see, I was driving Mr. Gladholland's Rolls-Royce on the lawn when he tried to take off in the little helicopter and . . . well . . . '

The scene could have gone on for ever, possibly ending with the inspector bursting a blood vessel, but the pounding footsteps of people coming up the stairs and the sound of a familiar voice told me that John of Special Branch was coming to my rescue.

'You missed him then?' he said, walking right into the room, past me and over to the bed. 'But got her. This is the one we wanted to question?'

'Yes — Hazel,' I said. Then added as a warning, 'She's not wearing anything.'

Like the lecher he was, John whipped back the sheet and had a good look at the girl. Though she was in a deep sleep her body was reacting to the atmosphere and goose pimples appeared on her arms and legs and she shivered.

'She's cold. Get her down to my car. We'll get her to a doctor straight away.'

'There is a doctor here,' I said, pointing to the wide-eyed young man in the corner.

'Oh, you're a doctor, are you. Shove a pump down her, there's a good lad. I must get a statement before she passes out for ever.'

'May I, sir, ask who you are?' the inspector said, addressing John in a dangerous tone.

'By all means. Better still, ask my assistant; he'll give you all the details you want about me, even a photostat copy of my passport if you think it important. Meanwhile what I'd like from you are a few able men to search the grounds. We're looking for a criminal — escaped.'

When John wanted to make people sick he had just the right smile. The inspector didn't actually allow his lips to curl but his moustache did a very unpleasant little dance, a sort of quivering twist.

'I suggest we go down and sample

Gladholland's brandy now, Flute, and discuss our next move. Who, by the way, is the poor idiot sleeping on the lawn?'

'The chauffeur.'

'Ah yes. Used him as a decoy. Clever man Gladholland — cleverer than you anyway.'

I followed John down to the drawing-room, where I got an unexpected surprise; it was even a shock. Mary Ellen was sitting there, cross-legged, deep in a winged-chair, sipping a glass of brandy.

'You two have met, of course. Mary Ellen, Adam Flute.'

'You found her then,' I said and immediately regretted the remark.

'Found her? Oh come now, Adam, Mary works for us. Didn't she tell you?'

'No,' I said, trying a smile. It hurt.

'She wouldn't, of course. Yes, she's been after this crowd for over a year.'

'Then you knew, when I rang you up.'

'Of course we knew.'

Mary Ellen graciously got to her feet, handed the half-empty bottle of brandy, which was on the table beside her, to John and then led the way through a door to a book-lined study.

Cupboards and drawers had been unlocked and pulled open and three clerk-like men were busy reading through the various files they had found. On a desk, piled high, were some hundred 'artistic' photographs, featuring, at a glance, quite a number of well-known persons.

'I'll have a look at those later. You'd best take everything back to the office. Anything new?'

'Most of his income came from rents. He owns quite a lot of property,' Mary Ellen said, opening a file.

'Didn't we know that?'

'We knew that Coven and Gladholland were property dealers before they bought up the Butts Construction Company some seven years ago, but we didn't know Gladholland owned the Barons Court block of flats, or the Pont Street house, or the terrace of houses which his offices occupy.'

'He owns them personally?'

'According to these documents.'

After being given a small tot of brandy I was allowed to look over John's shoulder at the various contracts and deeds which had been found in a safe behind the bookshelves.

'What part do Messrs. Coven and Butts play in C.G.B. now?' I asked.

'None. He bought them out, or used unorthodox methods to persuade them to retire. He is the main shareholder of the company and has a number of directors doing all the work. One can't dismiss a man like this. He had a lot more to offer the Americans than Alva-Lazells. He was responsible for that scientific project in the Hebrides.'

'Why waste his time with all this then?' I asked, looking through the first few photographs.

'He cut through the red tape with those. Every time he got stopped by some civil servant he threatened someone in a superior position unless he got what he wanted. He never used this vice business for personal gain, not directly. What he did he did for progress, strange as it may seem.'

'A sad reflection on our times, that one has to stoop so low to conquer.'

'One always has. I don't, personally, view his deeds as criminal; he didn't indulge himself, he just made use of other people's degeneracy. He went a bit far when he shot his colleagues though.'

A sharp knock at the door made us both turn round. The police inspector, with leather gloves now, was standing to attention. He had fifteen men outside in the drive awaiting instructions.

'Good. I'll leave it to you to deploy them, but we're looking for George Gladholland. We think he's somewhere in the grounds of the house, and we know he is armed. I want him alive.'

'Sir!' The inspector did a smart about turn and left our presence.

'Where do you think he'd run to?'

'Gladholland?' I asked.

'Mmm.'

'Abroad, if he got away.'

'He didn't get away, thanks to you.'

'Oh?'

'He was down there in the garden with

Mary Ellen and his chauffeur when you drove at them. The moment he realized someone knew he was taking off in a helicopter he told his man to go alone. While Mary Ellen hesitated, not knowing whether to follow him or go with the chauffeur, as Gladholland would expect her to, you made your magnificent charge. He ran off in the dark. Unless he had another car ready and managed to leave the estate without making any noise, one of you would have heard him. Mary, after all, was keeping an eye on him all the time.'

'Except when he disappeared,' she admitted.

'So you think he's somewhere on the estate?'

'Yes. Like to have a look for him?'

'Wouldn't mind.'

'Go with my blessing, dear boy, but remember you are acting in a quite unofficial capacity. Don't get killed, I've enough corpses to explain away as it is,' John said through a sigh, then added, 'Mary thinks he has an armoury hidden somewhere. When we find that, we'll find him.'

I said nothing, but quietly did up the buttons of my jacket. I had no gun, no weapons, but I knew exactly where I was going.

13

I counted nine vehicles outside in the drive, two private cars, three police cars, one ambulance, two police vans and a fire engine. Half of them had their headlights blazing, which was a guarantee that Gladholland would not emerge from his hiding-place if he was anywhere in the vicinity.

He was a sufficiently well-organized man to provide himself with an escape hole and I decided that I would start by visiting the two towers, that stood on either side of the secondary entrance to his estate, where he stored his guns.

The walk across the dewy paddock was pleasant; dawn was breaking, a wind had blown the clouds away, the stars sparkled in the mauve blue sky and a crescent moon in the west lent a touch of the *Arabian Nights* to the scene — the lull before the storm.

I reached the far side of the paddock

and, with a twinge in my hip, climbed over the railings to join the driveway that encircled the estate. It was still dark enough for me to blend with the shadows and I walked on the grass verge to avoid making a noise.

The revving of cars and the shouting sounded far off now and the house, with lights shining from every window, gave one the impression that a party was in progress, rather than a group of men getting together to hunt out a dangerous criminal.

As I got nearer the gates with their two sinister towers, I kept as near to the bushes as possible yet carefully avoiding the uneven ground with its hidden tell-tale cracking twigs.

When I was a few yards from the armoury tower I stopped. I had struck lucky first time. A thin line of light was showing through a crack in the door, and as I cautiously moved nearer I heard the movements of someone inside, dragging heavy objects across the floor.

The light went off, there was silence, then unexpectedly a key was turned in the lock. I moved quickly, flung myself down flat in the long grass only a few feet to the left of the door and hoped for the best. It was not a hiding-place and if anyone looked in my direction I would be spotted.

Holding my breath, I watched the door opening and a tall figure emerging. It was Gladholland. He stood for quite a long time looking towards the house; then, presumably confident that he had tricked everyone, strode off determinedly towards the other tower, flung the unlocked door open and went in.

I didn't wait. Acting on impulse, I rushed to the armoury, went straight into the dank, cement-smelling room and tried to remember if there was anywhere I could hide. If he came back I would be trapped now, trapped in a secluded place where I would get no help and where my assailant would know exactly where to lay his hands on a suitable weapon to eliminate me.

I took out the small pen torch from my wallet pocket and allowed the narrow beam to dance around the walls quickly.

The large gun cupboard was open, but apart from that and a pile of cement bags there was little else that would afford me cover. Then I noticed a trap-door in the floor with a ladder leading down to some hidden room below ground.

I started to climb down it, but realized in time that this was probably Gladholland's hide-out. Down there I would be even more at his mercy.

The sound of something heavy being rolled along the road outside made me jump. In a panic I climbed over the bags and hid behind one of the large open cupboard doors. I held my breath and my heart beat loudly. Gladholland was having a field day and didn't care how much he disturbed the peace. He knew they could not hear him from the house. From a crouched and somewhat painful position I watched him roll a tin drum into the tower. It was heavy, containing a liquid, and he only just managed to up-end it to get it through the door. Once through he shut himself in, locked the door, switched on the light and wasted no time swinging the drum onto its side again and rolling it towards the trap-door. With a superhuman effort he then tipped it over and tried to slide it down the side of the ladder. He groaned, hung on for a few seconds, then had to let go. There was a loud crash, then the sound of the drum rolling along a passage. Gladholland's escape hole was more elaborate than I had imagined.

Without looking around, he went down the ladder after the drum and, again from the sounds that came from below, I gathered he was rolling it along.

I waited quite some time till his footsteps and the noise of the drum were in the distance, then left my hiding-place.

Lying down near the opening of the trap-door and lowering myself head first, I peeped round the edge and saw a long, straight corridor, lit by electric bulbs all the way, stretching for perhaps some five hundred yards. The passage, newly-cemented and wired, obviously led to the house.

It did not take a genius to guess what Gladholland might be up to. With his bellicose nature and his armoury it was not impossible that he was rolling a drum of high explosives along there to blow up the house, the snoopers and all the evidence of his crimes with it.

If a catastrophe was to be averted I would have to act very fast. To run along the narrow well-lit passage after Gladholland, who was probably armed, would be suicide. I would have to go down there with some form of protection, a weapon to defend myself.

Though he had a fine selection of guns, pistols and revolvers in his armoury cupboard, none had ammunition except a Very pistol. With no time to be choosy I smacked in one of the cartridges. Even if it wasn't accurate, it would make enough noise to draw his attention and stop him going any further with his diabolical plan.

The sound of the drum rolling on echoed and re-echoed down the passage and, though it was difficult to judge, I was fairly certain he hadn't yet got halfway to the house.

If he had no gun with him I would have the advantage, but if he was armed I would be in trouble. There was no protection for me down there at all, and, for all I knew, there might be a room or a space halfway along the corridor for him to hide.

Working feverishly, I pulled six cement bags to the edge of the opening, piled them on top of each other then pushed the lot over so that they crashed to the floor of the passage at the foot of the ladder. Two burst; they made a dull thud, but, surprisingly enough, not enough noise to draw Gladholland's attention. I was in luck.

Carefully I swung myself over the opening as though exercising on parallel bars, hung there for a few seconds, then dropped down and landed neatly behind the mound of grey powder and split paper containers. Not giving Gladholland a chance, I lay flat behind the barrier. It was dangerously low and afforded me little protection.

I waited for some time. Gladholland had heard something and stopped. He had turned perhaps and seen the cement bags. Now I would have to draw his fire or somehow find out whether he was armed or not.

Using an old ruse, I quickly slipped off a shoe and lifted it slowly above the line of the mound. There was a short sharp report and a bullet hit the sole and sent my shoe flying backwards out of my grasp. Gladholland was not only armed but was a good shot and in a good position to take aim. I waited.

Nothing happened for two whole long minutes. I decided I would not need my other shoe, so took that off and poked the heel round the side of the cement bags. A fraction of a second later a bullet zipped past, hitting the wall behind me. Gladholland was frighteningly awake. I tried another position directly above my head, and this time he got a bull's-eye. The bullet tore the shoe out of my hand and went straight through the half-inch of thick leather, splitting one of the ladder rungs before ricocheting off the wall and embedding itself in the cement only a few inches from my nose.

Shivering nearly uncontrollably, and contemplating the thought of dying, trapped in the gloom of this underground tunnel, I came out of my moment of fear hearing a strange scraping sound. Quickly I poked my head round the side of the mound and saw in a second what Gladholland was up to.

Cleverly and as silently as he could, he was coming back down the long passage rolling the drum in front and ducking behind. Now I had the advantage of being able to pot at him whenever he showed his face.

After sticking a piece of torn cement bag out at the side to make sure that he wasn't still in a position to shoot at me, I put the Very pistol over the top of the mound and fired a warning shot. It was an unpremeditated action, done on the spur of the moment in a state of nervous tension. I was to regret it.

The exploding cartridge thundered in the passage completely deafening me. The pistol kicked back in my hand — breaking my forefinger which got caught in the mechanism. The war-head blazed down the corridor, bouncing from wall to wall, sending a mass of bright pink burning sparks trailing behind it and filling the confined area with thick blue sulphurous smoke.

An agonized cry for help made me look up in horror. Gladholland, arms outstretched, was in the path of the ball of fire. Suddenly it hit him, catching his flapping jacket as he staggered backwards trying to avoid it. He fought it for a moment as though it were some strange attacking bird, then, amidst terrified blood-curdling screams, he caught alight like a torch and the purple sparks that exploded from him hit the cement walls, sent pieces of masonry flying and something hit the drum.

I didn't wait to see what it was. Leaping to my feet, I grabbed hold of the top rung of the ladder and pulled myself up. Only in the presence of death could I have had such a quick reaction and such strength. A fraction of a second later the very earth exploded beneath me. I rolled to one side; heard the walls of the tower crack all round me; saw the armoury cupboard lurch forward and crash to the floor and then was enveloped in a thick ugly black smoke that came belching out of the opening. From the roar of flames and the choking smell I guessed the drum had contained petrol.

I crawled to the door, unlocked it and stumbled out into the open. I managed to get clear of the building, then, like a volcano, the paddock in front of me heaved up and flames burst out for one brief moment before everything caved in with a sudden suffocating silence.

I was lying in the middle of the road aware that I might lose consciousness. I tried to get to the grass verge but realized I could not. My feet had been scorched by the volume of heat that had expanded in the narrow tunnel; my trousers were burnt; my socks dust to the touch. Afraid that ambulances and fire engines might rush to the scene and run over me in their blind enthusiasm, I made another effort and rolled over a few times till I could lie in the dip at the side of the road. I lay there too dazed to feel any pain and saw again Gladholland with his outstretched arms, his twisting, flame-enveloped figure battling with the clinging ball of white heat.

I have no idea how long it took them to find me, but it was John who helped me sit up and poured some water down my dry throat.

'Whatever happened, man?' he asked, trying to shake some life into me.

The noise I made with my mouth told me I was in bad shape. I couldn't see properly, my ears were numb; maybe I had been hurt more than I thought, maybe I was dying.

'Did you find Gladholland?,' he asked, insisting.

'Uhh,' I managed to say.

'Is he dead?'

'Yes,' I said, remembering. Then I pushed myself away from my friend and vomited in a ring of daisies.

For the second time in forty-eight hours I was lifted onto a stretcher and put into an ambulance. John got in and sat down beside me on a bracket seat, dabbing my smoke-blackened face with something damp while a male nurse picked bits of my charred trousers off my blistered legs. It was agony.

'He had a passage . . . under the

paddock ... leading to the ... house ... Ooh!' I said between gasps of pain.

'I know,' John said, patting me gently.

'You know?'

'We found a map in his safe, the plans of the newly built passage. We were waiting for him at the other end.'

'So you would have got him alive?'

'I doubt it. We didn't reckon on him doing a Guy Fawkes act.'

The ambulance driver started up the engine and we jogged off. The jarring soothed my nerves for some reason and I asked John for a cigarette. I was beginning to recover.

'How long has that girl been working for you — Mary Ellen?'

'Two, three years. Her mother used to run a drinking club but she went broke and ... '

'She told me that story. What's the true one.'

'That is the true one. Mary Ellen's a pro. Used to be a cabinet minister's mistress till he found out he wasn't the only one, but he realized her potentialities and passed her on to us. Clever girl, doesn't mind what she does either — very useful.'

'How long had you suspected Gladholland of being mixed up in this?'

'Not long. Fantastic a man like that behaving in such a way. Makes one wonder who you can trust.'

'Now all you've got to do is find out who he worked for The big ring. The international set-up. Natalie.' I tried to move but my ankles were very sore and stung as they rubbed against the rough blanket that covered me.

'We know all about the set-up now, Flute,' John said. The ambulance was doing about fifty and he had to hang on to the side of my stretcher. 'Gladholland was a tidy business man and had an elaborate but simple filing system.'

'Who is Natalie then?'

The ambulance swung round at the end of the drive in front of the house and came to a halt. The double doors swung open and the male nurse clambered in to see if I was all right. It was morning now and I found the bright light unpleasantly dazzling; maybe my eyes had been affected by the smoke as well.

'Got another casualty going to hospital, sir. Put her in here if that's all right with you?' The man wasn't addressing me but John.

'Yes, fine. I'll go.'

'Who is Natalie?' I shouted, managing to get up on one elbow and grab John's sleeve as he started getting out.

'Gladholland was Natalie. A fictitious character to help him control the people he had working for him. There was never anyone but him at the head, no one to tell him what to do, no vice ring, international or otherwise. He invented Natalie and spread rumours about her to sidetrack you and us. We might well have looked for such a woman for years if his family album hadn't given the game away.'

'How?'

'His second name was Nathaniel. George Nathaniel Gladholland. He was called Nat by his parents, and a photo of him at the age of five dressed as a little girl was subtitled 'Natalie'. Besides, we've never found anything to suggest that foreigners were involved in all this, except Babette who worked as an individual.'

'What about the threatening letter he received, the photographs they took of him and me?'

'Did you see them? Pure fiction! They raided the Brighton apartment about two hours ago. There was nothing. He spent all his ingenuity on the Pont Street set-up.'

A small crowd of uniformed men in the driveway announced the approach of my fellow passenger. Amongst grunts and conflicting directives a stretcher slid onto the rails next to me and clipped into place. More interested to see what John was up to, I looked out of the dark windows, but lost sight of him. Then I turned to see who Gladholland's other victim was.

'Hallo!' I said, surprised.

'Hallo,' she said. 'I'd heard you were dead.'

'No, I don't think so.'

'I'm glad.'

She was very pale, but even without make-up she could compete with all the beauties I had known. She drew her naked arm from beneath the blankets and held out her hand for me to take.

'Are you badly hurt?'

'Don't know,' I answered.

'What happened?'

On this touching scene the doors were closed and the onlooking policemen allowed their twisted smiles to broaden. I told Hazel. I told her the whole story, missing out the gory details of Molly's and Babette's deaths and Gladholland's end which I knew I could still not stomach. It had been a bloody business, a sordid affair, but talking about it helped pass the time away.

During the journey I noticed that John followed us closely in his Mini, and when the ambulance eventually stopped in a street outside a London hospital, we both craned our necks to see where we were, but every London hospital looked alike to me.

'What will happen now?' she asked.

'To you?'

'Yes.'

'Nothing. You'll be asked to make a

statement to the police, help in the various enquiries, then nothing.'

'What about Fred Bear's? Will they close that?'

'I expect so. It probably belonged to Gladholland along with all his other bits of property.'

'So I'm jobless?'

'Seems like it.'

'You did say . . . ' she started, then the hospital gates opened and the ambulance moved into the quadrangle. 'You did say that perhaps you might need a secretary.'

'Yes, I did. The trouble is I might be laid up for a while.'

'Well, if you change your mind,' she said, sufficiently astute to realize that I might have changed my mind about her — 'if you change your mind you could give me the keys of your flat and I could tidy it up for you, get it ready for your convalescence.'

I smiled at her and gave her hand a squeeze. I didn't know what I would want to do in the next few days; maybe it was a good idea, but I wasn't sure, so when the doors opened and they started sliding her stretcher out, I just smiled some more and blew her a kiss.

They dumped me on a clinically clean bed in a private ward and left me there with my thoughts and pains. Then John walked in, heartier than ever, telling me he couldn't stay but would be grateful if I could think of preparing a statement. Kindly he left me a copy of the morning's paper and wandered around the room examining the various hospital gadgets that intrigued him.

The headlines concerned a revolution in South America, but the secondary story was about the Californian under-water atomic reactor station project. Contracts had been signed after four months' hard negotiations, it said, and a Japanese firm had been chosen.

'Ever gambled on the Stock Exchange?' I asked John, remembering some money I would lose.

'No. I don't believe there's any way of making a quick buck — except by selling one's story to the newspapers of course.'

'If you've got one.'

'If you've got one,' he agreed.

'Have I got one?' I asked hopefully.

'Only if you want to ruin your business.'

'What about Hazel then?'

'Yes, she's got one. She'll make a fortune.'

I didn't think about it for very long, but asked him to pass me my jacket, dug in the pockets for my keys and handed them to him.

'Will you be seeing Hazel before you go back to the office, John?' I asked.

'Yes.'

'I wonder if you'd give her these then, the keys to my flat. She'll understand.'

'All right.'

'And give her my love.'

THE END

We do hope that you have enjoyed reading this large print book.

Did you know that all of our titles are available for purchase?

We publish a wide range of high quality large print books including:
Romances, Mysteries, Classics
General Fiction
Non Fiction and Westerns

Special interest titles available in large print are:
The Little Oxford Dictionary
Music Book, Song Book
Hymn Book, Service Book

Also available from us courtesy of Oxford University Press:
Young Readers' Dictionary
(large print edition)
Young Readers' Thesaurus
(large print edition)

For further information or a free brochure, please contact us at:
Ulverscroft Large Print Books Ltd.,
The Green, Bradgate Road, Anstey,
Leicester, LE7 7FU, England.
Tel: (00 44) **0116 236 4325**
Fax: (00 44) **0116 234 0205**

Other titles in the
Linford Mystery Library:

DEATH CALLED AT NIGHT

R. A. Bennett

Jimmy Ellis believes his parents have died in a car crash when as a young boy he is taken to live with relatives in Australia. The years pass happily, then the nightmare comes. Terrifying images flit through his mind in the dark — all through the eyes of a child, a witness to grisly events seventeen years before. He begins to delve into the past, and soon he finds himself on the trail of a double murderer — a murderer who is prepared to kill again.

THE DEAD TALE-TELLERS

John Newton Chance

Jonathan Blake always kept appointments. He had kept many, in all sorts of places, at all sorts of times, but never one like that one he kept in the house in the woods in the fading light of an October day. It seemed a perfect, peaceful place to visit and perhaps take tea and muffins round the fire. But at this appointment his footsteps dragged, for he knew that inside the house the men with whom he had that date were already dead . . .

DEATH IN RETREAT

George Douglas

On a day of retreat for clergy at
Overdale House, a resident guest,
Martin Pender, is foully murdered.
The primary task of the Regional
Homicide Squad is to track down the
bogus parson who joined the retreat.
Subsequent events show that serious
political motives lie behind the killing,
but the basic lead to it all is missing.
Then, three young tearaways corner
the killer in the woods, and a chess
problem, set out on a board, yields
vital evidence.

A HANDBOOK OF PASTORAL COUNSELLING

OTHER MOWBRAY PARISH HANDBOOKS

A handbook of
PASTORAL
COUNSELLING

by

PETER G. LIDDELL

Director of Pastoral Counselling,
Diocese of St Albans

MOWBRAY
LONDON & OXFORD

ISBN 0-264-66778 6

First published 1983
by A. R. Mowbray & Co. Ltd,
Saint Thomas House, Becket Street,
Oxford, OX1 1SJ

Photoset by Cotswold Typesetting Ltd, Cheltenham
Printed in Great Britain by Redwood Burn Limited

Contents

Foreword

I am glad to have been asked to write a Foreword to this valuable book. I have long known Peter Liddell both as a friend and colleague. There is no doubt of his dedication to the cause of pastoral counselling. He has studied and practised the ideas and insights which figure in this book, both here and in the United States.

His approach demonstrates an all too rare combination of technical skill and personal warmth: he is professional without being forbidding, and sympathetic without being soft. This book deserves the attention of all those involved in any form of pastoral counselling.

+ ROBERT CANTUAR

Preface

During the five years that I was associated with the Part-time Programme in Pastoral Counselling at the Westminster Pastoral Foundation, we received seventy-five students a year on to the half-day a week, two year course. They included teachers, social workers, health visitors, home helps, doctors, clergy, college lecturers, counsellors from Cruse, Life and the Samaritans, a municipal engineer, wives of clergy and diplomats, a verger, a publisher, a translator, astrologers, nuns, civil servants, personnel officers, a dancer and a hairdresser. The hairdresser came because she found that, while people were having their hair done, they told her their problems. She was concerned to become a better counsellor to them.

In the past two years that a similar course has been introduced in the Diocese of St Albans, fifty-five people have taken part. The opportunity is offered because (a) people seek training for their own development, (b) there are visible needs within the community, where individuals in distress benefit from the support of the ordinary person who can offer the right kind of listening, and (c) there is an increasing diversity of ministry within the parish, where there is room for parish life to be transformed by the contribution of pastoral counselling.

It is out of this background that this book comes to be written. I make the dedication of it within the body of the book to my wife and children, Mary, Jane and Timothy, who are the living spirits of my pastoral counselling world.

I also acknowledge the assisting ministry of my diocesan lay minister, Mrs Meg Hooper, who in sustaining the parish during my absence has sustained me; my former tutors and fellow students at the Institutes of Religion and Health, New York, and the members of Asbury United Methodist Church,

Crestwood, all of whom I have to thank for a new life in the new world; Edward C. Whitmont, co-founder of and training analyst at the C. G. Jung Institute, New York, who taught me the ways of man and God; my colleagues, staff and students, at the Westminster Pastoral Foundation, with whom I have shared the sometimes unnoticed excitement of creating new structures, defining a new practice and re-discovering old truths; the members of the parishes of Kimpton and Ayot St Lawrence, to whom I am present and absent.

From the family where I was nurtured to the new family settings where I have found a place, I find the strength to be able to ask, 'What is pastoral counselling?'

Peter G. Liddell
Director of Pastoral Counselling,
Diocese of St Albans

Chapter 1

What is Pastoral Counselling?

What is 'counselling'?

Counselling is an activity in which one person seeks the help of another in dealing with a problem.

This, of course, happens all the time without it being given a separate title. Some people are intuitively sought out for help because of their personal qualities. However, even these (like the hairdresser) usually find that they come to a point where they are unsure about how they are dealing with the situation. Other people find that being a counsellor is thrust upon them because of some role they occupy; they feel that they want to set about learning what is for them a new 'discipline', much as they might start going to evening classes. Understanding that there is an identifiable way of being 'with' another in distress helps both to supplement a counsellor's innate qualities and to uncover ones he did not know were there.

Counselling is not simply being a friend. A friend is able to offer listening, practical help, information and guidance; he stands alongside and shares the impact of a crisis, but he may be as much at a loss as the sufferer to know how to deal with it.

The counsellor takes up a different stance. He is more one

who stands 'over against' the other. He is not simply an ally but a 'third' person who mediates between the sufferer and his situation, so that the meaning of it may be more fully understood. A counsellor provides both a presence and a distance, draws attention to the value of them both and to the space in the middle.

The new ground to which the counsellor draws attention and on to which he invites the other to join him is the creation of the right trusting relationship between them, in which both may look at the difficulties and both try to find a way of resolving them. This will involve the counsellor in enabling the client to discover new strengths within himself, so that he will be able to lead his life more in a way that he would like.

This understanding of counselling is one which could be held by a marriage guidance counsellor, a welfare officer who sees an employee in a counselling situation or a 'pastoral counsellor'.

What is 'pastoral counselling'?
'Pastoral' has a general sense in which it describes the role of a welfare officer, a social worker or a teacher who is entrusted with 'pastoral' responsibility. It implies 'responsibility', in that the person is responsible for a certain population to a body of which he or both may be part. A welfare officer in the civil service is responsible for the pastoral care of a certain number of employees to the institution which is interested in their well-being. He represents the organization and some of its functioning. A welfare officer or a teacher with pastoral responsibility could be interested in pastoral counselling, even if they do not call what they do by that name.

To a number of people, 'pastoral counselling' represents a narrowing of the field within the broad area of counselling. 'Counselling' is a very widely-used word. It may refer to school counselling and careers guidance; it may include behaviour therapy, short-term workshops, learning active techniques by which a person's inner energies are released, reliving one's birth trauma and overt sexual exploration; a person may be seen by a 'counsellor' after having attended an evangelistic campaign. 'Pastoral counselling' to most people is less at the end of the spectrum which is 'fringe' and 'risky', and more to do with listening, talking, using religious terms and receiving gentle advice. This is a limitation on its understanding.

Another mistaken approach is to suppose that 'pastoral' implies the area of the counsellor's special interest. There are 'abortion', 'bereavement', 'drug-dependence', 'marriage', 'sex' and 'student' counsellors; it might be expected that a 'pastoral' counsellor's interest is limited to working with those who have a 'religious' problem. This again is a limitation. An abortion counsellor's function is to initiate a personal relationship with a client in order that both may agree on an immediate decision. The counsellor is safeguarding the institution's interests by seeing to it that the client fully understands the implications of the decision. The counsellor is likely to have decided views on abortion and may indeed influence the client one way or the other. This is understandable, and something which the client may be expecting, since she chose which agency to go to. The counsellor's task is short-term and focussed. If the client needed on-going help, the counsellor would have to enter another phase of relationship or refer the client to another agency. A pastoral counsellor could well be such an agency.

'Pastoral' certainly has a religious association, but even here there is a divergence of meaning. Every minister of religion may see himself as practising pastoral counselling. Some would say that it is not an activity which they would separate from the rest of their role, that they have been doing it for decades and their Faith before them for centuries. If a person comes to his parish priest for help with a problem, the priest sits down and listens. He looks at the situation from a different point of view and is of very real help to the parishioner. He has experience of other people in similar situations, draws on the teachings of his Faith, knows what is desirable, has insight and patience drawn from his prayer-life and has some of the strength which the other person needs in that situation; otherwise he would not have gone to him. The priest may be able to say some very valuable things as well as listen, and he may be able to mediate something, which he may not even recognize, which the parishioner takes away with him. It is right to call this 'pastoral counselling', just as it is right to include those situations where some counselling is able to take place within an informal context, where counselling is not being asked for and where it may not be realised that it is being given.

However, 'pastoral counselling' is taking on a new and specific meaning, to which, of course, there has been resistance, but which it is hoped will be seen as working with all other things for good. In this understanding, a pastoral counsellor is one who has undertaken an extensive training in counselling or psychotherapy. He may be religious and seek to relate it to his religious faith, so that he may share in the work of healing and being healed for the enrichment of individuals within the community and the corporate life of the body of believers of which he is one.

The components to this identity of pastoral counselling are as follows.

The religious tradition of wholeness in body, mind and soul

Religious tradition has always managed to retain the truth that there is more to healing than curing the ills of the body; if a person is to find healing for some of his illnesses, he must find where he is troubled in spirit. However, religion has always stood by the occurrence of miraculous cures, which to the sceptical makes it the province of the credulous and superstitious. The pastoral counsellor may be able to take a stand between the sceptical and the credulous and ask how each is challenged by the other. In the process, he may be able to find a conviction which has been refined by fire.

The medical tradition

One of the parents of pastoral counselling is the hospital chaplaincy. The hospital chaplain is in the position of seeing in a controlled setting those who are 'ill' or 'abnormal'. The separation of groups of individuals with some common characteristics from the rest of the community makes it easier to focus attention upon them and examine them in depth. The hospital chaplain works alongside medical colleagues, uses their disciplined approach and learns from their discoveries. He has the setting in which he may observe, record and analyze his interactions with patients, their inter-actions with each other and to the institution. It is a ready-made laboratory setting. There is up-to-date information and there are models to follow. In the United States, the Clinical Pastoral Education movement (CPE) has reached a sophisti-cated state of development, as reflected in the hierarchy of qualifications it offers to those who train under its auspices; CPE grew out of the work of hospital chaplains. In Britain, pioneering trainings in pastoral counselling were initiated by hospital chaplains (e.g. Littlemore, Oxford), while hospital chaplains are currently conspicuous in the advancement of the pastoral counselling movement. Some doctors and clergy have always felt able to co-operate. Their common purpose is expressed in the work of the Institute of Religion and Medicine, founded in 1963.

The educational tradition

In the United States, the theological seminary stands alongside the hospital chaplain as being one of the co-sponsors of pastoral counselling. Seminaries are interested in 'practical theology', that is how the faith may best be put into practice within a local setting. Departments of 'religion and psychiatry' were established in seminaries.

In Britain, within the Church of England, interest in pastoral counselling has often sprung out of the work of diocesan education officers who may have set up training programmes for the enrichment of interpersonal relationships.

In the 1960s, clergy and lay people were introduced to the field by having been members of sensitivity groups sponsored by diocesan teams.

The Protestant tradition

The American scene is again of great relevance, where pastoral counselling has developed to an advanced degree. While the American Association of Pastoral Counselors contains a wide variety of Christian denominations and Jews, and represents ecumenism in action, it has a certain Protestant heritage. Its members are 'pastors' doing counselling or psychotherapy, either as part of their role as parish ministers or working as professional pastoral psycotherapists in a pastoral counselling centre. In such a centre, the pastoral counsellor works with an interdisciplinary team; clients come for hourly sessions and pay fees. This role of the minister is a pioneering one and it has not emerged without upheavals and suspicion. Some see a radical separation from a previous role; others claim an authentic continuity. With an emphasis on the self-authenticating nature of the work being undertaken, the New Testament spirit of a new movement and the offer of a new salvation for the individual, there are at least some marks of a mini-reformation.

Protestant churches have a high standard of pastoral care. The pastor is looked upon as a person of high standing and skill. He is paid well and expected to perform well. He has a professional pastoral interest in the individual members of his flock. It is, therefore, understandable that he should equip himself to be as effective as possible and to make use of all recent advances. Therefore, he will give himself fully to whatever training is available in pastoral care.

In Britain, the Protestant tradition in pastoral counselling is represented within the Church of Scotland and the Methodist Church. In Scotland, the training of ministers remains within the universities, where the emphasis is naturally intellectual and theological; but it is not surprising, given the liberal and enquiring Scottish educational tradition, that courses in pastoral studies have been set up attached to university departments of Christian Ethics. It is similarly to be expected that the actual exercise of pastoral care should have received study and advanced application in the work of Scottish hospital chaplains. The quarterly, '*Contact*', which is concerned with interpersonal and social issues, was founded by the Scottish Pastoral Association. The first International Congress on Pastoral Care and Counselling took place in Edinburgh in 1979.

In the Methodist Church, pioneering work was begun by Leslie Weatherhead in the counselling service which operated at the City Temple. William Kyle extended the movement by establishing first the Highgate Counselling Centre and then the Westminster Pastoral Foundation, located originally in the Central Hall, Westminster. The Foundation offers both a training in pastoral counselling for clergy and lay people and a counselling service, which provides individual, group, marriage and family counselling.

The Catholic tradition

Pastoral counselling owes much to the model of confession. What a client learns in counselling is how to extend his confession. In learning to confess what is most difficult for him, he comes to experience the other meaning of 'confess', which is to 'witness' and 'proclaim'. In confessing his weakness, he confesses an authentic strength. In finding a proper response to his confession, firstly from the counsellor and secondly from within himself, he makes himself 'at one' with himself.

The pastoral counsellor draws from Catholic tradition a sense of the numinous in his work. In the nuts and bolts of dealing with very practical and concrete matters with a very alive person in front of him, there emerges a sense of the 'oddness' of it all. A conversation goes on between two people, the words of which are not unusual, but the interaction between the two people, the questions the counsellor asks, the impact of them upon the client, the replies which the client finds himself making suggest a sense of 'unusualness' amidst an ordinary setting. It is sensed that while things are going on on the surface, there seems to be something else going on underneath. This, of course, is the case, for the pastoral counsellor is there to appreciate the way in which something is said, what is not being said and what is being said only as a pointer to something else. From Catholic tradition, the pastoral counsellor draws a quality of receptivity.

The priestly tradition

The priest who can hear more fully the authentic voice of the suppliant is a more effective guide to the soul. The priest is a mediator. The pastoral counsellor mediates between the client and his problem, the client and the world with which he is at odds, but chiefly between the client and his inner self. The pastoral counsellor introduces the person to 'another' self and consecrates a marriage between them.

The pastoral counsellor may be aware that he is involved in the working out of some sort of liturgy. This may simply be that counselling with an individual or with a group follows an ordered sequence. However, if religious liturgy has any meaning, it is a reasonable hypothesis that it must have a parallel in interpersonal and intrapsychic (i.e. within the person) processes. If it is through the action of the priest that the liturgy is made visible, it is through the mediation of the pastoral counsellor that a living liturgy is enacted.

The 'unconscious' is a starting point in psychotherapy. The 'unconscious' may mean simply those parts of ourselves of which we are unaware and which are brought to light for the better functioning of the person. However, that is to state simply a bland intellectual observation. What is missing is awareness of the place of the 'feeling' response of the person himself to the emergence of the unconscious. This response is often one of surprise, wonder, fear, obedience, awe, accept-ance and belief mixed with disbelief. These reactions are traditionally associated with experience of the religious.

The evangelistic tradition

The pastoral counsellor, like any practitioner who commits his integrity to his work, believes in the essential benefit of what he has experienced and in what he is doing. The pastoral counsellor is clear that there are visible ills around and that there are empirically tested ways of being freed from them. People actually are suffering because their emotions are in turmoil and there is a way of healing, part of which lies in being able to put the illness into words; when something is put into a word, an order emerges from chaos.

The congregational tradition

The exercise of pastoral counselling is not something which is limited to a priestly caste, but a function which belongs to the people as a whole.

The Anglican tradition

Anglicans have been in the forefront of the development of pastoral counselling in Britain. A major step forward took place when Clinical Theology emerged as a movement in 1962. Dr. Frank Lake, a former medical missionary, created a blend of psychology and theology which brought a whole new understanding to a large number of people. Seminars were held in parishes and colleges of further education across the country. A considerable number of pastoral counsellors owe their beginnings to Clinical Theology.

The Diocese of Southwark appointed in 1970 a Director of Pastoral Counselling, the first of a handful of dioceses to do so. Consultation groups led by external consultants were set up in which clergy and lay people could discuss pastoral situations in which they were involved, receive support and work on their own interpersonal contribution. An educational programme in co-operation with the Extra-Mural Department of London University was established.

The national body, the Association of Pastoral Care and Counselling, may be thought to have taken on some Anglican qualities. It seeks to hold the tension between the urge for professionalism, accreditation and standards and retain the organization as a body to which voluntary workers and all who have an interest in pastoral care and counselling may belong. There is within the field a tension also between the exercise of pastoral care and the more thrusting promotion of pastoral counselling. It may be that Anglican experience in holding together tensions accounts for the way in which these energies have so far been contained within the organization.

The secular tradition

The rise of the psychotherapy movement in this century has been largely, though by no means solely, a secular one. This secular tradition asserts that religion is a neurosis. This is a challenge which brings vigour to detractors and supporters alike and man is the gainer. What Freud did in liberating man from that part of his religion which is neurosis was to increase his stature. Freud said that there are reasons, which had hitherto gone unnoticed, why man behaves in certain ways. He thus 'justified' him and became his advocate; in pointing to the fact that man has an ego, he gave man an ego.

This whole exciting tradition, which is humanist, has developed under the discipline of psychoanalysis, from which have grown supporters and opponents: neo-Freudians, Jungians, Adlerians, interpersonal theorists, followers of Klein and Horney, gestalt therapy, transactional analysis, the whole field of group therapy and family systems theory. All this tradition is available to the pastoral counsellor to accept, reject and refine.

The social conscience tradition

One of the major roots of pastoral counselling is the Richmond Fellowship, which was set up in 1959. It has established a network of half-way houses in this country and abroad for those who are making their way back into the community after having been institutionalized. The work is made possible by part-time and full-time courses in pastoral counselling for those who will staff the centres, but which are also open to others. Probably a fair number of students are motivated by religious faith and see such a service within the community as the most realistic setting in which to exercise their talents.

The Jewish tradition

While Jewish pastoral counsellors are more common in the United States than in Britain, it is certainly true that enlightened Jewish congregations have become interested in pastoral counselling and rabbis are increasingly encouraged to undertake training in it. However, it is probably those Jews who are analysts who are making the greatest contribution to the movement. Some believe that it is in the area of understanding suffering that the Jew makes a special contribution. For the Christian, it is possibly the fact that the Jew is able to stand between Christianity and the secular. There is certainly an affinity within Jewishness for pastoral counselling; perhaps it is in the awareness of what is religious combined with a distance from it. The conjunction of these two qualities is essential to pastoral counselling.

The individual tradition

This category encompasses the fact that most, if not all, of those who learn and practice pastoral counselling arrive at it from their own need to be healed and from their own conscious and unconscious experience of suffering. If pastoral counselling is about healing, it is also about the sense of carrying the wound. In the process of being involved with the healing of another, the counsellor recapitulates a healing for himself.

Training Programmes in Pastoral Counselling

One of the ways in which to describe what pastoral counselling is, is to say how a person might be trained in it. The pioneer of training programmes was the American Foundation for Religion and Psychiatry (now the Institutes of Religion and Health), which was founded by Norman Vincent Peale, Pastor of Marble Collegiate Church, New York and a psychiatrist, Smiley Blanton, who had been analyzed by

Freud. In the United States, pastoral counsellors are by definition clergymen; thay have been ordained or recognized in some similar way by their faith group. In Britain, the Westminster Pastoral Foundation offers the largest training programme, with the important difference that it is not limited to clergy, which means that it has many more students than the American Institutes. The American programme, however, is three years full-time; the Westminster programme one year full-time followed by two years part-time. The following description of an extended course in pastoral counselling is based on these two programmes.

A Professional Course in Pastoral Counselling

1. *Personal therapy*

Central to the training is for a student to have been a client himself, to have looked in depth at himself and his pattern of functioning. It is important that the student have the support which comes from such an experience during a course which challenges his way of life, outlook and very being. Because the student is involved in change himself, and learning to integrate it, he is better able to understand what a client is experiencing. Chiefly, however, the aim is to enable the student to have sufficient insight into himself to be able to protect the client from his own (i.e. the student's) inner problems.

Personal therapy takes place with an analyst or psychotherapist of a recognized institution outside the structure of the training programme. There is no consultation between the training institute and the person's analyst. Sessions are likely to be once a week and they may be supplemented by group therapy.

2. *Clinical Practice*

Counselling is learned by doing it. A student, therefore, has to see a number of clients and have his work supervised. It is important that he have a variety of experience, seeing some clients on a short-term basis, i.e. five to ten sessions, and some over a prolonged period, i.e. eighteen months or more, and that there be a cross-section of clients. Clients are usually seen once a week for an hour. Total case-load requirements may vary from four hundred (WPF) to two thousand hours (IRH). Supervision may be on an individual basis, but is more likely to be in a group of three to five students with a supervisor. In the supervision session, the student re-creates the problem he is experiencing with the client. He may do this in a way which is unnoticed by himself, but it is likely that one or other of his colleagues will be able to point to a number of issues about the client and about his response to the client which will be of help to him.

3. *Theory*

A considerable body of knowledge has been built up on the theory and practice of counselling. The many schools of psychotherapy are relevant, as is the practice of group therapy and marriage and family therapy. Trainings which follow an analytic model emphasize more frequent analysis (four to five times a week) and less theory (possibly two evening seminars a week for two years, these following the orientation of the particular analytic school). For a rounded experience, it is desirable to cover the discoveries of the movement as a whole. Seminars frequently have a dynamic character to them; that is, they involve not merely the presentation of theoretical material, but have the potential to be the context in which the theoretical material is applied or can be seen to emerge. If a particular concept is being talked about, it is possible and necessary to identify it in the processes which are actually taking place within the seminar.

The body of information which needs to be covered includes the following.

(a) *Development of the personality.* There are stages of life from birth (and before) through to death. An individual becomes 'blocked' at a particular stage in a particular area of his life. Counselling recapitulates in the interaction between client and counsellor the process of normal development and enables the client to be 'unblocked'.

(b) *Psychopathology.* It is useful to recognize that there are recurring recognizable states of being which have causes. Short-hand language is useful in order to communicate simply and clearly about them. This involves categorizing disorder. It does not mean that one is bound to a 'sickness' model of neurosis. The shorthand language is only understood by following full-length case studies of individuals who are suffering in different (and similar) ways.

(c) *Psychodynamics.* Different practitioners of the art have described what happens in the process of counselling in different ways. They have created new words to describe what they mean and they have emphasized different areas. Psycho-dynamics is the study of the movement or energy which stirs within and between people. Each theoretical system repays study and the student needs to be able to make the theory come alive by seeing the situation in the way the originator of the system saw it. A system is a way of helping a person grasp what is going on. Different individuals are described more easily in different systems. The more counsellor and client can state what is going on, the more beneficial the counselling is going to be.

(d) *Techniques of counselling.* The actual practice of counselling is put under scrutiny; attention needs to be paid to what is actually happening within the session. It is desirable that the counsellor have a 'strategy', without implying that that is superficial. It is important to know what he is doing, when and how. What is the beginning, middle and end of the individual session and of the process as a whole? How is the counsellor assessing the session as it is proceeding and what options does he have to change it?

(e) *Clinical Psychiatry.* The counsellor has to know the borders of his work. He needs to have a clear picture of more serious psychiatric conditions, what sort of drugs are in current use and what their effects are. He needs to begin to think how co-operation with a psychiatrist may proceed.

(f) *Intake and Assessment.* This seminar pays special attention to what takes place in the first session, before the client is allocated to a counsellor. The intake worker has to be able to set a client at ease, elicit information pertaining to current state and past history, factual details about state of health and hospitalizations, test the client's motivation for counselling, set the ground-rules for future work and possibly indicate referral elsewhere.

(g) *Theory and Practice of Group Counselling.* What actually happens in group process, what are the therapeutic qualities of a group which the counsellor needs to foster and the destructive conditions which he needs to resist? Can group process be conceptualized? What are group norms? Where does authority in the group lie, is there a group 'unconscious' which may be of service to the members?

(h) *Theory and Practice of Marriage and Family Counselling.* How does the counsellor conceptualize movement within a family or pair? How can he see the family as a system of forces rather than a collection of individuals? If the counsellor can conceptualize the system, he will be aware that his own coming into the setting changes the balance and flow of energies. He perceives that the family system is brought into the counselling room and is made visible in the way the members interact with each other; the counsellor has to see where he can best place his energies.

(i) *Community Resources.* An outline of statutory and voluntary agencies which are available.

(j) *Philosophy of Counselling.* An opportunity to explore, question and develop the pre-suppositions on which counselling is based and to set it in the context of art, religion, anthropology and the social sciences.

4. *Peer Group*

This is an experience provided by the institution where the student may test with his peers the feed-back he is receiving elsewhere from therapist and supervisor. It is an opportunity for integration of the course as a whole. A course in pastoral counselling is a demanding experience and brings pressures and buffetings as well as growth. Working within a new agency and learning within an institution can be a confusing and disorienting experience. A peer group is a place where some sort of centre to the experience may be created.

The person who has completed a professional course in pastoral counselling will have a specialized experience. He will have gained a substantial body of knowledge, been trained in specific skills, which are not widely available, and undergone an intensive personal experience, subjecting his life to some scrutiny. Since there is no obvious career structure to fit into when he has completed it, there is a considerable element of risk involved, which emphasizes the worth the individual places on the experience.

The pastoral counsellor is equipped to establish an in-depth relationship with a wide variety of people who are suffering from life's problems. He is trained to be supportive, that is, to maintain at a functioning level those who otherwise might be overwhelmed by external pressures and internal weaknesses and who would otherwise be hospitalized. He is also trained to help make whole those who have sufficient healing power within themselves to make considerable changes in their life-pattern.

Where do pastoral counsellors go? Some take their skills back into the job from which they came, adapting it so that they have the space to use what they have learned. Clergy may do this, using some of their time to do structured counselling with individuals referred from their fellow clergy. They may, however, address themselves to the parish and ask themselves, 'How is one a pastoral counsellor to the parish?'.

Clergy, however, are by no means the only professionals who can adapt their role, and usually clergy are in a very small minority on pastoral counselling courses. Pastoral counsellors have found employment as student counsellors, in the social services and in community projects. They have to explain what their training has involved and sell themselves and their skills. A large number of pastoral counsellors work in private practice. The reasons for this may be that they feel that the individuality they have gained is best expressed by working independently; they have not been prepared to convince established institutions of the worth of their training, and agencies both religious and secular have not yet recognized the worth of a pastoral counsellor; all of which is understandable, since we are yet in the very formative stages of the development of pastoral counselling.

What the future may bring is that training programmes in pastoral counselling will receive more formal validation from external academic bodies. This means that agencies will be offered a counsellor who has a diploma or other qualification in pastoral counselling, which is on a par and probably exceeds other recognized qualifications. An agency will then be able to choose whether it wishes to employ somebody with a qualification in counselling or one in pastoral counselling.

The Association of Pastoral Care and Counselling is one of the seven divisions of the British Association for Counselling. APCC is one of the few divisions which has yet produced an accreditation process. One would expect that pastoral counsellors will at least be on a par with whatever levels of competence are eventually recognized by the Association as a whole.

Shorter Training Programme
This type of programme is of the order of half a day a week for two or three years. The assumption here is that personal

therapy is not available for the student and therefore the only available experience of personal growth has to be included within the programme itself. This type of programme is often the stimulus for a local counselling centre and is described more fully in chapter 10.

Introductory Programme
This is simply a ten week series of evening sessions introducing the subject to those who have no previous experience. Each session is given over to a particular topic, e.g. bereavement, adolescence, basic principles of counselling, marriage and family, the unemployed, etc. On a practical level, the leader seeks to involve the students in the session. Merely moving from a situation where the leader is presenting material, to one where the individuals are asked to share their reactions and to experience the topic is a major shift.

Pastoral Counselling and Psychotherapy
What is the difference between (pastoral) counselling and psychotherapy? An immediate answer is that psychotherapy involves the students in having been in prolonged personal therapy himself. When a counsellor has not been in therapy himself, there is a different quality about the work being done. Such a counsellor is undoubtedly able to do valuable work, but there is a large part of his personality which is unavailable to the process. This means that there is some existential element missing, which has had to be there for the psychotherapist by reason of the demands which the training has made upon him. The duration, impact, expense and intensity, together with the risk as to future role, must mean that he has had to nail his existence to his profession in some fundamental way. There is some totality of commitment there, which means that the process is for him something where issues of life and death are worked out. The client's world has to be treated with that dimension of seriousness. It is therefore fitting that the process should be something to do with 'soul' (psyche) therapy.

It might be appropriate to describe an extended programme in pastoral counselling as 'pastoral psychotherapy'. The reluctance to do this arises from the desire to retain 'pastoral counselling' as an activity which spans a wide range of operation. This may reflect neurotic strivings for omnipotence, not unknown amongst those in the 'pastoral' field; or it may mean that 'pastoral counselling' is an unpretentious name, which falls easily aside in the everyday world, where there is no 'counsellor' and no 'client'.

Chapter 2

How Pastoral Counselling Works

Counsellors are rightly hesitant to talk about 'techniques' of counselling. Counselling is about being and becoming a person and any approach which impersonalizes one who is coming for help into an object on whom 'techniques' are practised is to be rejected. Secondly, what techniques there are may actually be used harmfully in the hands of an amateur. A vulnerable individual may be left rawly exposed and doubly resistant to further progress as a result of injudicious probing. Thirdly, what techniques there are have the unusual quality that being mere words, they appear to be no different from the rest of our language, so that one is left to conclude, 'So what? There is nothing there.' The corollary, however, is that if there are techniques, they are the more potent by their very ordinariness, which makes sense, because counsellors are interested in drawing attention to ordinary things which have previously escaped notice.

Counsellors also have their own neurosis in not wanting to talk about techniques, namely the fear that what they do will not stand up to analysis. This, of course, has to be challenged; and, as is the case with most neuroses, something better emerges. It becomes clear that a counsellor, like a musician, must learn the discipline of technique before he can achieve his own individual style, interpret the music and enhance the understanding of those who are sharing the experience with him.

Beginnings
Counselling often starts with a telephone call.

1. *The Explosion*

A familiar voice from the parish rings up and says, 'This is Gordon. Well, it's finally happened. After thirty years of marriage, she has finally left me.'

Priest: (stunned silence, in which he asks himself, 'Who is this? Yes, it's Gordon Wright. Who's he talking about? What is he talking about? Jean has left him. Yes, I could see that coming. But I don't want to get into this heavy situation.')

Gordon: '. . . There was this note left on the table. But no address. I've tried our sons and her sister. But no one has heard anything of her.'

Priest: 'I am still trying to take in what you are telling me, Gordon. What has happened?'

Gordon: '. . . she's taken only a suitcase. The place is all tidy. But she got what money she wanted.'

A great number of things happen in this conversation. The priest is initially coping with his own sense of shock. He is absorbing the blow of the news and does not wish to respond with superficial expressions of sympathy. As the conversation proceeds, it becomes his purpose to slow it down for himself and so catch up with his client, who launched into the middle of things and kept on going.

The priest begins to intervene with concrete questions, so that a lucid and coherent picture is built up. This is useful for his own good, but also for the client, who will eventually become more 'grounded', by having to spell out what he assumes the priest already knows. By having to acknowledge more fully the presence of the other person, he is brought more into real contact and more out of himself.

Whereas on one level, the news is a shock to the priest, it emerges that Gordon and Jean have recently divided their estate. If the priest had been able to hear fully the second sentence ('finally happened'), he would recognize the fact that Gordon wasn't as shocked as he was.

At some point, the priest may want to underline the relationship between Gordon and himself; Gordon has, after all, rung him up.

After the intitial force of the situation has been recounted, the question arises as to what is the next stage. The priest offered to go and see Gordon that evening, but Gordon did not feel it was necessary. A meeting was arranged for the following evening.

2. *A Tentative Beginning*

(Telephone): 'Is that the new vicar?' (hesitatingly).

Vicar: 'Yes . . .(silence). . . Is there some way I can help you . . .?'

Voice: (silence). . . 'I'm not sure why I am ringing. I don't know you . . .' (silence).

Vicar: 'Perhaps you thought somebody new might help . . .'

Voice: 'I haven't seen a vicar for a long time . . .' (long silence).

Vicar: 'But you are asking to talk to somebody now. I know it's difficult to begin, but if you can give me an idea of what's troubling you, I could see if I can help.'

Voice: 'It's my husband. He's planning to divorce me. But it's not right. We've been married twenty-six years. And I don't believe in divorce. I love him. You don't think divorce is right, do you?'

Vicar: 'He wants a divorce and you don't. That's a very hard situation. How has it come about?'

She: 'He's started helping down at the youth centre. And one of the other helpers . . . I suppose she's looking for more for herself than being a youth leader.'

Vicar: 'He's become involved with somebody else. You know, you haven't told me your name yet.'

She: 'I'm Mrs. Jones from Duke's Way.'

Vicar: 'I'd be very glad if I can be of help in looking at the situation. Would you like to come round and see me and we can talk further?'
She: 'Yes, all right.'
Vicar: 'How about tomorrow at three?'

One of the major underlying factors here is the pace. The vicar is able to take his cue from the pace of the caller and harmonize with it. He leaves a reciprocal amount of space to the caller, but also manages to be firm, ('I know it's difficult to begin'). He manages to avoid one certain trap ('You don't believe in divorce, do you?') and one possible trap ('I haven't seen a vicar for a long time.'). He gets a clear idea of what the problem is but does not allow the caller to go off into an unproductive account about the other woman. As a compensation for cutting her off, he tries to make a direct link by getting her name. She is initially surprised at his offering her an appointment. She would probably have preferred it if he had offered to go round and see her. But the suggestion of her coming to see him is made as a challenge to her system. If she can agree to come and see him and get out of her environment, she expresses an earnest of her motivation for growth.

First Session
The first session may be a continuation of such introductory telephone calls. It may be appropriate to acknowledge the connection or it may be just right to hold on to the fact that it is there. Counselling is often about recognizing connections, putting them into words and building upon them. Even if the client thinks it is not worth noticing, the fact that the counsellor articulates a connection may be the beginning of something registering with him. Or the client may say something.

1. Gordon: 'It was good of you to listen to me last night. And to come out and see me tonight.'
Priest: 'I was shocked, but also in some way it wasn't a complete surprise . . .'

The priest responds to the risk the client has taken in exposing his marital distress to him by offering a risk, 'It wasn't a complete surprise.' He is on fairly safe ground, because Gordon has implied the same ('It's finally happened.') and it gives Gordon the opportunity to elaborate.

The opening dialogue might have gone like this:

Gordon: 'It's nice of you to come round, but I don't know what you can do . . .'

Priest: 'Perhaps it's difficult to think that anybody can be of any help in this situation.'

Gordon seems here on the point of giving up and rejecting the counsellor. The counsellor refuses to collude with the client's hopelessness, but offers something back which may take the dialogue forward in a positive direction.

2. Mrs. Jones: 'I've just no idea why it can have happened.'

Vicar: 'Perhaps the best way to start is by telling me what happened.'

Here the counsellor focusses firmly on the situation as seen by the client, who is trying to dismiss the whole thing in her effort to escape the pain of it. It is the faith of the counsellor which enables a beginning to be made. Neither knows where they will reach, but the counsellor, from past experience, knows that beginning pays off. The focus is on the 'what', since the 'why' can only be understood in the light of it. Diversions and asides may be allowed, but only so long as the counsellor knows that they are giving space.

3. *Some Formal Beginnings*

Whether the counselling takes place in a formal structured session or with somebody who has informally asked for help, the underlying purpose is the same. It is the counsellor's job to turn an unpromising beginning into one where a counselling process, with the focus on the client, can ensue. It is important to bear in mind, that what the client brings is his first contribution, however much it may encapsulate the very problem he has.

The following are some opening statements and possible responses:

a) 'The Counselling Centre is very hard to find. I asked in the High Street, but nobody seemed to know where you were. Have you been here very long?'

i) 'That must have been irritating for you, if you had difficulty in finding the Counselling Centre.'

ii) 'Perhaps if you think we haven't been here very long, you are unsure whether we can be of any help to you.'

iii) 'I think you are saying that you like things to be very clear, and if they are not, you find that frustrating.'

iv) 'I'm sorry that the Centre is not yet well signed.'

b) 'I don't reckon much to this counselling idea.'

i) 'Can you tell me what you don't like about it?'

ii) 'Perhaps you have heard some things about counselling that you don't like?'

iii) 'It sounds as if you are looking for some help but are not quite sure whether counselling is what you need.'

c) 'Do you mind if I take my shoes off?'

i) 'That would make you feel comfortable?'

ii) 'I wonder what there is about taking your shoes off that makes you more at ease?'

d) 'How long have you been living round here? Do you like it here?'

i) 'I've been here four years and I do like it here. But I'm not sure whether you are saying something else?'

The client could be saying that he wishes that he was settled where he is; if the counsellor affirms his own contentedness with his setting, the client could feel even greater isolation. He could be saying that he finds it difficult to talk to somebody trustingly about whom he knows nothing. Or he could be saying that he was born and bred in those parts and doesn't think much of those who have been living there for less than two generations.

If the first session is part of a structured counselling process in a counselling centre, it will be a formal 'intake'. Here the emphasis will be on the gathering of information which is going to enable the centre to make a decision as to whether they can help this person. This gathering of information will be seen by the client as an expression of the centre's professionalism and caring. It also serves to point out to the client that he can hold the disturbing aspects of the problem until there is a more appropriate setting. The intake worker will respond to the feelings of the client and allow space for them, but he will not encourage them to be elaborated upon; his purpose will be to assess the strength of feelings and the client's ability to make use of them. The intake worker will want to gain a picture of the client's family background, his personal problem, his current relationships, employment, medical history and expectations of counselling. The counsellor will attempt to come to a personal assessment of what is the client's problem and relate it to his behaviour in session. He may try to motivate him by support or challenge. But he will not attempt to probe feelings too much. (For further discussion of intake see chapter 10).

If this is not a formal counselling situation, the counsellor can allow the session to be shared more equally between describing the facts of the problem and giving vent to feelings about the facts. These two components are as two 'limbs'. The counsellor assists them to walk apace and thus enables the 'body' of the counselling to move forward evenly. If there are too many facts without acknowledgment of the feelings, it becomes apparent that there is an important component missing 'in the weave', that is, what the 'doing' is costing the client and what the picture, as it is being built up, means to him. On the other hand, if there is only ventilation of affect and a scarcity of facts, the counselling gets heavy and bogs down in mud. It then comes as a relief when the counsellor encourages the client to step out with his other foot by saying to him, 'Now I can understand something of your feelings about what has happened; can we go back to where you were describing . . .'

The results of the first session are:

a) The client achieves some sort of catharsis. This is not to be underestimated. The ventilation of strong feeling in the presence of another person is a very important event and cannot go without being registered and valued by the client at some level. One of the most therapeutic events remembered by clients is the expression of anger and tenderness. If the client is able to get to this point in a single session, it means that a level of trust has been established or that the event itself creates the level of trust. The counsellor's task is to assist that happening.

(b) The client elaborates on his picture. The conscious setting out of the picture is a very therapeutic act. It is one thing to have a picture in one's own mind of one's problem or pain (or indeed not to have it); it is another to put it into words and set it out. Speaking in the presence of another is a potential and actual balancing force; the client is already in the presence of a third party, who, he recognizes, may see the situation from a slightly different point of view, however sympathetic he may still be. This dim awareness is the beginning factor in the creation of an 'observing ego' within the client, that is, the acquisition of his own other ego, by which he may look at his own troubled ego which is speaking.

(c) As the client tells his story, he is impelled by the story's own inner energy to say things and speak details which may even surprise him at this stage.

(d) The actual speaking of the story is strengthening. What has brought the client along is some inner weakness. The speaking itself is a strengthening act; it exercises the speaker's muscles in some way to say something which before has been left unsaid.

(e) The laying out of the story is the actual creation of a 'middle ground', which is a new territory for the client. Metaphorically speaking, a jig-saw is being laid out on the table, which the speaker must begin to recognize as an entity, a production of his own. It has some qualities of a third party, since it is separate from him, but it is a creation which he has produced. It may have the quality of a painting, or an artistic production; it may be a 'child', still attached by an umbilical cord to his body; it may be a symbolic expression of his own vomit or excrement, or a wound on his own body, or a diseased part of his body removed from him. But in relation to all these, there is an awareness that 'This is me: I have produced it; it is both me and separate from me.'

(f) Even at this early stage, there may be some insight by the client into what he is saying. 'Yes, I see that now, which I didn't before.' 'I never thought of that.' 'I never guessed that that was how he was feeling.'

Closing and Contract

As the session is proceeding, the counsellor will be asking himself how he is going to handle the closing of the session. If the counsellor has been used to hourly appointments in a counselling centre, he will probably follow the same pattern in the parish or office. Beginning counsellors often feel that they have to prolong the session until it ends when the client is content to go. However, it is part of the discipline of being a counsellor to be able to draw a session to a close, even if all the ground has not been covered. Part of the client's problem may be that he allows his response to situations to build up to unmanageable proportions. Learning, for him, will consist in deflating the pressure to a moderate degree, so that he doesn't feel that in order to be alive he has to be either filled with feeling or entirely devoid of it. It is therapeutic for this client to be able to feel life at a moderate and even level and realize that he is still alive. Beginning counsellors may extend the session out of their own sense of omnipotence, believing that they should be able to solve the client's problems of a lifetime in fifty minutes. Clients encourage them in this belief, out of their own need to have a perfect parent. Similarly, the counsellor may extend the session because he undervalues what has already been accomplished in the way of ventilation and picture-building, even if there has been no insight. Perhaps the counsellor needs to have the reward of the client acknowledging insight or progress, which may be inappropriate at this early stage.

There are, moreover, very positive values in limiting the time. Both client and counsellor may return to the problem afresh; both may find their concentration waning after an hour. If there is energy still left at the end of the session, there is motivation to come back to the problem another time. If the client leaves the session flat and exhausted, he may well have no motivation to return. Not least important is the fact that the period between sessions is itself a healing time. New thoughts and new feelings occur in the intervening period which bring some change, however slight, in the client's perception. The session is a time for fertilizing and germinating; the period in between is when growth actually occurs. Furthermore, if the counsellor is confident and firm about closing and can communicate the benefit of it, he models for the client the strength to go back out into the world. The client takes the session away in his consciousness and unconsciousness. He integrates the experience of it and carries around within him the dialogue of the session, the person of his counsellor and the person he himself was in the session. He needs the intervening period to move from these bodily presences to the point where these become an internalized presence. For the religious person this process of internalization is a religious process by which the individual incoporates his own spiritual self.

The rounding off of the session is important. The counsellor may think it right to explain some of the reasons for finishing now rather than continuing, at least putting it in a positive way that it is right to finish now. It is useful to summarize what has gone on and the counsellor may already be able to see some threads and link them together in a way that he thinks the client will understand. Or it might be good if the client can summarize the session himself by being asked, 'What has happened in our session?' When the client has said what he has seen, then the counsellor may respond, 'Yes, I agree with you that we did that,' or, 'I hadn't thought of that, but I think you are right,' or, 'I think we should add this as well . . .' This is the translation into counselling terms of a simple business transaction. Having gone to see one's solicitor or accountant or bank manager, it is right that at the end of the session there should be an agreed summing up, 'This is what we have done and this is what we have yet to look at.'

The act of agreeing is in itself a very important one. It may well be that one of the client's problems is that he is unable to agree when an agreement with another person is available, if only he had the right approach to be able to secure it. The counsellor, in asking for an agreement at this stage, however primitive it may be, is modelling a piece of behaviour which is useful to the client. Such a 'contract' is also another building brick in the construction of a 'third party' ego for the client. It adds to the 'something out there being built.' It is also a powerful recognition of the presence of the other person. Often a client's problem is his inability to recognize fully the presence, value and being of another person; he may undervalue the other person or undervalue himself. The act of reaching an agreement is an antidote to this state, for it causes the client to recognize that there is another person in the room besides himself. If the client tended to undervalue the other person, he is thus forced to acknowledge that the other must have meaning and power; if the client tended to devalue himself, he is shown that he is a person of value, who is thought by the other to be important enough to be a partner in a joint enterprise. Agreement is a word shared. It is, therefore, something which is remembered between the two of them and something which can form the foundation of a subsequent process.

At the end of the first session, there are a number of practical options: (a) no further meeting, (b) a further meeting at a specified time, (c) a further meeting at a time which either the counsellor or the client may subsequently arrange, (d) agreement to meet for a specified number of times, (e) agreement to meet with another person involved in the situation, (f) agreement to consult further and renew contact in the light of that, (g) referral to an appropriate place, e.g. social services, doctor, counselling centre, another clergyman. If a fee is being charged, it will form part of the contract to agree on what is appropriate. This is a very practical and therapeutic issue for negotiation, and when it is successfully agreed forms a solid expression of the contract. (For further discussion see chapter 10).

Referral elsewhere is an option which must be considered very seriously. Many people who come to their local clergy may benefit from help elsewhere, and many clergy, if they are honest, would be greatly relieved if they could refer them elsewhere for additional support. It is not unusual for the local clergyman to find he has a very dependent parishioner attaching him/herself to him. He may think it is his duty to give him every support and be totally available, and this becomes a very draining experience, which ends in guilt feelings on his part and anger on the part of the parishioner, when the latter does not find all that he wants in the relationship.

The act of referring a person to somebody else at some slight distance is a very therapeutic one all round. It is good for the client, whose dependency receives an initial slight challenge, but is also met with a degree of support, for the clergyman is saying, 'No, I can't give you all that you want, but yes, I can give you this very important support, getting you to someone who can be of more help to you than I can in this situation.' The effort to go a slight distance is therapeutic to one who looks only close at hand for total fulfilment of his needs. The referral is also freeing for the clergyman, who can maintain a relationship within stricter limits. He can remain a priest, without becoming mother, father, spouse and perhaps also God to his parishioner. The very act of separating out the needs is what is most therapeutic for the parishioner.

The referral is also beneficial in that it encourages good supportive relationships amongst the clergy. Isolation, suspicion, competitiveness and burdensome depression are the way of neurotic omnipotence; mutual support, respect and defined boundaries are the way of health.

Referral also has the advantage of conferring a sense of importance on the need of the client. By so doing, the priest is saying: 'The need which you are expressing is important; it is causing you some problems and it is something on which work needs to be done. It is not something we can solve by chatting about it informally. We must address it in a business-like way. And indeed, if we do so, that will be the most important step in solving the problem. It is because something has been allowed to drift that this situation has arisen. I want to co-operate with you in finding what will help you most.'

The Middle Course of Counselling

There are three important components in the process of counselling: silence, the counsellor's question and interpretation.

Silence allows the client to begin where he is 'at' rather than at some place where he is assumed to be by the counsellor. Waiting upon the client's silence allows some completely unanticipated factor to emerge, which is central to the client's concern. If the silence had not been there, he would have discarded it; however, it is the discarded bits of a person that the counsellor is interested in, which, if they are pursued, take a person out of his customary battle area into some more open and pleasant place.

A client comes to counselling after her marriage has broken down. Her husband has subsequently died, making it a period of double mourning for her. She would like to have an affair with her employer, but it isn't working out. She comes to counselling late for her appointment. She doesn't begin her session where she usually begins, in complaining about another secretary at the office who has supplanted her in her boss's affections, but there is a silence. After a while, the counsellor comments on it.

Counsellor: 'You seem to be very quiet today.'

Client: 'I haven't anything pressing on my mind . . .'

Counsellor: 'Perhaps there are some things there but they are different and you don't look upon them as being important . . .'

Client: 'Well, actually, what I'm thinking about is those brass fittings on your doors. They remind me of home, I mean where I grew up.'

Counsellor: 'You haven't told me much about that yet . . .'

Client then gets into an account of her relationship with her parents.

Waiting upon the silence places the onus on the client, who begins to realize that the responsibility for beginning rests upon him. If he can begin in session, then he can make a beginning on the pattern of his life. He may be irritated at the onus being placed upon him, but that becomes a factor to be explored in the counselling.

Counsellor: 'What is it about beginning which irritates you?'

Client: 'I find it hard to begin. It's heavy. I can't get going . . .'

Counsellor: 'What is the heaviness . . . ?'

Silence, by its unusualness creates a different sort of environment from what the client would normally expect. The session is immediately marked out as being different; the pattern of normal interaction is given a slight shake, which allows a different relationship to begin. If it puts pressure on the client, it also creates a situation in which the counsellor is seen clearly to reach out to the client, 'Can I help with this silence?' 'This silence seems as if it is becoming rather hostile.' 'I wonder what this silence means.' 'I see that this silence is bringing something very painful to you; I wonder if you can put into words what you are feeling now.'

It is important for the counsellor to remember that one of the reasons why the client may be silent is that he is afraid of the counsellor's reaction to what he wants to say. It could be a purposeful shot in the dark for the counsellor to say, 'Perhaps you are afraid of my reaction if you say what is on your mind.'

'Well, I hadn't thought about it as actually being afraid of you, but maybe in some way I am.'

'What is it you are afraid of in me?'

Once the client speaks out his fears and the counsellor accepts them, they are no longer fears.

Silence is the beginning of the process. It points to the potential for the future and provides the open space on which the future can be enacted. It is enigmatic and therefore accepting of paradox. It is a mark of respect to the other person, and it is also an expression of trust, for usually one can only sit comfortably with another person in silence after getting to know him well. By a degree of silence, the process of establishing trust is telescoped.

The ending of silence calls upon the other person for a response. The counsellor may end the silence and he may be mistaken in the interpretation he puts upon it. But if the client responds, he speaks out of a basic human instinct to co-operate, which might itself be worth exploring further.

Client: 'I felt that even though that's not where I was, I wanted to respond to your initiative.'

If the counsellor is right, however, in his interpretation, it carries the process a stage further:

Counsellor: 'It seems as if you have run out of energy.'

Client: 'Yes, I've lost it. I can't think why.'

Counsellor: 'What is it like to be lost?'

Client: 'Well, actually, it doesn't seem to matter. I don't usually allow myself to get lost, but now that it's here, it's all right. One may even enjoy it for a little while . . .'

Counsellor: 'One . . . ? Who is one?'

Client: 'All right, "I". I'll take it. I'll take the space.'

The counsellor's question is the complement to the silence. The counsellor's question, unlike the client's question, is neutral. The client's question asks for help or makes a misleading assumption about the other person. The counsellor's question is an offer of help to the client. It is neutral in that the counsellor himself does not know the answer to it. He may, in fact, in asking it be surprised if it does have an answer to it; he himself cannot conceive what the answer would be. Yet he asks it, trusting in the worth of his discipline and art, knowing that the process itself will bring forth the answer. The counsellor's question also indicates implicitly his empathy with the client, for he bases the question on his hearing of what has been said. The counsellor's question is a pointer to the 'middle ground' which the client needs to find for his growth and it is also an expression of the counsellor's preparedness to accept the negative feelings and thoughts of which the client may be ashamed or fearful. The counsellor's question is, in fact, a proclamation. It is not just the fact that the counsellor may have to risk asking the client something which no one else has yet dared; but the freedom which he expresses in asking it is the hope for and promise of the client's power. Every question which the counsellor asks is an implicit invitation to state a purpose for continuing to live; therefore, every question is an existential one. The counsellor's question is also a paradox, because it may well contain within it its own answer.

The following are two effective examples of the counsellor's use of silence and question:

(a) Client: 'Sorry, I'm late.'

Counsellor: 'Mmm . . . You had a problem in getting here?'

Client: 'Oh, it wasn't anything very much.' (Clams up, goes into himself, silence).

Counsellor: (after a little while) 'I'm wondering if you are holding on to something important.'

Client: 'Well, if you really want to know, the reason why I am late is that I had to come on public transport. And the reason why I had to come on public transport is that I crashed my car last week.'

Counsellor: 'Oh . . . it sounds pretty bad.'

Client: 'Yes, a write-off. I was so disgusted that I just left it there.'

Counsellor: 'Where? You mean on the street?'

Client: 'Yes . . . It'll be worse now than it was before. The

vandals will have been at it; the police will have put tickets on
it or towed it away. I haven't told the insurance company yet.
I'm just waiting for them to get in touch with me.'

Counsellor: 'So it seems that everything is catching up on
you.'

Client: 'Yes, I feel like running away. I didn't even want to
come here this evening.'

The session proceeded with the counsellor eliciting a more
detailed picture. He pursued the client's pattern of crashing,
abandoning and running away from the consequences. He
explored how the practicalities might be dealt with and what
it was from the client's past that was pursuing him (sense of
death, destructiveness and depression.)

(b) Counsellor: (breaking the silence). 'So you are going away
on holiday?'

Client: 'Yes, we're going to Tangier.'

Counsellor: 'Tangier! Is there something special about that
for you?'

Client: 'Not really. I saw this cheap offer in the local travel
agent's. They couldn't understand themselves how it was so
cheap. This'll be our last chance.'

Counsellor: 'Last chance?'

Client: 'Yes, my wife is expecting a baby . . .'

Counsellor: 'Oh, and things aren't going to be so good after
that?'

Client: 'Well, it's bound to be, isn't it. This is what they all
say.'

Counsellor: 'It sounds as if this'll be your last experience of
the good life.'

It emerged that for the client good holidays were things he
had had as an adolescent. The direction which the counsellor
was given to follow was asking where was the 'exotic' element
in the relationship between the client and his wife which did
not depend upon her being unpregnant and upon their going
to Tangier. What were the client's fears about the prospect of
being a father?

The counsellor's question points the way to interpretation.

The question prepares the ground on which an interpretation can be put and the interpretation itself may be said to be the answer to the question. Interpretation emerges from the process of counselling at the appropriate time. A number of factors have to come together. There has to have been sufficient material spread out; it has to have been sufficiently spaced out to be recognizable in its component parts; the client has to be on the point of being able to make the perception for himself. In these circumstances, the interpretation may be made either by the counsellor or by the client. Expressing the interpretation and having it affirmed by the other person solidifies the reality of what is being said and the relationship between the two people. The fact that the truth belongs to one of the persons makes it a personal truth. The counsellor himself has no investment in the interpretation other than as an expression of solid truth for the other person. If he does have an investment in it, which comes out of himself rather than the client, it will not be a truth.

The following interpretation is brief and to the point.

Client: 'My wife got this new job.'

Counsellor: 'How do you feel about that?'

Client: 'Well, quite good really. I mean it is a good job . . . and she has done very well to get it . . .'

Counsellor: 'But . . . ?'

Client: 'Well, yes, I suppose there is a "but". I do have some reservations about it. Yes, yes. I mean she got it so easily; at least, it seemed so. Here am I, slogging my guts out and I haven't got all that far really, and she has just gone straight back to work and landed this super job. I mean it annoys me a bit.'

Counsellor: 'I see, so you are in competition with each other, are you?'

Client: 'Oh . . .'

Interpretation involves relating current experience to historical causes. In this instance, the client was put in mind of his family background, where he felt in competition with his younger sister, and where the striving of each for recognition was an isolating experience; success was not achieved by general co-operation or celebrated by common rejoicing. Interpretation points to the possibility of rearranging the pattern. Questioning the old pattern is the first step in this client's being able to find total pleasure in his wife's success, which will improve their relationship and probably enable him to be more effective himself.

Interpretation may relate to the past and to the very events within the counselling session. The client in (a) began to explore the relationship between his recent accident and his more distant past. Seeing that there was such a relationship gave him hope, for it became clear that there were reasons for the hopelessness which he experienced and which seemed to be continually re-created in concrete events. It also became clear that the hopelessness had actually been brought into the session and that he had almost abandoned the session (by being late) as he had abandoned his car. The counsellor was inviting him to 'repair' the session by enabling him to make use of it and recount the details of his car. In so far as the session is 'repaired', there is a victory for the client. Interpretation actually reverses the flow of destructive energies within the client and is, therefore, a most potent tool of therapy. Counselling is the successive integration of interpretations.

Termination

(a) *Unsatisfactory.*

There are a wide variety of reasons why counselling terminates before a satisfactory solution has been achieved.

(i) A break may occur early in the counselling, e.g. client or counsellor may have planned a holiday or may be ill; counselling does not re-start.

(ii) The client came to counselling under duress from another person or from an external situation; he feels he 'does his bit' by coming once and does not return.

(iii) There is some factor early on which is not picked up by the counsellor. A client may have had another counsellor in the past and feels that his new counsellor does not measure up to the old one. The old one may have left, leaving the client feeling angry and abandoned, which he now holds against his new counsellor.

The client may agree to pay too high a fee out of his desire to please the counsellor, but finds that he has merely perpetuated his life's pattern of placing unrealistic demands upon himself.

The client may have been pressured into coming at a time which he did not realize that he did not like.

The counsellor may remind the client of someone whom he does not like. The client may have asked for a counsellor of the other sex and it is not fully explored whether they can agree to work together.

The client pressurizes the counsellor into feeling he has to come up with an early solution to his problems; the counsellor does not realize that he has the option to suggest that they meet over a prolonged period in order to assess the problem and that the procedure is a joint one in which the counsellor is there to assist the client.

(iv) The counselling goes on for several weeks with the client coming doggedly, while the counsellor is dimly aware that there is an underlying resentment, confusion, hopelessness and even determination to scuttle the process. If this issue is not recognized, the client takes away his disappointment with him.

(v) Even after the counselling has been going for a considerable time, apparently insignificant events can have a considerable impact upon the client, e.g. a change of room, or the fact that the client sees the counsellor leave the building with girlfriend or spouse.

(vi) Specific counter-transference problems of the counsellor exist; e.g. the counsellor may not realize that he is angry with the client and distances himself. If this is allowed to continue, the counsellor effectively precipitates the client out of counselling.

(vii) There are pressures in the counsellor's life which he resents; he deals with them by resenting first the counselling and then the client.

Unsatisfactory terminations are made satisfactory when some therapeutic benefit is derived from them.

(i) When a client fails to turn up, it is important to encourage him to meet for one more session in which termination can take place. This reverses his pattern, by which he has absented himself at the point at which some block has occurred. This may, in fact, lead to a working through of the problem, but this does not have to happen for some therapeutic value to have been salvaged.

(ii) The counsellor is able to identify something which he missed in what the client was saying, which was the probable cause of his leaving.

(iii) The counsellor is able to use the termination in a way which allows him to discuss and get rid of his own feelings about it.

(iv) The counsellor is able to recognize that the client may have achieved the level of his motivation.

(v) The counsellor recognizes that the client's termination is an aspect of his life's pattern and not something for which the counsellor has to take total responsibility.

(b) *Satisfactory.*

A satisfactory termination is prepared for a good way in advance, so that the end becomes a part of the process itself. The termination will be as valuable to the process as all that has gone before. It may raise the question of the value of the relationship between client and counsellor with a clarity which had not been previously apparent. The client will have to face feelings associated with any bereavement process, i.e. surprise, shock, anger, pain, tenderness, hope. The termination repeats other less satisfactory terminations which the client has had in the past, e.g. loss of parent, or spouse, leaving home. A satisfactory termination of the counselling enables the client to embark upon his new stage in life with the full availability of the new strengths he has discovered.

Chapter 3

Who Comes to Pastoral Counselling?

On the word 'client'

The advantage of using the word 'client' is that it establishes a professional relationship. A client is a person who employs another to achieve a particular end. The initiative lies with the client, the appropriate skills with the professional. Secondly, a client is also a 'customer'. He is buying certain goods and the counsellor is selling something. Thirdly, a client is also a dependant, asking for the protection of the other. This quality is also in the relationship between counsellor and client.

It is understandable that there are reservations about using the word 'client'. The alternative, however, is to accept that a person is looking for something and to accept his denial that he is. This is not an honest starting-point. Since counselling is about honesty, it is understandable that it encourages the use of the word 'client'.

However, there is the disadvantage that 'client' can easily become impersonal and have labels such as 'obsessive', 'hysterical', or whatever attached to him.

The word 'person' is acceptable, since it has the dignity of 'man' or 'Adam'; but it has the disadvantage of being easily ambiguous when one is talking about a number of persons at a particular time.

The best answer is to accept well-tried usage and to understand that counselling is about being, becoming and recognizing persons.

The following is an attempt to describe two clients, David and Margaret, and to say what happened for them in counselling. David and Margaret are partly imaginary and, therefore, unrecognizable, except in so far as they are in each of us. David is described because he is a young man and Margaret because she is an older woman, the intention being to cover a broad spectrum of human nature.

David

David was thirty-three; he lived alone in a bed-sitter and he worked in a local factory. He offered himself as a helper in a church-sponsored youth club. He was quite useful in that he was a very good photographer, with a special interest in 'trick' photography. For a time, this was of some interest to the boys, but he was very reserved and some of the boys laughed at him. He had no contact with the girls and one or two of them, when pressed, admitted to feeling uneasily wary of him. The youth leader was somewhat anxious, but also realized that he quite liked David. He went out of his way to engage him and to gain his confidence. David began to rely heavily on the youth leader and he admitted to him that he felt depressed much of the time; he agreed to go for counselling.

In the course of counselling, it became clear that David was the youngest in his family. He had four elder sisters, one of whom had committed suicide. The father was a fairly successful businessman, the mother had been reduced to something of a drudge, who now in later middle life had contracted a debilitating disease. David had some distant admiration for his father and only contempt for his mother.

When he left school, David did a course in catering, which he did not finish; he had also been a waiter. In fact, he had

had about ten jobs in twelve years. Some he had given up when he could not get out of bed in the morning. Some had ended when he had insulted a woman colleague or superior. He complained of pains in his back, legs, knees and ankles, about which he had consulted the doctor, but had been told that there was nothing physically wrong with him.

He remembered going to church with his father from about the age of six to twelve, and when he moved into his bedsitter a welcoming letter to newcomers from the local church arrived through his letter-box.

As the counselling proceeded, the level of David's distress began to reveal itself. It became clear that he had given up his career in catering because he was afraid that he would poison somebody. And when external pressures upon him increased in the course of the counselling, he complained that his neighbour had telephoned for the firebrigade when she saw steam coming out of his kitchen, as a result of which he threatened to the counsellor that he would poison her dog.

The counselling as 'mother'

The beginning phase of the counsellor-client relationship draws on the background of the mother-child relationship. To this setting belong stability, continuity, acceptance and being nurtured. The counsellor provides time and in the session gives his whole attention to the person. He tries to personify, may succeed and be seen by the client to personify, the 'good' mother. The counsellor telephones up the client when he misses a session, he does not retaliate to the client's negativity, he accepts the mess the client brings, he encourages the client to speak about difficult areas in his life. He probably provides an acceptance in areas of the client's life where the client did not experience acceptance from his own mother. However, it is not just the counsellor but the counselling itself, the sense of 'being there', which provides the matrix for the client.

The counsellor and David did have grounds on which they could begin. There was the distant, though positive relationship with father, the interest in photography, the fact that he managed to get himself to a youth club as a helper and the interest of the youth leader. David was also prepared to start talking about his depression. This was where the nurturing began.

However, it was not long before an 'antagonist' appeared from within David, who attempted to sabotage any good that was being built up; the antagonist metaphorically tried to 'poison' the process. David felt that what he was getting was insufficient; therefore, he looked upon the counselling as a 'bad' mother. He wanted relief for the physical pains he was suffering and when the counsellor could not promise to do this for him, he threatened to leave. What he was getting from the counsellor was time, attention, friendly concern, interest, support, encouragement, reflection, non-threatening insight, bits of wisdom and acceptance, but David had only contempt for his mother; therefore, he could give no value to what he was receiving. At the end of the session he may have felt better, but by the time he came the following week, the 'food' he had received had been poisoned.

Nevertheless, a relationship was built up with his counsellor. Even his complaints helped to solidify an attachment. Since his counsellor was a man, he assumed that like his father, he was successful and powerful. Therefore, he began to admire him. He wished to become like him and indeed at one point he began to feel that the counsellor's thoughts must be the same as his own. In David's mind there grew up a unity between him and the counsellor which was like the unbroken unity which exists between an infant and its mother. David became more clearly self-centred, as if he were the only thing which mattered in the in the counsellor's life. He began to ignore the fact that counsellor had a realistic private life.

The counselling as 'father'
As the 'mother' in the counselling relationship encourages closeness between client and counsellor, so there arises a 'father' who brings about a separation between mother and

child. The counsellor has to begin to mediate external reality and encourage the client to acknowledge responsibility for his own behaviour. Having invited David to speak about the pains in his knees and ankles, he asks him what he thinks they mean. What does his interest in trick photography mean? What does his succession of jobs mean and the reasons why he left them? David is asked to reflect upon himself, which means setting a wedge between him and his blind, dependent and passive relationship with the world around him. As he gains strength by doing this, more sensitive areas are looked at, e.g. his difficulty in getting on with women. The 'mother' unites, the 'father' separates. These are useful figures for the counsellor to bear in mind as well. He may recognize that he is getting too close to the client, in which case the 'father' in the counsellor allows him to draw back. Conversely, the counsellor may recognize that he is not being sufficiently supportive and active; he will then reach out more.

'Father' and 'mother' are two figures which have an existence in the process and it is in the co-operation which takes place between them that something happens for the client. The client may indeed have had a better relationship with one parent than with the other, and he will automatically try to structure the relationship with his counsellor to ensure that that situation is repeated. But the counsellor's integrity or 'oneness' depends upon whether he can mediate both parents satisfactorily.

Development: childhood, adolescence, adulthood
In the process of counselling, the client relives the developmental stages of his life. This begins with the experience of closeness, followed by separateness. When the client comes to experience the separateness of the counsellor, he can confidently accept his own separateness, which carries with it the promise of his own future destiny. This is the reliving of the so-called Oedipal situation, where the child finally understands that he cannot win either of the parents at the cost of

the other; he accepts that the best solution is for them to be a unit for themselves and for him to be separate, though joined in their affection.

As the child grows, he learns to crawl and walk; he experiences physicality, movement and power over his environment. This experience is parallelled for the client in the 'steps' he takes. He moves outside his familiar world by actually coming to the counselling session; as he learns insights and gains confidence, he interacts differently with his environment and achieves a measure of new control over it.

The child learns to talk. In effect, the client learns to speak a new language. Things are drawn to his attention which previously did not have a name. He did not notice that certain behaviours by other people came about by reason of some things he did himself. It may be a whole new concept for a client to understand that there is a way of looking at what people do, which is different from constructing buildings, making political decisions and even creating art. Understanding what is happening in counselling is trying to put words on to unnoticed experience.

The child learns from the experience of his own body; he achieves a sense of control over it, he can experience pleasure, pain and shame in relationship to it; he can be secretive. All this encourages his ability to be assertive and to gain territory for himself, which he can defend against rivals. He can enter wars and gather allies to himself. He can be industrious and build up his own empire.

This stage may be marked by gathering information, collecting stamps, learning to swim, being a member of a gang. In the client, it represents an important stage of positive growth, but one which is as yet unexamined by the person's ego. A client may make great strides in his progress, but it may be attended by a sense of 'inflation'; the client may give up smoking and leave therapy as a grand gesture.

In adolescence, the child grows to a stage of maturity where he is beginning to make a relationship with a person of the opposite sex; on the cognitive level, his faculties reach a stage of full development where he is able to subject his own 'system' to scrutiny. As the client grows to maturity, he is able to 'check out' his own responses against those which other people have of him and he is able to make a harmonious relationship with a person who is an opposite character type to himself.

The young person reaches full sexual power and enters upon the full bloom of adulthood. So the client grows out of his protected, monochrome world to where he is challenged by the fresh winds of the external, real world. Here he has to distinguish real threat from the threats which hung over him from childhood and he now has full powers to be able to confront the world with confidence.

As the client goes through this process of growing up again, he not only experiences change but can stand back and look at 'change' itself. He can understand how change happens and why it is not happening. Growing is an experience of receiving a greater number of more varied experiences. The old categories are insufficient to hold new information, which means that new categories have to be created. Just as a separating of information takes place, so also there emerge new connections between the new categories and the old ones. Therefore, change not only takes place within the client, giving him new categories of experience, but there is a category or understanding of 'change' itself, which he can grasp to face the future.

The inner person

As David grew away from his infantile state, he began to offer information about himself in a new way. Instead of having to be prodded and encouraged, he began to 'walk' of his own accord. He said to his counsellor, 'I can admit to you that I feel lonely. I hadn't noticed it before; I just assumed that that was the way life was. But now I notice it and I want to look at why my life is like this. It's as if I walk in a bubble. Between me and myself I feel alienated.'

David speaks of two inner persons ('me' and 'myself'), and

this is a discovery for him. Up to this point he has spoken simply of himself as one person. All his reporting came from 'himself', a being which generally had the quality of weakness and unreflective dependence. Now in speaking of himself as 'me' and 'myself', he puts into dramatic form the theory of the neurotic 'split'. This asserts that at some point in its early development, perhaps before birth, perhaps during the trauma of birth or perhaps afterwards, the personality undergoes a split. This is brought about by increase of external pressure (e.g. difficulty of being born) and by a decrease in internal resources (e.g. physical weakness). The 'person' feels he has to retreat inwards in order to survive; part goes on to function in relationship to the outside world and part goes inwards and is lost to consciousness. If the 'split' is severe, the two parts become disconnected. The fact that this happens deprives both parts of each other's strength. The conscious part may appear acceptable, but, in fact, is fragile, brittle and superficial, because its strength has gone elsewhere. The unconscious part carries the overriding fear of external reality and intense anger at what has happened. Because part of him has been unconscious, David has to this point not known about it and has spoken simply as one conscious person. What it has meant for him has been that he has felt in a 'bubble'. The reason why he has felt disconnected from the outside world is that he has felt disconnected within. Other people, no doubt, could have told him that he appeared to be disconnected, but that would not have meant too much to him. He would probably have just consigned that piece of information to a dark bin of forgetfulness, where it would have served to increase his basic anxiety and superficial brittleness.

When he says 'me', he means the usual 'me' that he has known up to this point. 'Myself' carries with it a new emphasis and sturdiness, which has not yet been apparent. This points to the truth that the source of his new strength must lie in the possibly frightening energy which he has not yet met within himself. His hope lies in being introduced to his own other self. The fear is, of course, both for the client and the counsellor that this other self, when brought to the surface, will prove to be as unacceptable as was feared. The hope is that both client and counsellor will be able to mediate the other self so that it turns out to be more acceptable than was feared, or indeed, that it will turn out that client and counsellor can accept that which was unacceptable.

In fact, however, when David says, 'between me and myself I feel alienated,' he is speaking of *three* rather than *two* persons, i.e. he refers also to 'I'. His 'I' sounds as if it is in some vacuum in between the 'me' and the 'myself'. Perhaps the 'I' is the very barrier which stands between the two persons. This would be confirmed by people's impressions, namely, that the most obvious thing about David was his barrier. Therefore, it is in some transformation of this that his new 'I' lies. Indeed, this new 'I' has already begun to emerge in the very fact that for the first time he has recognized that there is a 'me' and a 'myself' and he ('I') is asking for help with the situation. Therefore, David has begun to break through the bubble in relationship to his counsellor. The purpose of counselling is to ensure that the 'me' and the 'myself' stand forth clearly and unashamedly. The 'I' is the bridge between them, or the priest who consecrates the marriage between the 'me' and the 'myself' so that the three become one.

What counselling does
There are within the client two 'persons', the 'me' and the 'myself', not yet in dialogue with each other; there are within the counselling session two persons, client and counsellor, who have yet to establish dialogue with each other. The counselling process is the 'I' by which counsellor and client are linked and by which the 'I' of the client, uniting his 'me' and 'myself', begins to grow. The counsellor engages the client's 'myself' as well as his 'me', both of whom become aware of each other and wish to meet with each other.

The means by which all this happens is initially the counsellor's capacity to listen. This is not simply a passive activity, but one which is purposeful and energetic. The counsellor tries to see 'what else' is being said; the 'what else' has to come from what the client is actually saying and not at all from what counsellor's distortions are making of it. The counsellor has to accept, nurture and nourish what the client is saying, rather than reject or belittle it in some way which is unnoticed by himself.

There are at least three levels of listening. The first is when the counsellor is able to remove the various barbs attached to what is being said and respond to the client's statement as if the barbs were not there. In this way, he avoids giving the negative reaction which everybody else gives.

The second is where the counsellor can accomplish some expansion of what is being said. He can develop the words in a way which is an authentic continuation and which is elucidating.

The third level is when the counsellor can hear something which is quite different from what appears to be there. The client is initially surprised and then astounded by the accuracy of the counsellor's perception.

Listening enables an enhancement of the client's inner persons to take place; it is also the means by which the 'split' is healed and by which something is instead 'put in the centre'. The developmental process began with the unity of the separate figures of 'mother' and 'father' in the experience of the client; the inner problem of the client is his split between 'me' and 'myself'. The healing process continues in the degree to which listening can bond the two separated parts of the client and establish a relationship between counsellor and client which allows both intimacy and distance.

For David, this meant that his 'myself', with all its fears and anxieties, became more approachable. It emerged that his mother had been schizophrenic and had behaved very bizarrely at times. He recounted his childhood fears of her. At the same time, he was able to remember positive relationships with his elder sisters and a teacher at school. He began to go to mixed social gatherings. Finally, there emerged some glimmer of understanding of the pain and isolation which his mother had suffered. At this time, she actually died, which caused him to regress; he deteriorated to the point where he suspected that his neighbour was trying to poison him. The counsellor wisely did not encourage him to expand on these thoughts and as his confidence was rebuilt, he was less bothered by them.

David illustrated some of the problems of manhood. As he grew, he came to a richer understanding of 'woman'. Paradoxically enough, by integrating a real understanding of womanhood, he became more himself, more of an 'I'.

Margaret

Margaret was fifty-nine when she came to counselling. She was facing retirement. She had been a science teacher, but after a few years, she realized that she could not control a class and, therefore, spent the rest of her career as a laboratory technician.

Her husband had recently died. Her mother had lived with them all their married life and did, in fact, just outlive her husband. Her son had started medical school, but after a year he dropped out and joined the Moonies. Her daughter had recently fallen in love with an ex-priest twenty years older than herself; they were now going off to live in Peru. Margaret had one brother, a little younger than herself. He had received a privileged education, which she had not. He had become a military attaché, and had now retired to write novels. His daughter had been arrested on a drugs charge, and his marriage had broken up.

Margaret came to counselling feeling very lost. What life she had had seemed to have been unsatisfactory, but even that had now been lost to her. She described herself as a 'flower crushed by a male boot' or a 'hosepipe with a kink in it'. She looked older than her years, she wore thick spectacles and seemed shrunken inside of herself, but when she spoke she had a light girlish voice and she easily broke into giggles.

Margaret remembered her father as a cruel man who beat her younger brother severely; her mother seemed simply to have 'been there' in an undefined way.

Counselling for Margaret was a process of encouraging her younger, girlish self to emerge and holding back some of the severity of age. The strength within her had to come from a growing young woman. This was the way by which she could gain a new inner centre, the lack of which had meant that she could not control her class. The lack of centre in herself had meant that her son too had been unable to find an authentic centre. He had begun a nomadic life based on some illusory pursuit. Her daughter had gone to a great distance and there seemed to be no firm relationship between them. If Margaret the older woman could recognize and accept her younger self, there was hope that their combined strength could withstand the figure of her hostile father so that there could be revealed some positive qualities within him of compassion and vulnerability. Having a male counsellor who would embody less hostility and more warmth than her father would contribute to the process.

Understanding Margaret's 'dual system' of health and neurosis

The 'theory of duality' is illustrated by holding in one's imagination one of those puzzling psychological test pictures which are ambiguous. The most common one is in black and white of two faces looking at each other; after a while, one perceives the space in between the two faces as a chalice.

The model suggests that the neurotic view sees only one image in a given life situation. The neurotic comes with an ingrained expectation and imposes his perception on the situation without seeing the whole or the *gestalt*. He omits to consider the 'spaces in between' and therefore does not see the alternative configuration.

The task of the counsellor is to perceive in the client the alternative configuration which his personality and his behaviour yields. Therefore, health for the individual does not involve the rejection of qualities within him but a reordering of their energy.

If one looks at Margaret more closely, the following are a few of the details of her pattern as they would emerge more clearly in a group counselling session:

1. She found it difficult to make use of a silence. After a moment's pause, she said, 'The subject I think we ought to talk about this evening is the distrust between the sexes.'

2. Rather than speak about herself, she found it easier to seize upon someone else, 'Tell us how you feel about that, Carol'.

3. She protected to the point of denial, 'Roger did not mean that, did you, Roger?'

4. She giggled and expressed her anger slyly.

These qualities, seen as different configurations, could be:

1. She was willing to take the initiative. If this was pointed out to her, she would probably reflect that it had always been expected of her that she should do so.

2. She was probably right in intuitively recognizing that Carol did have some strong feelings about a particular area, but she did not recognize the vulnerability of Carol at the time. She was attempting to ally herself with Carol, but was in fact putting her on the spot.

3. It is therapeutic to defend a person, but Margaret did so at the cost of avoiding some basic point.

4. Her indirectness, in its healthy configuration, becomes the ability to hold an appropriate middle ground between passivity and aggressiveness.

It is possible to outline a series of 'healthy' and 'neurotic' patterns.

Isolation in an individual is negative when it involves being cut off from personal relationships; in its positive configuration, it becomes 'objectivity'.

'Projection' is that mechanism of behaviour by which a person assumes that he knows what the other person is feeling, his assumption coming from within his own self. Projection is a negative expression of empathy. Empathy can arise where there is a genuine separation of persons and an authentic understanding of what it is like to be the other.

'Rationalization' takes place when a person explains away his responses with some plausible but unconvincing concrete explanation. 'I do not know when the end of the session has come because I do not have a watch'. In its positive aspect, rationalization becomes interpretation. 'I do not know when the sessions are ended because I do not like them to end. I do not like them to end because I do not wish to go back out into the external world. If I do not end them myself, I can get angry with my counsellor for throwing me out on to the street.'

In the process of counselling, Margaret was able to hear somebody else – in this case, her male counsellor – put a more generous interpretation upon her behaviour than she had done herself. She became less afraid of him and less inclined to see men as the 'male boot'. In coming to a more balanced view of man, she found a figure to mediate between her girlishness and her premature old age. She therefore found an authentic middle ground for her own 'womanness'.

Chapter 4

Change: Secular and Religious

The Manifestations of Change

Carl Rogers' descriptions of change are classic. He examines the type of statements which clients make at the beginning of counselling and compares them with ones they make at the end. Clients move from making statements about their problems and symptoms to making insightful ones about themselves and what sort of action they can take. To begin with, there is a more negative tone about statements, whereas as the person progresses, he makes more positive statements, reflecting his greater sense of self worth. As he progresses, he is more able to see himself as a 'perceived object'; to do this, he has had to perceive his feelings and abilities more objectively. He is more likely to arrive at decisions by standards which are consciously understood rather than the unconsidered ones he used previously.

At the beginning of counselling, there is a gap between the ideal which the person is striving for and the capacities he has to achieve it; in the course of counselling, the goal becomes less idealistic and the capabilities of the person more developed and more directed to an appropriate goal, so that that goal becomes more realistically attainable. The person becomes more able to distinguish feelings without resorting to distortion of data, and he becomes more comfortable in acting on his feelings. He becomes more independent, spontaneous and genuine. He is more differentiated, less abstract and less generalized in either an approving or a condemnatory way. He sees more relatedness both in the process of the session and in his pattern outside. He is better at problem-solving, because he has discovered that more options are open to him than at first sight appeared. He is more aware of experiences which he has denied. He is more able to allow inconsistencies to stand in his perception and, having experienced them, to reorder his comprehension to be more embracing. He experiences less physiological tension and is more comfortable and adjusted in his environment; he experiences greater inner calm.

The Subjective Experience of Change

The '"Aha" experience' is that of the 'penny dropping'. In a psychological test situation, a problem is presented; it is beguiling. If a solution is pursued along lines which the problem seems to suggest, it will prove to be a dead-end. If the subject looks at the problem in a different way with a different expectation, an easy and obvious solution is forthcoming. The '"Aha" experience' is the nuclear experience of therapeutic change. As the child grows up, he develops cognitively because he learns to co-ordinate new information with information he already has and to create new categories for old information as he distinguishes its elements. The experience of discovery he has in that process is the same experience which the client has in putting together his new awareness and in discovering that he can differentiate his feelings more exactly. An inner energy is thereby stirred and there takes place an evolutionary step forward.

In counselling, the experience may begin with a feeling of irritation. The feeling says, 'Leave me alone'. If the feeling passes unnoticed by the counsellor or – if in a group – the rest of the group, it subsides or goes underground. If it is noticed, the individual may be pressed and feel cornered. He gets into a familiar 'back up style' and withdraws or is aggressive. He now feels fear of the unknown or fear of what is too well-known, i.e. attack. There is tension and confusion unless someone interprets what is happening. This causes a lowering of tension and allows the individual to say, 'All right. Let's go ahead.' Because interpretation has lowered the tension, he understands that there is a safety-net for him. Whereas before there was a sense of speed and rushing, now there is a silent space which is available for anyone to expand himself unthreateningly.

A counsellor wrote about Jerry: 'With Jerry, the process of change came as a focussing down. The picture which comes to mind is of proceeding through a number of concentric circles until we finally got to where Jerry was in the centre. As tension rose for him, he tried to deal with it by becoming more adept in his distracting tactics, darting in laughingly with his rapier-like plunges. Then he got up and walked across the room to get an ashtray which he didn't need, remarking, as he did so, on the needlessness of his task. Then he sat brooding in his chair, closely examining his hand, lifting up the fingers of one hand with the other and letting them fall thoughtfully. At this point, he said, "I feel at the edge. I've never been here before." He was asked if he was afraid, which surprised him. The question was not one which anyone had ever dared ask him before and no one knew quite what he would do, whether he would get up and hit the questioner, or realign his familiar distracting defences, or crumple into tears. There was a moment of group awareness when sounds and movements, or the lack of them, were noticeable. Somebody commented upon the quality of the time, which seemed different, and nobody felt that they had to do anything about it. There had been a different quality about the question to Jerry on his fear, which made it not a challenge but a lead. He responded with initiative. He experienced that the posing of the question did not result in his destruction or that of anyone else. His fear saw the light of day. The group was attentive and present, but not

intrusive. Jerry replied that he was frightened. Again there
was a silence, in which another moment was discovered. The
group's memory went back to the time when Jerry had
recounted growing up in a criminal environment. Members of
the group gave reactions to Jerry, which reflected empathy.
In contrast to the hostile environment of his childhood, a
more responsive setting had been enacted for him. He saw
that his previous pattern was assembled to cope with a world
which he knew to be hostile.'

The Maintenance of Change

Change is likely to be followed by regression to familiar ways,
but it is also true that once a client has 'owned' something
about himself, he is thereby different and even though he may
repeat familiar patterns, he now has the ability to catch
himself at it and can ask for help when he needs it. The
experience of change will have to be repeated between client
and counsellor, but the first step has been taken towards the
time when the counsellor will be able to withdraw himself and
allow the client's strengthening ego to do his own monitoring,
remembering and anticipating.

One client said, 'I woke up one morning and I realized for
the first time in my life that I didn't have to be depressed, that
I was not going to lose anything by going out into the world
feeling happy rather than in my usual way of finding it hard
to stir from bed and walking about for the next two hours
with half-closed eyes. I remembered that I had experienced
another part of myself and that it was really there and it was
really me; nobody else could take it away from me but I
myself. So why shouldn't it be there this morning . . . ?'

Another client said, 'In the session, I felt as if a balloon
was filling up inside of me. On the outside, I had on a suit of
armour which was stiff and impenetrable. But, as I breathed,
the balloon filled up and touched the inside of the armour,
moulding itself to its shape, so that both became one. The
armour remained but it became alive.'

Change is possible when movement has taken place deep

within the foundations of the personality. Once this happens, the question of how to maintain change is not fundamental, since change has already happened and it will inevitably find expression in the life of the person.

How Change Happens

Rogers does not speculate on the inner processes which underlie change; he merely describes the conditions in which change takes place. If the conditions are present, change happens.

Change comes about when two people are 'in contact', that is, there is a real area in which they are communicating. The client is in a state of 'incongruence', which means that there is a discrepancy between how he perceives himself and what is his actual experience; he has feelings and qualities different from what he perceives. (The counsellor has his own state of incongruence but, by having some degree of awareness of it, it is held that within the hour's session he has sufficient insight into his state to be able to protect the client from his own malfunctioning.)

The counsellor feels towards the client 'non-possessive warmth' and views him with 'unconditional positive regard', which is defined as 'prizing a person irrespective of the differential value one puts on his behaviour.' The counsellor seeks to understand the client's 'internal frame of reference', that is, to perceive the subjective world of the client accurately, as if he were the other person, but never losing sight of the fact that it is a state of 'as if.' The counsellor retains his stance in his own internal frame of reference, but a full understanding of the other's internal frame of reference, i.e. seeing the world as he sees it, leads to a state of 'empathy', i.e. feeling 'in' the other's feelings.

By reason of the empathy which exists, the client experiences the counsellor's unconditional positive regard and is able to view himself with 'unconditional positive self-regard'. He recognizes the discrepancy within himself between his concept of himself and his feelings. He, therefore, reorganizes his concept of himself to take account of previously distorted and denied feelings, and becomes a more 'congruent' person.

The Ideal Objectives of Mental Health

One of the difficulties of religious language in this field is that it is allusive and metaphorical. People can read into it justification for their own state of being. Psychological language has an uncompromising definiteness. The following is a substantial statement.

'The ideal objectives of mental health are many. They require that the person be capable of deriving pleasure from creature comforts in life – from food, rest, relaxation, sex, work and play. He is capable of satisfying these impulses in conformity with the *mores* of the group. Mobilizing whatever intellectual and experiential resources are required, he is able to plan creatively and realistically, and to execute his plans in accordance with existent opportunities. This involves an appraisal of his aptitudes and limitations, and a scaling down of his ambitions to the level of his true potentialities. It includes the laying down of realistic life goals, an acceptance of his abilities and a tolerance of his shortcomings. Presupposed is a harmonious balance between personal and group standards, and those cultural and individual ideals that contribute both to the welfare of the self and of the group. The individual must be able to function effectively as part of the group, to give and to receive love, and otherwise to relate himself congenially to his fellow creatures. He must be capable of engaging in human relations without indulging neurotic character strivings of detachment, needs to dominate or to be enslaved, or desires to render himself invincible or perfect. He must be able to assume a subordinate relationship to authority without succumbing to fear or rage, and yet, in certain situations, be capable of assuming leadership without designs of control or power. He must be able to withstand a certain amount of disappointment, deprivation and frustration without undue tension or anxiety when he

feels these to be reasonable, shared or necessary to the group welfare, or when the consequences of impulse indulgence entail more than their worth in compensatory pain. His capacities for adjustment must be sufficiently plastic to adapt himself to the exigencies of life without taking refuge in childish forms of defence or fantasy. To achieve a healthy regard for himself as an individual he must have a good measure of self-respect, the capacity to be comfortable within himself, a willingness to face the past and to isolate from the present anxieties relating to childhood experiences. He must possess self-confidence, assertiveness, a sense of freedom, spontaneity and self-tolerance.'
L. Wolberg, *Technique of Psychotherapy* (Grune & Stratton) p. 834.

Neurosis, Religion and Change
If neurosis expresses itself in the personality, it must express itself in a person's religion. The same denials, rationalizations, projections, dependency and repressions to which a person is given in his daily life are not likely to have been resolved in relationship to his religious understanding and practice.

The following are some of the ways in which religion is used as a neurotic defence; that is, the person's behaviour is an expression of his anxiety, which, if it were responded to, would allow him a richer personal experience, and therefore, presumably, a more 'true' religious experience. (Indeed, religious behaviour is irreligious when it protects the person from meeting his real self and prevents him from being transformed by integration.)

(a) The religious practice which is used as a defence against achieving satisfactory personal relationships; religion allows the person to avoid intimacy.

(b) The feverish religious activity which arises from feelings of low self worth; the person is constantly seeking to achieve external validation, which is bound to be unattainable because the inner feelings have never been satisfied.

(c) The inner sense of isolation which achieves acceptable compensation by proclaiming that he alone is right; the paranoid person has the ultimate sanction for his truth, if he can say that it has divine authority.

(d) The condemnation of the guilt of others which arises from a person's unrecognized sense of guilt within himself.

(e) The acceptance of an overriding guilt upon oneself, which is an expression of one's sense of depression; if the depression were resolved, something would have to happen to the sense of guilt. But the person has been taught that he is a worm.

(f) The practice of religion which takes place because the person feels incapable of functioning fully 'in the world.'

(g) The practice of religion which is a 'reaction formation', that is, the person is reacting by doing the opposite of what he feels, but is constrained to do so by fears that his true feelings will be rejected. The person is basically at odds with the world, but it is not acceptable for him to express anger and hostility; therefore, he practises something which is associated with forgiveness and love and he gains a compensation for his rejected feelings.

(h) Avoidance of peer relationships.

(i) The practice which arises from an unresolved relationship with mother and father. The child did not experience his parents as a unit, but made an alliance with one at the cost of the other; the Church is 'mother', the world is 'father' and the two do not meet.

(j) The inability to belong within a relationship of authority, which also implies intimacy and 'being known'. It is acceptable to yield authority to God but not to men.

(k) The practice of religion which is an expression of some inner anxiety, which can then be avoided. A phobic symptom is an externalization of a person's inner anxiety. The person creates some external behaviour which he can avoid (see chapter 6).

Neurotic expression of religion must be capable of a healthy configuration. The following alternatives are offered.

(a) The religious practice which is not an avoidance of

personal relationships, but which expands them; there belongs to both a sense of excitement, reward and unfolding challenge.

(b) Purposeful activity which is effective and which arises out of the person's sense of inner validation.

(c) A sense of conviction which is not a defence against other people.

(d) An inner sense of awareness of wrongdoing which allows the person to feel and express empathy.

(e) A sense of religious guilt which is separate from a sense of lifelong depression; the person is not afraid to stand unashamedly upright.

(f) The ability to be fully assertive.

(g) A religion in which one can express the totality of oneself to others and risk rejection.

(h) Incorporation of peer relationships.

(i) The ability to separate former unsatisfactory relationships from the present; the ability to replay relationship with father and mother the way one would like it to be, and achieve affectionate unity where it is offered.

(j) The ability to sustain and rejoice in vertical relationships by which all are enhanced.

(k) The practice of a religion which is not a neurotic necessity but freely entered upon. The person enters upon it with the fullness of mature choice in order to participate in it and be transformed by it.

Psychological change effects religious change and psychological health promotes religious health. A religious person affirms that religious truth has its own healing contribution to give to psychological health, but it is probably as well to begin by challenging a religious person psychologically. In the first stages of the counselling process, this is likely to be most therapeutically effective and therefore most authentically religious.

Chapter 5

Conscious and Unconscious in Pastoral Counselling

Role-play

This is an activity which is more common in training a counsellor than in counselling a client. If a student does not understand what is happening between himself and the client, one way of untying the problem is for him to role-play the client. There is no reason why a client may not undertake a role-play within the counselling session either on his own or with the counsellor role-playing the client.

The client, Margaret, said that she could not understand why her son, Roy, had joined the Unification Church. The counsellor suggested that she role-play her son, that is, be him and say what he would say.

What happens before, after and alongside the action of the role-play is as important as what happens in the role-play itself. Margaret found it very difficult to think of putting herself in her son's place. She said that it was 'unreal' and that it would not be 'her'; the very name of 'play' meant that it was not worth serious consideration. All these reactions have therapeutic potential. Margaret was probably afraid of getting too close to her son; it may have recalled for her the time when he was a small child and physically dependent on her, which she found difficult. Getting this close to him aroused physical and even sexual feelings which she did not like. For this reason, she kept a distance from him in his growing up, which was all part of the cause of the present unsatisfactory relationship. The way the counsellor deals with Margaret offers in itself the therapeutic response. With Margaret, the counsellor said that he understood that it was difficult for her to contemplate role-play and that he understood some of the reasons why, but that in the past, he had found it something which was often very beneficial and he offered to help her get into an appropriate situation, 'Let us think how you would be meeting Roy, what you would be doing and how such a conversation might begin.' The counsellor firmly resisted Margaret's fears and the offer of co-operation was the model of outgoing initiative which she needed to be able to get into her son.

Essentially, what a role-play does is to put a person in a position where he is experiencing empathy. He is being himself within the other, drawing upon his own resources in order to understand the other.

What Margaret said in the person of her son was that he joined the Unification Church because it gave him a sense of inner certainty for the first time in his life; he had not felt the same conviction about his medical career. What the counsellor did was to follow up with 'him' on what his sense of inner certainty was like and what it felt like between himself and his companions, between himself and his family and himself and his mother. The role-play allowed Margaret to hear some authentic things from within her son for the first time and it allowed some link to take place where there had previously been a wall. The problem as she saw it, namely that he had become a Moonie, was not solved, but the very point of that was that it was 'the unthinkable' and she was at least now, like him, beginning to 'think it'.

It is important, when the role-play is completed, to allow

the person to 'de-role', that is, to stand back and comment upon what it was like for him. Sometimes it happens that a person gets very fully into the role and experiences an unreal exhilaration and inflation, allowing parts of himself to be released which he did not know were there. Later on, he may feel ashamed and therefore it is very important that he have an opportunity to settle, to feel from the counsellor acceptance and to hear some interpretative comment which is going to allow him to understand that this 'other self' will prove useful to him. It is also important that if, as the role-play proceeds, the person appears to be getting too caught up in his role, the counsellor be able to intervene and even guide him back to calmer waters. But it is likely that the counsellor will not invite an individual to undertake a role-play if he can anticipate that the person is going to find it too exposing.

Sometimes, the person playing the role comes to a stand-still within the role, and gets out of it. The learning in that situation consists in drawing attention to what was happening at that point. Or the person may say something which he quite clearly did not intend or of which he remains ignorant. The counsellor may gently note it and wait to see if the person finds any meaning in it.

Role-play, like many dramatic devices, can be a potent tool and it must be used by the counsellor with full awareness of the impact it is having upon the client.

Empty Chair

In this exercise, a person who has played a significant part in the client's life is imagined as occupying an empty chair nearby. The client may have been speaking about a dead parent and he discovers that there are things he would like to have said to him. Up to this point, he has not been aware of those feelings, but now he finds that he is approaching a nexus with his parent and his parent has become 'alive'.

The client speaks to the empty chair what is within him and experiences a catharsis. He finds himself saying things which, when spoken, are different from what they are when kept within; the inner words achieve a life when they are offered to the other person.

Having said what he wanted to the empty chair, the client moves to the chair and becomes the person within it, speaking in reply. The 'parent' may reply to the client in a way in which the client did not believe possible. This is apparent to the client or is underlined by the counsellor. The client may feel guilty towards the parent for having withheld from him affection over a number of years. The counsellor invites the client to take up the chair of the parent and respond.

What happens is that under the initiative of the counsellor, the client takes the dialogue beyond the point where it had previously rested.

Like role-play, the empty chair can be a powerful tool; it is important that it be used, not out of the counsellor's neurotic need to put the client 'in the hot seat', but out of his desire to put himself at the service of the client.

Sculpting

This exercise is more commonly used in a group or family situation. The client is invited to reflect upon his family and imagine how he would place them in relationship to himself.

One client placed his brother and sister at the edges of the room, as far away as possible; one was in South America, the other in India. Father was at a moderate distance with an invisible group, conducting a public meeting. Mother was sitting on the floor. The client himself was hidden behind a pillar. The family as a communicating unit hardly existed.

After a sculpting is arranged, the participants are asked to comment on what they have produced. Each person is asked what it feels like to be in the position in which he finds himself. The individuals take a turn in each other's position and see what it is like. Each member is invited to rearrange the group in the way he would like to see it and describe what the result is like. The group may be able to agree on what is an acceptable rearrangement for them all.

Body Language

A person's body language represents the 'other self' of which he is unaware. It is a rich source of information but needs to be used appropriately and not drawn attention to garishly like a series of bill boards along the main street of some western city.

A client never looks at his counsellor, but spends his time looking at the carpet. Even as he enters and leaves the room, he never makes eye contact. This facet of his behaviour graphically represents his depression. It ensures that he is not challenged and it expresses his deep fear of other people. Another client, when listening to his counsellor, watches him from behind arched hands, as if he were listening to a reprimand, which he is not taking in. Another client crosses and uncrosses his legs every time he says, 'on the one hand' and 'on the other hand', expressing his fear that he might say something which would leave him exposed. Another client coughs slightly at regular intervals, illustrating his timid moves forward followed by his timid moves back. Another client describes herself as being pretty from the waist upwards; from the waist downwards her overweight becomes less attractive. Her job involves sitting behind a counter and meeting members of the public, with whom she is popular. But in her sexual life she feels abused. Another client spends most of his sessions talking about his depression. One day he comes wearing a bright yellow pullover. Initially he does not acknowledge that it has any significance, but despite himself, a new ray of light subsequently appears in his life.

When attention is drawn to his body language, the person may feel particularly exposed, but given the proper trusting environment, he may well get to the point of being able to co-operate in looking at its significance. The client who is most prone to intellectualizing is most vulnerable when attention is drawn to his body language, if it is tight and bound up. The counsellor may be tempted to be caught up in the same anxiety, but after mature consideration, he will be able to find an entrée at an appropriate time. Body language is physical and, like physical interaction between people, can be felt to be natural at the appropriate time.

Statements and Questions

One of the ways by which a client avoids responsibility for himself is to ask a question when he is actually making a statement.

Harry, in group: 'Don't you think Sheila was wrong to . . . ?'

What is happening here is: (1) Harry is avoiding saying; 'I believe Sheila was wrong to . . .'

(2) Harry is appealing to the other members of the group for help.

(3) He is making a place for himself by putting something negative on to Sheila.

The counsellor can deal with this by saying (1) 'Harry seems to be asking for help.' This has the effect of side-stepping the dynamic and offering a communication on a different level.

(2) 'Would you like to make a statement out of the question you are asking?' The counsellor can move on to eliciting the person's feelings of not wanting to stand out.

If Sheila is a member of the group, the issue of 'what she has done' can be explored with her. If she is not, somebody may be invited to role-play her.

Thinking and Feeling

One of the fundamentals of counselling is to know the difference between thinking and feeling.

When a child has seen a toy hidden under a succession of cushions, he may be able to work out where it is by remembering under which one it was put previously and by observing the direction of his parent's arm. The process, by which he concludes where it is, is one of thought, which draws on his powers of observation. What he feels during the process is a sense of loss at being parted from his toy, joy when he uncovers it and claps his hands, anger and resentment that it was taken away from him, a quickening excitement mixed with fear as he moves towards its possible discovery, and relief when it is all over.

Thinking and feeling are two separate processes, but they are connected in that thinking has a feeling content attached to it. The child does not just 'think' where it is but also remembers the good feeling he had when he recovered his toy. Therefore, he is better able to think by reason of having had a good feeling.

A student came to his final examination in which he had to defend his dissertation orally. At one point, he said, 'human orgasm' instead of 'human organism'. Since the oral was in pastoral counselling, the event did not pass unnoticed. On reflection, the student said that he used the word 'orgasm' because the context in which he was engaged with the examiners was one where previously unrelated thoughts came together, which was exciting.

The difficulty for most counsellors and clients is in separating thinking and feeling. Even when a counsellor says, 'Not how do you think, but how do you feel?', the client may still say, 'I feel that . . . .' 'Feeling that . . .' is not different from 'thinking.' Feeling means hope, joy, sadness, excitement, wonder, bitterness, fear, pain and so on.

Feeling is a pool of emotion, which, when tapped, spills out in what may be a variety of outlets. Hence, once the pool is stirred, a variety of feelings are experienced. Even 'opposite' feelings are felt, which is confusing to the thinking mind, which seeks to forget all but one of them. The thinking mind asks, 'How can I experience sadness and joy at the same time?' Feelings do not answer questions; they just are. At a funeral a person experiences sorrow; but at the same time he may experience, to his surprise, even a sort of relief and lightness, which he does not feel it is right to acknowledge. The emotions having been stirred, a person comes to be able to express joy more easily as well as sorrow. It is the conjunction of opposite feelings which is transcending.

The importance of this for counselling is that a person's feelings allow his other, unacknowledged, side to be expressed.

Metaphorical Language

There are two types of metaphorical language. In the first, the speaker is referring to some external situation which is parallel to something which is going on in the counselling session. The metaphor is that the communication between client and counsellor is clear on one level but it alludes to another level about which the client may be unwilling to talk.

A client returned to counselling after a break which had been caused by the counsellor taking a holiday. The client began the session by expressing his hope that the counsellor had had a good holiday and then went straight on to say that his boss had asked him to be chairman of a new committee. As the conversation proceeded, it became clear that the committee was a troublesome one and the client did not like the 'position he had been left in.' His boss had branched out in some new direction, which the client would like to have pursued himself.

The external issue for the client was real enough and worth talking about in its own right. It did, of course, have a parallel in the situation between the client and the counsellor, who had gone away and enjoyed himself, giving the client no choice in the decision and leaving him to rely on his own resources to deal with whatever problems came up.

The two situations had to be given separate consideration. However, it was noteworthy that the client had not expressed any feelings about the counsellor's holiday. He had begun the session by having wished the counsellor a good holiday. It is a matter of observation that holidays on the part of the counsellor or the client do have an important impact upon what happens in the counselling; to imagine otherwise is not to give value to the quality of personal relationship which is established. The client uses the words 'position he was left in', which relates more exactly to being left by the counsellor than taking up the new committee.

Whether there is a 'metaphorical' communication or not, the way forward helps the client in both areas. If he can express his dismay to his counsellor about being left to cope with things on his own, he is more likely to be able to express himself openly to his boss and his new committee. This might produce support from his boss and affirmation of his authority. With the committee, he will be better able to confront its troublesomeness. The troublesomeness is in himself, in his own lack of confidence. In gaining his own confidence, he will be able to enable the committee to do the same.

In a second example, the speaker saw the metaphor for herself and made use of it. A group had begun the session by sitting in silence for about twenty minutes. Finally, a member said, 'If I may break in upon your thoughts . . . I was looking out of the window and I saw this old couple trying to get across the road. They were having great difficulty. First he took a step forward and then they had to step back; then she did. Something like this happened many times. And then I realized that that was what was happening inside me. But now I want to step out. And that's why I had to break the silence.' The speaker allowed her metaphor to help her by connecting the 'outside' to the 'inside.'

In the first type of metaphorical communication, the language itself is not metaphorical; the metaphor is in the communication. Metaphorical language also means language which is metaphorical. The importance here lies in noting the imagery and seeking to understand what it means for the individual or group. A metaphor which is used in a group allows the group the awareness of participation in its own life. The occurrence of a group metaphor is an evolutionary step forward which allows the group to become conscious of itself.

At the beginning of group process, members speak 'past' each other. Two members have a conversation in which each is not listening deeply to what the other is saying; they speak 'at' each other. There are interruptions and unnoted changes of subject. There comes a point, however, when the members begin to speak in a way which is supportive of each other and of the group as a whole. In one group, a member started to speak about the 'building' he was making; for him it was a cottage. Another decided that his building was the Statue of Liberty; another a castle. From this point, the image which the group had of itself was of a number of bricklayers laying bricks. A member would say something and another would lay something else alongside it or build something on top of it. They felt that hitherto they had been speaking different languages, whereas now they had a common language. The metaphor described what was happening in the group and became a source of energy for further growth.

Another group looked at the series of metaphors which it had produced. It began by talking about 'strangers being stuck between floors in a lift and not knowing what to say to each other.' This developed into 'being on board an aeroplane', wondering whether there was 'enough fuel for take-off', whether they had 'faith in the pilot', whether indeed there was a pilot, whether they were on 'auto-pilot', whether there was a bomb on board; this proceeded to 'impact', 'impacted teeth' and dentist. Looking at the metaphors themselves became like looking back at 'snapshots in the family album'.

The quality of the metaphor is that it is individual to the setting in which it occurs. It focusses a truth momentarily but the impact is extended. It is, therefore, a cross-section of the life of the group but it is longitudinal in that it is the result of a long process and it does itself fertilize further progress. In one group, the theme was marriage; individuals were speaking about their own marriages. A speaker used the name 'Sallyn', which was a conflation of 'Sally' and 'Carolyn'. Some of the affection which these two members seemed to have for each other became enacted in a 'married' word, in which consciousness and unconsciousness came together.

The Unconscious
One way of thinking of the 'unconscious' is of a 'compartment' within the personality, evidences of which occur sometimes in slips of the tongue and unaccounted-for

behaviour, but most of the time the 'unconscious' goes back to sleep. A better way of describing it is to say that the 'unconscious' is there all the time as an ever-present ingredient in every aspect of behaviour. If a person carries around with him unresolved feelings about the death of his father, he carries around with him a silent, unspeaking companion. Unknown to himself, his conversation is directed to this invisible figure. The reaction of other people varies. Some do not notice, since they have long ago concluded that life is like this, others have the feeling that 'something is amiss' and they avoid interaction in particular areas. By not having had the time to experience the loss of father and feelings of anger about it (because it somehow feels like being angry 'at' father himself), the anger accompanies the person. Tasks are undertaken with apparent willingness, but the 'unconscious' purpose is to experience father's continued approval, which, because it is impossible, leads to a continued sense of dissatisfaction, which further fuels the anger and disillusion. Tasks are undertaken to ward off the depression which would arise if there was space within the person's life. Therefore, the tasks themselves become hateful. Persons who appear within the individual's life find that they are greeted warmly to begin with, since the individual is looking for somebody who can do for him what he cannot do for himself, that is, create a project which is going to give unalloyed satisfaction. When other people inevitably do not live up to expectation, they find that they are rejected with a degree of coldness which they cannot understand. The relationship ends in mutual helplessness; 'father' has won again.

There are two levels of the unconscious. The first level is simply that aspect of a person's behaviour of which he is unaware. However, with insight he comes to realize that he has an unreal expectation and that he appears to other people to be more angry then he believes himself to be. He sees the 'shadow' which has been following him around. A person has to experience this level of unconsciousness before he can experience the other.

The other level of the unconscious is that which is unthreatening to him. It proves to be a 'horn of plenty', a treasure-house of imagery and energy which is unique to the individual. Once the person has become reconciled to father, the energy which went into the unconscious relationship with him and into current relationships becomes freed for use in a creative way. Accepting loss of father leads paradoxically enough to an integration of him, so that instead of his energy causing a destructive result to current relationships, a sense of peace and resolution is available. The 'father' has died, 'death' itself has died and the person has been recreated.

Because his inner energies have been freed, the person is now likely to be more effective practically and by reason of his inner sense of transformation, be more open to artistic and transpersonal truths.

Dreams

A person's dream is the most complete expression of his unconscious. Every person dreams, but, of course, not everyone remembers them. This is partly habit and partly the fact that they have not been recognized as being important. One can usually remember them once one grants the inner possibility that they are important and begins writing them down.

It is tempting for trainee counsellors to rush in and 'analyse' dreams, but it is important to sound warnings.

1. A prior question is 'What does it mean that a client has brought a dream?'
2. It is tempting to discuss a dream, drawing on particular schools of thought, and miss the client's very real current difficulty. The client and counsellor may be seduced by the fascination of a dream, while the client is at odds with his spouse.
3. It is tempting for the counsellor to impose his own understanding on the dream rather than enable the client to clarify what it means to him.
4. The counsellor may not have reckoned with the degree of fearfulness a dream can hold for a client. It is a mistake to

encourage a person who is very distressed or disturbed to recount his dreams; they are more likely to increase his anxiety and such a person is not going to receive insight from them.

With these provisos, a client's dream may be a most useful factor in his therapy. His dream expresses his personality just as much as everything else about him; the dream, however, is particularly rich.

The Beginning Dream

A client described the following dream which he had just before coming to counselling for the first time.

'I was in the Alps. It was spring. There was snow and sunshine. It was very beautiful. The air was crisp and clear. There were Swiss chalets around. You were there. You were dressed in Swiss Alpine clothing and you had skis. But I noticed you had a hole in your sock.'

A few weeks later, the client had the following dream.

'I was on the North Sea, on a trawler, going up to Iceland. It was very bleak and stormy; the sea was very rough.'

The counsellor asked the client his associations to the dreams. In relationship to the first one, the client replied that he had visited the Alps occasionally and had also had one skiiing holiday. He generally felt rather exhilarated in that setting. It was very much out of his normal way of life. He was surprised to see his counsellor there all ready in skis. And he wasn't sure whether he should include the detail about the hole in the sock.

What was important for the counselling was that in the session the client should experience and enlarge upon the feelings he had had in the dream. What did the Alpine air feel like? What was it like to see that his counsellor was there? What did he feel about his counsellor having a hole in his sock? How did he feel when he himself had a hole in his sock?

It was of secondary priority whether the client saw any connexion with the beginning of counselling, whether counselling was a 'winter skiing holiday'. It was a third priority at this stage that the counsellor saw a mythological allusion to Achilles' heel. The confidence of the first dream made possible the second dream a few weeks later. The counsellor noted that the client seemed to be all alone on the trawler. The client replied, 'That's me; that's my life story. I am at home on the North Sea. I am alone, but I am not afraid.' The counsellor continued, 'Deep-sea fishing in hazardous waters without a crew is quite a task.' The client was able to reflect upon the size of the undertakings he got himself involved in.

Working Dreams

These dreams belong to the 'working' stage of counselling.

In this dream, the client was walking along a city pavement. He came to a building where there was scaffolding erected. He had either to go into the road or go into the house. He went into the house and a large Alsatian dog came bounding along the hall to meet him. He was afraid, but he held out his hand towards it.

The client had no particular associations with the house and the scaffolding (which for the counsellor meant the reconstructive work which was going on in counselling), but he was able to re-experience his fears about dogs. The counsellor noted that sometimes it was realistic to be afraid of dogs and asked why he had felt able to reach out his hand to this one. The client remembered that an acquaintance had once asked him to look after his Alsatian while he was on holiday and had told him that although he was fierce, if he stretched out his hand towards it, it would become friendly. The counselling pursued what were the fears in the client's life and in what way he might stretch out his hand towards them.

The dream allowed counsellor and client to participate in a metaphor.

In another dream, a client dreamed that he was in Washington DC. Around him, there were dark giants building a huge temple; it was like Stonehenge or the

Parthenon. The client's association to Washington was that it was the seat of secular, political power and the temple was the fabric of state. The dream expressed for the client his own desire for and inability to involve himself in a search for power. He had not claimed his own inner power.

The Transformation Dream

The same client who had dreamed about the Alsatian dog some time later dreamed that a friend was coming towards him on crutches. The friend explained, much to the amazement of the dreamer, that he had always had artificial legs, but today he was on crutches because the legs were getting mended. The friend then moved off and the dreamer was amazed at how quickly he could move on crutches.

The dream pointed to the transformation which was coming over the client and this was confirmed by the fact that the client, having recounted the dream, on his own initiative said, 'I can confess to you that I am the person. I didn't realise that I had artificial legs and I have been able to function very convincingly.'

The Big Dream

These dreams have a unique power. Their significance extends beyond the immediate context of drawing the person's attention to his unconscious behaviour. They are felt by the person to be part of his religious experience, on which they draw and which they expand. They waken the person up, leaving him with the question as to what is more real, the world he has woken up to or the world he has woken up from.

After a considerable experience in counselling, a client dreamed the following.

'I was returning home from school. I was about fifteen. When I drew near, I noticed a figure coming towards me. It was my father, carrying his walking-stick the way he used to. Much to my surprise, when he saw me, he threw away his walking-stick and ran towards me and embraced me. But then I thought, "This is crazy, because he is dead." As I said that, the visible person left me, gradually, like the smile of a Cheshire cat, but the feel of his invisible embrace remained constant and was even more unmistakable. It was iron-like in its strength, but human in its firmness. I woke up, still feeling the embrace around me.'

The dreamer had a number of associations to the dream.

1. The healing miracles of Christ, in whose presence the afflicted were made whole. The father threw away his walking-stick.

2. The parable of the prodigal son, in which the father ran and 'fell on' his son's neck.

3. The Resurrection, since the dreamer's father was, in fact, dead, but now appeared to be very alive.

4. The Ascension, when the risen Lord was removed visually from the disciples but remained with them with an undiminished and even redoubled power.

The dreamer concluded that he had for an eternal moment seen into the 'world of the Resurrection', where parables and miracles were living events; he reflected that the events of his day-to-day life had an aspect which 'shared in' an eternal life; it seemed that parables and miracles were alive and his own life shared in them.

Styles of Counselling

It is perhaps helpful to conclude this series of chapters, which have been on the practice of counselling, with an overview of the styles or 'levels' of counselling which might be adopted. I am indebted to David Holt, a Senior Supervisor at the Westminster Pastoral Foundation and a member of the International Association for Analytical Psychology, for permission to use the categories which he formulated and which are in everyday use in assessment at the Foundation.

Style 1 The focus is on a particular problem which the client brings. The counselling may be short-term, e.g. a girl has received an invitation from an estranged father to go back to the USA with him after his forthcoming visit, where he will set her up in business.

Style 2 The counselling proceeds beyond an immediate focus to look into the history and background of the client. In order to be able to readjust himself, the client needs to look at the influences which have been brought to bear upon him.

Style 3 This is 'interactional' counselling. The problem which the client brings is brought into the session itself. The dynamics of the client affect the counsellor and the counselling; the counsellor interprets these and responds to them. In fact, the client cannot fail to bring into the session the pattern of functioning in his external life, but it depends upon the ego-strength and the level of relationship between client and counsellor as to whether he can make use of insight.

Style 4 is supportive counselling. The aim here is not to achieve considerable insight or life adjustment on the part of the client, but rather simply to maintain the client at an acceptable level of functioning. Into this category may fall the heavily depressed, some elderly, and those with fragile personalities. It is useless to offer insights to those who cannot hear them, or to those who can only receive them as an additional burden. It is dangerous to offer more than support if a person might be overwhelmed by uncovering his fears.

Style 5 Ongoing assessment. No clear picture has emerged in intake of what level of counselling is going to take place. The client may not know what counselling is about, but he is prepared to come back for a few more sessions to see what may be achieved.

Style 6 is individual counselling leading to group, or individual and group at the same time.

Individual and Group Counselling

The following views are taken in relationship to individual and group counselling:

1. Individual counselling is wholly sufficient for the client. In

examining the client's relationship with his counsellor, there will emerge many other figures in the life of the client.

2. It is helpful for a person to be in individual and then in group counselling. In individual, the person gains the experience of basic trust which he can take to the more dynamic setting of group, where he can appropriately work on his peer relationships.

3. It is not necessary for a person to be in individual counselling at all. A group, with its more varied membership, is a setting in which a person is more likely to be able to settle down. The group itself has an identity to which a troubled person may relate more easily than to an individual. Every person who can benefit from individual can benefit from group.

One of the ways in which these arguments most commonly have to be resolved is on grounds of availability and cost. Most pastoral counselling centres offer mainly individual counselling; a minority offer only group.

There is much to be gained from having the experience both of individual and group. What is important, however, is that the client does not sabotage the one by the other. It is not permissible to take an issue, which arises in one setting, to the other.

It is a further point of discussion as to whether the counsellor in individual and in group should be the same person. The advantage from the counsellor's point of view is that he can get a clearer picture of how the client is functioning by seeing him in group. But there is integrity in the view that the client should have to make his way in two separate worlds; he himself has to put the two together and cope with whatever disparities there are.

Chapter 6

Who We are:
Various Characteristics

Depressive

Depression is a normal reaction to a bereavement. The person has profound inner feelings, which may be expressed in changed behaviour. A bereaved spouse may take up the interests of the dead person, going for long walks which he never did before, even beginning to speak like the dead person did. Depression of such a kind requires support but the individual's ego remains intact and over the course of time he is able to readjust himself. It is not a question of reordering a character structure.

At the other end of the scale is the person who is psychotically depressed. He is agitated, he wrings his hands continually and paces the floor. He goes up to strangers and asks for help. He sits down for a meal and immediately pushes it away. He complains that his insides are rotting away, about which it is useless to try and convince him otherwise.

In the middle, is the person whose depression does not prevent him from functioning adequately, but it is an ingrained part of his personality or it has arisen from a particular event and has stayed. The person has about him a continuous air of gloom. He has lost a large part of his interest in life. He goes through the motions of eating, sex, work and play, but with little enthusiasm. He smiles sadly at someone else's humour; his own humour is more cynical and contemptuous. There is also an unmistakable air of anger about him; he complains bitterly and hopelessly that he is unloved and by so doing makes himself unlovable. He ruminates at length about life's afflictions and hopes that some omnipotent force will intervene; hence he may turn to religion.

The depressed person finds it difficult to maintain social relationships, for although he strongly desires them, he is unable to offer anything. He is slow. He answers questions but does not offer new avenues spontaneously; instead he is defiant and offhand. He may have physical symptoms, such as difficulty in falling asleep, fatigue, loss of appetite, headache, aches in the joints.

The depressed person suffers from a deep sense of loss, which was probably formed in the first twelve months of his life. Every infant suffers a sense of loss in relationship to his mother, when she does not feed him or when she is not present when he wants her. But usually there is sufficient good experience to carry him through his temporary deprivations. However, if the deprivation is greater than the rewards, the experience becomes ingrained. The person carries around with him the sense that he has lost his state of well-being. Inside is a hungry emptiness. Strength appears to rest in other people. They move in a greater and more real world, with which he does not have the resources to cope. Therefore, he goes back into himself. He is understandably angry that other people seem to have the good things, but it is no good being angry with the outside world, because he has learned that his powers are ineffective. His anger, therefore, 'eats away' within him. The psychotic believes that he is being eaten away; what he means is understandable in the light of the neurotic's metaphor.

Because the neurotic's anger derives from a primal experience, which was out of his hands, his anger feels continually larger than himself. On some level, he may be aware that his anger is inappropriately directed, and that leads him to feel guilty. This redoubles his impotence and anger. But for him that is all right, because he feels that that is only what he is worth. Life is about suffering, which is another reason why such a person may seek a resolution in religion; he accepts himself as the sacrificial lamb or the scapegoat. This is, however, only a temporary resolution, because he is left with the underlying feelings of being badly done by. The fact that other people plainly do not go along with him further isolates him and allows him to be disillusioned in them. They do not measure up to his standards and therefore he looks down on them. This may be complicated by his tendency to do the opposite of what he feels (i.e. a reaction formation); he attempts to 'love' them, but this does not work and he is left in his isolation.

Counselling with a depressed person is a great challenge. The person may have built up a massively impenetrable structure; he is dedicated to proving that any sign of hope or change is doomed. Implicitly this includes the purpose of counselling. Indeed, the counselling session itself represents the 'good object', which the person has lost, for although the session may provide a space for one-to-one communication at a more open level, the end of the session arrives and overwhelms the client with loss.

Counselling may remain at the level of being supportive, or the counsellor may be able to gain the alliance of the person to look at his patterns and the causes of them. This clearly places the responsibility on the individual rather than accepting it for the counsellor, for it is the person's neurotic pattern to place responsibility outside of himself.

Group counselling may be an additional or alternative support. A group offers a place where the depressed person who is heavily bound up with himself can be exposed to peer relationships in a controlled setting. His 'heaviness' is less likely to weigh down a group than an individual session.

Suicide

If a client talks about suicide, or if the counsellor suspects that a client might be contemplating it, it is important to explore the possibility fully. The client may be making a special bid for the counsellor's attention, but he may be seriously intending suicide. The counsellor needs to know whether he has made any attempt before, how he would do it and when. The various means signify something different and it is important to explore what the meaning is for the client. It is significant whether the client already has the means at his disposal or whether they are available to him. The counsellor may have formed some judgement as to how impetuous or how determined a person he believes the client to be. It is important whether the client knows somebody else who has committed suicide.

Exploration of the whole issue is more likely to build up the relationship between client and counsellor and thus make suicide less likely. If the client has no significant relationships and he finds the counsellor alienated from him, holding on to his life is more difficult for him.

It is important to acknowledge that in contemplating suicide the client may for the first time in his life be claiming control of it. Once he realizes that he can do this, he may have less need to do it.

The counsellor needs to clarify with the client whether he wishes the counsellor's assistance in preventing suicide. This is likely to be so, since the person has come for counselling. In which case, it is important to consider with him what preventative measures are available, e.g. medical treatment, hospitalization, carrying the Samaritans' telephone number.

However, there are situations in which the individual has already decided to commit suicide and he is asking that his counsellor understand.

Electric Shock Treatment

This suggestion is sometimes raised by clients or their relatives. A decision regarding such treatment is, of course, in medical hands. Shock treatment can often have beneficial results in the case of severely depressed hospitalized patients. The interest of the pastoral counsellor, however, lies in what such treatment means to the client. It may seem to offer a quick, magical cure in which he does not have to participate himself, or it may represent some punitive approach which he thinks he deserves.

The Phobic

The phobic person causes the beginning counsellor anxiety because of the dramatic quality of what he is presenting, namely, a symptom. A counsellor may feel that he can listen, offer insights and make interpretations, but when it comes to working with such an obviously 'sick' person, his skill will be being put very much to the test. The client, via his symptom, is putting forward an objective gauge of the effectiveness of the counselling.

If the counsellor takes on this implicit challenge, he falls into the client's trap. In focussing on the symptom, he gets caught up in the same anxiety which the client has. The counsellor may have to explain that he does not see it as his primary task to resolve the symptom, but he would be willing to explore with the client some of his feelings and conflicts. It is the job of the counselling to enlarge the picture, so that the size of the symptom is symbolically reduced. If a trusting relationship with the counsellor is built up, the conditions are created in which healthy forces can assert themselves.

People are afraid of a wide variety of objects and experiences: being out of doors, travelling more than ten miles from home, travelling on the underground, being enclosed, height, cats, dogs, spiders, going into a public lavatory, eating in a restaurant, having a haircut, crossing the street, knives, driving a car, touching money, cinemas. A person may lose one phobia and take on another.

What he does is to externalize an inner fear on to some concrete object or situation, which he can then avoid in the hope that he will avoid his fear. This may be successful for much of his life. He can avoid going up Blackpool tower or crossing the Atlantic by sea, but when he feels that he can only go to the toilet when there is a friend nearby or when the door is left open, it becomes a problem. In any case, he plainly sees that his phobia is not actually helping him to avoid his fear; it actually makes his fear more obvious.

The development of a phobia relates to the experience in childhood when a child has difficulty in distinguishing himself realistically from external objects. When a child is afraid of the dark, his inner fears and external reality are confused. When an adult is unable to cross the street, there is an unrealistic assumption about the experience; a parent may have said to the child that it is dangerous to cross streets, but the injunction is no longer realistic to the adult. The connection lies in the child's relationship to the parent.

The phobic has typically grown up in an environment where external danger was emphasized; he was warned about traffic, bullies, walking in the dark, riding his bike, walking in the park and crossing the road. The fear mediated from parents was colluded in by them; when the child did not want to go away to camp with the cubs, parents unquestioningly agreed; when he was afraid of school, they kept him away. The anxiety of the parents in relationship to the external situation is communicated to him. In avoiding the feared situation, the person recreates the nurturing warmth he received from his parents; this compensates for his guilt at the avoidance. The symptom is a symbol of guilt, fear and desire.

The counsellor becomes a new parent who is interested in locating the fear itself and not letting the client avoid the external situation. The process of building up trust with the counsellor is the context in which the issues can be teased out and looked at unthreateningly. The client who had to keep the lavatory door open recalled how she had suffered sexual abuse at the hands of an uncle. She realized that her phobia was an expression of the fear that this would recur; she needed someone to be present. But it was also a semi-exposure of herself again. It was therefore a neurotic compromise by which instead of avoiding fear, she put herself in the situation which re-enacted her fear. The counselling separated the reality of her childhood and her adult reality, which once she had acknowledged, she was no longer able to perpetuate the pattern.

The Hysteric

The hysteric and the obsessive are at opposite ends of the personality spectrum; each represents the unlived part of the other. For this reason, they may marry each other, the hysteric usually being the woman and the obsessive the man.

The hysteric is an extrovert; she appears to be open and communicative, but after a while, one has the impression that she is tailoring her presentation to what she believes the other person is looking for. Her unspoken response is, 'Tell me what you want, and then I will be able to reply.' She receives her validation from outside; her basic need is for affection and approval. This helps her to relate to others, but it also makes her hostile in that she is dependent upon them to fulfil her needs.

The hostility to her environment, together with her need to evoke a response from it, may cause her to be somewhat disordered; structure in her life comes from outside. She may not carry a watch and be late, whereas for the obsessive to be late would be a shameful humiliation. In receiving a response from another person, she takes it as a sign that she means something to him. This, however, is a neurotic compromise, since she is actually looking for affection, but may receive weary acceptance, which covers hostility. On the unconscious level, she perceives that she receives hostility, which further affirms her isolation, which makes her try harder to appease her environment. So the cycle continues.

The hysteric appears to be a 'feeling' sort of person. Her language is vivid and dramatic and she may talk a lot about feelings, but this is often more to attract the feelings of others, which she needs. When confronted with profound, confusing, paradoxical, fearful or even tender feelings of others, she may be curiously out of her depth and, to the surprise of those present, pass on as if they had not been mentioned. She has problems over intimacy. Although she is attractive, seductive and apparently responsive, she has difficulty in achieving genuine sexual pleasure. She both attracts and flees. The men on whom she depends for admiration seem to be too powerful for her; she remains girlish and hostile.

The hysteric is the product of the unresolved Oedipal situation. Mother and daughter have built up a strongly protective relationship; father remained distant. To him she was a little princess to whom when she grows up he transfers the affection which was missing between him and his wife. When she was small, she received from him a semblance of himself, and now that she has grown up, she can receive no more than a semblance of a partner. She seeks sexual experience, but it does not touch her. Indeed, this may have a physical manifestation; she may not have feeling in the genital area of her body, illustrating in negative form the importance to her of body as a means of expression. The hysteric is lacking in true inner purpose for herself and she comes to counselling depressed and directionless. She feels pain, but this is part of her way of life, for pain is punishment; having grown up trying to please, she has failed and feels guilty.

Recent researches have pointed to the influence of the mother's psychological state upon the child in pregnancy. Certainly there is a degree of hysterical personality which seems to reflect that the person has never separated from mother; the person is a raw, unformed bundle of primitive rage and has, metaphorically, to be held until safe defences have been allowed to grow.

Hysterical 'conversion' takes place when a part of the person's body physically expresses the conflict of the individual; e.g. she becomes blind after seeing something which horrifies her. By this means, the person achieves a symbolic punishment, which is visible to all, of what she believes herself to be guilty. Note that here also there is a lack of separation, for the emphasis in the hysteric is not objectively on what she sees, but her own responsibility in seeing it. She is unable to separate herself from the scene in the same way as she is unable to separate herself from mother. When one considers that in the hysteric it is possible for a part of the body to decay out of a sense of the person's guilt, one can understand how some miraculous cures take place after sins have been forgiven.

In the same way as a part of the hysteric's body may be 'split off', so may a facet of her behaviour; e.g. she may take flight, walking for miles and not knowing where she is going. Just as the hysteric loses feeling in part of her body, so she 'freezes' in part of her activity. Some relative has to go and retrieve the lonely soul who has wandered off, but after many such experiences is probably desperately angry; thus she receives a sign of affection from her environment, but it is mixed with hostility.

Counselling with the hysteric involves building the initial relationship between mother and daughter. As the counselling progresses, it introduces 'father', in that the counsellor has to provide the structure and groundedness which reality demands. The counselling has to be penetrative and focus on true feelings of anxiety, fear and depression. When this is achieved, a rewarding process occurs and there takes place a genuine exchange of warmth and understanding.

The Obsessive

If the hysteric is characterized by a lack of structure, the obsessive is over-structured. He is rigid, orderly, conscientious, reliable and humourless. His central conflict is apparent in that he is obsequious to authority and at the same time defiant of it. Whereas the hysteric gives to another person the responses that are felt to be wanted out of a desire to please, the obsessive is obedient to another out of a sense of shame that he will not live up to expectations. Being isolated within, he fears that, if the response of the other is withheld, his isolation will be complete. He is fearful of punishment and therefore his way of life is based on avoidance of it. He punishes himself by repressing himself and is therefore hostile to those who have power over him. He receives gratification in maintaining the status quo, since he may not allow himself to envisage personal advancement. The successful achievement of tasks is the reward of which he feels he is worthy. But it is an isolated reward; he knows its worth within his own mind and does not feel that other people's estimations are to be expected. Therefore, he does not expect that an exchange between people takes place on the level of feelings or of intimacy.

Being incapable of feelings himself, he looks to others to supply them; therefore, he is attracted to the hysteric. When he discovers, after a little while that her outward display of feelings covers a difficulty that she has with her own range and depth of feelings, he feels disillusioned and angry. He, therefore, retreats into the isolation with which he has been familiar all along, and substitutes success in work for the interpersonal gratification he had begun to look for. At this point, his marriage may fall apart, he may take to drink or begin the life-style of middle age which is going to end in a heart attack.

Many obsessives function well, for hard work and dedication to an ideal are culturally accepted. It may be that the ideal he is working for has interpersonal aims, e.g. a charitable trust. He, therefore, gains indirectly a success in a field where he has not been able to release his own personal qualities.

The obsessive is an intellectualizer. He has learned that his rewards come from achievement in this field; therefore, he pursues this direction with all his energy. Basically, he is an introvert, used to having conversations with himself rather than with others, but he acquires a facility for language, which, in fact, communicates very little. The listener receives a flood of information but is rather confused by the detail of it. The amount received is rather unwieldy, which has the effect of keeping the listener at a distance and not wanting to get involved with this person, who, when once he opens up, reveals that he has rather large needs. The cautious listener, therefore, is switched off or cuts off the speaker more directly, who is then left feeling his usual isolated self. His greatest attempts at communicating have failed miserably and he loses the object of his striving. He retreats into his own system, which may be scientific study or religious involvement, which is now neurotically buttressed by reason of his external disillusionment.

In some more dramatic cases, apparently opposite tendencies coexist. The orderly person, for example, is orderly in only a particular field and is very disorderly in another; he is totally particular about whether his shoes are clean or his trousers pressed, but has dirty personal habits; he apologizes at length for dirtying a clean ash-tray and then drops ash on the carpet; he is meticulous about arriving on time and then spends many minutes writing out a cheque.

The example of the obsessive helps in understanding the difference between a 'personality disorder' and a 'neurosis proper'. The word 'neurosis' is used in a general sense meaning the basic 'flaw' in every normal personality, in which sense it has been used up to this point. It is important to note, however, that in proper clinical terminology, it alludes to a state of being which is likely to have been brought on by precipitating circumstances and which is pointed and dramatic, whereas a personality disorder relates to a lifelong, ingrained pattern of functioning. An example of the obsessive neurosis proper is the person who becomes obsessed with the idea that she will poison food when she is cooking and is therefore unwilling to keep in the kitchen any household chemical which could get into the cooking, or the person who has the recurring thought that she will stab her children and therefore keeps knives and scissors locked away. The particular condition is likely to have been brought on by precipitating stress which, if it is lifted, allows the person to subside into less noticeably troublesome ways.

Obsessions are thoughts, compulsions are actions which are sometimes associated with the thoughts. One of the most common compulsions is hand-washing. The person is obsessed with the fear of germs and when he uses the toilet, has to wash his hands until they are red-raw. He turns off the tap, but in so doing wonders if he has exposed his hands afresh to infection and has to start washing them again.

The obsessive personality derives its dynamics from that stage of life where there is conflict between parent and child, e.g. over toilet training, eating or sleeping. The child has seen that behaviour is a win or lose situation. If he wins his struggle, he loses, in the sense that he goes hungry or suffers rejection of affection. If he loses, he nurses his inner sense of defeat until the next battle. The intial battles with mother are replayed with father, who enters the scene as another against whom he cannot win. His only way forward is to comply and hurt inside.

When the obsession leads to a compulsion, the inner conflict assumes bodily shape. The battle of wills between authority and himself becomes enacted in a physical act, just as for the hysteric there was a physical manifestation of an inner conflict. The person who compulsively washes his hands, has to do so; he does not wish to do so. If he is prevented from carrying out the ritual, which he recognizes as inappropriate and maladaptive, he suffers extreme anxiety. His ritual is an enactment of his fearful obedience to the voice of authority.

The obsessive is likely to keep the counsellor at a distance. The relationship between the two is set up by him as one of authority and obedience. He is out of touch with his feelings and keeps the experience of the session within a narrow limit, which, if it is broken, causes him to retreat and absent himself from the process. The counsellor feels bored, angry, cut off and powerless. However, it may be possible for him to divert the client on to some non-threatening ground, where he feels a genuine and spontaneous interest for the client. When the counsellor understands the degree of the client's isolation, he will be able to communicate that, without being put off by his isolating tactics. When the counsellor discovers that the client is going back to his old game of intellectualizing, he will not cut him off abruptly, but divert him back to the area where he felt within himself a warm response. The client needs to experience a relationship which is not based on obedience on his part or on a need for him to dominate the other.

As the client proceeds, he begins to understand that there is a middle ground based on interpretation. This discovery may appeal to the obsessive's intellectualism and may make possible a contract to work in that area. Being accepted as a partner in an enterprise offers him higher value and stimulates feelings of acceptance, which he would not have before when he worked in his own isolated world. When trust has been built up, the client can look at his own feelings of shame and experience an external authoritative voice which does not place injunctions upon him. The process provides the qualities necessary to dissolving the person's conflict, namely acceptance, warmth and good-will.

Paranoid

A paranoid person is nearest to the popular understanding of somebody who is disturbed or mad. The extreme state of paranoid schizophrenia describes somebody who believes he is Napoleon, or that he has a radio in his head, or that the preacher is delivering to him secret messages of sexual intimacy. The pastoral counsellor will probably not work with such clients, but it is helpful to understand the basic paranoid personality, who is common enough in the community and the counselling-room.

The paranoid person is distrustful, distant and aggressive. He is an unwilling client and comes under duress because his marriage is threatened or because he has been made unemployed. If he comes on his own accord, he probably comes because of his depression and it is only in the counselling that his paranoid character is uncovered. As long as his system is working, he has no need to come, since it is not he who is at fault. If something has gone wrong, it is because he has not yet had time to get his plans straight or he has been misunderstood. Projection on to others and denial of his own input are part of the weaponry of the paranoid. He has learned to cover himself by attacking others, indicating his inner feelings of emptiness. He feels that he has nothing to give and nothing worthwhile to accomplish; he externalizes this feeling and 'proves the prophecy true.' He compensates for his sense of inferiority by an over-large estimation of his own value. This grandiosity is an expression of a childhood state of self-centredness. The paranoid is the centre of his own world and he is protected by his own thick blanket, just as the depressive, the hysteric and the obsessive in their own ways.

The paranoid person has grown up feeling that he is in some way different from the rest of the community. Some children are very much desired by their parents and grow up feeling special to a degree which alienates them from their peers. The feeling of specialness, however, conveys a sense of weakness. If the child was born, for example, after siblings had died, he picks up the basic vulnerability of being a child and of himself in particular, by reason of the special protectiveness bestowed upon him. The family system of the paranoid person buttresses the individual's individualistic perception; e.g. failures are blamed on to teachers and other children. The over-protectiveness appears on the surface to be a nurturing environment, but is lacking a genuine easy warmth. The parents fluctuate between possessiveness and emotional coldness. The child's valid achievements go unrecognized by the parents, because they do not believe in his inner strength. In earlier days, the parents' coldness may even have been sadistic, for which later over-protectiveness is a compensation. The child, therefore, received contrary messages and learned the experience of an irrational reversal. The mother may have behaved seductively with the child, but denied to herself the impact of her behaviour. The child, therefore, learns the experience of denial and forges a separation in his own mind between the effects of behaviour upon him and what he is allowed to show. In the male paranoid, the homosexual dynamic is often noticeable. The child failed to receive a proper nurturing from mother and turned towards father, whom he loves, but from whom he does not receive the totality of his wants. Hence, the male paranoid is likely to be attracted towards his male counsellor but he cannot express it and in any case, hostile feelings are more familiar to him. The client, therefore, may tend to copy the counsellor in some way. His message is, 'I am doing what you want me to do; therefore, I am cured.' The message also means, 'I am doing what you do better than you do; therefore, I don't need you.'

In the paranoid person, the counsellor is confronted with anger, resentment and self-centredness. The client is likely to sit in sullen silence or to harangue the counsellor about the world and the counsellor's behaviour towards him. If the client does show an apparent opening, the counsellor may be tempted to rush in thankfully with some warm response. This is a mistake, which the client will be quick to spot. The client is fearful of warmth and he will see 'over-warmth' as a basic untruth. The counsellor is being more honest when he says that he is in fact a total stranger to the client and there is no reason why the client should see him as an ally. However, he can express his compassion for the way the client feels. The paranoid's basic difficulty is in knowing whom he can trust; if he receives a response which is over-expressive, he is further convinced that the other person is someone he cannot trust. By accepting the reality about there being no grounds for trust, the counsellor shows his understanding of the situation.

The counsellor has to tread a similarly fine line in relationship to the client's suspicions of the world. It is important that he be not trapped into fully accepting the client's perceptions, and that he does not appear to reject them. The counsellor responds to the difficulty which a situation is causing the client and at the same time notes that other people may view it differently. 'I understand how you feel about your neighbour lighting his bonfire there, but I wonder if there might have been other explanations.' If the client feels a genuine recognition from the counsellor of the central issue, namely his difficulty, he may be willing to let go of his mis-perception. He will be glad to be let off the hook in a way which allows him a dignified withdrawal. Since some of his basic dynamic relates to covering his feelings of shame, the process of allowing him a dignified untangling of himself is the most therapeutic thing which can happen to him.

Schizoid

The description, 'schizoid,' relates to a degree of 'split-ness' within a personality. The person appears distant and removed, to the degree that a large part of him is not present. In some early stage of his development, it is believed that he suffered an increase in external stress or decrease within his inner resources which caused him to be 'split' in two; he functions on the surface, but a large part of him has retreated from the world he experienced as hostile. Indeed, his whole inner energy may have been lost to him or it has been converted into a relentless force for his own destruction. The depressed person is in a state of mourning; he has had the experience of something good, however fleeting, but it has been taken away from him. The schizoid person has not reached the stage of having experienced a positive life force. There is a fragility and emptiness about him. He may be able to hold down a job, but there may be long periods when he cannot function.

The schizoid person is shy and seclusive. He finds it impossible to express strong feelings; he is as unable to express hostility as he is incapable of building up a sustained intimate relationship. The healthy introvert can form a few close relationships and can make use of an inner richness to experience a fruitful life, but to the schizoid person, life is largely meaningless. You are damned if you do and damned if you don't; so what is the point of any of the alternatives which face you? One may as well be the executed as the executioner. What satisfaction there is in life comes from day-dreaming. Life passes him by without making much of an impact upon him, but he does have the strength of having acquired a way of being in the world and he does recognize reality. However, he is unable to participate in it and he does not have any particular feelings about it.

The degree of schizoidness determines the extent to which counselling is helpful. David (chapter 3) showed a degree of schizoidness, but not to the extent that inner resources could not be uncovered. Where these resources are less accessible, supportive counselling in individual or group sessions may maintain the person and present some modicum of improvement.

Schizophrenic

It is not likely that a pastoral counsellor will do prolonged work with a schizophrenic. It is important, however, to know what schizophrenia is and to be aware of those times when we come across schizophrenic-type behaviour in ordinary neurotic persons. It is also important to recognize that to counsel a schizophrenic person in the same way as one counsels a neurotic is harmful.

The classical description of schizophrenia is Bleuler's 'four A's': disturbance of affect and disturbance in association; autism and ambivalence.

Affect (emotion): The person shows a lack, flatness or inappropriateness of affect; e.g. he laughs when describing a sad situation, or he generally describes events without any show of feeling.

Association: His thinking is disordered; e.g. 'Tell me about your wife' is answered by, 'Blue is my favourite colour.' There may be a connection there (i.e. wife-favourite) but there is a step missing. In mild forms, the gaps in thinking are not so obvious. The listener may feel that his attention has wandered and will supply the gap himself. The gaps in thinking may not be apparent until he sees the client's written thoughts in the form of a letter.

Autism: The client lives in his inner world and substitutes fantasy for reality. His words have meaning only to himself.

He may compile words. His humour appears hilarious to himself but nobody else gets the joke.

Ambivalence: The client finds it difficult to make a decision. The normal neurotic experiences ambivalence, but the schizophrenic is ambivalent about almost everything.

The secondary feature of schizophrenia is delusions. The person may suffer delusions of persecution (that somebody is 'out to get him'), delusions of grandeur (the experience that he is a famous person), hallucinations (usually voices speaking to him) or ideas of reference (the belief that other people are talking about him, e.g. tv announcer, or newspaper headline).

It is useless to try to convince a person of the unreality of his delusions; they are real to him, perhaps the most real thing in his life. The disbelieving listener merely puts himself in the client's rejected world. The counsellor needs to elicit what their meaning is without causing the person to expand them so that they become more florid and raise the anxiety of both client and counsellor.

Schizophrenia in these descriptions is fairly simply recognized and there are a number of factors which are thought to contribute to it. (a) A child may be more predisposed if he has had a psychotic parent. (b) Illogical and extreme inconsistent behaviour by parents is a factor, particularly those situations where the child experiences a 'doublebind', that is, where he was punished whatever response he made. For example the parent withdraws when the child does something unacceptable and is openly angry when the child attempts to do what he thought the parent wanted. The child experiences panic and rage and has no outlet for his true self. (c) Poor social environment, where there are few opportunities for advancement, is another factor. The person reaches adolescence and finds it a time of great isolation. He withdraws into his own world, loses ambition and begins to fail at work. He gives himself up to strange cults or interest in extraterrestrial bodies, or he starts collecting knives. He has day-dreams about mass destruction, grandiose accomplishments or sexual orgies and has strange dreams about weird animals. As he speaks about himself, he sounds like a spectator of himself.

Counselling with a neurotic person demands probing, uncovering and interpreting material which is produced; it is a mistake to probe into the bizarre world of the schizophrenic, for it removes the person further from reality. He senses that the counsellor has become involved in his world and that the ground has become shaky. The counsellor needs to focus on the day-to-day functioning of the client, so that the reality which is there is extended. The unreal world has to diminish in size as the person senses a growing trust and can look at some of the meaning of his own world.

In considering the schizophrenic, two important issues relate to pastoral counselling. (a) A counsellor does not recognize that he is working with a schizophrenic and that he is being harmful to him. (b) A client who presents as a 'normal neurotic' begins to show signs of schizophrenic behaviour.

The former situation occurs when a trainee counsellor is not in touch with his own feelings about what is happening in the session. His enthusiasm and intellectualism outstrip his awareness of the impact he is having on the client, who withdraws or becomes more agitated. The best means of prevention is for the counsellor to have regular consultation, so that colleagues and supervisor can reflect back to him what he cannot see for himself.

As regards the latter possibility, the client David (chapter 3) began to speak about his neighbour trying to poison him, and about seeing a goat on his bed. The counsellor responded less to these than to David's fears of the night, going to bed, darkness and what the day was like to him. From exploring his childhood fears, the counselling moved on to David's current difficulties in holding down a job.

The schizophrenic may be especially interested in religion and mysticism, which is a particular trap for the pastoral counsellor. In avoiding getting into this area, the pastoral counsellor has the advantage that he may at the same time be able to communicate his understanding of the importance of this area for the person.

Overweight

There are some psychological factors in overweight and these relate to the earliest stage of the child's development, the oral stage. The child receives nurturing from the mother's breast; the most primitive means of contact and communication with her is via his mouth, while he is being held by her in full bodily contact with her. Eating, therefore, and putting on weight may help a person recall feelings of acceptance, security, the pleasure of physical touch, being alive, being between the womb and the breast, 'outside' and yet still 'inside', next to the mother's heart beat, totally accepted. In between feeds the child begins to feel frustration; feeding is an end to rising anxiety as to whether the child will survive, just as it is an attempt to return to the total security of the womb. People who have suffered great deprivation at this stage of life may overvalue oral activities. Having been deprived, they seek to claim what they did not have and make themselves unwelcome by their demandingness. They become 'only' a mouth or stomach, like chicks in the nest. Finding themselves object- ionable, they feel of low value, which they compensate for further by eating more as a consolation. They are thus angry with those around them who reject them.

It may be that in the family, physical attractiveness was highly prized or that one sibling was regarded as attractive. The overweight person may be rebelling at this scale of values and against the envied sibling.

Overweight may give a person a sense of his own power, which he has been unable to achieve by other means. Size and bulk convey assurance and certainty, a way of buttressing his own sense of right. They also give a person a reason for not engaging in certain physical activities of which he does not feel himself to be capable, and in relationships of which he does not feel himself to be worthy.

Counselling may help by responding to some of the psychological factors. If a person feels less rejected and unworthy in counselling, his self-image improves, which leads to an improved bodily image. If the person finds that there is no realistic reason for his hostility to his environment other than his inner sense of weakness, he may be able to decide that it is unnecessary to deal with his environment in the same way. If the person experiences some of the freshness of moving, he may be able to renounce some of his dependency needs in favour of a more invigorating and active way of life.

It is important that other aids to improvement be sought. Individual counselling is more likely to benefit if the person is a member of Weightwatchers, if he receives some education as to what is a good diet and if there is some agreement about physical exercise.

Anorexia

Counselling responds to anorexia as a symptom of a psychological disorder. What the underlying dynamic is has to be uncovered in each case. An adolescent may have an extreme fear of obesity, which is possibly associated with a particular person in her life, she deprives herself of nutrition to escape ridicule and to maintain self-respect. Counselling aims to achieve a self-respect for her which is based on an enhancement of her qualities as a person as well as upon her bodily image. Her self-starvation may be an expression of her unworthiness, a rejection of her small size or an expression of hostility against her parents in a belated attempt to determine who wins the battle about feeding properly. It may be a fear of her emerging sexuality and what she sees as the costs of it, that is, involvement with the opposite sex. This may be based upon hostility towards father. The child may feel that she has never achieved full acceptance in her parents' eyes, and her self-starvation is an attempt to reduce herself to the size she believes herself to be.

If the person experiences unthreateningly being 'fed' in counselling she is less likely to need her symptom.

Alcoholic

Counselling may be an adjunct in the treatment of an alcoholic. However, counselling alcoholics is a specialized business and many counsellors avoid it, recognizing the fact that those who have been alcoholics themselves (and regard themselves as 'still alcoholics') are often the most successful counsellors.

It is important to understand the effects of alcohol which the client needs. It relieves anxiety and tension; it increases the ability to express aggression; it changes the mood – some people become more cheerful, some morose; it weakens inhibitions and facilitates social contacts. It also has a self-destructive effect and may be sought by those who wish to punish themselves in some way.

As with overweight, the basic dynamic is feeding at the breast. Dependence on alcohol represents comfort and acceptance. The alcoholism may, however, be a compulsion, when it occurs amongst hard-working characters, who treat their drinking with the same determination with which they treat their pursuit of success and recognition.

Counselling may be able to respond to the alcoholic's low self-esteem and thus deprive him of one of the elements in his neurotic structure. The basic aim is to substitute dependence on counselling for dependence upon drink. For this to happen, it is better that there be a variety of resources. Membership of Alcoholics Anonymous is important. The person needs to be encouraged to differentiate his activities, e.g. to take up some sport. There is a specific educative role to be undertaken with the alcoholic; he needs to be taught that alcohol for him is poisonous and that effectively he has an allergy to it; it is actually more destructive for him than for another person. Counselling the alcoholic demands that the counsellor be more active than with the 'normal neurotic'. The counsellor has to decide when the active style of counselling is simply perpetuating the client's infantile demands. He has to reflect back to the client when he believes this is happening, which will involve incurring the client's anger. Possibly many counsellors avoid working with alcoholics because they do not wish to face the client's anger, to state that they do not think that counselling is helping him move forward or be prepared to be 'merely' a support in the alcoholic's relatively unchanging pattern. To state that counselling has failed is not easy for the counsellor, but the realization may be even more poignant for the client and it may also produce the necessary energy for a move forward.

Homosexual

Traditional labelling puts homosexuality in the categories of 'disorders' alongside fetishism and pedophilia. The contrary view is that homosexuality is not a deviation but a way of life which is as acceptable as the heterosexual, and that the problem lies in society's refusal to accept it. In recent years, more people seem ready to acknowledge that there are within the person both a homosexual and a heterosexual tendency, which is physiologically based as well as psychologically influenced. It is, however, understandable, taking into account the model of neurotic denial, that heterosexuals may find a distaste in acknowledging a repressed homosexual quality within themselves. This is to their loss, since it deprives them of a full recognition of their own attachment to members of their own sex and a full understanding of people whom they regard as 'different' from themselves. It is reasonable to be hesitant about making statements that people are 'different' from ourselves, lest the statements turn out to be projections. And it is not unknown for a minority in society to proclaim a truth and to suffer injustice for it.

Having said this, the homosexual is as subject to neurosis as the heterosexual, and counselling may benefit him or her in those areas of life which he may not see as being related to his sexual functioning. It may also emerge that there is a psychological component to his sexual orientation. This, of course, is as possible with the heterosexual, but it is open to both to choose what use they are going to make of insight into the psychological causes of their state; they may decide to change, they may not.

The following are the psychological causes which are often uncovered in male homosexuality.

1. An over-possessive, controlling mother and weak father. This leads to a conviction in the child that he will avoid a repetition of a relationship with a person of the opposite sex. This may be expressed on the surface by saying that mother was so important that no other woman could take her place.

2. Some research suggests that there is a correlation between excessive birth trauma and male homosexuality.

3. Some male and female homosexuals relate that parents desired a child of the opposite sex.

Counselling work with the homosexual may relate to: (a) ordinary neurotic difficulties in interpersonal relationships; (b) freeing some of the individual's libido and stemming some of his hostility; (c) enabling him to achieve a more free and acceptable expression of his sexuality; (d) recognizing his capacity for sensitive affection and helping him to value that within himself; (e) enabling him to separate homosexuality realistically from rebellious complaints against society: (f) helping him to define for himself the special nature of his own sexuality.

Chapter 7

Learning to be a Pastoral Counsellor

Becoming a pastoral counsellor; criteria and selection
Many people, of course, already practice pastoral counselling
and in some sense they have already been selected. There are
others who wish to train and they are confronted with a
selection process. The procedure may seem mystifying to
those who have had little contact with the counselling world,
and confusing when a candidate is turned down and given no
reason; he is understandably shocked and sometimes angry.

The selection criteria vary according to the type and
intensity of the course, but it is possible to say that there are
some things which help and some which don't.

It helps: to have had some experience of therapy oneself, to
know what counselling is like from the inside; to be able to
acknowledge some of one's own denials and rationalisations;
to be able to show that one can build up constructive relationships even when under pressure; to be able to show that one
knows one's own boundaries and can indicate to others where
they are; to be able to show that one has options in this world,
and also that one is reasonably clear on one's commitment to
a preference; if one can envisage a realistic setting in which
one is going to make use of the training; to be grounded as
well as to be imaginative; to have a glimmer of justifiable

delight in one's own individuality, as well as to be appropriately open to dialogue about one's own blind spots; to have
had some areas of one's life in which one can take some
realistic satisfaction in achievement and, if one is leaving
behind a way of life, to be doing it not as an escape but with
some realistic appraisal of its benefits and its shortcomings; to
realize that however much one prepares for an interview, it is
going to catch one's blind spot, the evaluation of which lies in
the heads and hearts of the selectors.

It does not necessarily help to have had a career in a
counselling-related field. Some of those who are turned down
for a training in pastoral counselling might be those who
consider themselves to be three-quarters of the way there, e.g.
social workers, doctors, psychiatrists, clergy, probation
officers, youth and community workers. There are two views
on this. One is that it is important to help those who are
already doing it to do it better, so that even if they are doing it
badly their impact may be lessened. The other view is that it is
perfectly possible for somebody already in a helping profession
to have an ingrained approach which is a hazard when
working with a wide variety of people, and giving the person
a training gives him credentials to proceed. Selection process
has to weigh these alternatives.

It does not necessarily help to have high academic qualifications even in psychology. The capacity to 'over-think' may
have been achieved at the cost of repression of one's
feelings. However, it is important not to encourage a reverse
prejudice in this area; counselling needs people who can
pierce woolly thinking and who can bring a discipline to the
practice.

If a person is turned down, it may mean a number of things.
1. The selectors feel that he is not yet ready and would like
him to have more time to uncover some of his latent strengths.
2. The selectors feel that counselling is not actually the right
direction for him to pursue. As painful as this is at the time,
he may be able to be thankful that someone else has helped
him find the right direction in life.

3. The selectors are wrong in their decision. Selectors can get caught up in their own assumptions and projections and come to unwarranted conclusions, just as they can make the decision wrongly to accept someone.

Perhaps the most important factor about training in pastoral counselling is the principle of self-selection, by which those who are unsuitable drop out and those who are suitable stay. Taken by itself, this is an easy rationalization. There have to be a number of obstacles on the way and the trainers have to be prepared to take the step of discontinuing a person's training. This process should be a positive step and one which should have therapeutic value for the individual and for the organization.

Selection on to the course carries with it a significance which is sometimes lost on even those who achieve it. In the case of a course which involves practical pastoral work and/or counselling, it implies that the student is thought capable by the organization of engaging in that work. This is often one of the first questions which a student asks in supervision, 'What happens if they ask if I'm a student?'

Seeing one's first client

The assumption of the foregoing question is that being a student will be thought by the client to be a second best. What has happened is that client and counsellor have got caught up in the same plaintive feelings of inadequacy. The counsellor has not learned to separate himself from the client and to keep the focus on the client's feelings, e.g. how the client would feel about being counselled by a student. The student himself has not given value to the fact that having been selected, he is considered fully capable of seeing this client within the agency with the available support. The fact that he is a student and that this is his first client may actually be very positive indicators; the client may get rather a lot of attention, which he might not get if he were one of a case-load of fifteen of a tired counsellor ten years on. This objective comment does not answer the real point for the counsellor, which is his anxiety at seeing his first client. 'Will I be good enough? Will I say the right thing? Will I give the client value for money? Will I understand what he says? What if . . .?'

Supervision provides a place where these questions are raised. Supervisor and group as a whole will provide the setting in which the student's anxieties may be heard and seen, so that he receives from the group what he needs in order to counsel. What he needs is not, 'Well, you say this or that', but perhaps, 'I wonder what it is like for you beginning to be a student . . .', or, 'It sounds as if you are experiencing some of the anxieties the client will probably be feeling when he comes to his first session. Let's look at what those anxieties may be', or, 'What is wrong with the answer you yourself would give?'

The client asks, 'Will this counselling help me?' The student asks, 'What are the things I need to know for the first session?' The questions are parallel; each is asking for a specific answer in order to be able to continue. The supervisor responds, 'Where do you feel you are lacking?' which might enable the student to reply to the client, 'How would you like counselling to help you?' or 'What is it like to be helped?'

Both student and counsellor at some point say, 'But you never answer any of my questions'. The supervisor may answer, 'What is that like for you?' or, 'I can see that it is not easy for you when you don't see any answers to your questions,' all of which may help the counsellor to go back to the client and keep the focus on him. The beginning student assumes that in order to be helpful to the client he is bound to the client's expectations. In fact, the hope for the client is for the counsellor to be able to remain outside of his old world. But while the counsellor may take fairly easily to this approach as a means of indirectly expressing his own aggressive instincts and hostility to dependency, he needs also to be able to go half way to meet what is the client's unspoken feeling when he experiences disappointment or disillusion.

Supervision is an attempt to enact an experience, rather than provide a lesson in which answers to certain likely situations will be told him. What is told has to come from within the student. It is the purpose of the supervision to respond on a fundamental level. But, having done that, it must deal very matter-of-factly with concrete information, e.g. fees, time, contract. It is no good the supervisor being 'counsellor' to the student and not deal with whether the student 'forgot' in the first session to begin the negotiation of what is an appropriate fee, and how long each sees the counselling proceeding, and the necessity to be present each week and to give adequate notice on either side of breaks. It is also important to uncover what relevant facts may not have arisen in intake, e.g. hospitalizations, medications, illnesses, current marital status, etc.

Various hazards in the supervisory process

1. Supervision actually increases the counsellor's anxiety. By seeking to anticipate some of the pitfalls, it presents the counsellor with a shopping-list which he feels he has to get through. The pace of the first session becomes too fast and the counsellor's anxiety is passed on to the client. This will not happen if the supervision session addresses and interprets the student's anxiety, rather than seeks to allay it in the student's own terms by providing answers to actualities.

Rather than the student not know what to do, it is quite likely that he will know well enough what to do; he will trust his intuition and the beginning of a satisfactory relationship will be made. The hazards then become less obvious but remain equally dangerous.

2. The counsellor listens to all that the client says, but finds that all he has done is to take into himself the client's monologue. He comes to supervision and proceeds to repeat the monologue. The group sits in silence for some time, until at last someone notes the boredom. What has happened is that the counsellor has been virtually obliterated by the client's tale of woe. He has felt that he has had to sit and listen to it; the client has spilled out all over the place and not felt anything back from the counsellor, and so has gone away feeling as if

nothing has changed. The counsellor has been afraid of what the client's reaction would be if he intervened, and ends by being as depressed as the client. The supervisor has to intervene earlier in the monologue in order to help the counsellor intervene.

3. The counsellor probes too deeply. He has understood that questions are important, but all he does is question. He offers no time for reflection or comment. In some intuitive and destructive way he becomes aware of the client's weakness and he exposes it, to which the client may agree in the session, but goes away with an uneasy feeling that he didn't like it. The supervision group has to take it upon itself to hold back the counsellor and protect the client.

4. The counsellor is too distant. He feels he has to live up to some image of a 'blank screen' but does so in order to conform to his own neurotic character structure. There is a positive way in which the neutrality of the counsellor may convey a different type of 'being present' to the client; but it can also reflect the fact that the counsellor actually is unaware of what impact is being had upon the client's life by the events he is speaking about. Distance in the counsellor is necessary as the hook to bring to light the client's dependency needs, but it is not distance from the feeling which is thereby evoked.

5. The counsellor is involved in an erotic transference. The counsellor may not realize that his special feelings of affection for the person are causing him to deal with the person in a special way. Counsellors can feel flattered by the feelings which clients have for them. There is a right time in a counselling relationship when a counsellor may draw the client away from indirect dealings with the external world and say, 'How do you feel towards me?' But that question may come out of the counsellor's needs rather than the client's. A counsellor may feel competitively towards the spouse of the client and thus get in between a relationship; the counsellor can easily take the client's description of the spouse at face value. A woman client who is in the habit of choosing a mate who turns out to be unavailable for her, either because he is

impotent or is actually married, will unwittingly attempt to put pressure on a male counsellor. He may agree to see her for an extra session, or, if she is in group, see her for individual sessions, without being able to interpret what is going on. The integrity of the counsellor lies in his being able to ask himself what is in the client's best interests.

6. The counselling focusses on the counsellor rather than on the client. The client may want to know about the counsellor's personal life, his philosophical system and what he would do in certain situations. The counsellor may not be directly asked these questions but offers his own views with the intention of showing support and understanding. It is realistic for the client to want to know the counsellor's qualifications, but it is important for the counsellor to be able to respond to the level of doubt or trust the client is feeling. The counsellor needs to be able to recognize when the client's questions are ways of keeping the counsellor at a distance or of retaining some power position without which he feels unsure. Generally speaking, the more the counsellor talks, the less he is allowing the client to talk and, by speaking at length, he allows the client to distance himself from the present. If the counsellor begins to speak about his own philosophical system, what is likely to happen is that the client will begin to pick holes in it and the counsellor will be called on to defend it. The counsellor is then on the run. The counsellor has been unable to cope with his own anxiety about letting the client sit with an anxiety he has never before had to face. In over-nurturing the client, the counsellor has not been able to allow him a space for expressing his frustration and finding out where it comes from, probably because the counsellor does not like to face the person's frustration.

7. Counsellor and client get too close, so that the counsellor does not see the client's pattern and gets caught up in it. This is a danger in any counselling, but particularly when client and counsellor are similar character types or of similar age. A young woman counsellor and a young woman client may initially make a very good relationship, but the counsellor

finds that she is having difficulties in separating herself off
from her. She allows the client to bring her baby to the
session without questioning what makes it difficult for her to
find a baby-sitter; she does not see the relationship between
this inseparable union between mother and child and the
mother's difficulties in making a new life for herself. Client
and counsellor have become as inseparable as mother and
child.

8. The client makes the counsellor angry and the counsellor
does not know how to handle it. A client may criticize the tie
a counsellor is wearing or make it clear that he is deficient in
education or artistic appreciation or whatever. In fact, the
counsellor may be caught on a sore point and reply with less
than his usual firmness or objectivity. For the counsellor who
hasn't come to terms with his own homosexuality the homosexual client may present difficulties of being competitive and
needy. The anger of the counsellor will cause both to feel
rejected, yet if the counsellor does not experience his own
anger, he will not be able to separate himself from the client;
but where to experience his anger? In supervision. One
counsellor was used to working in a setting where all sessions
were tape-recorded. When his homosexual client perceived
this, he brought along his own tape recorder the following
week. A student might have felt this as (a) too intense an
imitation of his own behaviour, (b) a threat to his role as
counsellor.

A more experienced counsellor might be able to elicit from
the client how listening to his own tape recording helped him;
and when they had established a sufficiently trusting relationship, could look back and see what bringing a tape recorder
into the session meant to the client.

9. The client successfully torpedoes the session. The client
begins by announcing that none of his relationships have
worked out. As the session unfolds, it seems to be going quite
well, with the client assenting to all the things he should do,
but as the session draws to a close it appears that he is not
invested in it. He proves that the counselling is not going to

work out for him just as with the rest of his life. If the counsellor is not able to see what is happening and explain to the client that it is actually taking place before their eyes, the session ends in mutual disappointment.

The way forward

The purpose of training is to ensure that the counsellor's old patterns are noticed and that he adjusts them. This has to happen in the life of every counsellor and it is a critical time. For example, a client brings it about that in every relationship she enters, she becomes the victim. She marries three times and each one does not work out. She comes to counselling in fits and starts. So long as the counsellor accepts this pattern, the client remains a victim and the counsellor remains a victim to the client for being at his beck and call. Only when the counsellor is able to move out of being the victim can the client do the same. Counselling demands that the counsellor come to a point where a change has to be made within himself so that the client may benefit. This shift within one counsellor was vividly expressed in his dream. In it he saw a type of prehistoric sea creature fished up from the depths of the sea and laid on the dock side; it was being examined by a group of professors. As he looked at the dying fish, he noticed that its eye moved. The counsellor understood that hitherto he had been treating his client as a fascinating scientific curiosity, but now he understood that the client was attempting to catch his attention with the single movement of which he was capable, which caught his inner feeling. Thereafter, the counsellor was able to respond to the client as a human being who was barely able to keep alive, rather than as a 'client'.

The way forward happens in two ways. (1) The counsellor discovers something between sessions and brings a new approach to a subsequent session. (2) The counsellor is able to make a shift within the session. He realizes that darkness is coming over the land, and he has to make a definite shift in order to find some positive ground. He says, 'It looks as if we are getting into a disagreement in the same way as you were saying has been happening in your family. I wonder how that happened . . . Can you take us back to some better place?'

Chapter 8

Pastoral Counselling in Group

For many people, counsellors and clients alike, group work represents a progression from individual counselling. Clients feel that they can be in a group once they have had some individual counselling; counsellors feel more confidence in leading a group when they have gained some security in working with individuals. This is understandable, but it is only part of the picture. Although it may seem more threatening to be part of a group of people, there are more 'points of entry' for a client, who has the choice of making a relationship with an individual member, with the counsellor or with the group as a whole. Similarly the counsellor finds that instead of having ten 'clients.' looking to him for some unknown 'help', there are potentially ten co-therapists with him. The group itself has an independent therapeutic energy which the leader enables to be released.

Irvin Yalom[1] has drawn together ten 'curative factors' of group therapy. They are as follows.

1. Imparting of information. Individuals answer each other's factual questions about how long the session will go on, how many times, what is the most convenient way of getting there,

[1] I Yalom, *Theory and Practice of Group Psychotherapy* (Basic Books)

where they can get lunch, and even why they are coming and what the group is for. The exchange of information is a symbol; it alleviates anxiety by expressing the fact that somebody else has 'been there before'.

2. Instillation of hope. Those who come with positive prior anticipations are more likely to benefit from the process. Supportive groups such as Alcoholics Anonymous nurture hope within members by statements of individuals' success.

3. Universality. Group members learn from listening to other members that they share some of the problem which is being talked about. The individual realises that in 'him' there is something of 'me'. Most people's problems fall into the categories of (a) sense of inadequacy, (b) sense of isolation, (c) sexual secret.

4. Altruism. The act of being supportive to another person within the group is therapeutic in itself; it draws out from within the troubled person some resource of strength which was previously unexpressed.

5. Corrective of primary family group. Within the group, an individual recreates his family scene. He relates to the leader in some of the ways in which he related to his parents; he finds his siblings among the members. If he was used to being quiet at home, speaking when spoken to, if he was secretive, if he attempted to win over one parent against the other, he repeats all these patterns in group. The family, by its very nature, had its usual way of dealing with his pattern, for it was itself part of the pattern. But the group is different; it is a place where patterns are not simply played out but looked at and a place where the individual learns a different way of dealing with a situation.

6. Developing socializing techniques. The individual discovers for himself those areas in which he is inadequate, e.g. he finds that he is stiff and bumbling in some of his initiatives. Some episode in group illustrates this, or a role-play may have brought it to light. A further role-play may enable the person to improve upon himself.

7. Imitative behaviour. An individual watches others in

group and 'tries on' some of what they do, rather as he takes a suit off the peg to see if it fits. If it fits, he keeps it and uses it in his own way, if he doesn't like it, he discards it and looks somewhere else.

8. Interpersonal learning. In the setting of ordinary life, the individual makes assumptions and proceeds as if his assumptions are reality. Within the group, there has to take place, some 'consensual validation', that is, it becomes clear whether the group perceives what the individual is doing in the same way as he does. For example, the individual may think he is issuing an invitation, but it may be clear to the group that there is a considerable barb attached to it. Consensual validation occurs where there is a coming together of the individual's and the group's perception of an episode.

9. Group cohesiveness. Cohesiveness is the therapeutic quality of the group. The individual has a relationship with other individuals, the leader and the group as an entity in itself. Cohesiveness is the degree of relatedness which occurs. It is a measure of the group's morale. It is the 'quality which defends the group against internal and external threats.' the 'resultant of all the forces acting on all members to remain in the group.' Cohesiveness is the pre-condition of effective therapy. It is the setting in which there can take place the expression of strongly positive and negative feeling.

10. Catharsis, the ventilation of feeling. For one person it may be an achievement just to say something in the group; he feels he has participated if he does so. It counteracts some of his feelings of isolation. Another person finds benefit by recounting some external situation which has been troubling him, or drawing attention to some episode in the group which he felt was unresolved and unsatisfactory. This enables a step forward to be taken towards resolution.

Yalom's 'curative factors' are some of the rationales for group counselling.

Additional factors are as follows.

1. It is easier to see an issue for the client being enacted within group, where it is only reported in individual counselling.

2. There is economy of time, effort and money, without there necessarily being a loss of benefit.

3. There is less chance of collusion between client and counsellor. The group itself acts to point out those things which the leader misses, especially when he has a blind spot in relationship to a particular individual.

4. Yalom's categories do not do justice to the inner experience of the person in finding space for himself amongst a group of people.

What happens in group process

Beginning

Who establishes the group? How does it come about? Was it advertised; where was it advertised; what flavour is given to the group by the way in which it was advertised? Are all the members known to the leader but not to one another? Are members coming to a pastoral counselling centre of which the leader is an unknown employee, or are they coming to a person whom they know in some way? What sort of place is the group meeting in – a clinic, a church hall, a consulting-room, a private house? Is a fee being paid? Is it an expensive group or a cheap one? Who gets the fee?

All these factors exist, but they may have been very little spoken about at the beginning. At some point in the group process they are likely to come up for investigation. Issues are present in the beginning but their relevance is not understood. Group process is the uncovering of what is already there.

Practicalities

The practicalities form the perimeter of the group; they help mark out the boundary in a concrete way, when it may not yet be possible to discover where the functional boundaries lie. It is easier to exchange names, even though it is unlikely that most people will remember them. This is the stage of 'imparting of information'. The leader may encourage this; he may be silent or he may ask to understand what is going on. There is usually some attempt to ascertain what he thinks should happen, coupled with a denial that this is necessary. He may then note that disagreement has become possible in relationship to the leader, whereas the members seem to have been expressing a sort of unity by exchanging names. Has the leader given his name when his turn came? This again might be taken up by the group for comment and disagreement. The beginning of a leader-centred episode may be under way, which may give way to something less emotive. Somebody may have commented on the curtains, or the seats or the way people are sitting. If cohesiveness is the desirable group factor, the leader has to decide what is the best way in this opening time to achieve it.

Task

In some settings, the agency or the leader gives an outline of what the task of a counselling group is. The outline states quite directly that it is the task of the member to share his feelings and reactions to what goes on within the group. The alternative is for the leader to encourage and underline such behaviour so that it becomes established as the norm.

Authority

Who decides what shall take place within the group? Is the leader a member or not? Is he expected to disclose himself in the same way? When the group has been going for a little time it may be judged the best time to explore these latent issues. Probably it will emerge that the leader regards it as his task to assist members to share their feelings and reactions when it is difficult for them, and to draw attention to it if it means that they can only do so when he does so himself. The leader uses his feelings to understand better what is happening, but if he speaks about himself at length he draws the energy of the group to himself rather than create the setting in which the individuals may confront the present. It is desirable that the leader be able to be both opaque and transparent. By deciding when that shall be, he gives encouragement to members of the group to decide that they do not have to say more than they want. The negotiation of this process may be prolonged; it may be verbalized before it takes place or put into words as it is happening or after it has done so. Less tension arises when explanations are given first, but if he does this, the leader may be doing the group's work.

Middle Stage

In the middle stage of group process, members bring to the group external situations which are a problem to them. They see that the problem they bring is actually enacted in the group by the way they bring it, or other members see a parallel between the way an individual brings a problem and the way he has already interacted with another group member.

Gloria comes to group saying that her boy-friend does not understand her; he seems to be interested only in sex. She feels abused by him. She is pretty, but to herself she is overweight. She is Jewish, her latest boy-friend is Iranian.

In individual counselling we would hear about her home background, her escape from eastern Europe, where her father remained while mother and daughter fled to Israel; mother remarried, someone older than herself, who is now senile; daughter came to this country and got a good job and has recently travelled to eastern Europe to find her father. These facts may also emerge in group, but what would also be clear is that Gloria relates in the group mainly on the basis of her sexuality. She flirts with the younger men, with occassional jabs of her sharp tongue; with the women of her own age she is at best silent, at worst, cold and cutting; with older women she is patient and familiar; she attempts to 'snuggle up to' the male therapist. It is clear that when others begin to speak at a more feeling level, she loses interest; she is dismissive and thinks them soft. She appears often to be angry and quite depressed. She gets increasingly depressed about her weight and describes periods when she stuffs herself. This makes her less attractive, she loses confidence in herself and contact with colleagues.

The group may interact with her at a number of points.

(a) Her tendency is to relate in the group on the basis of her sexuality. She may acknowledge that that is as far as relationships go with her.

(b) Some members distance themselves from her; the one man in the group she finds most difficult is most attracted to her.

(c) Her depression increases within the group.

(d) What does she want for herself? When does she 'get' something in the group which she might previously have scorned but which now appears to be a genuine and undemanding support?

This process involves a cartharsis and ridding herself of some of the shame and anger she has been carrying around with her. She may begin to lose some weight, make herself attractive in a different way and involve herself in more rewarding relationships.

This is a compressed process as described here. Such a process is more likely to happen in a shorter time where the counsellor takes a very active role in relationship to individuals and their dynamics, working with the individual, pointing out what is happening, holding up the group process as a mirror to the individual, eliciting responses from other group members, underlining the ones which are supportive to the client, relating what is happening in the present to what the client has said about herself, asking what she understands from what is happening and how she might do the episode again differently, underlining what is different and how she feels about that. The purpose of this approach is to give clear directions; it points a model to the client and it underlines success; all rejoice.

The other model of group process is not to focus on the individual directly but to point to what is happening in the group and allow the individual to grow for herself. When Gloria describes her problem with her boy-friend, the group might be silent. The leader then draws attention to the silence and asks what it means or what it feels like. Somebody might say that it feels heavy, or it feels sensitive and vulnerable; it might indicate that members of the group do not know whether they wish to proceed or whether they are afraid of what might happen if they say more. For this reason, group process is understood as a series of 'focal conflicts'. At any given time, there is a conflict between what is a group wish and what is a group fear. The wish in this case is the wish to hear more from Gloria, the fear is that she will crumble and no one will know what to do. If the fear is greater, someone may come in and cut across, introducing a new topic. In so far as the wish or fear is unresolved, it re-emerges at some later date. The resolution at this stage may be a decision to proceed or a decision to interpret what is happening and leave it at that. Interpreting lessens the anxiety and makes it easier to take up the topic on another occasion.

When the focus is on the group process, the individual is not deprived of an opportunity to contribute; it means that the therapist is consciously building a group entity and allowing the individual to come forward as he wishes. There is probably in the end no great difference in the outcome, for if the therapist were working in the group with an individual, he would only do so if he intuitively felt that the group was 'with' him and was being sufficiently supportive to the individual. What the leader seeks to do is to be fully aware of the anxiety level of the group. If there is insufficient tension to promote creative activity, he increases it; but if it is already too high, he needs to be able to reduce it by referring to it or by focusing attention away from a vulnerable member.

There is within group process a 'unit' of experience. A particular issue is dealt with, and when it resolves itself, there is a lowering of tension. When the issue is not fully resolved, tension still attaches to it.

Group process causes the group identity to be built up. It may be scarcely possible for members to state what is happening, since it is a new experience for them; otherwise they would not be there. Group identity comes from the realization that the group is a safe place to be, where risks can be taken and encouraged and where a new mystery may unfold itself to the members. For this reason, the boundary of the group is a *temenos*, the perimeter which marked the precincts of an ancient temple. This is the religious description which attaches to the important psychological concepts of confidentiality and maintaining the group structure.

One way for a pastoral counsellor to conceptualize group process is by using the image of the labyrinth. The labyrinth is an important pre-Christian and Christian religious symbol. It represents a sacred journey and occurs on the floor of Chartres cathedral, where it could be walked as a symbolic journey to the Holy Land.

1. The individual approaches the perimeter of the maze, and paces out its circumference. He concerns himself with practicalities, boundaries of group, seating, setting, etc. As he approaches the perimeter he begins contemplating the task. (What do we do here?).

2. In so doing, he begins to ask, 'Who decides the task?' (authority). By asking the question, he indicates that he has already taken his step inside the maze.

In a number of mazes one goes in quite a long way initially as if straight towards the centre, and then finds oneself apparently coming back out towards the edge, but going round just within the perimeter. The group process (middle stage) has started.

3. In this stage members are proceeding from wish to fear, balancing one against the other, seeking a resolution.

4. If one looks at the maze, one sees that it is composed of segments balanced against each other. As the segments fill up, agreement takes place within the group on the extent to which wish and fear are balanced.

5. The individual proceeds towards the centre, which in some mazes is an open space. In other mazes there is a fearful monster which has to be slain (the group fear). In others, there is no apparent centre; one passes it without noticing that one is already on the way back out.

6. There is the return journey. That is accomplished when one can put into words where one has been. The agreed words are the 'thread' which bring the person back out.

The Leader

The leader is responsible for selecting and convening the members. Six to ten is the best size, with a balance of sexes and ages. Some clients will be more promising than others. Yalom summarises those who are least suitable: the paranoid, the extremely narcissistic, the hypochondriacal, the suicidal, those addicted to drugs or alcohol, the acutely psychotic, the sociopathic. They are less able to make relationships and thus less able to benefit from a group. However, there are also very practical considerations, e.g. who is available and what is the tolerance level of the group leader, and what are the expectations of the group. A group may be able to have a containing effect where there are limited expectations of insight and personality change. It is probably important to avoid having one person in the group who is markedly at a different level from the others. This again depends upon the style of the leader as to how much he is prepared to balance the one in relationship to the others. But even so, a person who has considerably less ego-strength than the others is likely to draw the energy of the group to himself and become a block for the others.

The leader provides the structure in terms of time and place. If there is a fee, it may be payable to him or to the counselling centre. In the former situation he represents only himself, his reputation and experience; in the latter he represents the counselling centre. In this case, he bears in mind the figure of the agency behind him and what the feelings of the clients are towards it. He remembers that the clients are clients of the counselling centre.

By his presence the leader provides a degree of commitment and is an expression of hope. There is also some anticipation in the client that he is a 'healer'; there is an expectation of some skill. This is not just some neurotic dependence on the part of the client, but something to which the counsellor needs to respond with realism and humility. If he acknowledges it realistically within himself, he is more likely to be able to get in touch with the strength it conveys.

In the exercise of his role, he provides a balance between stimulating and allaying tension.

He fosters behaviour which increases cohesiveness and discourages behaviour which is destructive of cohesiveness; e.g. he draws attention to lack of attendance, lateness, and any tendency to sub-group (i.e. meeting at other times) which draws energy away from the group as a whole.

He encourages individuals to participate, or if he decides that this lessens the individual's capacity to find energy within himself, he will refrain from encouraging.

He restrains members who are taking over the group and inhibiting others.

He slows down the process if it is getting overheated.

He keeps the focus of attention within the group. Description of external activities is allowed only if attention is drawn to what it means within the group. What is important is the impact of what is being said upon members. The parallel between behaviour outside the group and behaviour within the group needs to be drawn.

He interprets the meaning of behaviour within an individual and within the group.

He nurtures the setting in which an individual may see himself and in which he and the group may reach 'consensual validation'.

He moves the focus and interest from individual to group and vice-versa.

He separates where there is collusion on the part of members, and forges a common theme where others are pursuing dissension.

He fosters the setting where an individual may discover his 'other self' through his experience of others.

He seeks to put into words the identity of the group-as-a-whole.

The individual member
The experience of group counselling for the individual member includes some of the following.

He experiences 'unreality' within 'reality'. The reaction of many individuals in a group for the first time is: 'This is weird. This is odd. Here were are sitting around and we are talking ordinary language the way we do the rest of our life, but it doesn't seem the same. After all, where does it happen that when you ask a question, you don't get an answer? Where does it happen that when you say something, somebody else may make a comment which at first sight does not appear to be related to what you were saying? It is very strange. I do not understand it, but it draws me to it and allows me to speak in a way that I did not know that I was capable of. It is very rich. And in some way it is totally real.'

He experiences confusion. In other situations he has been able to dismiss this confusion, but in group he will have to deal with it in a different way, allowing himself to stay with his confusion and allowing it to lead him where it will, to where he has not been before.

He makes alliances. It is natural for an individual to make alliances with others with whom he feels some affinity. But in group he is in the position of integrating, within those alliances, those whom previously he would have rejected.

He may well be drawn into a group alliance against the leader and only realizes it when it has happened.

He discovers that what is complementary to himself is what is alien to himself, that those whom previously he had spurned hold the key to his further development.

He discovers that something happens when it appears not to be happening.

The group is a very potent therapeutic force. Understandably, individuals may fear it. It can appear to be threatening, and it can be imagined that it will have a negative power, e.g. to expose, threaten, reject and exclude. Such power is undoubtedly there within the group. Awareness that this is so imparts to the occupation of being in group a sense of seriousness and bestows on the participant that respect which those who are used to working with natural forces have for the energies with which they come in contact. Occasionally, somebody gets hurt, but this does not discourage the human spirit from seeking its own power within the force with which it is co-operating.

Chapter 9

Marriage and Family Pastoral Counselling

One of the commonest occasions when a person seeks counselling is when he is having a problem in his marriage or when a member of the family has become a 'problem'. The underlying assertion of marriage and family counselling is that whatever problem there is belongs not just to an individual but to the partnership or to the family unit. An individual's problem is contributed to by the relationship of which he is a part and his problem in turn affects the relationship. Therefore, it is the relationship or the unit which is properly the focus of the counselling.

The second justification of marriage/family counselling is that the individual's environment is a very powerful force. Even if he benefits from individual counselling, when he goes back into his environment he may succumb to the same forces which previously moulded him.

Not only do marriage and family counselling have adequate justification for a separate existence, they have also evolved their own genre of counselling. Some practitioners would say that there is a radical difference between individual analytic therapy and the modern 'family-systems' approach; others would say that there is a complementarity and that the two can be used in conjunction. On the one hand, individual therapy is linear and historical; it attempts to stimulate insight in the individual into the causes of his functioning and it relies on him, in co-operation with his therapist, to uncover within himself the strength to rearrange inner forces. On the other hand, family therapy is interested in current interlocking relationships and circular interactions; it is the counsellor's task to intervene in these patterns as they occur in the session itself, and he has to be quite directive. The family counsellor acts as a communicator between the people involved and to do this he must be clear, simple and transparent, not just in what he says but in what he actually does. When this happens, interlocking patterns are changed, which in turn causes the underlying attitudes of the persons to be changed. It is an incomplete understanding of marriage therapy to practise an individual approach, just as it is insufficient to behave as an individual counsellor within group; both the group and the marriage have a therapeutic force of their own which is over and above what is available in an individual relationship.

There is a polarization of views here, and it is right to respect the professionals who hold to one extreme or the other; probably they have their skills for the very reason of their dedication to their view and they would not be so proficient if they felt that they were holding to some pale synthesis. However, there is no reason why a pastoral counsellor should not be able to achieve some moderate practical integration of the two views.

The interlocking nature of relationships
One of the major contributions of marriage counselling has been to draw attention to the interlocking nature of the relationship between partners. Each supports and is supported by the other in his maladaptive pattern. The counsellor, therefore, is faced in the session with not just the resistance of one person but of the two as individuals and of the interlocking unit itself. If 'she' gives up her depression, it not only has to happen that she finds new strength within

herself, abandoning old ways, but 'he' has to confront the idea of having somebody around who is less dependent and more interested in sharing power within the family agenda. Therefore, they both have an investment in maintaining the status quo.

The following are some interlocking patterns.

1. He is aggressive, sadistic and out to humiliate her; she is dependent, submissive and enduring.

He has a perfectionistic view of life and is lacking in the inner warmth which comes from having received easy affection. She has grown up in a situation where she has been largely ignored and has had a dominant parent; she has never felt worthy of receiving value. He was attracted to her because he felt that she was somebody who would do as he wished and affirm his sense of power. She was attracted to him because he was somebody who had qualities of drive which were lacking in her.

2. He is seemingly self-sufficient and is emotionally detached; she makes an intense demand for love. Her demand arouses his fears, which cause him to retreat and become even more detached. She perceives this as a humiliating rejection and gets the very thing she wanted least. She was attracted to him because she was looking for strength and saw his calm as strength. He saw her vivacity as independence and thought that she would be able to look after herself and achieve the same self-sufficiency as he felt he had. However, he did not realize that the vivacity was not the strength itself but the means by which she could gain the strength. She discovers that beneath his calm exterior, there is a turmoil of distress. There is mutual disillusion.

3. He and she are involved in a battle for domination over each other. They are severely critical of each other and most of their life is spent in arguments. They probably come from similar cultural backgrounds, where they have had to struggle for survival. What they recognized in each other was a fellow-sufferer; not having had the experience of equal and reciprocal friendships, they felt that they would be able to

face the hostile world together. However, they discover that the pattern of hostility to outsiders is one which can also operate between them. They cannot separate, because they would each be deprived of the source of their security and hope for survival. They continue to lead independent lives without gaining the recognition which would come if they were able to pool their resources.

4. She suffers from some chronic weakness and expects him to care for her, since she looks upon him as omnipotent and perfect. He has grown up as the only child and received adulation from his parents. He encourages her to think of him as omnipotent, since it affirms his inner sense that he is unboundedly special. However, his sense of specialness came at the cost of isolation from his peers and was fundamentally unreal. This he realizes and concludes that he can only get the reward he needs from somebody who is giving it to him neurotically. He is angry at her but cannot express it because he would then lose the reward he is getting. He is subject to depression, which has psychosomatic symptoms, which gives him a fellow-feeling with her in her chronic illness. The fact that both end up the same way affirms his pattern. Meanwhile, she becomes disillusioned when she discovers that he is not omnipotent, which causes her to be further depressed, and this increases her bodily ailment. He and she are both depressed and gain companionship from their inevitable state, which sets the seal on their individual patterns.

Into these situations comes the counsellor. The following are some of the steps open to him.

1. He works with one partner alone. The counselling follows the course which has been outlined in previous chapters. The purpose is to find those parts of the person which are repressed and allow them to speak.

The other spouse is encouraged to see a different counsellor. The separation of the work, two people working with two counsellors, lays the model for differentiation and initiates the process by which the neurotic interlock is prised apart. The individuals gain the idea that there are benefits in separation from their previous mode.

2. The counsellor sees the couple together, but in the session actually works with them separately, so that at times one partner is an observer to the process. There are advantages in beginning this way. The partner who speaks has the experience of setting out his story in a less threatening environment than before. The counsellor encourages him to go into areas which are new to him and to the partner. The observing partner begins to see that there are reasons why the other has behaved in the way he did; if there is sufficient co-operation between the two, he can continue after the session helping his partner explore new ground. Meanwhile, the counsellor's mediatory stance, which prevents him from making those reflex responses which took place within the marriage, is something for the observer to note and integrate within himself. The new middle ground is a metaphor in which all can share.

3. The counselling shifts from a linear, historical approach to a present-centred approach, e.g.

He: . . . (ending long account) . . . and that's why I didn't do it.'

Counsellor: (to her) 'How do you feel about what he says?'

She: 'I've heard it all before. There's nothing new in it . . .'

Counsellor: (to him) 'How do you feel about what she says?'

He: 'It seems as if I said the wrong thing.'

There are a number of options for the counsellor in this little vignette.

(a) He can focus on the fact that neither answered him when he asked how each felt. They each gave a reflex answer. To focus on the feeling begins to establish a space which may prove to be shared and, being a step back from the reflex interaction, begins to prise the system apart.

(b) He can say to her, 'What would be something new?' This confronts her system more forcibly. It takes the pressure off the husband, so that he does not have to play his 'badly-done-by' game. It is an invitation to her to co-operate and seeks something from her; it prevents her from being dismissive.

(c) He can say to him, 'Did you say the wrong thing?' This invites an adult acknowledgement rather than a childish plea from him and helps break his 'child' system.

(d) The counsellor can recognize the quality of what is being said and like a good parent provide some nurturing to two needy children. 'From what you are both saying, I get some unpleasant feelings – bitterness, resignation, frustration, weakness, helplessness. This is the way you are both feeling. We can sit with those feelings and recognize them.' The couple have been prone to battle with words and miss the feeling content of each other.

(e) The counsellor can point to the impasse which has been reached and invite them to describe it. If successful, this becomes a joint project. It may take on pictorial language. What does the impasse look like? Where is it? What sort of impasse is it? Where is each person in relationship to it? How would one describe it? What sort of materials is it made of?

If there is a metaphor, which is agreed, the life of the metaphor becomes the middle ground in which all participate. If one is not able to participate, this becomes a question for negotiation. What is there about the present which makes it difficult to join in? The impasse itself is used as the vehicle for communication.

The success of the counsellor's approach depends upon the tenacity with which he can hold on to the direction. If he goes too fast, somebody gets left behind. Then he has to ask, 'Where did we lose you?' 'Can you find your way back to us?' or, more cajolingly, 'Now we set out with an agreement to try and work on our difficulties. What can you put into the pot at this stage?' The counsellor has to judge when some positive direction is needed and when he may be doing all the work himself rather than getting the others to find new resources within themselves.

When confronted with conflict, the counsellor's strategy is:

(a) try and uncover the antecedents,
(b) space out the episodes,
(c) stay with the present feeling,
(d) encourage movement through the impasse,
(e) identify what common quality is there.

The counsellor has some more directive responses which are available to him. He can invite one spouse to role-play the other. In this case, the woman is invited to recount her husband's dismal life story, which she has heard so many times before. It is better for the counsellor to make an introduction. Thus, for instance, 'I know this is going to be unusual for you, but we find in marriage counselling that it sometimes helps to do these rather unusual things. When two people live together, they develop strong interlocking patterns. Doing something like a role-play has the advantage of getting us out of these established patterns.'

Securing the agreement of the two people for this exercise is a major factor in itself. It is a process of negotiation in which the counsellor is both gentle and firm. His firmness is what is needed to penetrate the collusive resistance of the pair. Having gained their agreement, something important in itself has happened. They can be congratulated and affirmed in the step they have already taken. The counsellor gives them warmth and nurturing which they have not been able to give to themselves.

What the role-play achieves is:
(a) a realization of some of the feelings which her partner is having,
(b) an awareness of what the outside world looks like from within his internal frame of reference.

Another possibility is for the counsellor to get the couple to sculpt themselves in some way which makes a picture of their relationship. 'He' is asked to place 'her' in the way that he sees her. He may place her with his back to him, cowering in a corner or passing beside him, looking behind him when he is past. As the tableau takes place, each is asked how they feel in that position. She is invited to arrange the tableau in the way she sees it. They are then invited to make a synthesis of the two presentations.

If doing the tableau is unreal to them, they could be invited to imagine it and describe it.

A similar approach is to make use of art therapy. Each draws the event as he sees it. The two pictures may be set alongside each other. The counsellor may make connections between the two or invite them to do so. If this is like 'play therapy', there is justification for it, in that each has missed out on a formative stage of communication.

Communication

At some point, 'she' is going to say something which 'he' hears in a different way from what she intended; he picks up the wrong half of what she said or she gives him the wrong half of what she meant.

'Don't you think it is about time that you got a new suit?'

This may have the desired effect or it may not. It consists of three blows:

'Don't you think . . .?', 'it is about time' and 'new suit.'

In fact, what she may mean deep down is:

(a) 'It is important to me how you look. I like you to look your best.'

(b) 'I shall come with you and help you choose.'

(c) 'Since you haven't bought yourself a new suit for some time, you may be feeling not at your best.'

(d) 'I too am feeling down and in need of some brightness.'

In (a) to (d), the speaker speaks out of her own feelings; she puts herself into the scene. Having the strength to do that means that she does not have to look to him for strength. Since she speaks out of her own feelings, she is able to recognize his more authentically.

'Why does the car never have any petrol in it?'

'Because you never give me the money to put any in.'

This exchange leads to looking at how the family finances are set up. It emerges that she always has to ask him for money and he is always left to fill up the tank after she has used the car. Awareness of the situation may lead to a re-arrangement. But it may be necessary to look at the situation more closely. How has it come about that he retains supreme power over money? What are the family and cultural influences, what is the feeling of power he needs to retain, what is his anxiety? How has it come about that she feels unworthy to have equal control? What has been the trade-off for her? For instance, she is able to continue feeling hostile towards him for withholding power and distances herself from him. He can do the same and they end up leading separate lives connected by hostility.

There are 'rules' in the relationship. He fills up the petrol tank; she gets the car during the day. He keeps the bank state-ment and the credit cards; she can have the cheque book and bank card with the £50 spending limit. She does the shopping. When the overdraft reaches a certain limit, there is a non-productive confrontation. There is a 'stand-off' for a few days, until the salary gets paid in, when there is a lowering of temperature until the cycle starts all over again.

One of the basic rules has been not to look at the pattern itself. This arises from a feeling of helplessness which is common to both. But it might also mean that, if they did look at the pattern, they might end up being together more and he would have to give up his squash and she her bridge.

However, once the rules are brought into the open, there is necessarily a changed situation. It is no longer the same game. Either the individuals have to change or they must make a silent pact with each other against the therapist not to change, continuing to come and continuing to complain to him. In this case, it may be that the therapist cannot be of any further help. Withdrawal at this point makes clear his integrity that he is unable to continue to work in such a situation, and it may be the best means of giving the individuals the determina-tion to effect a change. However, it may not have to proceed to this point. Pointing out the silent pact and inviting comment and a shift may accomplish a change.

Neurotic Conflict and Healthy Co-operation

The couple bring their neurotic conflict to counselling. What they do not recognize and what is the purpose of the counselling to expose is where they have a common enterprise.

(a) The 'petrol tank'. Both are afraid. He is afraid of what it will be like if she has more control over the money. She is afraid of the same thing. Both are afraid of moving forward. The joint enterprise is to explore what fear is like. The neurosis consists in the fact that, not recognizing fear, they become separated and their fear becomes clothed in hostility against the one who can help most. The symptom of the neurosis is self destructiveness.

(b) The 'new suit'. He has lost some sense of his own worth. She does not acknowledge that his low sense of worth has caught hold of her. She attempts to make herself better by making him better. If she recognized his situation for what it was, she would be able to see it in perspective and would be able to respond to it; she would realize that her own situation did not have to be bound by his. But, in fact, she attacks him and thereby increases his low self esteem. She probably recognizes this on some level and dislikes herself for it. They both end up feeling badly. He is bound to his status quo and she to him; both act out of their passivity. The way forward is for each to differentiate him/herself, he from his depression and she from her dependence upon him. The same forces for neurosis and health are in each. Once this is recognized by them, there is some hope that they can embark upon a joint enterprise.

Family Therapy

Mr and Mrs K. came to counselling when their teenage daughter, Joanne, became a 'problem'. She had previously been a model child. But now she had stopped doing her homework, she had started smoking and was going around with a 'bad crowd'. There was tension in the household, which was making life difficult. Mr K. was a busy executive,

Mrs K. a teacher. There was a second daughter, Susie, aged thirteen.

The Process

1. The couple came to speak about their problem with Joanne. Towards the end of the session, the counsellor asked the couple, who were somewhat surprised, that the whole family come the following week. Mrs K. doubted whether Joanne would come.

2. In fact, they all came, Joanne rather more reluctantly than Susie. The counselling would have had less chance of success if only mother and Joanne had come in the first place. The fact that all came gave the possibility of some restructuring of the family dynamics taking place in the session.

3. The counsellor was able to hear some of the parents' story and by gentle investigation to draw out some of their background, which the children had not heard before. The counsellor was careful not to expose the parents and it had the effect of taking some of the pressure off the 'identified patient'. Joanne began to feel herself as part of an 'adult' discussion, the agenda of which was the family. She was more prepared to talk. The counsellor sought to ensure that her story received an unthreatening response from the group, and, instead of allowing the session to become stuck in a parental-disapproval/teenage-rebellion syndrome, the counsellor moved on to hearing what the impact upon the family was. Susie was helpful in being able to say something of what the rows between Joanne and her parents did to the atmosphere in the house. The counsellor concentrated on what it was like for the family and how each felt about it. The focus on the central theme meant that no individual was being threatened. It became possible for the parents to speak out of their concern rather than behave as attackers.

4. Once some beginning rearrangement of the family dynamics had begun to take place, the counsellor asked to see mother and father. They could well have said at this point that they saw the problem as Joanne's and, if she was not

going to come, there was not much point in their coming. The counsellor agreed that it was important that they should meet together as a whole family and with various combinations, but suggested that because of the special relationship which parents have, it would be an advantage if there could be some sessions with parents alone. The parents agreed.

5. The work with the parents assumed that Joanne was a symptom of some dynamic that was operating within and between the parents. This could be variously conceptualized. e.g. Mr and Mrs K. co-operated on a fairly authoritarian stance. They had both grown up in deprived circumstances and had achieved success through hard work. They were living out of the expectations of their own parents and had short-circuited their own adolescence. Family life proceeded fairly smoothly so long as the children fitted into their efficient routine. Since their own feelings had been repressed, it was difficult for them to give value to emerging ones in their children.

There was room for some individual counselling to be done in order for them to explore their repressed inner selves. They had married fairly young without much experience of other members of the opposite sex. It would be helpful to them to explore their sexual feelings.

It became clear that the restrictions which were placed on themselves were contributing to the way in which they were dealing with Joanne. She was becoming the embodiment of their fears. But she was also leading them to get to know each other in a way they had not previously known.

Joanne came along to the counselling sometimes with the family as a whole and sometimes with a particular parent. Coming along with one parent was a symbolic push in the direction of rearranging the dynamics.

For her, coming along meant receiving some validation from her parents, whereas she had been looking for it exclusively from her peer group. The counsellor was trying to firm up the links within the family and contribute to nurturing the centre of it rather than allow energy to be drained away.

Overall, his strategy was:

(a) support the individuals, by giving each a warm response which they probably did not receive from one another;

(b) place his weight in different places, so that the imbalance was corrected;

(c) listen to the anxiety of each individual and follow it up in a historical linear way;

(d) focus on the unit as a group and lend his strength to the positive identity which the unit had.

The therapist

The family therapist is likely to have very clear values as to what is a desirable relationship and how it is to be achieved; he will probably feel that it is part of the process for him to say what his values are. The individual therapist is more likely to respond to a client's question by saying, 'What are your values?' 'What would you believe my values to be?' 'What are values?' 'Whose values are important to you?'. The family therapist is more likely to say: 'The purpose of these sessions is to provide a place where each individual may begin to find his uniqueness. Everyone must manifest uniqueness in himself, validate it in others, settle differences according to what works rather than who is right and treat all differentness as an opportunity for growth.' (Based on V. Satir). When he hears this, the client implicitly agrees to enter the internal frame of reference of the counsellor in the expectation and belief that he will be healed. The very openness of the counsellor is challenging and evokes confidence. The counsellor is saying, 'I am laying myself on the line; I expect you to do the same.'

The family therapist, therefore, is likely to be 'transparent' rather than 'opaque'. He will respond in terms of his own immediate reactions to what happens. He may give a running commentary on what he is doing, e.g. he will turn to the parents and say, 'Now I am going to ask your child some questions because I believe it is important that he be given a place of full value in this session.' To the child he may say, 'I think it is important that I speak to your parents and let us see if you see them in a different light from previously.'

The family therapist may prescribe certain tasks for the family members to do. Where there is difficulty in their achieving some agreement, he may ask them to write down what agreement has been reached during the week. This may mean that they cannot find anything, in which case the agreement they have made is 'not to find anything.' They may acknowledge that they did agree to something negative, e.g. they agreed that they would not decide who washed up. Sometimes the therapist will give a directive which requires them to do what they say they do not like. A family discovers that it always has a row on Saturday morning, when the freedom of the weekend is beginning. The therapist gives them a directive that they should have their row and, at the same time, he expresses doubts whether they would be able to cope with the freedom not having a row would bring. The family is challenged into changing its pattern. The family rule has been brought into the open, which means that the situation cannot be the same again. Saturday morning came and no one was able to start a row because everyone was watching for the first move.

The family therapist provides a refreshingly new direction in counselling. His advantage is that he can move from a longitudinal, historical stance to a present-centred, interactional, circular understanding of the process. By incorporating a shift within the counselling, he encourages the family to make a similar shift in their own interactions. However, opponents argue that if he pursues only an action-centred approach, he may only achieve some temporary change in behaviour, leaving the foundations of the person-ality unmoved; at worst, he could be accused of pursuing a gimmick.

It is probably important that a counsellor be able to shift backwards and forwards between an individual analytic approach and an interventive 'systems' approach. After all, if 'uniqueness' is part of the family therapists' creed, one would expect that the 'individual' approach would still have something special to contribute.

Chapter 10

A Local Pastoral Counselling Centre

The purpose of setting up a counselling centre is to suggest that counselling is a business-like function. Distress in a person is something to which it is important to give full attention and something to which hope is allied. A counselling centre states this purpose.

Name
There are as many as thirty counselling centres in Britain which would see themselves as doing 'pastoral counselling.' They have varying titles, e.g. pastoral counselling centre, counselling centre, pastoral foundation, pastoral centre, neighbourhood centre or some proper name.

Trustees
The centre is likely to be an independent charitable trust or a part of a larger trust which is offering other services. A group of people who are interested in the field may come together, a group of churches may sponsor a counselling centre or it may be the agency of a diocesan board. The trustees are the persons who have general control and management of it; it is their duty to ensure that the purposes of the trust are properly carried out. Such purposes may be expressed as 'the promo-

tion of pastoral counselling for those in need in the community with the object of assisting persons to lead more useful and purposeful lives by overcoming their personal difficulties within their families, their personal environment and their work.' Another stated aim is 'the promotion of maturity and wholeness of personality through a partnership of educational, religious and community services.'

Management Committee
The trustees may be expanded by the addition of various representatives from the community to form a management committee.

Director
The director of the centre needs to be a trained pastoral counsellor. The director reports to the management committee on the progress of the centre. The role of the director is to oversee the work of counsellors, oversee the training of counsellors, promote the work of the counselling centre within the community and relate to statutory and voluntary organisations.

Psychiatrist
It is important that there be freely available a psychiatrist whom the agency can consult. Psychiatric evaluations are needed on selected clients at intake or occasionally in the course of counselling. Counsellors need to be able to consult him. In a larger counselling centre, the psychiatrist would participate in a weekly staff meeting and client-allocation meeting.

Supervisor
Counsellors need to be members of a weekly supervision or consultation group. The supervisor will be somebody who has completed a full-length training in pastoral counselling (such as outlined in chapter one) or be a graduate of a recognized institute of psychotherapy or, in addition to a recognized

professional training, have undergone a prolonged period of personal therapy. If not trained specifically as a pastoral counsellor, he will be able to bring his own background into harmony with the world of pastoral counselling. It is desirable that the supervisor have gained accreditation through the Association of Pastoral Care and Counselling. This will have involved presenting to the accreditation sub-committee an account of a piece of work of supervision, a description of methods and aims of supervision, an account of his philosophical or theological position and a recommendation from two references. This accreditation has to be renewed after five years.

Counsellors

A counselling centre is more likely to grow when there is a group of people wanting to learn about counselling rather than when there is a group of people who want to begin counselling others. Therefore, the beginning of a counselling centre may lie in the creation of a training course in pastoral counselling. A minimum course is that mentioned as the Shorter Training Programme in chapter one. Such a course is for three years, thirty weeks of the year, half a day per week. If the half day is divided into seminar (one and a half hours) and group-work (one and a half hours), this produces 135 hours of each. If a student joins a weekly supervision group for his second and third years for forty-five weeks of the year, this produces 135 hours. If a student sees six clients during his two years in supervision for an average of twenty weeks each, this produces 120 hours' work. This degree of experience brings a student within reach of attaining the Certificate of Competence in Counselling awarded by the affiliates of the Westminster Pastoral Foundation, the minimum requirements of which are: seminars 150 hours, self-awareness work 90 hours, supervision 150 hours, counselling experience 120 hours. The Certificate is not a qualification but only a licence to practise within an affiliate centre under continuing supervision.

The seminar work has to cover the following areas:

Practice of counselling, what happens in the session.

Dynamics of counselling, the theory of counselling.

Patterns of growth and development, the stages of life.

Patterns of interpersonal interaction, understanding personality.

Philosophical/theological basis of counselling.

Theory and practice of group-work and family/marital counselling.

Community resources.

A group of people who undertake a training for themselves form the nucleus of a team of counsellors who will staff a future counselling centre.

It is desirable that the counsellors seek accreditation as pastoral counsellors with the Association of Pastoral Care and Counselling. This involves keeping a log-book over a six month period of work with clients, submitting it to the accreditation sub-committee and meeting with an accredited APCC supervisor during this time.

An increasing number of those working in the pastoral counselling field take out malpractice insurance policies. The author is not aware of there having been a lawsuit involving a pastoral counsellor in this country or in the United States; nor is it clear what would be the grounds of such a lawsuit, since it is questionable whether 'advice' or 'treatment' is given. It is debatable whether such malpractice insurance is a wise precaution or whether, by initiating it, the counsellor is claiming a role for himself which is inviting the risk he is protecting against.

Intake
The intake worker needs to be a counsellor who has wide experience and preferably someone with a medical or social-work qualification. The intake worker needs to be able to:

(a) make an effective link within a single session between the inquirer and the agency;

(b) elicit, within a limited time, the information which the centre needs in order to decide whether this is the right place for the person to receive help, since some clients require more support than a counselling centre can give;

(c) respond effectively to referring agencies;

(d) hold potential clients until a counsellor becomes available for them.

Appointments Secretary

This person receives the initial telephone call and makes an appointment for a potential client to meet the intake worker. This process is critical, since many clients do not know what they are looking for when they telephone; they may be even less able to outline why they are coming. The appointments secretary needs to be a person of training and experience, who can begin to relate to an individual in a counselling way, i.e. motivate and challenge, if necessary, and guide to a firm appointment. The appointments secretary may also act as receptionist, receiving calls from clients who wish to cancel. This is further reason for training and support. Many reception workers complain that they are put into situations by clients which they do not know how to handle.

Fees

Most counselling centres operate on the understanding that a client will pay a fee for the counselling. Usually this is on a sliding scale, and is something which is arrived at by discussion, perhaps over a number of sessions, between counsellor and client. The policy is that no person is turned away by reason of an inability to pay a fee; but also it is important that the client contribute something as an expression of his commitment to the process. Counselling is not something he can just receive. In practice, client fees go down if the client's ability to pay goes down, and up if the client and counsellor become aware that what he was paying is not a realistic contribution when set against his way of life as a whole.

Fees are, of course, an important economic factor in the running of a centre. They enable members of staff at least to receive expenses of office. It is also more likely that funds will be forthcoming from other sources if it is seen that the centre is paying some of its own way. A library may be built up for the use of counsellors; training events become possible; the counselling centre can have money spent on it so that it becomes a more attractive place to be in.

In a more elaborate counselling centre, there will be a reception desk, which expresses a business-like relationship between the agency and the client. It may be the practice for the client to pay his fee to the receptionist and present a receipt to the counsellor. Some counsellors believe it is more therapeutic for the counsellor himself to receive the fee on behalf of the agency, thus pointing to the reality of the transaction which is going on between counsellor and client.

Location

The building which houses the counselling centre proclaims its own message. Some counselling centres operate out of a number of buildings in different parts of the town, or even in different towns.

Some buildings are anonymous, which has its own benefit. Some long established counselling centres have a purpose-built suite of rooms. Highgate Counselling Centre, now twenty-one years old, has converted the upper floor of a church hall into a suite of seven counselling rooms, with a spacious waiting area and office space.

The rooms, of course, need to be sound-proof and be able to accommodate three persons. The furnishing needs to suggest warmth and comfort, but also business-like purposefulness. The location and decoration depend upon how the agency sees its purpose and its clientele. Some agencies will wish to be identified as ecclesiastical organizations; others will want to ensure that those who might be wary of such an identity will also make use of its services. One pastoral counselling service meets in the local health centre.

The counselling centre needs to express confidentiality, acceptance and lack of pressure. Where hourly appointments are kept, there can be difficulties in change-over between one session and another. It is advantageous if the counselling centre can show that it has grown to cope with its own hassles.

Type of counselling

Most counselling centres will offer individual counselling, and feel that they can graduate to group and marriage and family. This, however, need not be the progression. At least one centre is set up to offer only group counselling. It sees itself as a community service and believes that the most suitable mode to offer is group.

Training events

Once established, the counselling centre may well feel that it can sponsor events in the community, e.g. lectures on related topics and courses of an introductory nature. The centre becomes involved in educating the community to the issues in the pastoral counselling field. The centre could become the base for a field group of APCC. It also has much to offer in the way of help for the local church. Counsellors are able to go and speak to local organizations, help run projects in pastoral care and perhaps interpret a spirituality which has grown out of the experience of pastoral counselling.

Chapter 11

Pastoral Counselling in the Parish

If the focus of pastoral counselling is the mental, psychological, spiritual and physical health of individuals, groups, marriages and families, it must have something important to offer the local situation, which gives a new understanding to 'care of souls'.

The following are possible directions.

1. There are quite clearly individuals who may benefit from formal pastoral counselling. If there is a mode of effective help which has grown up as a result of psychotherapeutic practice over the past seventy years, it is a question of educating people to the awareness that they do not have to live with their problems for the rest of their lives. This involves positive referral and active support of the source of help.

2. Those who know something about pastoral counselling will be able to incorporate their approach into their everyday pastoral care. A pastoral counsellor may be able to recognize a need and mediate something authentic. His informal intervention may provide the individual with more options.

3. It is becoming increasingly popular to run ten-week evening courses which introduce pastoral care and counselling, (see chapter 1). Involvement in such a course will enable a person to understand that there is 'another way'. Interaction

with a person is not simply a question of having to 'provide' something for him. When a person complains, it is not a matter of giving a reflex answer; it is more important to try and understand what it means that the person is complaining. The listener does not have to take on board his complaints. It will be better for him to understand that a person complains, for example, out of a repeated inability to get for himself what he wants. The listener may be able to relate to the feeling of what it is like when life is not what one wants it to be. The basic need of an individual is thereby recognized. It is the business of a local congregation to be a place where a basic need can receive an unthreatening response. A person also complains, if that is his pattern, because he has grown up in a context where he has been the recipient of complaints. He has not lived up to the expectations of those who were important to him. Therefore, he is going to do the same to other people. If the listener does not realize this, he is going to feel that he has to respond specifically to the complaint itself. He becomes rather busy in responding to the complaint, which is a fruitless task, because it is simply replaced by another.

4. It may be possible to become aware of some of the underlying dynamics within the parish and to realize that just as a family may have certain maladaptive patterns of behaviour, which produce an individual who is a scapegoat, so the parish may function in the same way. Some examples of such patterns are as follows.

(a) The parish where there is a hidden war going on but nobody speaks about it. It has not been the practice to be able to speak about negative feelings; they go underground, the participants become involved in entrenched positions and the rest leave. There is evident disharmony in the family and the neighbours keep clear, (schizoid position).

(b) The parish where there is no intimacy and no true friendship; there is a distantness and a lack of involvement, (ditto).

(c) The parish whose message is that it is safe within, but it is unsafe and unrighteous outside. The mechanism of projection operates so the internal insecurity is attached to the external, forbidding world, (paranoid position).

(d) The parish where there is a scapegoat. Sometimes the congregation may scapegoat the minister; their own guilt feelings and sense of inadequacy are projected on to him, which he accepts because of his over-idealistic expectations of himself. There takes place a neurotic collusion as between two spouses, as a result of which the children grow up never feeling good enough and the whole cycle repeats itself, (ditto).

(e) The parish feels that nothing will make any difference; the resources it has are not going to change anything for the better; external forces are that much greater, (depressed position).

(f) The parish which believes that the golden age of the church is past; it existed in some previous century, but since then, all is lost. We can look forward, but a good future does not seem to be within reach, (ditto).

(g) The parish which is frenetically busy. It seeks to ward off consideration of its inner feelings by repeated tasks, (the obsessive position), or it attempts to gain its own inner sense of worth by fulfilling the expectations of others, (the hysterical position).

(h) The parish in which a particular organization becomes isolated, e.g. the choir, the Sunday School, the men's group or the women's group. The particular group becomes the rebellious child in the family; it does not feel valued or part of the whole and therefore becomes 'awkward', (the 'identified patient').

(i) The parish where the team of ministers have not resolved their interpersonal differences, which then 'overflow' on to the congregation, who do not know what is happening and understandably are frustrated by something of which they do not know the cause, (projection, denial).

After such a list, one might well ask, 'Who can be saved?'

It is a daunting task for a group to examine itself, but there is no reason why the courage should not be forthcoming. The confidence of the pastoral counsellor is that the parish contains within itself the resources to be able to move itself forward.

The steps towards growth might include the following.

(i) Recognizing and accepting the particular pattern which the group has evolved. This is more than half the solution. Insight into the situation brings its own strength rather than leads to further depression. It is the lack of recognition of the true state which is debilitating.

(ii) Allowing the expression of conflict. This is likely also to produce mediators.

(iii) Encouraging the expression of tenderness. This is more likely to follow strong negative feelings.

(iv) Allowing the assumption that it is the purpose of the individual to achieve a true individuation. It requires basic trust to enable this to happen. For the individual to achieve individuation, the unconscious has to free its powers; the power of the unconscious is autonomous, it has its own direction, which will come as a surprise to those around. But having said that, the trust is that 'all things work together for good'.

(v) Drawing attention to the 'metaphor' which expresses the life of the group.

This metaphor relates to religious language or experience, but it arises from the unconscious in a way which is unpredictable and which is not according to familiar past experiences.

A programme might be undertaken which would assist a parish to grow.

1. A trained pastoral counsellor meets over a prolonged period with a group weekly for at least six months. The group is agenda-less; it is not a Bible group, a visiting group, a quasi-psychotherapy group or a group for the exposure of personal problems. It follows the agenda which arises within itself from the interaction of members. The leader is likely:

(a) to encourage group cohesiveness,

(b) to allow an amount of feeling which is appropriate to the group,

(c) to relate the process of the group to the needs of the

parish and an understanding of religious faith; i.e. instead of asking 'How do you feel about that?' or 'What does that mean to you?', the leader may say, 'I wonder how what is happening now is important/important to the parish/important in our religious faith.' The focus of the group is on the emerging group identity and how that is understood by the members in terms of their faith.

2. The individuals in the group become leaders of the other similar groups within the parish. The leaders remain in weekly consultation with the pastoral counsellor, who ensures that any vulnerable members within the groups do not become over-exposed, or that heavily defended or aggressive individuals do not take over the group.

The purpose of the group is to promote the mental and spiritual health of the individuals and of the parish as a whole and is a contribution to the 'cure of souls'.

3. As the groups continue, attention is drawn to the 'metaphor' of the parish as it emerges.

4. The groups are encouraged to follow the direction which seems right to them. One may feel that it is its specific purpose to undertake a particular task. It is probably better if the group feels free enough to say that it will undertake the task for a specific length of time. It may wish to invite other groups to join it, but it is also hoped that they will feel free enough to refuse.

5. The groups are able to die without unrealistic guilt, appropriately satisfied at what has been achieved and providing the space for some as yet unknown successor to emerge.

Appendix 1

(Pastoral) Counselling Centres and Networks

Alton	Mr Ken G. Hunt, Director, Alton Pastoral Counselling Service, Friends Meeting House, Church Street, Alton, Hants GU34 2DS Alton (0420) 85996 or 63566
Beverley	Revd Peter Jaquet Leconfield Rectory, Beverley, North Humberside HU17 7NP. Leconfield (0401) 50188
Birmingham	Carrs Lane Counselling Centre, Carrs Lane Church Centre, Birmingham B4 7SX. (021) 643 6363 or 6151
Blackpool & Fylde	Mrs P. M. Cardew, 430 Ashfield Road, Bispham, Blackpool, Lancs. (0253) 867197 or 866976
Cambridge	Cambridge Consultancy in Counselling (0223) 67631 St Columba's Centre, 35A St Andrews Street, Cambridge. (0223) 357221

Chelmsford	Mr Frank Cooper, Chairman,
	Writtle Pastoral Foundation,
	31 Maltese Road,
	Chelmsford,
	Essex.
	(0245) 353590

Chesham   Peter Litrizza,
             20 Mount Nugent,
             Chesham,
             Bucks.
             (0494) 772282

Crawley   Revd Peter Addenbrook,
             Adviser in Pastoral Care & Counselling,
             Diocese of Chichester,
             The Vicarage,
             Colegate,
             Horsham,
             W. Sussex RH12 4SZ.
             Faygate 029 383 362

Crowborough Mr Colin Riley, Director,
             Crowborough Counselling Service,
             Crowborough Hospital,
             Southview Road,
             Crowborough,
             East Sussex TW6 1HB.
             Crowborough (08926) 2223

Croydon   Mrs Pat Branford,
             Croydon Pastoral Foundation,
             United Reformed Church,
             Sanderstead Hill,
             Sanderstead,
             Surrey CR2 0HB.
             01–651–1779

Derby	Secretary, Francis Centre, 125 London Road, Derby. (0332) 366863
Enfield	Enfield Counselling Service, Revd David Jamison, The Vicarage, Forty Hill, Enfield, Middlesex. 01–363–1935
Haslemere	Mr Reg Woods, Director, Haslemere Pastoral Centre, Methodist Church, Lion Green, Haslemere, Surrey. Client enquiries: (0428) 3762 Other enquiries: (0428) 4665
Hastings	Revd Edward Houghton, Hellingley Hospital, Hailsham, Easy Sussex BN27 4ER. (0323) 844391 Ext 322
Ipswich	Revd Christopher Gane, Counselling Leader, Concern Counselling Centre, 32 Constable Road, Ipswich IP4 2UW. Ipswich (0473) 54937

Leeds   TEMENOS,
Revd John C. Lacy,
8 Clarence Road,
Horsford,
Leeds LS18 4LB.
Horsforth (0532) 585827

Lichfield   Ms Kathleen Foster, Director,
Lichfield Counselling Service,
30a Tamworth Street,
Lichfield,
Staffs WS13 6JJ.
Lichfield (05432) 23370

Liverpool   Revd Miles Parkinson,
COMPASS,
25 Hope Street,
Liverpool L1 9BQ.
(051) 708 6688

London
Hammersmith AXIS Group Counselling,
  & Fulham   Mr Nick Owen,
Social Service Department,
Cobbs Hall,
Fulham Palace Road,
London SW6.
01–385–7971

Harrow &   Harrow & Wembley Counselling Foundation,
  Wembley   Sudbury Neighbourhood Centre,
809 Harrow Road,
Sudbury,
Middlesex.
01–902–7831

Highgate   The Director,
                  Highgate Counselling Centre,
                  Tetherdown Halls,
                  Tetherdown,
                  London N10.
                  01–883–5427

Kensington   Westminster Pastoral Foundation,
                  23 Kensington Square,
                  London W8 5HN.
                  01–937–6956

                  Richmond Fellowship,
                  8 Addison Road,
                  London W14 8DL.
                  01–603–6373

Southwark   Ms Pat Gibbon,
                  Director of Pastoral Care & Counselling,
                  Diocese of Southwark,
                  29 Fontenay Road,
                  London SW12.
                  01–673–8326

Tower Hamlets Salvation Army Counselling Service,
                  177 Whitechapel Road,
                  London E1 1DP.
                  01–247–0669

Westminster   Dympna Centre,
                  24 Blandford Street,
                  London W1H 3HA.
                  01–486–1592

Loughborough Loughborough Pastoral Centre,
                  169 Forest Road,
                  Loughborough.
                  (0509) 230499

Maidstone	Revd Peter Marden, Maidstone Counselling Centre, 60 Marsham Street, Maidstone ME14 1EW. Maidstone (0622) 55014
Marlow	Mr Alan Greening, Administrator, Marlow Pastoral Foundation, The Farmhouse, 52 Marlow Bottom Road, Marlow, Bucks. Marlow (06284) 2799
Milton Keynes	Revd John Keonig, 22 Stratford Road, Wolverton, Milton Keynes ME12 5LJ. (0908) 313162
Newport	Gwent Counselling Service, Mr Wilfred Bevan, Volunteer Bureau, 8 Pentonville, Newport, Gwent NPT 5XH.
Northampton	Revd William Simons, Director Northampton Pastoral Counselling Service, 54 Park Avenue North, Northampton NN3 2JE. Northampton (0604) 713767
Norwich	St Barnabas Centre for Christian Counselling & Healing, Derby Street, Norwich NR2 4PU. (0603) 25222

Nottingham	Clinical Theology Association, Lingdale, Weston Avenue, Nottingham NG7 4BA. (0602) 785475
Orpington	Revd L. Virgo, Adviser in Pastoral Care & Counselling, Diocese of Rochester, The Rectory, Chelsfield Orpington. (0689) 25749
Oxford	Isis Centre, Little Clarendon Street, Oxford OX1 2HU. (0865) 56648
Penarth	Dr E. F. Griffith, Director Penarth Pastoral Foundation, 34 Salop Street, Penarth, South Glamorgan CF6 1HH. Penarth (0222) 707738
Redditch	Revd Frank Godfrey, Counselling Centre, Ecumenical Centre, 6 Evesham Street, Redditch, Worcs. B97 4AN. Counselling Centre: Redditch (0527) 69582

St. Albans	Revd Dr Peter Liddell, The Vicarage, Kimpton, Hitchin, Herts SG4 8EF. Client Enquiries: Centre: St. Albans (56) 51748

Stroud   Michael & Diana Carey,
Pensile House,
Pensile Road,
Nailsworth,
Glos.
(045 383) 2114 or 4433

Southampton   Revd David Porter,
Southampton Pastoral Counselling Service,
Union Road,
Northam,
Southampton.
Southampton (0703) 39966 or 432295

Uxbridge   Revd Martin Eggleton,
22 Belmond Road,
Uxbridge,
Middlesex.
(0895) 33997

Warminster   Ms Lalage Fair,
The Grange,
Chitterne,
Warminster,
Wilts. BA12 0LG.
(098 55) 623

Welwyn   The Director,
  Garden City   Magdalen Centre,
                Gooseacre Health Centre,
                Welwyn Garden City,
                Herts.
                Groupwork only

West Kent   W. Kent Association for Pastoral Care &
                Counselling,
                The Revd Geoffrey Hyder,
                24 Commonside,
                Keston BR2 6BP.
                Farnborough (0689) 53186

Appendix 2

Association of Pastoral Care & Counselling,
  Revd J. Foskett,
  109 Monks Orchard Road,
  Beckenham,
  Kent BR3 3BJ.

British Association for Counselling,
  37A Sheep Street,
  Rugby CV21 3BX.

Contact (Journal sponsored by various pastoral counselling
  organisations)
  Mr C. M. Campbell,
  Branwood,
  Manse Wynd,
  Stour,
  Galashiels TD1 2QS.

Bibliography

Freud
Freud, S. *New Introductory Lectures on Psychoanalysis* (Penguin)
    On Psychopathology (Penguin)
    Two Short Accounts of Psychoanalysis (Penguin)
Brenner, C. *Elementary Text Book of Psychoanalysis* (Doubleday)
Brown, J. A. C. *Freud and the Post-Freudians* (Penguin 1967)
Clark, D. Stafford *What Freud Really Said* (Penguin 1977)
Hall, C. S. *Primer of Freudian Psychology* (Octagon)
Jones, E. *Life and Work of Sigmund Freud* (Penguin 1964)

Jung
Jung, C. G. *Memories, Dreams and Reflections* (Fontana, 1967)
    Man and His Symbols (Aldus)
Campbell, J. ed. *The Portable Jung* (Viking 1971)
Fordham, F. *Introduction to Jung's Psychology* (Penguin 1979)

Interpersonal Theory
Sullivan, H. S. *Interpersonal Theory of Psychiatry* (Norton 1953)
    Psychiatric Interview (Norton 1970)
Pearce, J. & Newton, S. *Conditions of Human Growth* (Citadel 1974)

Client-Centered Theory
Rogers, C. *Client-Centered Therapy* (Constable)
    On Becoming a Person (Constable)
Hart, J. T. & Tomlinson, T. M. *New Directions in Client-Centered Therapy* (Houghton Mifflin 1970)

Holistic Theory
Angyal, A. *Neurosis and Treatment* (Wiley 1963)

Gestalt
Perls, F. *Gestalt Therapy* (Penguin)
Fagan, J. & Shepherd, I. *Gestalt Therapy Now—Theory and Techniques* (Harper Row 1970)

Reality
Glasser, W. *Reality Therapy* (Harper Row 1965)

Transactional Analysis
Berne, E. *The Mind in Action* (Penguin)
    The Games People Play (Penguin 1964)
Harris, T. *I'm O.K. You're O.K.* (Pan 1973)

General Books
Colby, K. M. *Primer for Psychotherapists* (Ronald Press 1951)
Egan, G. *The Skilled Helper* (Brooke-Cole 1975)
Faber, Herje *Psychology of Religion* (SCM 1976)
Frank, Jerome D. *Persuasion and Healing* (Schocken 1963)
Frankl, V. *Psychotherapy and Existentialism* (Penguin)
    Man's Search for Meaning (Hodder)
Fried, E. *Active and Passive* (Grune & Stratton)
Fromm, E. *Fear of Freedom* (Routledge 1950)
    Art of Loving (Allen & Unwin)
Fromm-Reichman, F. *Psychoanalysis and Psychotherapy* (Univ. of Chicago 1959)
    Principles of Intensive Psychotherapy (Univ. of Chicago 1950)
Ford, D. H. & Urban, H. B. *Systems of Psychotherapy* (Wiley 1963)
Haley, J. *Strategies of Psychotherapy* (Grune & Stratton 1963)
Janov, A. *Primal Scream* (Sphere)
Kennedy, E. *On Becoming a Counsellor* (Gill & Macmillan 1977)
Laing, R. *The Divided Self* (Penguin 1965)

MacKinnon, R. A. & Michels, R. *Psychiatric Interview in Clinical Practice* (Saunders 1971)

May, R. *Man's Search for Himself* (Souvenir)
Art of Counselling (Abingdon 1939)

Menninger, K. *Love against Hate* (Harbrace)

Stort, A. *Integrity of the Personality* (Penguin 1977)
Art of Psychotherapy (Heinemann)

Truax, C. B. & Carkuff *Towards Effective Counselling and Psychotherapy* (Aldine 1967)

Wolberg, L. *Technique of Psychotherapy,* vols 1 & 2 (Grune & Stratton 1967)

Development of the Personality

Axline, V. *Dibs in Search of Self* (Penguin)

Baruch, D. *One Little Boy* (Dell 1964)

Bettelheim, B. *Empty Fortress* (Free Press 1967)

Bowlby, J. *Loss—Sadness and Depression* (Penguin)

Erikson, E. *Childhood and Society* (Paladin)

Flavell, J. H. *Development and Psychology of J. Piaget* (Van Nostrand)

Spitz, R. *First Year of Life* (International Universities Press 1965)

Wadsworth, B. J. *Piaget's Theory of Cognitive Development* (Longman)

Werner, H. *Comparative Psychology of Mental Development* (International Universities Press 1964)

Winnicott, D. W. *The Child, the Family and the Outside World* (Penguin 1973)
Playing and Reality (Penguin 1974)

Pastoral Nature of Counselling

Campbell, A. V. *Rediscovering Pastoral Care* (Darton, Longman & Todd 1981)

Clinebell, H. *Basic Types of Pastoral Counselling* (Abingdon 1966)

Jacobs, M. *Still Small Voice* (SPCK 1982)

Lake, F. *Tight Corners in Pastoral Counselling* (Darton, Longman & Todd 1981)

Lee, R. S. *Principles of Pastoral Counselling* (SPCK 1978)

Weatherhead, L. *Psychology, Religion and Healing* (Hodder & Stoughton 1963)

Wright, F. *Pastoral Nature of the Ministry* (SCM 1980)

Group Psychotherapy

Bion, W. R. *Experience in Groups* (Tavistock 1961)

Durkin, H. *The Group in Depth* (International Universities Press)

Whitaker, D. S. *Psychotherapy through the Group Process* (Aldine)

Yalom, I. *Theory and Practice of Group Psychotherapy* (Basic)

Marriage & Family Therapy

Ackerman, N. W. *Treating the Troubled Family* (Basic 1966)
    Psychodynamics of Family Life (Basic 1958)

Ard, B. N. & Ard, C. G. *Handbook of Marriage Counselling* (Science and Behaviour 1969)

Bach, G. & Wyden, P. *Intimate Enemy* (Avon 1968)

Ferber, A., Mendelsohn, M. & Napier, A. *Book of Family Therapy* (Aronson)

Haley, J. & Hoffman, L. *Techniques of Family Therapy* (Basic 1967)

Laing, R. D. & Esterson, A. *Sanity, Madness and the Family* (Penguin 1964)

Lederer, W. I. & Jackson, D. D. *Mirages of Marriage* (Norton 1968)

Satir, V. *Peoplemaking* (Souvenir)
    Conjoint Family Therapy (Souvenir)

Skymer, A. C. Robin *One Flesh, Separate Persons* (Constable)

Index

Cat Toy
Copyright©2006 Illian Obsidian
ISBN 1-60054-034-1
His and His Kisses Edition
Second Print Edition

Published by
loveyoudivine 2006
Find us on the
World Wide Web at
www.loveyoudivine.com

Dedication

Emerald

Sabrina

Marquie

and the lovely Ms. T

– always there for me

Cat Toy

by

Illian Obsidian

He ran. He ran and ran. He could hear the larger being, couldn't call him an animal, could he? Tree limbs crashing behind him. He tried not to let fear overtake him. How had it come to this? But he didn't know. He ran on.

He didn't know what the other wanted. He knew these people were aggressive, manlike humanoids, bigger than he. In fact, he had been sure he'd forfeited his life to the ugly, smelly one that had had him by the back of the neck. And then this one had happened along.

Yes, he'd been struggling then. The creature, the man? Either way he'd found him hiding in the forest, asleep. He'd been safely ensconced in the wreckage of his little shuttle. Well, perhaps not as safely as he'd thought.

Suddenly, he'd felt himself being jerked, tugged out of his little cubby. He'd managed to squirm free but the overlarge creature had tackled him and lifted him by the back of the neck.

For several minutes, he had dangled from the thing's hand. But the closer they got to "civilization," the more he'd worried. How would he ever get away if they managed to lock him up? What if they ate him? And this thing smelled so bad, so bad.

He'd just begun to struggle wildly when the other had come upon them. He almost looked dapper, the new one, black hair fluffing about his head in a dark mane and brushing his shoulders, framing his dark, fur-covered face. Both wore clothes but this one was clean, neat almost. He wore a long tunic, cinched at the waist and what looked like leather boots, hard to tell from his vantage, kicking three feet off the ground. The fur-covered face was lean, but broad across the nose, and his eyes were dark yellow, overall, much more attractive than the one that held him.

The new one said something to his captor. Offered him

something. The captor had made a sound that could have been a snort of derision.

The large man, that was all he could call him, a man, had reached out and somehow sliced the stinky captor. The yowling one let go and he took off.

Now though, his breath was coming in short, urgent puffs. He was frantically searching for which way to go. Right? Left? It didn't matter, he just ran.

Something, a tree branch, a clump of dirt, something tripped him. He hated nature as he careened toward the leaf-covered ground, rolling, sliding, and then, "Ooof!" the breath whooshed from his lungs.

A heavy weight landed on top, rolling him underneath. He felt a long, hard body pressed against him. Taut, densely packed muscles, a pounding heart, or was that his own? Terror whipped through him as he forced himself to look up.

The eyes looking down at him were almost black, though as he watched, yellow-green edged in around the long pupil. Cat's eyes. Not quite, almost cat's eyes.

He couldn't speak, could only gasp, but still he struggled, trying to worm away. Then he heard the warning growl. Yes, a cat's growl, low and tense. He froze and this man, this thing, cat man, bared his long pointed teeth in either a smile or a threat. He took it as a threat.

What could he do? He was trapped under the solid, lean body of a predator. Biting his lip, he looked deep into those leonine eyes for a long moment. He did the only thing he could think to do. He closed his eyes and angled his head, baring his jugular and trying not to cringe. He would die like a man.

Tryl stared at the vision of light underneath him. The slight form, warm, heart beating like a hummingbird's under his body. The hair, it was as bright and golden as a sun's ray, lighter even than that. As it slid across his fingers, it felt like flowing water, cool and slick. Those eyes - as blue as the deepest spring - how they stared in terror, in fear, and finally, in resignation, up into his own.

And then, this beautiful, bright creature did the unthinkable, offered his throat, gave himself to Tryl. And what could Tryl do? Only the one thing he most wanted to do. He accepted.

He opened his mouth against that fine, soft, hairless skin and tasted, running his tongue up the jugular to the jaw. The sweet smell, the fine, light, musky taste…. He licked, he nipped, and the body so beautifully fitted to his own collapsed.

It was as if the air, the substance drained away. In one smooth motion, Tryl stood and lifted the pale, light-haired creature in his arms. So sweet, so fine. He cradled the smaller body against his broad chest as he made his way from the trees and back to the city.

"Take me home Stft," he informed his driver once he arrived back at his conveyance. "Send a healer to my den, I will stay there today."

Too often, he'd been urged to choose a slave. Only the finest, only the most rare specimen would do, however. Until today, none had ever been good enough. Once again he tasted the soft flesh in his arms. Yes, this was a rare find. He would be trained. He would wear Tryl's mark. Tryl had finally found and chosen his slave.

No sooner had he arrived back at his den, placing the slight form gently in his bower, had the healer arrived. On his heels came Tryl's assistant, Narn, up in arms and concerned.

"Sir, is everything okay? I heard there was a disturbance…"

Tryl stepped forward, into the den's opening, and held up a powerful hand, eliciting silence from the other man. "Everything is as it should be. In fact, better than I would hope. Please go into the city offices in my place and make sure that my appointments are postponed," he ordered.

"Sir? What…." A moan from the other room cut his question short.

Tryl turned on his heel and strode back into his bower, leaving Narn hovering at the entrance. He saw the healer bending over his slave as the light, pale body twisted in the nest of soft skins.

"Shhh," he soothed, sliding down beside the light one, slipping his foot coverings off and gathering him up.

He wanted the slave to wake against him, his smell, his feel the first thing to penetrate his consciousness. He shrugged out of his tunic so that the small body would be in contact with his.

"Can you remove those coverings?" the healer asked. "I think he's been injured."

Tryl had suspected as much. It was clear to him that this new being was an off-worlder. Their entrance here was never easy.

Gently, his fingers skimmed the closures on the single stitched cloth that the pale creature wore. It covered him from neck to wrist to ankle, though it was torn in places. One hand slid down to his feet and slipped the heavy footwear off. He reached up again and worked the fastener down and slid the fabric off. Every centimeter of skin he uncovered was pale, white and pink. His little slave had light fur, no - not fur, hair, of gold and silver, dusting his arms and chest, legs, and even a little on the top of his feet.

"Out," he hissed at Narn over his shoulder, turning back again to look at the white-gold hair on the pale chest, and the darker pink nipples poking out from the soft thin tangle of light hair.

As he tugged the one-piece covering off, he found yet another lightweight covering at the slave's midsection. He slid that cloth over the thin hips and down, stopping a moment to stare at the quiescent appendage nestled in the downy, curly nest of white gold. His hand shook almost imperceptibly as he raised his fingers to touch the soft flesh, to touch the tight fur around it, lingering, so beautiful. Tight little furred sacks of skin hung below, like his own but small and soft, so soft and unprotected.

This body, this slave, was his property now; he resented even allowing the healer to look on this bounty of pink, gold, and pale beauty. And his scent, the sweet musky scent, he growled low and warning at the healer when he heard him inhale deeply.

"Look," the healer pointed to darker purple marks on the sweet pale skin.

"What is that?" Tryl asked, his hand still lightly cupping the limp sex of his new slave.

"He has hit something with his body, something hit him, he is injured. I've seen such things before. They aren't as visible on you or I," the healer explained, speaking rapidly. "Most of us are darker, and you can't see under our fur."

Tryl lifted his arm, trying to imagine what he'd look like without the short black fur that covered his arms, legs, torso. He couldn't. He knew his skin was dark even underneath and that no marks could ever be seen.

The hand that wasn't cupping his new slave's exposed sex trailed up the pale body to the throat offered so resolutely to him only an hour before. "He was injured today. The other marks may be older but these came today, when the poacher caught him. I saved him and I claim him," Tryl looked into the healer's face, challenge clear in his voice.

"Yes," the healer bowed his head in submission and Tryl turned.

And yes, Narn, too, inclined his head, his sleek, dark gray hair glistening in the half-light of Tryl's den. He'd snuck into the bower, well, not snuck, but come in. So now he knew.

"Mmm," the slave moaned again, stirring under Tryl's hand. He mumbled something. Words in another language and Tryl gathered him carefully up.

Those jewel blue eyes opened and he looked around

wildly, white gold hair slipping and sliding. One look into those vivid eyes and the healer gasped, so unusual they were.

"Be still," Tryl tried to calm him and those eyes, the color of a night sky, went wider still. "Don't, you are safe here. Don't fight."

The slave struggled even more wildly, water filling the blue and dripping down, causing yet another gasp from the healer and from Narn, who had moved further into the bower.

"Out! Get out, both of you!" Tryl hissed angrily. "You, to work," he growled at Narn. "You wait there," he ordered the healer.

The naked creature in his arms shook and Tryl could smell his fear, his panic. Those midnight eyes fixed on Tryl, knowing there was no escape, desperate.

Tryl reached down, pulling up thick furs and wrapping the slight body in them. "Don't worry now," he purred, stroking the long, slick hair. "You're safe here with me."

He continued to purr, the deep rumbling warming him, warming the slave, calming him. As he purred, he stroked the frightened creature, soothing him, lulling him. His own body, his own sex had grown painfully hard as he'd looked upon this creature of light beauty. He would take much pleasure in this soft, almost hairless body. Much pleasure.

First, the slave would need care, training. He would learn his place, which was wherever Tryl wanted it to be – within feet of him all the time. He would learn that he belonged, body and soul to his master. But holding him close, stroking and calming him, Tryl wanted more than pleasure. He wanted much more. He didn't know how much he could get from this lithe beauty, but he would take every bit he could and coax ever more from him. It wouldn't be easy, no, but he would force the bond.

The slave would get food, drink, warmth, punishment, all from Tryl. He'd wear Tryl's mark. His collar. He would learn, starting now.

The poor little thing must be exhausted, Tryl realized. Only a few minutes of stroking and purring and his eyes stopped leaking the water, though they seemed puffy. They would close and then he'd open them again, looking around, but Tryl continued to stroke, his deep purr rumbling through both their bodies.

His breath hitched a few times, Tryl knew he was fighting sleep. Finally those deep, gemstone eyes drifted closed and the breathing evened out. He stayed where he was for a few moments, noting the purple markings under the eyes, and seeing other scrapes and injuries on the fair skin.

Slowly, carefully, he lifted the sleeping weight away from him, tucking the furs closely around the new slave. A name. He'd have to name him soon. There were many things he should consider, he realized, as he edged away from the other. And as he did, a pale arm reached out to him, an unintelligible murmur from between those full, pink lips.

Tryl gently tucked the arm back under the furs and strode into the other room. There, talking quietly, he found both Narn and the healer.

"I thought I told you to go to the city offices and make my excuses?" Tryl growled, low and menacing. "You are not the only among us qualified to assist me."

Alarm shone in Narn's eyes and Tryl was glad. He'd long felt the younger was becoming complacent, too sure of his station. The only one among their number who should be sure of his place in this community was Tryl himself. He was the leader, the strongest. Not only was he the most intelligent, he was the most deadly among them. Strangers to their pride learned such things quickly. Those coming to trade were aware.

"Sir," Narn bowed in submission, "I simply wanted to ask – to learn what you knew of this slave. If I can help somehow to gather information for you."

"Where is *your* slave, Narn?" Tryl's voice was soft, a caress, almost a purr.

"She remains outside, sir. She awaits me," he bowed again, making sure his eyes remained low.

"Tend to your own and know that I have chosen. He will be my most valuable possession, do you understand?" Narn nodded his understanding. "Thank you. It showed much foresight of you to consider exploring the forest to gather information. Please do send someone to collect what you can," he praised. Now that things were clear, he would be nice. "Also, make my offices ready to accommodate him. He will remain at my feet at all times."

"Yes, sir," Narn answered, backing away to turn and make his way out of the room.

"You," Tryl turned to the healer. "What can you tell me now?"

"Your chosen is what we call a furless biped. He is compatible, certainly, and obviously male," the healer dipped his head at this; perhaps worried that Tryl would be angered at any reference to his slave's genitalia. "He will need to be fed and treated as we do our young. The teeth of this type of biped are softer, more blunt than our own. His meat must be cooked. He will need to eat plants for the fiber. He won't have claws, only soft fingernails."

Tryl nodded. He'd suspected some of what he was being told. The slave's eyes were round, the pupils within also round. He wouldn't be able to use the low light as their kind could. His almost hairless state would mean that he'd be cold and would need covering. Most slaves did wear covering but Tryl would have to consider long and hard how he would clothe his new slave. And no claws... He would be defenseless but for Tryl.

"His health? Is he in pain? Do we have medicines for him? What of his genetic makeup? Will our herbs hurt him?"

"I have some knowledge of these furless ones," the healer began. "My father knew of another who had a furless slave. I can treat this one for you. I can give you herbs for his pain and to help him sleep and heal. His ribs are damaged and we'll need to treat them. If he can be made to move only moderately, we should simply let them heal. He's softer than we are but we will care for him."

Tryl sighed in relief. He'd been most concerned. It made him feel a little better to know he did have the means to provide for this being. One of his deepest fears, knowing himself as he did, was that he'd choose an exotic slave and grow attached to it, only to have it die because he couldn't meet its needs. He was intense and committed. Those traits, along with his physical strength and cunning, had guaranteed him leadership of their community. Sometimes those traits were a disadvantage, too.

"Do you speak the language?" If someone could, Tryl was certain that would be helpful.

"That's another thing," the healer began. Tryl narrowed his eyes at him. "Uh, his palate, it's not formed as ours is, his tongue – he won't ever be able to speak as we do. Maybe approximate, but never speak our language. And I doubt you or I can ever speak his."

Tryl nodded abruptly. He'd expected that might be the case when he heard the strange sounds the little slave made.

"There's another problem, sir," the healer faltered. Tryl glared at him. Another problem was NOT what he wanted right now. "I'm sure Official Narn will be of some help, but," the healer faltered. "We don't know how long he was out there, sir. We don't know how malnourished he is, and," he faltered again under Tryl's low growl. "he has a bruise on his head, sir," the healer finally blurted. "It's wide, at the edge of his hairline. I feel certain he hasn't suffered a brain injury; there shouldn't be any... swelling. He would be ... dead... by... now..."

Tryl's low and rumbling growl grew louder with every uncertain word.

"He's going to be okay, sir," the healer promised nervously. "He cleaned himself. His reactions to us are within normal parameters. His speech, though we don't understand it, is still known to him." He expelled a relieved sigh when Tryl stopped growling. "It is possible that he doesn't remember exactly who he is or how he came to be here, but his intelligence isn't harmed."

"Okay," Tryl took a deep breath. "Okay, I would have you prepare anything I will need for his treatment. And then leave."

"Sir," his thin hand swept toward a collection of medicines on a nearby surface. "It's ready for you, but I or an assistant..."

"No, I will treat him. You may return on the morrow to check on him. Understand? And be available should I send for you."

"Yes, sir," the healer fidgeted. "I'll call by at the evening?"

"In the morning," he countered firmly. "I will send for you

if I need you."

"Yes," The healer nodded reluctantly, backing toward the entrance to Tryl's den and then out.

He opened his eyes cautiously, reluctantly. He was so warm, warmer than he'd felt in... well in a while. He hurt, but that wasn't new. For as long as he could think back, he'd hurt. Still, he knew there was some other way to feel.

A noise drew him and he shifted, closing his eyes against the pain. He really didn't want to stir, but he knew he must. His very survival depended on it.

Opening his eyes again, he found the source of the noise. It was that man, the cat man. Well they all were, weren't they? They were all cat men. Someone, in his childhood perhaps, had had a cat. He knew cats. He liked them fine. And so far it seemed they liked him. He wasn't the mouse. He hadn't been eaten. Unless...

He met the eyes of the cat man, struggling to sit up, to move away. But the man reached out a fur-covered hand and laid it on his shoulder, shaking his head from side to side.

He bit his lip and stopped moving. The cat man stroked the hair back from his temple with two fingers, brushing a sore spot there. He winced and the large man stroked his cheek with the back of his hand. The fur felt good on his skin and he closed his eyes briefly, enjoying.

The cat man moved closer to him and he jerked, thinking he should pull back, but he managed to hold himself still. This self-control earned him another stroke on the cheek and a short purr.

He felt his lips curve in a smile. He couldn't help it. He'd always liked praise. Well, he thought he did, anyway. He wanted to think about that. How did he know what he'd always liked? There was something besides his living in the woods in the broken shuttle, but what?

The cat man tapped his cheek lightly and he looked at him, into those yellow-green cat's eyes. "Tryl," the man said, tapping his own chest.

He bit his lip.

"Tryl," the man said again, pointing to himself. The man lifted a finger and tapped him on the lips.

Oh! He understood now. He was to try to say the other's name. "Til?" he tried.

"Tryl," the cat man said again.

"Tril?" he asked.

"Tryl," was that a smile on those dark, leonine lips?

"Try l?"

Yes! A purr. He'd earned another purr! He smiled. The cat man, Tryl, stroked his cheek again. He then tapped his chest and tilted his head. But... nothing. He tried. He knew he was called something.

He tried so hard to remember. Something. He was called something. What? He furrowed his brow, trying hard to think. To remember. It hurt though. His head hurt and he felt his eyes fill. He shook his head, grabbing it with both hands.

"Shhh," Tryl purred to him. "Shhh," he soothed, pulling him close.

He knew he should be afraid. Some part of him was. But he hurt so bad. And he didn't know what he was called. Tryl seemed to care. Tryl held him against his warmth and rubbed his back, purring and making comforting sounds.

He relaxed against Tryl, sniffling, accepting the comfort and trying to get hold of himself.

"Yai," Tryl said. He brushed his hair back and said again, "Yai."

"Me?" he asked. "I'm Yi?"

"Yai," Tryl said.

"Yay?" he asked.

"*Yai*" Tryl insisted, and licked his temple with his sand-papery tongue.

He felt the hot blush creep up his chest and neck, burning his face. "Yai?" he asked, scrubbing at the moist spot with the heel of his hand.

Tryl purred loudly, pulling his hand away and licking him again, holding him close against his warmly vibrating body.

"Yai," he murmured, sinking against the furry chest, "I am Yai?" It didn't sound familiar but he liked it just the same. He had something to be called. He was more than "he" or "him" -- he was Yai.

Tryl sat holding his new slave, holding Yai, and smiled, purring. He wore only covering for his loins. He didn't want to scare the timid little thing. Every move, every sound made him hungrier for the beautiful creature. He was just so sweet. Yes, so adorable.

He could tell that Yai was tiring fast, the pain, no doubt. With a comforting rub to Yai's back, he slid away, going to collect the medicine that he knew would soothe him and help him heal and rest.

When he returned with the elixir prepared by the healer, Yai looked at him expectantly. He carried also a broth for him, hoping to get some nutrients into his malnourished body while he was at it. In all probability, he no longer felt hunger since he hadn't been eating regularly.

Tryl held the container of broth to Yai's lips and tipped it. Yai lifted his hands and held it in place, opening his mouth to drink. He took two gulping swallows before Tryl tugged it gently away. Disappointed but obedient, Yai let go and Tryl placed the vessel on a nearby surface.

Next Tryl pushed the elixir against Yai's lips. A little pink tongue snaked out, touching the small container of elixir. Yai made a moue of disgust, wrinkling his nose and pushing at Tryl's hand, turning his head away.

He had to drink it. Tryl couldn't allow him to push it away. His body needed the healing agents and the pain numbing medicines. Tryl growled a warning.

Those gemstone blue eyes opened on him and filled,

betrayal clear in them. The chin wrinkled and the lower lip began to tremble. Yai bit his lip as the water spilled over his long, sparkling lashes. Tryl groaned, brushing his thumb over the trapped pink lip and freeing it from the blunt white teeth. Never had his warning growl elicited such a reaction.

Tryl groaned again, knowing he was right but feeling brutal just the same. This slave was different, not of his species. Some things were bound to seem different, more threatening to him. And he was injured, Tryl reminded himself. The sweet little creature had started this day running for his life and ended it revealing that he didn't even know his own name anymore. In point of fact, the day hadn't actually ended yet, had it?

"You must," he entreated Yai. "You must swallow it so that you can get better."

Yai simply stared at him. After a long moment, he raised his arm and wiped the water from his face. Finally, he closed his eyes and opened his mouth.

Tryl tasted a tiny drop of the elixir and found it not unpleasant. With a shrug, he brought the vial to Yai's lips and tipped it, pouring the healing herbs into his mouth. The slight body in front of his tensed and shuddered.

Yai made coughing and choking noises, eyes scrunched, closed tight, and both hands clapped over his mouth. After a moment, he moved his hands, gasping and coughing as if he'd developed a hairball.

The faces he made were alarming, as was the bright pink and finally dark red color that stained his cheeks. He continued to make snuffling and sneezing noises, clinging to Tryl, no doubt fighting the desire to expel what apparently was a foul tasting liquid to him.

Tryl brought the broth back and pressed it to Yai's lips. He took a tentative sip, and then two. Finally, he finished the cup, a grateful glance aimed at Tryl. Purring in approval, Tryl stroked his back, giving him a moment to calm and let the medicine work.

Suddenly, Yai reached up, tugging at the fur of Tryl's ruff. He looked worried. No, he looked panicked. He was once again biting his lip, but with his free hand, he was cupping his genitals. At the same time, he brought his thighs together, one knee slightly above the other, pressed tightly. Ah, the universal signal for the need to urinate.

Tryl hid a smile and lifted him, carrying him to the back of his den where running water could always be found. On one side was a draining spring where one could urinate or defecate and the waste would be washed immediately away.

On the other side of chamber, a steady fall of water, lukewarm, allowed anyone who chose, the opportunity to clean themselves.

Setting Yai on his feet, Tryl stepped back, taking the fur Yai had been covered in with him. He watched as the naked pink and gold figure reached between his legs and lifted the rigid appendage, holding it and aiming a stream of yellow at the draining spring. Finished, he then turned and squatted, his back angled away from Tryl. And Tryl wouldn't deny a hint of disappointment. Yes, he wanted to watch this as much as any other thing his new slave would do. Anything that entered or exited this body was his domain now.

"Ayiee!" He heard. How had he missed the little pale figure plunging under the waterfall?

Yai turned this way and that, yelping from the pain and the almost cool water. Tryl stepped into the fall, reaching to capture his little possession and take him back to bed.

"Kean tho, Tryl, wan e kean," he made out. He wasn't sure what Yai meant but it was clear he had a purpose. And he was pleased that Yai had called him by name.

Alarmed, yes he was, though the dousing of water had cooled his libido just a little. He wrapped the almost hairless slave in the fur he'd been wearing earlier and strode back to the bower with him.

Laying him down on the bed, Tryl covered him in furs and went to find his communicator. Lifting it, he entered a code, and as soon as he heard the connection open, he snapped, "Send the two strangers to my den now. Make sure they're prepared for me. They can enter and wait."

That done, he settled down next to Yai and began to lick the long, slick hair dry. At first, Yai twisted away, but when Tryl began to purr, he settled, going so far as to open his arms and legs, almost in the manner of a sacrifice. Tryl was sure that the opiates in the medicine had finally kicked in and Yai was well and thoroughly anesthetized.

All his needs had been met. He'd been fed, medicated, bodily functions attended to, and now, he would sleep. While he slept, Tryl would clean, dry, and explore his body.

He licked the golden, satin hair dry with his rough tongue, combing it at the same time. His lips and tongue trailed down the delicate throat and over the prominent clavicle, brushing through the soft hair on Yai's chest.

The dark pink nipples, how they called to him. He gently rasped his rough tongue over one, delighting in how it peaked and hardened at the first touch. He licked his way across to the other, toying with it, teasing it.

Yai stirred, his hips flexing up, insensible though he was, mentally. Physically, his alabaster beautiful body was stirring to life, even if he was unaware of it.

Tryl's rough tongue followed the trail of golden hair down to the fully aroused sex of his new slave. His first impulse was to suck the tube of flesh into his warm mouth and savor the flavor. And then he got a closer look at it.

He gasped in horror as he took the velvet-skinned rod in his hand. The purpled head was mushroom shaped and leaking sweet, clear fluid. But the foreskin! Someone had mutilated his slave's sex. Tryl slid around next to Yai's hip to look more closely.

It seemed so bare and defenseless, a small scar at the hood where the glans was. Who would do such a thing? Had Yai been fleeing his abusers? Is that how he'd come to be in the trees at the edge of their settlement? Even Yai himself didn't know any longer. Tryl stroked the length of it, wondering.

Obviously it was still functional. It was full and engorged now. Tryl leaned down, touching his tongue to the shiny bulb. Oh, Yai tasted so good, so musky, but sweet. Much sweeter than any of his own kind tasted. He licked up the shaft, earning a little moan and another flex of the hips. He trailed his tongue through the exquisite golden curls, reaching under his loincloth to adjust himself.

Moving down to lay between Yai's legs, he lifted and

spread them. He slid his hands down to cup the round globes of Yai's rear and spread them wide with his thumbs. He stroked the puckered opening with his rough tongue, pausing at the tight sacks to taste, savor, suck, and then he took the entire six inches of rigid erection into his mouth, sucking and purring. At the same time, he pushed a thumb at the tight bud between the cheeks, breaching the muscle just a little.

"Uh, uh, uh," Yai groaned, pumping his thin hips up. The little sacks gathered and tightened still more as Tryl pushed his thumb in a little deeper, gently sweeping his tongue back and forth, and still purring. "Oh! Oh!" Yai cried out. His blue eyes flashed open as the cream spurted from him.

He deflated like a punctured sphere, collapsing boneless against the furs, drained and unconscious. Tryl carefully licked him clean and pulled the furs over him, leaving a last lick on his cheek. As he pulled away, Yai's mouth turned up and he muttered, "Ank oo."

Tryl didn't know what it meant but he knew it was something good.

Tryl wasn't just hungry. He was ravenous. Beyond ravenous. He needed to sate himself, quench his hunger on someone. That was why he'd sent for the two. So he could drive his aching flesh into their willing bodies and quench the flame his new slave had built in him.

He stalked into the front room of his den. There they were, the two slaves, just as ordered. Two male slaves from another area, a different community. While they were the same as he, furred, biped, they were a subspecies. Not exactly the same. They belonged to a slave-letter, someone who shared slaves for a price. There was no charge for Tryl. The slave-letter still lived. The price was paid.

They were of lighter color than Tryl's kind. They were similar, however. Their claws were smaller, their fur shorter. Brown flecked coats and lighter build, but they were hardy, just the same. He'd never heard them purr, didn't care to. And growl? That would be a mistake.

They would do for his purposes now. "Disrobe," Tryl growled.

They wore the typical garb of the slave, similar no doubt, to what he would clothe Yai in. The pants were thin, they slipped off and on easily. The tunics were just as thin, they slipped over the slave's head. Later Tryl would decide if he wanted a tunic that opened at the front or went over Yai's head. How he loved those pink nipples, he would handle them often.

The first one, he didn't care what their names were, had dropped his pants and was wriggling out of his tunic when Tryl grabbed a hip. The man froze. Tryl parted the furred globes of his rear and slid a finger into the man's hole. Yes, it was well lubricated.

With one hand, he reached into his loincloth and caressed his wide, hard sex. The other hand found the second slave, pushing his back so that he bent at the waist.

With no discussion, he slid two fingers into him, pulling his engorged staff from his covering, and aiming it at the first slave's anus.

"Spread wide," he growled and the slave did.

He slid his blazing length into the tight hole, pushing forward until he could go no further. Still sliding two long, thick fingers in and out of the other slave, he pulled back and plunged forward again. This unexpected movement caused urine to spill from the first slave, little dribbles hitting the floor.

He pulled out. "Hold yourselves open, both of you!" he rumbled. "You!" he swatted the parted cleft of the errant slave, causing a squeal. "Squat and bend forward and clean that up." Turning to the other slave, he pulled him nearer, fingering the hole between his open cheeks. Sliding a finger into him, he reached around and grabbed the slave's cock. "Watch him, look at him as he bends."

"Yes," agreed the slave.

"Do you like to look at that?" Tryl felt the slave grow even harder in his hand; he forced himself back onto Tryl's finger and his short, thick rod jumped in Tryl's hand.

"Yes," the slave sighed. "Yes, I like it."

Tryl added a second finger. "Lean over and hold his cheeks apart." The slave did as instructed, his stubby cock leaping and twitching in Tryl's hand. "Stroke him with your finger," he ordered, pulling his fingers out and moving behind the slave.

"Sir?" He looked over his shoulder and back at Tryl.

"Stroke his hole," Tryl ordered again.

"Yess," hissed the slave, drawing a finger down over the puckered, slightly open and leaking hole before him.

The other slave wiggled his rear end back, asking for more. Tryl lined up behind the slave, releasing his cock and holding his cheeks apart. He rubbed the head of his shaft up and down the puckered entrance in front of him.

"When I fill you, push your finger into him," Tryl told him.

"Yes, oh yes," the slave breathed. The other one kneeled

on the floor now, his ass in the air, holding his own cheeks wide.

Tryl could see the oil leaking down the kneeling slave's cheeks and over the furred sacks between his legs. The dim light of the room did nothing to obscure his view of the finger resting at the slave's hole, poised to enter.

Grasping the hips of the one in front of him, Tryl pushed forward until he was all the way in. As the broad, round head of his cock breached the tight ring of the slave's anus, the finger entered, slowly, steadily until both Tryl and the finger were buried as far as each could go.

"Fuck him with your finger, slave," Tryl hissed.

Holding the hips in front of him, he began. In and out, fucking the slave, quenching that hunger, watching the finger sink into the hole and come out again. His eyes slid to half-mast and he pictured fucking his own slave, soon, in, out, losing himself in that pale flesh.

He wasn't finished when he felt the smaller slave begin to orgasm. He pulled out and pushed the slave to his knees, dislodging the finger and causing the transgressing one to spill his semen down his legs.

"Bend over for him, he will finish inside you," Tryl growled, "I will finish inside him."

Hands on hips again, he guided one slave to fill the other. Pushing him to bend over, he sunk himself deep, ready to finish, needing to come. He slid out and in, faster and faster, causing the one slave to service the other at the same time. Harder and harder, building he felt the tingling, the tightening. And then, one, two jagged thrusts and the explosion.

Tryl flexed his hips, emptying inside the slave, feeling the tightening as the slave emptied inside of his other. Finally, he was done.

"Clean yourselves up. Clean the floor," Tryl ordered. "And tell your master his debt is paid."

Tryl turned his back on the two, going to the waterfall and rinsing the sex off his body. He didn't want his slave to wake in his arms and scent another on him.

He was in bed beside Yai before the two sex slaves had finished doing as they were told.

Yai stirred in his warm cocoon. He felt clean and comfortable. He didn't hurt as bad as the last time he'd awakened. He felt like... Like he had a hangover. And he felt like he'd jacked off the night before, to a really good image.

What was a good image? He didn't know. He'd never actually had sex with another being, not human and not any of the humanoids he'd met on his journey with the ... well his journey. He wasn't sure how he knew THAT, but he knew. He also knew that he'd jacked off a lot. That he had. Oh, wait! He did have a really good image. Yes. More than once, he and Karl, his academy roommate, had stood side by side and jacked off... um masturbated. He was older now, of legal age. Not jacked off, masturbated. And why could he remember Karl and not himself?

But he was Yai, wasn't he? And he didn't fly or have anything to do with any academy. Academy was school, yes. He knew that – and he didn't have anything to do with them. They weren't part of his life anymore.

Tryl, the cat man, he was part of his life. And Tryl had lay next to him throughout the night, purring. It had been warm and he'd felt safe. Those were two things he hadn't felt in a very long time. And he didn't wake up hungry in the night, either. That had happened often enough over the last... recently. That had happened a lot recently.

He felt a broad hand push the hair off of his forehead and looked up. Tryl. Yai tried to smile. He was still just a little nervous of Tryl. He'd growled at him last night. That was a little scary. Still, he'd cared for him and given him a name. And now look. Here he was, caring for him again.

"Ssss eee prrr, Yai," Tryl said. But then he probed at the sore spot on his forehead.

"It does still hurt a little," Yai confessed, making a face.

He struggled to sit up and the room moved wildly. Tryl

quickly wrapped an arm around him, easing him up, pulling the fur back from his chest to prod at his ribs.

"Owww," Yai complained, reaching a hand out and resting it on Tryl's wrist. "Hurts," he explained, rubbing at the abused area with his other hand.

Tryl looked hard at him for a moment and then nodded. At least he wasn't mad. He seemed like the kind of guy who was used to being in charge and wouldn't take kindly to being told what to do or how to do it, by anyone.

With a flick of a furry wrist, the fur wrap was removed from around him and Yai found himself sliding forward. He flushed scarlet, knowing that he was hard. Morning wood, Karl had called it. And he had it. Stiff as a board.

He tried to cover himself with his hands and Tryl grabbed his wrists, gently pulling them away. Exposed. He was completely exposed.

Tryl gathered both wrists in one hand and tapped the tip of his morning wood with his finger. Yai looked at him, wide eyed. And why didn't that wood wilt? He knew damned well that Tryl had some very, very sharp claws attached to those soft, furry fingers.

Tryl tapped Yai's erection again and then tapped his own chest. The meaning was unmistakable. His. Yai bit his lip. A warm palm encircled his erection and oh, it felt so good.

"Yai," Tryl said his name.

Yai looked into his eyes, nervous, unsure, even yes, even afraid. He'd never had anyone touch his sex before, maybe not even his mother. He didn't remember. And had he ever wanted anyone to touch him there? Karl? Not really, maybe a little. But Tryl... Yai didn't know how he felt, though it seemed that how he felt was superfluous.

Tryl cupped his balls and fondled them.

"I…. I have to go to the bathroom," Yai said in desperation. And he did, really. But that wasn't all he felt.

"Yai," Tryl said again, stroking him, still staring into his eyes.

Yai wanted to close them, he wanted to look away, but he didn't dare. Still staring into his eyes, Tryl dipped his head and licked the tip of Yai's shaft.

"Ah!" Yai yelped, alarmed and... Something.

Turned on. Yes, he was. That felt good. That thick, rough tongue, rasping over his so-tender hood. That did feel good.

Suddenly, Tryl sucked his entire dick into his mouth. "Ah! Oh! Oh, my!" Yai babbled, spreading his legs wide, unable somehow to even control his movements.

That leonine mouth opened wider and he felt the rasp of that sandpaper tongue caress his balls. Tryl released his hands and Yai fell backward, catching himself and leaning back, propping himself on his hands. Now he was even more exposed and open. Just at that minute, however, he couldn't be overly concerned about it.

Tryl began stroking Yai's inner thighs, running his tongue lightly back and forth, up and down Yai's genitalia. He couldn't help it, Yai was so absolutely overcome with the feelings singing through him.

And then Tryl cupped his ass cheeks and spread them. That's all it took. With a shout, Yai felt the heat explode in his balls and he was coming. Coming in Tryl's mouth. Coming and coming.

He collapsed against the furs and that's all he knew.

It was definitely too soon to fuck his little slave. Definitely. Still, he'd brought Yai to climax while he was awake. That would be a good thing… unless he'd killed him.

Tryl ran a hand across the sparsely haired chest settling on one of those delicious pink nipples. The heart below it beat on, erratically? Maybe, but it was beating.

He'd heard of this happening of course. It was rare that anyone, even a slave, would loose consciousness during sex. Something in Yai's eyes though. Something told Tryl that this had been new for Yai. If only he was sure how experienced this little slave was… Or wasn't.

Yai began to stir. Tryl leaned over and licked his forehead, an eye, the side of his mouth.

"Uh," Yai moaned, eyes popping open to reveal the deepwater blue.

No sooner did the eyes open than a dark pink crept up his chest, neck, and finally his face, staining even the tips of his ears red. Tryl could see because his affectionate licks had pushed the long straight strands off of one rounded ear.

Yai mumbled something unintelligible, as if Tryl would understand *anything* the little thing ever said. He brought both hands to his face, trying to cover himself from Tryl.

No, that wouldn't happen. Hiding from him would *not* be allowed. Tryl pulled the hairless, fine boned hands away from Yai's face.

"You are mine," he told him, licking up one palm and then the other.

In the absence of his own hands to hide behind, Yai tried to bury his face in Tryl's chest. Laughing, Tryl lifted his little slave and carried him to the back of the den, setting him down again as he had the night before, but keeping a hand on his shoulder.

Yai was none too steady on his feet right now. The call of

nature distracted him a little and he focused on his own needs.

When Yai finished, he turned; Tryl was almost done. His eyes were fixed on Tryl's large member, unashamedly? Possibly. Regardless, he couldn't look away. Once finished, Tryl unhanded himself, turning to look at Yai.

Yai gulped and looked up nervously. Tryl let out a short purr and took his hand, leading him to the cleaning water. It was warm and sluiced through his fur easily, soaking his thick mane of hair and trailing in rivulets down his pelt.

"It's okay," he soothed, realizing that his new slave was, in fact, completely inexperienced. "Touch me, Yai," he crooned, pulling the pale body against his muscled thighs.

Yai looked up into Tryl's eyes and then down to his full erection. Gently, carefully, Tryl placed one of Yai's hands on his rigid cock.

Yai's hand shook but he kept it in place. After a second, he lightly ran his pale fingers up to the tip, feeling the wrinkled foreskin gathered under the engorged hood. His touch so light, his fingers skimmed all over, as if cataloguing every ridge, bump, and wrinkle.

Tryl moaned, it felt so good and he wanted, needed more. Holding himself in check, he let the slave explore. Yai glanced quickly up, checking no doubt to see if Tryl was angry.

Tryl rumbled an encouraging purr and Yai smiled. Those full pink lips tipped up at the corners, and the little pink tongue poked out.

Reassured, Yai focused on Tryl's cock, his other hand coming up to stroke his heavy sacs as he took a firmer grip on the length of Tryl's rod. Yai's fingers barely met around it as he gripped, causing another nervous glance up.

"Mm," Tryl purred, stroking a hand through Yai's hair, another cupping his shoulder.

Yai concentrated once again on his task, on exploring and playing with Tryl's painfully hard shaft. He slid his grip up and down over the length, gathering the foreskin and pulling it up, sliding it down again as he did.

Backing up, Tryl spread his legs, bracing himself against the wall. They were out of the water now, covered in warm mist but not deluged. The sight of those alabaster hands skimming his dark flesh was so erotic to him.

The feel of those small, fine fingers, cuddling his balls, skimming his length, squeezing him – so good. So good. He wouldn't last much longer, that he knew. Yai's fascination, his very concentration as he pleasured Tryl, it was clear that this was new to him.

Sparks of heat, zaps of intensity, up and down his spine, gathering between his legs and then… he knew he was leaking. Pre-come clear and copious, weeping from his slit. He watched riveted as Yai scooped a finger through the liquid and carried it to his mouth, rounded pink tongue licking it off, blue, blue eyes closing to savor.

Tryl gripped Yai's hips as he came, urged even more by the feel of a stiff appendage prodding his thigh. Through slitted eyes, he watched himself come, purring and rumbling, entranced by the look of pride, accomplishment on Yai's face. And then… then the hot spill against his thigh and he knew that Yai was more than proud; he'd been excited, too.

When he finished, when his sacs were empty, he gathered his little slave and herded him back into the water, rinsing them both. Back in the bower, Tryl treated Yai with elixir, this time having sweetened it. That went much more smoothly than the previous night's treatment. He also managed to feed Yai half a container of milky plant mush before the elixir did its job, leaving Yai snoring softly in Tryl's arms once again.

"How will you mark him?" Narn spoke after a pause in the conversation.

Tryl had been in his den work area, talking with Narn. Narn's slave, Min, sat quietly at his feet, sewing.

They had determined to store the little shuttle found in the woods and Tryl would decide at a later time whether or not to let his slave see it again. He wasn't worried about more off-worlders. He'd spent a great deal of time and study ensuring that they didn't land on his part of the planet on purpose. He was the leader here and it was his duty to protect his people. All of them. From everything. Off-worlders crashed or even landed near his area from time to time, but it was always by accident, not invitation.

"His throat, I think," Tryl mused, after a few minutes. "I might have him engraved. I'm still considering."

"You could have him pierced as I have done with Min," Narn reached down and caressed a pointed, downy ear. Min looked up in adoration, purring softly.

"I could, but it wouldn't be seen. His ears are small and pink. His hair covers them."

Tryl was unwilling to divulge more about his slave than that. Already he could sense Narn's interest. If he described them any further, Narn would want to see. He wasn't sure he could keep from harming Narn after that.

"What of the marking ink? Could he become ill from that?" This was why he'd chosen Narn for his assistant. He was very detail oriented.

"I'll have to ask the healer when he arrives. I will allow no doubt that he is mine. No doubt at all."

"And how is…."

A noise stopped Narn's question and even Min looked up when Yai staggered into the room, tripping on the fur he was wrapped in. Tryl surged to his feet, attempting to intercept when Yai careened into him.

"Tryl," Yai gasped, grabbing at him. "Mere, az ost," he said, making no sense at all to Tryl.

"Yai? Why are you up and around?" Tryl asked, though he'd never told Yai not to get up.

Tipping Yai's head back and looking more closely into his eyes, he could see that something wasn't right. There was barely any of the deep blue showing, his round pupils seemed to take up the entire eye.

"S'loan, Tryl," Yai answered, seeming sure that Tryl would understand. When he didn't, the pale beauty began to get agitated, tugging at Tryl and babbling incoherently.

Tryl lifted Yai, both white arms snaking around his neck; sunlight head dropping to his shoulder in something like relief. "Contact the healer," Tryl snapped to Narn, "something is wrong."

"I'm here, sir," the healer spoke up from in front of Tryl.

"Follow me," Tryl growled.

He carried Yai back to the bower, bending down to lay the exhausted young slave among the furs once again.

"Na! Z'antz! NA!" Yai cried, bouncing up again, clutching at Tryl in panic. At the same time, Yai was brushing at his legs, slapping at his midsection, reaching around, squirming as if something were crawling on him. "Keen, Tryl, z'antz!"

"Oh no, oh no, no," the healer moaned, perhaps as sorry for what might happen to him as what *was* already happening to Yai.

"Speak," hissed Tryl, lifting Yai into his arms again, rocking him, attempting to soothe the near hysterical man.

"He has taken too much elixir," the healer explained. "His constitution," he sighed heavily, "I have erred sir, I have erred. He is seeing hallucinations."

"And what good does your honest confession do to my ailing slave?" Tryl snarled, only barely preventing himself from injuring the healer by remembering he needed his expertise, such as it was.

"It is his slight build, sir, his lower metabolism. I misjudged the dosage. But I can give him something to knock him out," the healer's voice had a pleading quality to it now.

"Do it," Tryl growled, "And see that you don't kill him, or be prepared to join him in the afterlife."

Visibly shaken, the healer scurried away to prepare another medication while Tryl applied himself to calming and placating Yai.

"Z'antz, Tryl? R ta antaz?" Yai asked, hands shaking, head nodding.

"No, Yai, there aren't any an… whatever, there aren't any. Shh, it's okay."

"S'oki, Tryl?" he looked wide-eyed at Tryl, his black pupils making his eyes look even wider. So trusting.

"Yes, Yai, it's all okay, I'm right here with you. Everything is okay."

"S'oki…." Yai sighed, calming still more, settling against Tryl's chest, seeking safety and reassurance. Tryl stroked his hair, murmuring to him softly.

"Sir?" the healer returned, timidly approaching the pair huddled in the furs.

"Yessss?" Tryl hissed.

The healer leaned forward, a sharp implement in his hand. Tryl reached out and stopped him.

"This will make him insensible, sir," the healer pleaded.

"He seems quite insensible already," Tryl sneered.

"Sir," the healer whispered. Tryl released his wrist and he pricked Yai with the implement.

"Aowwww, Tryl," Yai complained. The healer flinched, looking nervously at Tryl. Before Tryl could react, Yai's eyes began to droop, even though he fought it, in seconds, he'd crumpled against his master and was once again fast asleep.

"Sir," the healer spoke up again.

"What is it?" Tryl growled, patience at the breaking point. The day had started with such promise. He sighed. "What?" he managed to reign in his irritation.

"Official Narn suggested that you'd like to mark your new slave?" the healer ventured.

"Yes," Tryl agreed suspiciously, scooting out from under Yai and tucking him in once again.

"With this reaction, I think the ink perhaps might be unsafe, sir, but I offer another solution."

Tryl arched a brow at the healer, "Well?" he urged, growing impatient again.

"You can brand him sir. He won't know what is happening. The drugs," he explained. "Here, perhaps," the healer lay two fingers just below Yai's sternum.

Tryl growled a low warning. The healer snatched his hand away.

"He won't know, sir," the healer assured him.

Tryl nodded slowly. If he could mark Yai without causing him further pain or damage, it could ensure his safety later. And truthfully, he wanted some permanent symbol of his claim for all to see. Something that couldn't be taken off or put away.

"You're sure?" Tryl verified.

The healer nodded enthusiastically. "I'll prepare it, sir."

The world had become a very confusing place. Yai was certain he was dreaming. He'd woken only a while ago, completely sure that biting ants were crawling all over him.

He'd tried to explain this to Tryl but the giant feline hadn't understood him. He felt closer to drunk than sober, a lot like when he and Karl had inhaled the injector cleaner for the Laspician saucer.

He'd known what he meant but he just couldn't spit it out. He'd known where his feet were supposed to go, he just couldn't seem to operate them properly. But Tryl had been there. Tryl....

This morning, Tryl had touched him... hell he'd sucked him. Tryl had sucked him off. That's what Karl called it. A blowjob. But there had been a complete lack of blowing. Why didn't they call it a suck job?

And he'd touched Tryl. He'd been so big. Huge! But exciting, it had felt good to touch Tryl that way. His dick had gotten hard when he'd touched Tryl's. Would Tryl touch him again? He'd done it right, Tryl had come... shot his wad... he'd liked it anyway. They both had, he'd shot his own wad, too.

But someone was touching him now.... Not down there, but touching him. Yai fought to open his eyes; they were so heavy. Someone was putting something on him. Something gold. Shiny gold, some goldish metal. On his chest. He worked harder to open his eyes.

What was that cat guy holding? It wasn't Tryl. Who was that? Oh, no... fire? Fire. Fire! He had fire on the gold thing on his chest.

Shit! *Shitshitshit!* "Holy fucking SHIT!" he finally managed. "Shit! Ohmygodohmygodshitohmygod!" Yai shrieked, finally getting some kind of traction and scrambling backward.

The cat man holding the fire had dropped it, but the gold thing had melted into his skin. He tried to get away from it. After a second, two of his brain cells got together and informed him that he couldn't outrun something attached to his chest.

He couldn't claw it off, couldn't get close to it. All he could do was scramble frantically for the door to the waterfall. Where the fuck was Tryl? Had he abandoned him?

"Tryl!" he bellowed, running, stumbling, somehow making it to the water. "OhgodTryl!" he was sobbing now, the water running over him, steam sizzling from the gold thing in his chest. "Tryl?" And why did he trust Tryl? Just because he'd brought him sexual pleasure?

Tryl let this happen to him. He was a very assertive cat man. He probably made this happen to him. And there he was. Reaching a giant cat hand out to him. Yai couldn't help it. He wanted to stand and fight. He wanted to be a man. But he *was* a mouse just now.

He cringed out of Tryl's reach, sinking to his knees and falling over on his side. "Nonononono," he chanted. "Nonononono," he curled into a tight ball. He'd just make himself small; maybe he could disappear. The warm water would flow over him and wash him away.

The last thing he heard was the earth-shaking roar of a jungle cat ratcheting, ricocheting around the cavernous room.

Cat Toy

Yai was in some kind of a limbo. He sat on Tryl's lap, lay in bed with him, sat at his feet, whatever. Tryl spoke to him, though Yai didn't even bother to try to understand. Tryl soothed, purred, petted. Whatever.

Yai wasn't angry. He wasn't hurt. He wasn't happy or sad. He wasn't anything. He moved when Tryl propelled him forward or back. He sat when urged to. Urinated in the proper place at the proper time. He was just there.

Tryl dressed him in soft, loose fitting pants and a short sleek tunic that cinched at the waist. His boots were some kind of skin that fitted closely around his feet and were comfortable and warm. Tryl touched him. He fed him. And Yai just went along. Maybe eventually he wouldn't feel this way. Or maybe Tryl would kill him. Whatever.

He knew, somewhere inside, that Tryl was frustrated. Knew he was sorry about what had happened. Knew that Tryl cared about him. But he was property wasn't he? To be tagged and marked and put on a shelf. No, he wouldn't think about that. It made him feel funny. He liked the safe place he'd found.

Right now he was seated on his cushion on the floor between Tryl's feet. He rested his head on one muscular thigh as Tryl stroked his hair. He wasn't really asleep and he wasn't really awake. He'd been that way for days. Longer, maybe. He expected he'd stay that way a while. Unless Tryl killed him. He might. Yai wasn't good for anything was he? Whatever.

Yai sat listening to the hum of cat voices around him. He'd never understand what the hell they were saying would he? Except…

"They're just animals," he heard a whisper. "They don't know."

"They seem intelligent," another voice spoke now.

Yai froze. That was human. That was his language. He felt

Tryl shift against him. Maybe in reaction to his surprise.

He heard the same voice again, but it was speaking an odd cat noise. And then the whisper again, "We'll promise them to leave but we'll surround the area. Araspa, we have to. We need those metals."

Yai's limbo was over. He didn't like the sound of that. He didn't recognize that voice but he knew those words. Someone was going to cheat. Someone who spoke his language.

"Tell them we're just passing through, they'll let us by and then we'll attack later," the whisper came again.

They were going to attack. Hurt people... Um cat people, but still... they would hurt Tryl. Tryl who'd cared for him. Looked after him. Let him be hurt, yeah, but he didn't mean to. Probably. But these people were going to attack, maybe hurt him. No... he couldn't let that happen.

Yai tapped on Tryl's thigh frenetically. Surprised, even shocked, Tryl moved his chair so that he could look down. Yai could see him holding up one broad hand.

"Yai?" he asked quietly.

Yai shook his head frantically from side to side, but Tryl didn't understand. So he ducked around Tryl's massive leg and stood, brushing any wrinkles out of his fine clothes. Gasps could be heard around the room. Apparently it was a big deal for one of whatever he was to stand up and move around like that. There were several others sitting at the feet of cat guys all around.

Yai took advantage of the element of surprise and moved around the table. One quick glance told him that Araspa had a translator and the other guy didn't. He wished he could get his hands on one of those things. Right now, though, it was more important to pretend that he and the cat folk understood each other perfectly.

"Araspa?" he asked, sticking out his hand in invitation for a handshake. Stunned, the humanoid in question, not a human it seemed, took his hand and shook it.

"Greetings," the one called Araspa responded in English, the word coming through the translator at the same time and sounding quite a bit different.

"I am Yai, of the House of Tryl," Yai introduced himself.

Hoping that nobody... well, he was just hoping.

"Of the ... House of Tryl?" Araspa faltered.

Grinding his teeth, Yai tapped the gold symbol embedded in his chest, inclining his head toward Tryl. Tryl growled low in his throat and Yai dropped the other man's hand and stepped back.

"Now, Araspa, and whoever you are?" he looked at the companion. "I'm afraid I didn't catch your name. I did, however, catch that you want some of our metals? You want to tell us about that?"

The other man took a step toward Yai, eliciting another, angrier growl from Tryl.

"Metals?" Araspa tried to bluff.

"I heard you two talking about attacking, for the metals, why didn't you just ask?" Yai stepped closer. He knew his words were amplified over the translator. He hoped everyone was paying close attention.

The other man-type person stepped forward. He could have been human, Yai couldn't tell. "The House of Tryl," he spat. "You're his bitch, aren't you? You're that tomcat's boy toy, aren't you?" Yes, he had to be human. The phrase "tomcat" was pretty specific and "toy boy", yeah, that, too.

Yai could feel his face flush but he didn't back down. Maybe he *was* Tryl's toy boy. So what? Behind him he heard growls and gasps. Vaguely he wondered what "toy boy" translated to in cat language.

Tryl had been reluctantly watching the proceedings from a few feet away. That ended abruptly when Yai felt Tryl step up behind him, a large, warm palm settling on his shoulder.

The other hand he raised, and one finger at a time, extending his razor sharp claws. He stroked the side of Yai's face with his warm, safe hand, tipping the claw of his other index finger under Araspa's chin.

Yai couldn't make out what the other man was hearing, but his sidekick was unceremoniously escorted from the room.

The negotiations began again, with Yai sitting next to Tryl this time, and Narn on his other side. There were enough pauses, stops, and starts, so that Yai could tell that the translator that Araspa wore was not one hundred percent fool proof.

He still wished he had one. Some language between himself and Tryl was better than no language at all.

"This you can both use, of course. Any of you can," Araspa was saying. Tryl had been thinking along the same lines, it seemed. "It will translate for the one who wears it. Just know that it is flawed. Not all words can be understood. Not concepts, you see?" He shrugged, palms up.

Yai nodded, eager, pleased. He doubted that the translator would have prevented all that had happened since he'd joined Tryl. However, it certainly would have come in handy.

"We thank you for your forbearance, for your shrewd intervention and tolerance for our zeal in providing for my crew. I regret that I only have one translator to spare. Perhaps it will help?"

Tryl responded and Araspa held out a hand to shake, dropping it to bow to each of them. When the trio walked outside, two large cat creatures dressed in tunics similar to Tryl's came forward. They were followed by several smaller cat people who were pushing or holding or maybe just guiding some kind of trolleys loaded with ore. Yai assumed it was ore, anyway. It looked pretty dirty, as if it had come from the ground.

A group of human types met the cat types and relieved them of their ore. Araspa unhooked the translator from his ear and his tunic and offered it to Tryl. Tryl angled a curt nod toward Yai.

"This goes in your ear," Araspa murmured, showing Yai a little roundish, oblong thing. "This," he handed Yai a thin, flat, mesh-like square. "This goes on your tunic. It's pretty durable. It doesn't have to be too close. It's activated automatically when they are both worn."

"Thank you," Yai said solemnly.

"You're welcome," Araspa said just as seriously. For a minute Yai was sure he would say something else. Instead, his eyes landed on the gold crest embedded into Yai's skin. "Good luck to you," he said finally. And then he was gone.

Tryl kept an arm tight about Yai's shoulders as he escorted him to his, their, to their conveyance. He nodded at Stft, giving him a stern look. He wanted his to be the first voice that Yai understood.

Everyone seemed to realize that and avoided them. Even Narn, who began to move toward them, turned away after a moment. He would have to discuss with Narn all that had taken place. Later.

Right now, he was feeling a little bowled over and found himself fighting elation. He'd resigned himself to Yai's near catatonic state days ago. He'd gone so far as to contemplate intercourse – as a form of intervention of course. But when he'd fondled Yai and gotten no response, he just couldn't consider anything more.

It wasn't just the sex, though he wouldn't kid himself. The sex, and lack thereof, would certainly have played a part in his decision-making processes. No, he'd also missed Yai. In the short time he'd known his little sunlight slave, he'd grown to care for him.

In truth, part of the reason he hadn't killed Araspa and his entourage, especially the aggressive one with the big mouth, was because their treachery, certainly their language, had snapped Yai out of the state he was in. For that reason only, he'd held back. The knowledge that they had a device that could allow him to understand Yai's speech or vice versa... He had to have it.

Neither spoke as Stft transported them to Tryl's den. Neither said a thing as they went inside, leaving Stft to his own devices. Finally, Tryl turned to face his little slave, determined to end the silence.

"Um, hi," Yai glanced up at him through the filter of his long, golden lashes. A soft pink crept up his cheeks and Tryl realized that he was feeling shy.

"Hi yourself," Tryl answered, tipping his chin up and sweeping a thumb across the soft skin of his jaw. "I've missed you." Yai took his bottom lip between his teeth, something he'd done before when unsure or uncomfortable.

"I... Um, I didn't mean to go anywhere," Yai mumbled.

Tryl bent over and licked the golden brand on Yai's chest. If nothing else, he was pleased that it had at least healed quickly. "This was ... I never wanted you to be hurt, Yai," he said finally. Whatever was between them in the future, he would always regret what had been a painful abuse when Yai was helpless and injured.

Yai nodded, turning his head away. Tryl saw the glistening blue in the low light.

"What is it, Yai? The water in your eyes, it only happens when you're frightened or sad."

Yai chuffed a laugh, inhaling a sniffle. "You're supposed to pretend you don't notice the water. It's not very masculine."

"I don't understand." Yai sighed heavily, turning away from Tryl. Of course, Tryl wouldn't allow that, turning him back. "Explain," he ordered resolutely.

"Kids, our young, or maybe women, they're allowed to cry when something is wrong," he explained impatiently. "Big, strong men are not supposed to ever show fear or anything."

"Well, you aren't a big, strong man," Tryl countered matter of factly. "You're my beautiful, small Yai."

Yai rolled his eyes and huffed impatiently. "You could at least pretend," he said through clenched teeth, causing Tryl to lose his composure and begin to laugh.

"Rrrrr," Yai growled at him, though Tryl ignored him completely.

Pulling him closer, fitting Yai's body to his, Tryl slid his hands into his pants, cupping his rounded bottom. It felt so good to him that he began to purr. One hand slid around in front to ease its way up under Yai's tunic.

Yai's breathing sped up, his body hardened against Tryl, soft skin smooth under one hand, a little nipple hardening to a point under the other.

"Tell me, Yai," Tryl purred, his own body heating with urgency. "Who has touched you this way? Who has touched you before me?"

He urged Yai closer, his small member rubbing against Tryl's larger organ. "Nobody," Yai panted.

"Nobody?" Tryl purred. "Only me?" His finger slid into Yai's cleft now, and how Yai clung to him, rubbing against him, tortured lungs gasping for air.

"Just only... Was ever only... Only you," he got out finally, golden head thrown back, one leg wrapped around Tryl's, holding on.

With a beleaguered groan, Tryl lifted Yai, carrying him into the bower to lay him down among the thick furs. He loosened the fastener on Yai's tunic, letting it fall open. One tug removed the first soft boot and then the second.

Slipping out of his own long tunic and knee length foot coverings, Tryl pulled off Yai's pants and then slid out of the loose cover he wore to protect his privates. His actions had been quick and efficient and now he lowered his body to cover Yai's.

The younger man still wore his tunic, though it was open around him. He wanted to hear what Yai would say, he wanted to understand his gasps and groans this first time he fucked him. And yes, if there was pain, he would know that too. He was very large; he was under no illusions there.

He stretched out alongside his little slave, stroking one thigh and the other, fondling his taut sacs while he sucked on Yai's left nipple and then his right. Tryl leaned over the top of him, licking and nipping at his lips, his fingers straying back down to that sweet, warm division between his cheeks.

"Spread your legs, Yai," he purred, cuddling the tight satiny balls in one hand. Yai did, reaching out for him, stroking Tryl's hard erection with his fingertips. "Feels good," he praised in a soft rumble, "I like it."

He stroked the soft balls again, his finger finding its way behind them. After a moment, he tugged Yai up and then across a thigh. "I want to see you, Yai. I want to look at you, taste you."

"Down there?" Yai gasped, as a large, furry hand swept

down his back and settled on one round globe, the other hand following suit.

"Yes, there," Tryl pulled the plump, muscled cheeks apart, staring at the pink and white pucker, tightening at the thought of burying himself in it. "So beautiful, Yai. I want you more every time I touch you."

One long finger stroked over the tiny hole dragging a deep groan out of Yai. He leaned down, running his rough tongue lightly over the nerve rich area. So sweet. Never had anything tasted so sweet. Every bit of his slave was perfect, he was convinced.

"Oh, oh, oh my. Man, oh man," Yai babbled, his leaking cock jerking against Tryl's thigh.

Reaching over to a little pot of oil, Tryl dribbled it on, rubbing it into the wrinkled opening, his finger sneaking in a little and a little more each time.

"I want all of you, Yai, you're mine," Tryl rumbled, sliding his finger in even deeper, urged on by Yai's sighs and moans. He would lose himself in that tight pale flesh. He would claim Yai tonight.

"F'ls good, Tryl, ah!" Yai's enthusiastic encouragement punctuated Tryl's locating and massaging his prostate. Tryl took full advantage of that to slide another and still another finger into him. As he stretched him, he applied a light coating of topical anesthetic to the muscle ring. He was so big, Yai was so small, and he ached, just thinking of easing his cock into the tight satin heat his fingers were even now caressing.

When Yai began to push back at the invading fingers, Tryl eased him forward, onto his knees, lining up his large cock and removing the fingers at the same time. Slowly he pushed up, pulling Yai down onto his burning length bit by bit.

"Oh, oh! Oh, oh, oh, Tryl!" Yai panted, "Oh! Oh!"

Tryl had to hold him still, easing him slowly, fighting the urge to slam upward rapidly at the same time. So hot, so tight, so viselike tight. Finally, Yai was impaled fully and seated on Tryl's lap, gleaming head thrown back onto Tryl's broad, black, fur covered shoulder.

"Okay?" Tryl rumbled. He was so close, struggling in a tight velvet he'd never before encountered.

"Yeah, yeah," Yai panted, "Oh, yeah."

"Sure?" Tryl had never cared before if a slave was okay, if he was enjoying their pairing. But this was *his* slave. His Yai. And it was his first time. Ever. What a gift. Such a precious gift. And, oh, how good it felt, unbelievable.

"Feels full, I... can't, can't believe I'm doing this...can't believe..." he groaned.

"Why?" Tryl asked, pulling back slowly, his own breath tight, staccato purrs like machine-gun bursts, so tight.

"Never, um, thought anyone would, never wanted anyone to... just never... Ohmygod!"

Tryl had pulled back and steadily moved forward, hitting Yai's prostate and grabbing his cock at the same time. With one hand across Yai's stomach and chest, the other between his legs milking his swollen cock, Tryl held him firmly while he began rocking in and out of him steadily.

"Tryl! I can't, Tryl!" Yai wailed, his balls pulling tight, his shaft spasming in release as his sphincter locked tight around Tryl's wide length.

Tryl couldn't control himself, wanted to be so careful with Yai but, oh how tight, small, and hot, burning hot the passage was. His hips pumped erratically of their own accord. Three, maybe four or five jagged thrusts and he emptied himself into Yai, holding him tight against his chest, front to back.

He sat, holding Yai against him, letting his own breathing return to normal. Finally, he leaned himself and Yai forward, pulling out of Yai carefully as he laid him down on the furs.

"Zit ways l'k that?" Yai asked. Tryl took a moment to decipher the mumbled question.

"No," he said finally, smiling. "This was very special."

"Mmm," Yai answered, rolling onto his stomach. "'m gonna be sore tomorra, huh?" he inquired.

"I'm afraid so," Tryl laughed, removing Yai's tunic. He could barely understand him anyway.

"G'd thng, g' a pilla," Yai mumbled, drifting off into a snore.

Tryl shook his head, licking a trail down Yai's back before going in search of a cloth to clean them both with.

Yai leaned back against Tryl's muscular thigh under the table. He could hear, and thanks to Araspa, he could understand what was being said.

He smiled to himself, blushing in the dim hideaway where only the other slaves would see. Yes, he was sore back there. Not horribly sore, but he was lucky that he didn't have to sit up straight like Tryl did.

Of course, Tryl wouldn't be sore. And he'd checked Yai back there this morning. That had been pretty embarrassing. He'd awakened to find Tryl bending over him, cheeks parted and a finger making its way into his well-used hole.

When he'd squirmed and protested, Tryl had delivered a stinging slap to his left cheek. His yelped protest earned him a smack to his right cheek. He'd wanted to be upset, but he was so hard, he thought he'd come. Tryl's finger was deep inside him, and rubbing that lovely place.

One, two, three, staccato spanks to each cheek, that finger rubbing him, and that was all it took. He couldn't hold back. He hadn't thought he could come anymore after the night before and there he was, creaming all over Tryl because of a spanking. A *spanking*. He'd gotten a spanking and it had turned him on.

He'd been so humiliated. When Tryl scooped him up to carry him to the "bathroom", the waterfall room, he'd turned his face to the cat man's neck. Tryl had watched him closely during his morning ablutions, but Yai had refused to meet his eyes.

He hurried from the flowing water, anxious to get away when Tryl caught him by the arm. The larger man was dripping when he grabbed Yai. He shook himself off, spraying water everywhere, making Yai twice as wet.

Tryl had hooked a finger under his chin, looking into his eyes, but Yai looked away. Unspeaking, Tryl grabbed a large cloth and rubbed him down. Finished, he wrapped him in it and guided him back to the bedroom – well the sleep room. There wasn't any bed, really. Just a huge pile of comfy furs.

Still saying nothing, Tryl helped him into his pants and tunic, at last handing him the ear bud. When everything was in place, he crossed his muscular arms over his broad, fur-covered chest.

"Well?" he rumbled. Yai was sure he could see an eye-brow arched, but it was hard to tell with all that black fur.

He'd kept his eyes down; hating the heat he felt creeping up his face. "Dunno," he mumbled, suddenly longing for the recent past when he couldn't talk to Tryl and never had to explain himself.

"Yai," Tryl growled, his tone slightly threatening. "What has you behaving this way?"

Yai groaned. No getting out of it. He had to explain. Why all this upfront honesty anyway? What was wrong with avoid-ance?

"I'm embarrassed," he gritted.

"Why?" And why wouldn't Tryl get dressed, speaking of why.

Yai rolled his eyes. He glanced suspiciously at Tryl. Was that cat bastard smiling? No, probably not.

"You... you spanked me and," he didn't want to do this. He didn't want to explain. Why was Tryl making him explain? He turned away.

Tryl slid his big hands around him and pulled him close. "I slapped you, here," he punctuated this by easing a large hand into the back of Yai's pants and cupping the abused area. "It made you harder, here," he reached his other hand into the front of Yai's pants and caressed his slightly hard cock.

"I know," Yai mumbled. Tryl slid two fingers under his ball sac and he looked up. He got it. He understood. If he didn't spell it out for Tryl right now, he was going to be sexually tortured to death. On some level, that sounded in-triguing, however, he knew it wouldn't just go away. "Stop that, or I'll... you know. And I can't because I already did."

Tryl rumbled a purring laugh. "You're a young male, Yai. You can probably come as often as there are minutes in the day. Tell me what distresses you about this morning."

"I can't believe you spanked me," Yai had huffed. "Well, I can kinda believe that," he'd amended. Tryl was the very definition of Alpha. Yeah, he could believe that, all right. "But I can't believe it got me excited and that I… well, I creamed myself. Okay, I didn't cream myself, I creamed all over you!" he bit his lip. It was just completely humiliating, that's all.

Tryl looked at him in confusion for a long minute before realization dawned. "Yai, you are my slave. It is my duty to see to your needs. And my pleasure. You needed care this morning. When I was treating you and making sure you suffered no ill effects from our fucking last night…."

"Aw jeeze, Tryl!" Yai couldn't help it… that's what it was, fucking, but it sounded so bad.

Tryl pulled him close again, purring, running his fingers through Yai's hair. "You, my sweet, little slave, are a romantic prude, aren't you?" Yai moved to look away again, but Tryl caught his chin and licked one side of his face and then the other. "It was your first time and a rare and precious gift to me, as you are. Everything about you is rare and precious to me." Yai found himself staring at Tryl's face now, assessing his words. "You belong to me, mind, body, and soul. Every bit of you. It is my responsibility and my privilege to see that you are cared for in every way. You needed treatment, and in administering it, I caused you sexual excitement. You needed to come, Yai. And your excitement rewarded me."

"I don't see how," Yai said in confusion. He really *didn't* see how. "I got off, all over your leg. But you didn't. You didn't get off."

"Get off?"

"Shoot your wad… um, you didn't come," he said finally, when Tryl looked at him shaking his head.

"Shoot my wad?" Tryl chuckled. "As a matter of fact, I did, uh, shoot my wad. Exciting you excites me a great deal."

"Wow." What else could he say? That alone had blown him away. All right, so he wasn't in love with being called a slave, though it sounded like Tryl really got the short end of the stick there. "So, if I'm your slave, what am I supposed to do?" he'd asked then.

"You do what I allow you to do, what I ask you to do." While he was speaking, Tryl had slid a fine, platinum and gold collar, well it seemed to be those metals. Anyway, he'd slipped a wide, fine, precious metal collar around his neck.

"What are you going to ask me to do?" Yai queried, not understanding the slave thing at all.

"Stay close to me. Eat your food. Be careful," Tryl ticked off on his fingers. "When I think of more, I'll tell you." And then he *had* smiled. "Fuck with me. I like that very much."

Yai sat under the table, shifting uncomfortably on his pillow, considering everything Tryl had said that morning. He might be called a slave, but somehow, he didn't really feel all that enslaved.

Yai moved against Tryl's leg again, shifting his weight from one cheek to the other. Tryl brushed a hand under Yai's tunic, caressing across his chest and causing a nipple to pebble as he stroked over it.

"We have many matters to attend to this day," Narn was speaking to him now.

Tryl had to fight a satisfied grin when he thought of the previous night, pretending to attend Narn's words. How worried he'd been about his slave only hours earlier yesterday. Yai had been completely unresponsive, no interest in or reaction to anything.

When Tryl had felt Yai's startled jerk during the meeting, and then his agitated tapping, he'd been shocked, stunned, alarmed. Even more so when Yai had snaked around him and walked right up to that alien. Off-worlder – not alien. That was an improper term. If Araspa and his assistant were aliens, then that made Yai one, didn't it? He wasn't anything bad. He couldn't help where he was born.

The best he could make out, Yai's brain had been overwhelmed from all the abuse he'd suffered in such a short time. First he'd been mutilated by his own kind, Tryl assumed it was his own kind, then he'd been sent away or else he'd escaped, only to crash into the wilds outside of the community proper.

"I've assigned soldiers to police the wilds on the outskirts, sir," Rahld, in charge of keeping the peace, spoke up.

Tryl shuddered running a hand through Yai's soft sunlight mane--no not mane; it was hair. Anything could have happened to him alone in the wilds, anything *had*, in fact, happened. It was only luck, both his own and Tryl's, that had saved Yai from unspeakable harm.

Ah, but last night, Tryl's eyelids drooped, remembering the feel of burying his aching cock so deep inside of his beautiful, willing little slave. The yielding ivory body welcoming him, urging him on - oh, what a reward that had been. Every moment of worry, every hard fought battle of patience, the coaxing, the care, all had been repaid the moment he'd heard Yai's voice, just saying hello. And when Yai hardened against him, then later sprawled across his lap, perfect body open to him, what a gift that had been for Tryl.

Their fucking—joining, he smiled to himself remembering his little slave's prudish embarrassment, their joining had been something very special.

"The health of the ruling community must be considered, sir," Narn interrupted his thoughts.

Yes, for now, he had to focus. A new healer was needed. Tryl growled, a high-pitched tone that spoke of his still boiling anger. The last healer had erred badly. He was currently seeking the services of a healer for his own injuries.

In point of fact, the previous healer was fortunate to be alive, depending upon how one measured quality of life. Regardless, Tryl would be responsible for procuring a new healer for the ruling community. He would need to visit his outlying realm and interview the healers in various prides.

Choosing a new healer was too important a task for anyone else. The leader had to be the one to decide who was best capable of treating the variety of species, including off-worlders, who inhabited the ruling city. He also needed to ensure a healer was available to remain to treat the patients left behind.

"I will conduct this day's affairs and leave on the morrow. Narn, you will stay behind to see to the order of our offices. Mank, you will accompany."

Tryl caressed Yai's shoulder. He could practically feel the questions Yai held at bay. That was funny in its way, considering that he and Yai had thus far shared so few comfortable hours together just relaxing and knowing one another.

His pronouncement made, Tryl slid his chair back and stood. As he did, he reached out and pulled Yai to his feet.

"Bring me a fowl. Bring cheese and fruit for my slave," Tryl spoke over his shoulder.

"Fruit?" he heard gasps throughout the room. In general, their kind did not eat fruit, though they did eat cheese. Yai needed fruit, however. He was different.

"Yes," he growled. "Cut it in slices for him."

He led Yai into his private work domain and pulled him against him. Laying one finger across his lips, Tryl stopped him before he could get started.

"We must go on a journey," he informed Yai. "It will last several days and you will see many parts of my community."

Yai rocked forward to his toes and planted his lips on Tryl's cheek, closing them. Quickly he pulled back, making funny faces.

"Ptuie!" he spat. "Ptah!"

"What was that?" Tryl laughed, seating himself and pulling Yai forward to straddle his lap.

"I was gonna kiss you on the cheek. But you have all that hair on your face," Yai explained.

"Kiss?" Tryl asked, confused.

"Um, you press your lips against someone – usually on a hair-free spot, and… press, kind of," Yai seemed at a loss now and his explanation trailed off.

"I don't have hair on my mouth," Tryl smiled.

"Oh!" Yai exclaimed. "You don't! Oh…" his excitement fizzled out.

"What's wrong, Yai?" Tryl purred.

"I've never actually kissed anyone for real," he fretted, his brow wrinkled as he considered Tryl's lips.

Tryl pulled Yai forward so that their groins met. "Put your lips on mine, Yai. I haven't ever kissed anyone either."

"Oh. No?" Yai asked, a half-smile flitting across his mouth.

"No," Tryl purred.

Yai leaned forward and placed his lips on Tryl's mouth. Carefully, slowly, Tryl parted his lips a little. Yai touched his tongue to Tryl's lower lip before tentatively letting it venture forward.

Tryl closed his eyes, purring softly, letting Yai be the aggressor for now. He knew who was in charge, but this was so sweet. So special. His own tongue searched, touching Yai's.

Gathering the smaller man closer still, he wrapped both arms around him. Yes, he liked kissing. He and Yai would become very experienced in this new endeavor. Yai groaned and leaned back in Tryl's arms. It was Tryl's turn to be aggressive as his tongue searched and tasted Yai's mouth.

Yai was sucking on his tongue, aggression passed back and forth like a winning baton when a voice interrupted their pleasure.

"Sir! Sir! Are you okay?" Perhaps Narn should learn about kissing, too. Later.

Yai sat on the floor of the conveyance. It was a hover car, he realized, and suspected that it had some kind of magnetic propulsion system. Thinking about it too hard made his head hurt, though.

He didn't even realize he was biting his lip until Tryl's fingers feathered across his mouth. When asked what was wrong, Yai just shook his head. He didn't want to think or talk about it.

Tryl gave him a hard look that promised questions later and then went back to talking to the other cat guy. That one made Yai a little nervous. His name was Mank and he looked at Yai like he was steak on the hoof. As a matter of fact, Tryl often gave him that feeling.

It was okay when Tryl looked at him hungry, but nobody else. He was used to Tryl. He liked Tryl, in fact. A good thing he did, too, because he belonged to Tryl. He fingered the medallion of precious metals embedded in his chest. Mind, body, and soul, Tryl had said. Yes. Mind, body, and soul.

His fingertips strayed up to the light filigree choker, well really, it was a collar, no getting around that, and would he rather it be a necklace or a collar? He didn't have a clear answer for that either.

As he sat on the floor at his master's feet, Yai watched the scenery go by, reflecting on his new lot in life. The cat people wanted happy slaves, so the windows of the car went all the way down. He could see out fine. And that was part of his new lot in life, wasn't it?

He was a slave. A slave. A sex slave? Maybe, but more than that. He was a companion, a pet of sorts. But Tryl didn't treat him like a pet. He was important to Tryl. Anyway, that wasn't what was on his mind now. Right this minute, he wanted to consider how he felt about being a slave.

He didn't remember much about his life before he met Tryl. All he could clearly remember was Karl. That was pretty informative in his mind.

He'd liked everything that Tryl had done to him, with him, sexually speaking. And he remembered Karl. Karl's face. Karl's smile. Mostly though, he remembered Karl's hand on Karl's dick.

Was that because he'd had a thing for Karl? Or had he been attracted to Karl's dick? Mulling it over, he realized that he had been attracted to Karl's boldness. He, Yai, was shy about sex. Karl had urged him to whack off together. Any time Karl had been aggressive, assertive, Yai had been powerless to resist.

So what did he have, what was his life? Simple really, his life was here now. His life was with Tryl. As his slave.

Absently, he stroked Tryl's thigh, making curlicue patterns with his index finger as he turned that idea this way and that in his mind. He often found himself embarrassed or intimidated by Tryl's actions or his responses. The reality was, though, that he needed what Tryl gave him.

"Yai," Tryl rumbled.

Yai smiled at him. Yes, he needed Tryl's aggression, needed his dominance. And maybe Tryl needed his subservience.

"Yai!" Tryl growled.

Maybe nothing, there couldn't be a top without a bottom, could there? Of course Tryl needed him, too. They were…

Tryl grabbed his hand and hissed, "Yai!" one last time.

"Oh!" his face heated a dark red. He'd been so lost in thought that he hadn't realized what he was doing.

His fingers had gone swirling and wandering up Tryl's leg and under his tunic, under his loin covering, and… Tryl lifted him up into his lap where the very hard evidence of Yai's wandering mind and fingers was apparent.

Yai squirmed a little, trying to get comfortable seated on the ridge of Tryl's erection. Tryl slid a hand under Yai's tunic and pinched his nipple.

"Be still, Yai," he hissed.

"Sorry," Yai hung his head and looked up at Tryl through

the fan of his lashes, deliberately flirting.

"Ugh! Stop that, too!" Tryl moaned under his breath, nipping at Yai's ear.

Yai relaxed against Tryl's broad, muscled chest, covertly dusting his fingertips over the shorter abdominal fur.

"What were you thinking of so deeply, little slave?" Tryl purred in a low voice.

Yes, that was another thing that turned him straight to mush, Yai acknowledged. That whole purring thing did it for him, no question. Mind, body, and soul. Yes, he was owned, property of Tryl the cat man.

"Tell me, Yai, what had you so distracted?" Tryl looked at the young man on his lap thoughtfully. He had a secret all right. Some private knowledge that wasn't forthcoming. And now he hid that secret behind an enigmatic smile, cuddling up to Tryl's chest, stroking his stomach.

Tryl glanced over at Mank and down at his complacent slave. Yes, it was time for a lesson in humility. Mank had lost his slave over a year ago and had an eye for Yai. But he knew his place. It wouldn't hurt to give Mank a treat while Yai got a reminder of his place.

"That's it!" Tryl rasped, tugging Yai until he lay sprawled across his lap.

With the sweep of one hand, Yai's loose pants were bunched around his knees, his tunic short and stopping at his waist. A bounty of pink flesh lay exposed over Tryl's thighs, half-hard penis between them, rounded ass defenseless.

"Tryl!" Yai yipped. "What the...."

Swat! "You belong to me!" Tryl growled. Smack on the other cheek. "Your thoughts belong to me!" A biting snap to the other cheek, now a rosy pink color. "Your body belongs to me."

Back and forth, right and left until both cheeks and thighs were a flaming red. Yai's astonished yelps had turned to sobs now. He didn't understand, and he was truly being spanked. Worse in Yai's mind, no doubt, he was hard as steel and wanted to come. But Tryl wouldn't allow that either.

Stroking the hot skin with one hand, Tryl slid a finger between the burning globes, inserting that fingertip into the clenching hole.

"Shh, Yai," he murmured, stroking, purring, finger resting just inside the muscle ring. "Shh," he crooned.

His open palm caressed the small of Yai's back, soothing, calming. He could smell the sexual excitement pouring off of

Mank who shifted on the seat facing his and Yai's, relieving the strain on his erect cock. Their eyes met as Mank stroked himself once through the thick fabric of his long tunic.

Finally, when the urgency lessened and Yai relaxed somewhat, Tryl removed his finger from Yai's warm and satiny hole, easing his pants back up the burning flanks. He carefully turned Yai around and settled the hiccupping young man at an angle on his lap.

In a gentle voice, he purred, "What were you thinking about so deeply, little slave?" Tryl repeated his earlier question.

Yai inhaled deeply and released a jagged breath. "Bout, bout my life," he sniffed. His chin trembled. "Just, I only remember a little," he sniffled. Aiming an accusing glance at Tryl, he mumbled, "Thought maybe we needed each other," and looked away.

"Hmm, is that what you thought?" Tryl purred. He gathered Yai against him, ignoring his shrug and his stiff response. "Well, you were right. We do need each other. First and foremost, though, you need to answer me when I speak to you and remember which of us is in charge." Yai took in another deep breath and expelled it, nodding sullenly. "Do *you* want to be in charge, Yai?"

"Huh uh," Yai sniffed.

Tryl forced himself not to smile or to tell Yai how very beautiful he thought those night sky eyes looked with the water swimming in them. He knew how much Yai hated when his nose went that bright pink color and how much he hated when the water dripped down.

Yai thought himself tough and strong. In his own way, Yai certainly was those things, but he was happier letting Tryl take care of him, and that was very appealing to Tryl. He was controlling and he liked to be in charge. That was probably putting it mildly. He was focused and obsessive. The fact that he'd found someone unique and in need of the very attentions he so longed to lavish on another, yes, Yai was a blessing.

Still, he would need reminding from time to time. He was a slave. Where Tryl was too hard, too rigid, Yai was too trusting, too easily hurt. They would balance each other out.

Yai angled a shoulder toward his face, meaning to wipe the water off. Tryl beat him to it, his rough tongue cleaning the salty tracks from his puffy, hairless cheeks.

"What else were you thinking about?" Tryl wondered, settling Yai more comfortably in his lap. Both he and Yai were still hard, though not quite painfully so.

"Was thinking," Yai yawned widely, nestling a little more closely into the crook of Tryl's arm. "Was thinking I like your fur, and I remember Karl's cock, and um, I like when you purr," he yawned again, rubbing the edge of his hand against one eye.

"Karl's cock?" Tryl locked eyes with Mank, who had a brow lifted in curiosity. "Did you...have much interaction with Karl's cock?" Tryl asked, breaking eye contact with Mank to look down at Yai again.

Another jaw cracking yawn, and Yai rubbed his face on the fur tufting out from the vee of Tryl's tunic. "Um, just, y'know, we jacked off together and I looked at his sometimes. Don't remember his face, just his dick," Yai mumbled. "Think he had darker hair than me and green eyes. His dick was bigger, only a little."

"Jacked off? Dick?" Tryl glanced at Mank who shrugged.

"Means," a yawn, "means masturbate. And cock. Dick means cock," Yai supplied, more asleep than awake.

"I'm going to fuck you later, little slave," Tryl gritted.

"Kay," Yai agreed with a soft snore.

Another quick glance told him that Mank was wrestling a smile though he seemed to be winning.

It had been such a long day. Yai didn't know how much time had passed while he slept during the lengthy ride. His rear end was sore and Mank made him very uncomfortable. Even more so now that the other cat man had watched him get a spanking.

Mank had watched Tryl pull down his pants, spank his ass like a badly behaved child, and to make matters worse, Yai had cried like a baby, too. Even worse than that, though, had been … Yai had to shift against the cushions. Just considering it made him uncomfortably hard—embarrassed, but hard all the same.

Mank had seen Yai get hard. Had seen Tryl put his finger in his hole.

"Are you in pain, slave?" Mank's smooth voice came from behind him, still in the seat across the way.

"No," Yai murmured, rolling to sit up, not looking at the other man.

He was a little shorter than Tryl, maybe bulkier; it was hard to tell. His fur was a bit fluffier, or maybe it was just not as black.

"You are ill? Hungry?"

"Um, I'm okay. Where's Tryl?" he did his best to avoid looking at the other man. A soft tap on his cheek brought his eyes up to meet Mank's.

"Ah, good. I feared you were unwell."

He was smirking, Yai was sure of it. He felt the despised blush staining his neck, his face. Definitely smirking. Doubtless that asshole was thinking about *his* asshole.

Yai was sure his head would burst into flames when the door opened and Tryl entered the small space. He sat down and pulled Yai over to straddle his lap.

"Mank, go assist Stft please. We have been offered accommodation here."

Tryl leaned forward and nipped at Yai's lips, lathing the small hurt with his sandy tongue, resting his lips against Yai's.

"He makes you uncomfortable, doesn't he?" Tryl asked when Mank left the vehicle.

"Yeah," Yai breathed against Tryl's lips, his face still warm, just thinking about it.

"It's because he saw you being disciplined, isn't it?" Tryl pressed.

"And, and, then he saw you um… you know, touching me back there," Yai stammered. Tryl knew him inside and out. He'd made it clear that he owned his mind as much as his body. Yai didn't know why he was nervous about speaking his fears to Tryl.

"He only saw what I allowed him to see," Tryl rumbled. "And that wasn't very much. He has been without a slave for more than two years now."

Yai didn't know what difference that made, but he felt a little better so he relaxed against Tryl and mumbled, "That's um, too bad for him."

"He has, ah, abstained for quite some time," Tryl went on, leaning forward again to dip his tongue into Yai's mouth.

"Oh," Yai sighed, touching Tryl's foraging tongue with his own.

"Who do you think is the more dominant? Mank or Stft?" Tryl asked, taking another taste between Yai's lips.

"Well," Yai wasn't going to take a chance on not answering another direct question. "Um, they're both the strong, silent types, but Stft doesn't take any crap off of anybody. He's pretty tough."

"I think Mank will come out on top, in more ways than one tonight. Shall we go see?" Tryl countered.

"See?" Yai was confused now. "On…Top? Oh! On top!" he went along easily as Tryl put him on his feet and led him out of the conveyance. "We're going to watch… well, watch Stft and Mank…." He let the sentence trail off, not really able to get his mind around what Tryl was suggesting.

Though they entered the den quietly, Yai supposed it wouldn't have mattered how much noise they made. The two cat men appeared to be fighting, Yai thought, but no.

Tryl stood behind him now, his hand dipping into Yai's pants, cupping his half hard genitals. Yai began to harden more feeling the girth of Tryl's excitement pressed against his rear.

Standing in the darkened doorway, Tryl's hand stroked his cock as the other cupped his balls, together watching the two in the room beyond.

"Suck it," was that Mank's smooth voice, an edge to it now? "Make it wet, Stft, that's all the lubrication you will get from me."

That *was* Mank! A warning growl low in his throat and Stft sunk to his knees, his long tunic all but shredded as he shrugged out of it, a loincloth his only covering now. Mank's flowing tunic draped open, cock proudly erect and full as it disappeared into Stft's mouth, reappearing shiny and wet seconds later.

"Again," Mank hissed. There it went, slick with saliva, as Stft sucked it down again.

Then Stft stood, turning his back to Mank, stepping out of his loincloth and then bending at the waist to brace himself on a wide shelf. Mank sucked two fingers into his mouth, pulling them out glistening as he parted Stft's cheeks with his thumb and index finger.

Yai looked on as those dripping fingers plunged between the dark and rounded mounds and deep into Tryl's driver's nether hole. And now he felt an oily finger enter him from behind. Tryl's easy grip fondled his cock as the two men watched their counterparts through the door.

Mank stretched Stft with his fingers briefly, and then replaced them with the head of his wet cock. Stft grunted as Mank entered him, and though the larger cat man slowed, he didn't stop.

"You okay?" Mank ground out, obviously holding back.

"Slow," Stft panted. "You are not small."

Yai, still staring in voyeuristic fascination, heard Mank chuckle dryly. At the same time, Tryl pushed Yai's pants down, pulling his hips back. He parted Yai's cheeks, sliding a well-lubricated cock between them.

"Ready?" Tryl purred into his ear.

Yai nodded, still riveted to the scene across the room, ten feet, maybe fifteen feet away. He bit his lip, swallowing a groan as Tryl's large, wide cock filled him. Stft was groaning non-stop now as Mank slid in and out of him.

"You like that?" Tryl purred.

"Mm, yeah," Yai fought to keep his eyes open, Tryl's cock caressing his button, feeling so good as it did, spreading him wide.

Stft was obviously feeling pretty good, too, and positively answering the question Yai had wondered about whether or not cats had a prostate. "Please, Mank, harder," Stft moaned, "Touch me."

"Since you ask so nicely," Mank smirked, reaching around him, his thrusts speeding up. His cock could be seen embedded in Stft's hole, thrusts pushing it in deep, pulling it out again.

"Ahh," Yai groaned when Tryl moved one hand from his hip back to Yai's weeping cock.

"Good?" Tryl inquired, mimicking Mank's actions, if not his words.

"Oh, god," Yai breathed, his balls tightening, his orgasm near as flashes of feeling whipped up his spine.

Tryl's large cock pumped in and out of him smoothly as Mank pistoned into Stft, both couples rushing toward completion.

"Uh, uh, uh," Stft grunted, creamy white spraying the wall in front of him.

Yai began to come, spurting over Tryl's dark hand as Mank began to jerk erratically. Seconds later, heat suffused Yai's insides as Tryl froze, spilling his seed inside of his slave.

Tryl slowed his purring, gathering furs and pressing them in around Yai as he backed away from his sleeping slave. The younger man was restless, his breathing still hitching and uneven from his long and emotional day.

Finally, Tryl eased out of the bower and into the adjoining room. Mank, too, was maneuvering away from his sleeping partner, though Stft's slumber appeared to be undisturbed by his leaving.

Once outside, the two walked together, naked, ready to hunt. Although someone would have to cook Yai's food, which was less palatable for him, Tryl could still feed him the same things the rest of the party ate. Their hosts would willingly provide for their needs, but Tryl liked to hunt, missed it, needed it.

"Stft gave in pretty easily this time," Tryl observed, glancing at Mank who matched his stride almost exactly.

"He's never sure what he wants. He just knows he wants it," Mank answered dryly.

"How long are you going to keep this up?" Tryl asked, stopping to lean against a nearby tree.

"Until I find a slave like yours, I guess," Mank shrugged, crouching in front of him, picking at something in the dirt.

"There aren't that many around," Tryl observed wryly. "You sure it can't be you and Stft?" he pressed.

"No. I like Stft, but he's not right for me. I'm too dominant and so is he. I don't want to fight for it every single time."

"That's what I thought you'd say," Tryl sighed. "Well, you could be in luck."

Mank looked up sharply. "Oh really?" he asked, eyes narrowing.

"The community leader here tells me of off-worlders, heading this way. Hairless off-worlders. Three of them. Their conveyance is similar to the one Yai was found in."

"Hmm," Mank observed. "And you plan to be here when they arrive?"

"I not only plan to be here, I have the bait," Tryl declared dryly.

"You think they'll... You think..." for once, Mank seemed to be at a loss for words.

"Maybe, just maybe, *you'll* get a look at Karl's dick," Tryl growled, pushing himself upright at the sound of a breaking twig.

The sound of Mank's amused chuckle was lost in the noise of pursuit as Tryl ran down a hooved beast, his colleague a few paces behind him, tackling another of the same.

Yai looked around the clearing. It was so nice and quiet. The birds called to each other in the distance. The hum of insects could be heard, though Tryl said it was the end of the warm season and they'd be gone soon. He'd also reassured Yai that the insects around here wouldn't hurt him.

Yai didn't hate nature, but he'd never had a lot of interaction with it. He was a space baby, never really living long on a home planet and never really living among any indigenous populations either.

He sat up straight. Another thing he knew about himself. He was remembering! He couldn't wait to talk about this with Tryl. He stood and took a deep breath. What was keeping Tryl? He'd eaten breakfast with Yai out here and then told him that he'd be interviewing a healer.

He'd bring the healer to meet Yai afterward, to see if the healer would be able to treat Yai's health as well. He wanted to interview the man or woman, whatever; he wanted to talk to them alone. If they met all of Tryl's other criteria, then they could meet Yai.

Yai didn't know what had happened to the last healer. He didn't ask either. Something about Tryl's body language whenever it came up, and the low growls, just warned him off. He reached up and touched the embedded medallion.

"Johnny?" Yai heard a whisper from the trees. He whipped around.

"Who's there?" he called, startled.

"John? Johnny?" He knew that voice. Who was it? Karl! It was Karl!

"Karl?" he turned this way and that, blond hair flying about his head. It had grown so much since the crash. Definitely not regulation anymore. "Karl!" he exclaimed, wrapping arms around the thin, slightly taller young man who grabbed him.

"Oh god, John-John, I thought you were dead! Shit!" Karl was babbling now. His light, chestnut colored curls bounced, they were a little too long, too, really, and his emerald green eyes sparkled happily. Yai looked into the face of his oldest, maybe only friend. "Damn Johnny, it's good to see ya!"

"John! My name is John... John Sailor. I'm ... John?" Yai stood in Karl's embrace, trying to make sense out of what he knew. It made his head hurt. He pulled away from Karl, rubbing his forehead. "I have to tell Tryl," he mumbled. "Tryl!" he called out.

"John! Shut up!" Karl jerked him around, holding him by both shoulders.

"But... I have to tell Tryl. He'll want to know. I belong to Tryl now," he explained, still rubbing above his eyes. How it hurt, like a brain cramp.

"Johnny, what's wrong with you? You don't belong to anybody. Well, maybe the government, but not... okay, maybe The Captain. Johnny!" Karl gasped his name. "What the hell is that? What happened to you?"

He was tentatively touching the gold embedded in Yai's chest. "Um, I'm pretty sure that was an accident. But I'm used to it now." Yai pulled away from Karl. "Why are you here? Did you come back to get me? Did you come back for me?" He didn't mean to sound hopeful. He really only wished that they cared enough about him to go to all this trouble.

"No, our power cells...." Karl began artlessly, "I mean, um," Yai stopped him before he could say anything further.

"Its okay, Karl, I don't want to go. I like it here. Tryl really cares about me."

"Who's this Tryl, Johnny?" Karl stepped close to him, reaching for him again. "I always thought maybe you and I could get together."

"Tryl is... um, he's... I guess he's my master. I'm a slave now, but that just sounds worse than it is. I have it pretty good here. Um, Karl, these people are cat men. So if The Captain is here, well, I'm pretty sure she's gonna piss 'em off. You know how she is."

"Master? Slave? Cat men?" Karl plunged a hand into Yai's silky blond hair. "Johnny, I think you got hurt pretty bad, huh?"

"Yai!" There was Tryl! Yai sighed in relief, turning to smile at him. "Who touches you? Come to me!"

Yai pulled away from Karl who stood, mouth gaping, looking at Tryl and then at Mank, who stood a few paces behind him.

Tryl held out an arm for Yai, who came to him nervously. "You aren't mad at me are you?" He turned, a sweep of his arm indicating Karl. "This is Karl. I've known him since the Academy."

"Karl, whose cock you've seen and liked to look at?" Tryl teased him.

Yai's eyes went wide, "I like yours better, I swear!"

Tryl cupped Yai's cheek with one hand. "I believe you. I heard you tell him that you liked it here with me and didn't want to leave. That pleases me very much, Yai."

"And Tryl, I was remembering things even before he got here," Yai told him in excitement, ignoring Karl almost completely.

"Johnny! What are you doing? We have to get out of here!" Karl had snapped out of his stunned stupor. "The Captain and Commander Lighter are just over the next rise! We have to get to them!"

Karl turned, giving every indication that he meant to run. Tryl nodded at Mank who was on the newcomer in a flash, taking him to the cool carpet of grass with a flying tackle.

The air whooshed out of him and Yai would have run to him but for Tryl's restraint. "He's not going to hurt him, is he? Karl's a good guy, Tryl, really!"

"He'll be fine," Tryl soothed. "Mank likes him, see?"

Mank smiled down into Karl's mottled face, delivering a lick to the tip of his nose.

"Damn it, Johnny!" Karl growled in anger, "How could you do this to me? How could you let this happen?"

"Yai didn't do anything to you, slave. He has only sung your praises," Mank's heavy body covered Karl's struggling one, in no way bothered by the other man's determination to break free.

"He can... Mank sounds like us. How is that?" Yai was confused.

"We had copies made of the translator you wear, Yai," Tryl explained. "When you were sleeping one night, I allowed specialists to examine and copy it. When Karl is more comfortable here, he will be allowed to wear one."

"Karl's staying?" Yai breathed. Tryl couldn't tell if he was happy or surprised. That was a matter for another day, however.

"Yes, I believe he is. Mank finds him… appealing. Do you mind that?" Tryl asked casually. He had to know. He didn't know if it mattered much, but he did need to know.

"I just hope Karl finds him appealing back," Yai murmured, looking away from the two struggling in the grass.

"Go get your boots," Tryl instructed, nodding toward the soft skin boots Yai had removed to feel the cool grass on his bare feet.

Tryl turned to help Mank lift Karl to his feet, the young man wearing out, though still struggling.

The small party returned to the den, Stft standing by the door, letting the trio pass him.

"Won't Stft be upset if Mank gets someone for a slave?" Yai whispered as they passed.

Tryl glanced up in time to see Stft smile. The other man seemed pleased that Yai would worry about him. Tryl smiled back at the driver, nodding as they passed.

"No, he'll be okay. He isn't ready yet to devote himself to one as Mank is. As I am," he looped an arm around Yai's shoulder and gave him a half hug.

Mank propelled Karl in one direction as Tryl led a fretting Yai the opposite way.

"I suspected that you would meet someone you knew here, Yai," Tryl told him, settling him on his lap in a community area of the den.

Yai looked at him in surprise. "You did? How?"

"I was told yesterday that a conveyance similar to yours was seen not far from here. Three such as you were spotted briefly."

"How come you didn't tell me?" Yai pulled back and looked into Tryl's face. "I mean I guess you didn't have to…"

"There are a couple of reasons, Yai," Tryl lifted his hand and licked it. "I wasn't sure you'd be happy to see them," he told him. "I wasn't sure why you left and," he heaved a great sigh, "It is obvious that they mutilated you. I was concerned that it would be traumatic for you. Of course, you might also have wished to return to them. That, too, was a possibility."

"Mutilated me?" Yai seemed at a loss. "Um, I'm really not sure why I left, but I'm pretty sure that's not it."

"Your genitals, Yai," Tryl's voice shook. "Your foreskin?"

"Oh, um, oh. I … I don't remember when they cut that off." Tryl winced in sympathy. "I'm pretty sure that happened a long time ago though. Karl's, too, I think…." He trailed off, rubbing his head. "That's something that they just do to us. But me and Karl, we're shuttle drivers. That's just what we do. Pilots."

"Remembering still causes you pain?" Tryl asked in concern, a hand covering Yai's as he rubbed.

"Guess so," Yai murmured. "But I think, I think they sent me because pilots are cheap. That's probably why Karl got here first. He's expendable."

"I'm not sure I understand," Tryl murmured, all too afraid that he did.

"Every big ship has dozens of pilots. You have to be a certain intelligence to be a pilot and if you live, you might make higher rank. Almost every officer can fly. But you can send pilots out alone on intelligence gathering missions. They can send information back and if they don't make it, there's plenty more."

Tryl pulled Yai against him, rubbing his back, licking his hair. No damned wonder he had headaches when he thought about his life.

Mank tried not to laugh at the posturing young man. He was so cute. That abundant caramel colored hair curling all over. Those dark green eyes flashing. He was going to enjoy this slave. He felt drawn to him already. More so even than the sunlight colored slave of Tryl's.

This one did have fair skin and very little hair, like Yai. He was lean just as Yai was. A little taller, but when Mank had lain atop him, they had fit well. And he could smell fear behind that bravado. Teaching this one his station, and how to please his master, that would be such a reward.

"Don't fight little slave. You won't be hurt here with me. You're safe here," Mank soothed, to no avail.

"Karl F. Redmond, Lieutenant, Junior Grade, Pilot, Essex Class I," he repeated for the fourth time.

Mank walked up to the stubborn man, forcing him to back up until he was pressed against the wall. One large, furry hand on either side of him, Mank pressed his face to the slave's neck, opening his mouth wide displaying an abundance of sharp teeth.

He scraped down the jugular with one pointed tooth and then he smelled it. The slave's bladder had let go. His one piece covering had a spreading wet spot at the juncture of his legs.

Karl looked at him with wide, grass colored eyes, fear pouring off of him. Mank lifted one hand and extended his claws. The frightened slave slid down the wall and dropped his head into his hands.

Mank lifted him by one arm and sliced down his clothing, shredding it. He gently tugged off the heavy boots and sliced off the thin fabric covering his genitals. He poured a pitcher of water over the slave and then wrapped him in a thick sheet of fabric.

In a corner of the room was a nook, thick with furs. Mank

lifted the shivering, almost hairless creature and carried him there. He sunk down, holding Karl against him, pulling the furs around them.

"You're safe now. I won't hurt you," Mank crooned, rubbing his palms up along the lightly haired arms.

"Doesn't matter," Karl mumbled. "Johnny was the only one ever cared and they sent him off to die. Doesn't matter."

"Do you mean Yai?" Mank asked, pulling the fluffy head to his shoulder.

"Whatever. He's dead to them. Now I will be, too. They probably saw me come in here. Probably saw Johnny. Figure we're worthless now. Probably," Karl said, voice monotone.

"How much were you worth before?" Mank inquired, truly curious.

That seemed to seize Karl's attention. He pulled away from Mank's shoulder, looking into his yellow eyes.

"How much?" He stared for a minute. "Damned fucking little," he pronounced. "Damned little."

"Yai spoke of you," Mank pressed his advantage. "You were his friend. The only one he could remember when he couldn't remember his own name."

"Yeah?" Karl asked, pleased. "I always thought... well, I just knew we were something to each other. I guess I never knew what. Thought we'd be lovers one day."

"No," Mank said levelly. "You will never be lovers."

Karl looked at Mank, confused. "But you said he liked me?" He sounded hurt.

Mank hid a smile and stroked a soft, firm hand through Karl's curly hair, down his naked back, under the fur wrapped around him, and stopping to cup the naked globe of his posterior.

"Did you plan to fuck him, Karl? Would you put yourself inside him? Or he inside you?" He stroked the curve of Karl's cleft with his fingertips.

Karl shifted, his sex beginning to stir. "Well, I, um. He's smaller so I thought he'd go inside me. I mean, I wouldn't want to hurt him," Karl's face tinted red.

"Have you never fucked another?" Mank asked, not unkindly.

"Um, I did once, I ah, well, fucked a girl before. But I thought I might like it better with Johnny." Karl seemed uncomfortable with the conversation. Mank explored the parting with a fingertip.

"Why did you think you'd like it better, Karl?" Mank persisted.

"Um, well, I liked Johnny better than her but … um, I don't know," he dipped his head, flustered and embarrassed.

"It seems that Yai likes someone inside of him. Would you like to do that?"

"M-Maybe," Karl hedged, both hands grabbing Mank's shoulders as Mank's index finger pressed the hidden entrance to his body.

"Has no man ever touched you here, Karl? Would you like to feel that?" Mank pressed a little.

Almost automatically, Karl pushed his hips out, spreading his knees wide, straddling Mank's lap, at a squat.

Mank withdrew his finger and gently urged Karl to lay on his side. "What are you doing?" Karl rasped in a whisper.

"Let's see how you like this, Karl," Mank said, his voice soothing, calming.

He reached across Karl to a small ledge upon which sat a small stack of cloths and a covered pot of lubricant. Setting the lubricant beside him, he turned Karl onto his back and lifted his legs so that they were bent at the knees, and then spread them wide, stroking his thighs.

The younger man's penis was erect and proud, Mank could see the shiny hood, dark and slick with pre come. As he feathered his fingers over it, he noticed the complete lack of foreskin.

"Ohhh," Karl moaned. "Ahhh."

"Does this hurt you?" Mank asked, fingering the area below the lip of the hood. He didn't know how long ago this had happened, but there was a scar there, so it wasn't a recent injury.

"Mmm, feels good," Karl groaned.

Mank smiled, dipping his finger in the pot of oil. "This will feel good, too," he crooned, exposing the pink hole with one hand.

With the other, he began to stroke over the wrinkled pucker, his finger sliding in a little, and then a little more. He withdrew to gather more oil, and slid his finger in further.

"Oh, oh man, oh," Karl tossed his head back and forth, moving so much that Mank had to pin one thigh with his own to hold him in place. Mank had found Karl's prostate, rubbing it, and wondered if he could make him come that way.

He stroked the soft, lightly furred sacs below the other man's cock, beginning to fuck Karl steadily with his finger, in, out, stroking deep. "Spread your legs further," Mank purred, one hand cuddling the sacs.

"Ohhh, I'm gonna come, I'm gonna come," Karl chanted breathlessly.

"Yes, come, its' okay," Mank encouraged, finger sliding in, a second one joining it.

"I- I," Karl seemed unsure, tossing his head, resisting.

"Do you want me to fuck you, Karl?" Mank purred gently. "Do you want me inside you?"

"Ahhh, ah!" he was leaking so copiously now. "Yes," he hissed, "Yes, I want that, yes," Karl begged.

"Shh," Mank soothed, pulling his hand out of Karl's anus, stroking his thigh gently.

"Don't," Karl's voice broke. "Don't go, please," his deep green eyes filled. "Don't leave," he pleaded.

Mank reached down and ran a hand through his hair, calming him. "I can't fuck you, Karl, it wouldn't be right," he reasoned.

"But, but why?" Karl was nearly whining now, his shaft only half hard, wilting in dissappointment.

"I am not your master, you're not my slave, are you? Shh, it'll be all right. You want to go back to your people, don't you?" Mank continued to stroke a nearby thigh, still sitting between Karl's legs.

"No, no, I don't!" Karl propped himself on his elbows, imploring Mank. "Nobody there has ever made me feel like this. No, don't make me go back. They don't care about me. You won't hurt me, will you? Johnny likes it here. I want to like it here, too."

"It's a big decision, Karl," Mank purred, edging a little

closer, lightly stroking Karl's hardening length. "You would belong to me. You would be my slave. Mine to keep, care for, punish, mark as my own."

"Marked like Johnny?" Karl's voice was barely a whisper now.

"Not just like him, that was a mistake. But you would wear my collar, maybe a brand."

"A brand?" he seemed shocked, not frightened, but shocked.

"Yes," Mank brushed Karl's clavicle and two inches below with the tips of his fingers. "I'd want everyone to know that you were mine," he explained, looking into those green, green eyes.

"Would you... would you change my name, too?" Karl asked hesitantly.

"Would you like your name changed?" Mank asked, suspecting that he was on the verge of something important.

"Yes," the young man whispered.

"Why?" Mank asked, his hand wandering up to cup the soft face.

Water ran unchecked down the soft skin and over his fingers. Mank pulled him close, remembering the day before when Yai had been spanked and in pain from his punishment. The water had poured from his eyes then. He'd had trouble breathing and his nose had turned pink. These things were happening now, though this young man hadn't been punished. Perhaps this was what these hairless slaves did when they were upset?

"I want to matter," the slave whispered. "I want to have a name someone will remember. A name someone will want to say. I want someone to want me for myself."

Mank wrapped his arms around the shivering body, holding him close as he laid them both down among the furs. He licked the salty water from the slave's face.

"I will call you Karri and you will be my most valuable and prized possession," Mank murmured, stroking the slave, pressing the supple body tightly to his own. "I will burn my mark into your flesh here," he touched the place below the prominent bone of his neck. "You will wear my collar. I will make you mine and you will be much wanted every single day of your life."

"Really? You want me?" the younger one asked him, hope in his voice.

"Very much, I want you," Mank purred, his entire body rumbling as he stroked down the lean back, cupping the tender rounded flesh of his new slave's rear.

The look on the young man's face almost broke Mank's heart. "Karri," the slave murmured, awe shining from his eyes. "I'm Karri." He pronounced it Car-rhi, as Mank had done, simply replacing the letter L with an R and I.

"I'm going to make you mine, Karri, right now," Mank rumbled, rolling the young man under him.

Karri slid his fingers up through the fur on Mank's ribcage, wrapping his arms around him. Mank reached down, tugging at his own loincloth, pulling it off and allowing his full erection to spring free.

Karri looked down at it and up at Mank's face, his expression uncertain. "Wow, you're awfully big," he breathed. "Will it hurt?"

"Maybe just a little," Mank told him honestly. He moved to his knees, taking one of Karri's pale hands and placing it on his engorged staff. "This is only for you now, Karri."

Karri smiled. "I belong to you and you belong to me?"

Mank leaned down and licked his face. "Yes, Karri. I meet your needs and you meet mine."

The slender hand ghosted over the firm flesh, mapping the length, the width, the wrinkles. Flicking tentative glances up at Mank's face, he began to explore, testing the weight of Mank's sacs on his fingertips, stroking.

"Turn over Karri," Mank purred softly, urging the younger man onto his stomach.

"I want to watch you," he protested. "Can't I watch you? See your face?"

Mank considered this a moment. The first time might be more painful this way but the younger man needed the reassurance. He would make it good for him. He'd been too lonely for too long and so, apparently, had Karri.

Mank leaned down, licking at Karri's nipples and rubbing

his heavy erection against the slave's smaller but just as hard staff.

"Mmm," Karri moaned, arching his back, opening his legs wide to wrap them around Mank's hips.

Sucking on a tight pink peak, Mank propped on one arm while he captured more of the lubricant with the fingers of his free hand, carrying it to the cleft between Karri's nether cheeks.

He was already relaxed and somewhat prepared and it wasn't long before Mank had three fingers in his hole, spreading him. When Karri began to strain against them, Mank slicked his aching cock and pushed into his smaller lover steadily.

Slowly, so slowly, he pushed in. Karri's eyes went wide and he caught his breath, a hint of pain and uneasiness on his face. Mank stopped, resting not halfway in, waiting for him to adjust. The clamping muscles squeezed him and he had to fight for control.

Soon, the muscle relaxed, Karri released his breath and wriggled a little, encouraging Mank to continue. Mank pushed forward again and Karri did, too.

"More!" Karri demanded. "I like it."

"Oh, is that so?" Mank purred, a smile in his voice. "More it is, then."

He began to move faster, the tight heat massaging him, feeling so good. Never had anything with one of his kind felt like this. He knew his climax would be powerful when it hit. So tight, so hot. This was heaven, surely.

His full cock caressed Karri's button with every thrust. He would be coming soon, as well.

"Ohmigod, ohmigod!" Karri chanted, his sacs tight, his own cock leaking between them.

"Come for me, Karri. Come for your master," Mank rumbled.

The effect was spectacular. Pearly white ropes of semen erupted from his shaft as his rectal muscles clamped down on Mank's pumping cock. Only one jerky thrust and Mank was coming, too, stars flashing before his eyes.

Mank collapsed onto his side taking the hairless slave over with him, so as not to crush him. He knew he'd have to get up and clean them both before long, but for now, he would savor the moment.

"Wow," Karri sighed. He snuggled up close, pressing his face into the crook of Mank's neck. "Thank you," he whispered.

Mank smiled. "You're welcome," he answered, reaching past the young man to the towels resting on the shelf where he'd found the pot of lubricant. He'd have to leave a gift for their thoughtful hosts.

Tryl looked up as Mank joined him, settling next to him above the bank of a shallow stream where the two slaves splashed and chattered. He'd taken the ear and tunic piece from Yai. This way he'd know what both slaves said and still be understood by Yai.

"They're something else, aren't they?" Tryl nodded at the laughing and playing pair in the water.

"It's amazing how sweet they are. I just can't believe anyone would ever mistreat them," Mank shook his head, eyes trained on his own slave.

"Yours has been... cut?" Tryl asked carefully.

"You mean his genitals?" Mank looked over, nodding. "Yours, too?"

"Yes. I wondered if that was why he'd left but Yai said he didn't remember when it happened."

"I think I'd forget such a horrific thing, too, if I could. Karri said they'd sent Yai off to die. That they weren't worth much to their people except for their skills," Mank filled him in.

"Barbarians," Tryl hissed. "Abusive, vile users, wasting young men that way. Defiling their own kind. Wasting lives."

"Karri said as much before he asked to stay," Mank agreed, obviously working to keep his anger in check.

"Ah but he *is* staying," Tryl nudged his friend. "Not that I had any doubt. I knew you'd persuade him one way or the other. What happens if you like one of the two remaining furless ones better?" Tryl asked, doubting, but still having to ask.

"I am most taken with Karri. *Most* taken with him. The remaining ones, they sent him ahead to see if he would survive. They deserve the least of our consideration. I wouldn't put them out as relief for the lowest workmen. Nothing."

The two dripping young men were emerging from the water now, Karri looking shyly at Mank. He was pulling on an extra pair of Yai's loose pants, reaching for a tunic of Mank's that had been cropped to stop at his waist.

Yai had pulled on his own pants, a boot covering one foot, it's mate dangling loosely from his hand as he turned, startled.

"Run, Kar!" he shouted, giving the taller man a shove.

In the time it had taken Tryl to gain his feet, Yai had run in the other direction, golden brand glinting on his bare chest, sunlight hair flying back. Tryl absently noted that he'd abandoned his second boot.

The world seemed to turn in slow motion now as he saw what Yai was doing. The young slave, bright and sunny as he was, was dazzling against the background of green grass and trees and blue sky.

The two furless beings emerging into the clearing couldn't help but train their eyes on Yai as he ran. One of them, smaller in stature, turned and spotted Tryl. Good. He had intended to be seen.

These creatures had already sent Yai off to die once. Tryl would not give them a second chance to kill him. It seemed however, that Yai had other ideas.

The smaller of the two pivoted toward Tryl lifting what he assumed was a weapon in its hands. He couldn't tell if it was a male or female but with the weapon aimed at him, he didn't much care.

He wasn't that far from Yai. Instead of continuing toward him in hopes of intercepting him, Tryl zagged, intending to draw attention away from his foolish slave.

"No! No, no, no!" he heard Yai bellow.

The next thing Tryl knew, his little ray of light collapsed in front of him. The creature had fired at Tryl and Yai had blocked the shot. Before it could fire another round, he had it in his claws.

Roaring, all he could see was his Yai, falling like a rag toy in front of him, crumpled and lifeless like the forgotten boot he'd dropped as he'd shoved his friend out of the way.

He was vaguely aware of screaming, yelling, roaring, and all sorts of cacophony, a great deal of it from himself. It couldn't be possible for the first creature to live through Tryl's anger and he tossed it aside like the refuse it was. Though it seemed hours, lifetimes had passed, it could have only been a few minutes from the time that Yai had sprinted away barely dressed.

Mank was forcibly restraining the other creature, claws drawing red trickles of blood under his chin. This one was clearly a male.

"Yai?" Tryl croaked a growl, looking around at Mank.

"There," Mank nodded to a little pink and gold heap barely visible under the covering body of the other slave.

Tryl hissed at the sobbing young man, he couldn't help it. He needed him to leave, to move away. Reluctantly, the slave did back away, but only a little.

Stft appeared, no doubt responding to the roaring and screaming. Some part of Tryl noted that Stft took over the prisoner while Mank moved forward, picking up his despondent slave, purring to him and offering comfort.

Mank moved them back while Tryl ran his fingers over Yai, reluctant to do him further injury but desperate to find some sign of life. When he didn't, he refused to give up. These furless bipeds were different than his kind in some ways.

Purring jaggedly, he lifted the limp form, cradling the cool body against his warmth, blood from the vile creature that had shot him rubbing onto Yai's pale skin.

"Mank, send for the healer," Tryl ordered. "Stft, bring the prisoner." Licking a smear of blood from Yai's alabaster cheek, Tryl turned toward the prisoner. "Your life for his," he growled. "If you can save him, you live."

The furless prisoner nodded, pale himself, carefully reaching into his clothing and coming out with what appeared to be a communications device.

Tryl turned, Yai in his arms, not caring what went on behind him as he walked away.

Tryl had parted company with Mank moments ago, knowing that Mank needed to go to his little curly headed slave. Karri loved Yai and was traumatized at the very least by all that had taken place.

The male prisoner had identified himself as Commander Lighter and had demanded to speak with Lieutenant Junior Grade Redmond, with Karri. Mank had refused but Karri had been right there.

"You can just fuck off and die, *Commander*," Karri had growled, doing a fair imitation of one of their kind.

The Commander had nodded, as if Karri's very anger and disrespect had answered an unspoken question. He'd watched Mank stroke Karri's hair, calming him again, soothing him with purrs and licks.

Looking back at Tryl, Commander Lighter shrugged as if he'd felt bound to try. Shortly after that, Stft left to retrieve the furless healer who'd been summoned. He worked over Yai with their own healer for hours.

Now, Tryl stood in the shadows, watching as Karri snuck up to the bower where Yai lay, not dead, but not safe either.

"John-John?" Karri whispered. "Johnny Yai?"

Mank sidled up to Tryl quietly, neither saying anything.

"Uh?" Yai responded. Tryl grabbed Mank's forearm, clutching tightly. He hadn't expected Yai to answer, to understand.

"You, you gonna live, Johnny Yai?" Karri croaked.

"Dunno," Yai rasped in answer.

"I'll kick your ass if you don't," Karri said determinedly.

"Won't care 'f 'm dead," Yai forced out.

"Why'd ya do such a crazy thing, huh? You know The Captain!"

"Love Tryl. Dint want him t' die. 'N you, n'Mnk," he supplied with difficulty.

"I think he loves you, too. He went pretty savage. Ripped her to shreds," Karri informed him, awe in his voice.

"Good. She 's a bitch," Yai wheezed, what little energy he had fading fast.

"Don't die, 'kay? I need you and I think your Tryl would … well, he needs you a lot. I'm sure of it. He might not make it if you die, so you can't all right?"

"'Kay," Yai's voice was a thread of a whisper now.

Tryl nudged Mank who moved forward, retrieving his slave, taking him away.

Tryl watched Mank and Karri leave. All was silent for a few minutes. Tryl moved forward slowly, almost hesitantly.

He shrugged out of his long tunic dropping to his knees next to Yai. Still, pale, he seemed dead. But no, the furs stirred, he was alive.

"Don't leave me, Yai," Tryl carefully edged under the furs next to his slave. "I do need you, Yai, Karri spoke the truth."

Tryl gathered the barely breathing figure against him, purring. Yai liked it when he purred.

He lay in his cocoon of warmth, surrounded by... what. What was that? It was fur and a noise. A rumbly noise. He liked it. His head felt like it was on a string floating above his body. He didn't like that so much.

He, him, his. Who was he? This was a do-over wasn't it? A deja vous. He remembered Kar. Was that right, Kar? But Til – no...

"Tryl," he squeaked. He smiled in triumph. That was right. "'s Tryl."

"Yai, I'm here," came a deep voice. A rough, gravelly voice that he liked.

"You're Tryl and I'm Yai," he sighed, everything falling into place again. A surrealist painting brought sharply back into focus by the rumbling words of the fur surrounding him.

"Yes, that is so. You're my Yai," the voice confirmed.

Yai forced his eyes open, looking into the glowing yellow-green eyes of the black furred face above him. He remembered. He remembered everything. *Everything*.

"I belong to you," Yai's voice was husky, raspy.

"Yes, you belong to me," Tryl agreed.

"I dint do what 'm s'posed to do," Yai felt his eyes fill. He was in trouble. He knew it. He hadn't cried over being in trouble for many years. But this time... this time was bad. "You told me to be careful and I dint." He felt the hot tears spill over. "'m sorry. But, but I just, I just couldn'," he sniffed.

"Shh, Yai," Tryl soothed, his voice like satin against Yai's tattered nerves. "None of that matters now. For now, you must rest."

Yai sniffed again. It didn't matter? Maybe, maybe, "Do you still want me? I, I'm a bad slave, huh?"

He closed his eyes against the rush of hot tears, but they didn't stop. What would he do if Tryl didn't want him? Where would he go? And besides, he loved Tryl. He knew he did. Would that help his cause at all?

He forced his eyes open. He made himself look at the stern expression on Tryl's face.

Gut deep fear brought with it a rush of energy. "I'll try harder," Yai bit his lip. "I, I only… it's cuz I, I'm pretty sure I love you and I just couldn't, couldn't…."

He couldn't go on. He was begging. What kind of a man was he? Begging someone to keep him. He had known what he was supposed to do, hadn't he? Tryl had only told him three or four things to do. That was all. And he couldn't even do those and now he was begging Tryl to keep him.

"I'm sorry," he croaked, turning his head away. Everything felt so heavy now. So big and heavy. Like he was going down a long tunnel. "Was bad. 'll go 'way. Sleep first, kay?"

Cat Toy

Tryl was stunned. What had just happened here? Yai thought that he was going to get rid of him? Was that what he thought?

He leaned down to lick the trickling tears from Yai's swollen eyes. What could he do? It wasn't even certain that Yai would survive.

Both healers used words like "hopeful" and "probable" and phrases like "entirely likely" and "good chance". He supposed it was an innate condition of all medical professionals. Right now he had very mixed feelings about the vocation.

The thought that Yai could still die squeezed his heart like a vice. The idea that he could leave this world thinking that Tryl didn't' want him, oh no... no, no, no, that just couldn't happen.

Yet, Tryl couldn't wake Yai up to tell him. He needed his healing sleep. Purring loudly, Tryl wrapped himself around his little sunlight blonde, deciding that if he did live, he would spank him later just for suggesting that he might give him away.

Tryl was awakened by the shadow of someone bending over him. He reached out and snatched the hand that touched Yai, tempted to snap it off.

"Sir, Mr. Tryl, it's me. It's Doctor Brown. Please," came the half pleading, half angry voice of the furless healer.

"What time is it? What brings you here?" Tryl demanded, waking up completely now.

"Its been four hours since I last checked on him and it's

time for me to see how he's doing. I can tell he's been agitated," Dr. Brown shot a reproachful look at Tryl.

"How is he otherwise?" Tryl growled, making no excuses. He hoped the healer he chose to take back to the capital learned much about furless bipeds. This one would have a short lifespan if he stayed behind.

"Emotional upset notwithstanding," this along with another reproving glance, "His vital signs are a little stronger. If he wakes again…"

"When," Tryl hissed.

"When," Dr. Brown rolled his eyes. "When he wakes again, try to say something positive to him rather than whatever you said that upset him, would you please?"

Tryl growled high and threatening, like a tightening wire that would snap at any moment.

The doctor seemed unimpressed. "Just give him something to live for, hmm?"

"You may go," Tryl hissed.

Dr. Brown rolled his eyes again and left after patting Yai's hand.

"'z always been a pompous bastard," Yai croaked.

"Yai," Tryl leaned over him, brushing the hair back from his face. "You want a drink of water? You sound like your throat is dry."

"Mm," Yai agreed, closing his eyes.

Tryl could've kicked himself. Offering Yai water and telling him he sounded bad would *not* give him a reason to live. Still, he helped Yai sit up a little and let him sip at a container full of cold water.

His face had a little more color when he was done but he didn't look at Tryl. Not knowing what else to do, Tryl moved in beside him and gathered him up, cuddling him close.

Science had come so far just since Tryl had grown. There was a time when medicines and treatments would have to be injected constantly, patients cut open and made to wait long weeks to mend. Now, healers could restore the body through elixirs and non-invasive means that worked much faster, as long as the patient had the will.

Yai had to live. He just had to. Tryl's life had been so

much more full with him in it. He was inquisitive, trouble-some, beautiful. He was everything Tryl needed in his life.

"Yai," Tryl purred, nervous, a little unsure of how to proceed. Yai turned his face into Tryl's chest. He didn't want to be seen. "Yai, I need you, don't leave," he blurted. He cleared his throat. Yai pulled his head back and looked up at Tryl, mistrust, on his face. Why? "Yai?"

"You don't have to be nice to me," Yai mumbled.

Anger surged through Tryl. "If you weren't at death's door, little slave, I would spank you now and then I'd fuck you senseless. You are mine, mind, body, and soul, you can't have forgotten that already," Tryl growled. "I love you and I'll be damned if I'm going to give you up because you are stubborn and foolish sometimes. If I choose to be nice to you than I will. Why? Because you belong to me and I will treat you any way that I choose, do you understand? Do you?"

Yai's blue, blue eyes filled with water again and Tryl groaned. Now he was yelling at him. He surely would be the death of this little slave.

"You love me?" Yai sniffed. "You want to keep me?"

His lip trembled and water dripped down his face in little tracks. Once again, Tryl licked up the salty water, stopping at the trembling mouth, dipping his tongue in and tasting Yai, reveling in him.

"I don't want to live without you in my life. I want you with me. Need you, as you need me. Master and slave. Mind, body and soul. Together."

"Mind, body, and soul. Together," yai sighed, snuggling up. "Property of Tryl The Cat Man," he mumbled.

Tryl shook his head with a smile, laying his sunshine burden down. "Property of Tryl The... What's a Cat Man?"

And Yai answered him with a gentle snore.

Printed in the United States
100812LV00002B/214/A